To our long-time friends,
Dave & Florence ~

warm wishes always...

Jayne Rattray Murdock

December 1993 ~

The way I walk, I see my mother walking
The feet secure and firm upon the ground.
The way I talk, I hear my daughter talking
And hear my mother's echo in the sound.
The way she thought, I find myself now thinking,
The generations linking in a firm continuum of mind.
The bridge of immortality I'm walking,
The voice before me echoing behind.

Dorothy Hilliard Moffat
LHJ - 1966

OTHER BOOKS BY THIS AUTHOR

I Painted On A Bright Red Mouth: The War Years, 1941- 1945
Brief Infinity - A Love Story in Haiku
Love Lines - A TRUE Love Story (with Dick Murdock)
Until Death and After: How to Live with a Dying Intimate

Wind Chimes

The Story of a Family

Jayne Rattray Murdock

May-Murdock Publications - Ross - California

First Printing, January 1994

LIMITED EDITION

Library of Congress Catalog Card Number 93-33526

International Standard Book Number 0-932916-17-1

Library of Congress Cataloging-in-Publication Data

Murdock, Jayne, 1918-
    Wind chimes: the story of a family/ Jayne Rattray Murdock.
      p.   cm.
    ISBN 0-932916-17-1 : $14.95
      1. Family--California--History-- Fiction. 2. California-
-History--Fiction. I. Title.
PS3563.U72515W56   1994
 813' .54--dc20   93-33526
                  CIP

Published by
May-Murdock Publications
90 Glenwood Ave
Ross California 94957-1346

Printed in the United States of America

DEDICATION

To the memory of those who have gone – some before their time – my parents and grandparents, my brother, uncles and aunts, cousins, a beloved niece.

To those who are still here – my sisters, my children, my dear husband, grandchildren, great-grandchildren, nephews, nieces, grand-nephews and grand-nieces. And to friends who have been part of the story.

To those yet to be – to show them how it once was and to let them glimpse from whence they came.

My memories and perceptions may be biased. Forgive me if they differ from yours. This is the way I remember it.

INTRODUCTION

On a Christmas boat trip to Mexico in 1980, my nephew, Greig Shepard, was traveling with us. We were sitting on deck one night, sharing tales with the rest of the passengers. As I finished an ancedote about my father giving a piano performance with the Marin Symphony, Greig said, "I didn't know Grandpa Bill did that!"

Suddenly I realized there was a wealth of information about my parents that my five children, all their Shepard cousins, and the growing group of grandchildren, didn't know about the lives of these two very human remarkable people. And if their decendents were to learn of them, it was up to me to write the story. No one else was left who knew as much as I.

So the idea for this book was born.

I chose to step back and write in the third person. It has been a fascinating journey, recreating the story of the early days of this family. I knew the facts and had only to figure out, or imagine, the reasons and motivations of our parents that caused them to behave as they did. I've based much of the book on what my mother told me in countless hours of sharing plus studying writings in her little red book. I sincerely apologize to any family member who I may offend with my singular interpretation. This is offered in love. I hope you enjoy the story.

JRM

FAMILY TREE
(Abbreviated)

James Rattray - Ellen Greig	George Murdock - Susan Fuller
married in Dundee, Scotland	**married in San Francisco, California**
1885	**1879**

children	children
Bella Rattray - m. Ernest McRitchie	Hamilton (Tone) Murdock-
Greig - Steele	m. Bess Valleau
	Bobbie - Geordie
Alec Rattray - m. Bertha Enderly	Laurilla (Rill) Murdock-
	m. Oscar Schlesinger
	Otis
Lottie Rattray - m. James Panton	Charles Percy (Perce) Murdock -
Ronnie - Jamie - Betty Anne - Tottie	m. Catherine Warfield
	Steve - Dickie

Bill Rattray   -   married   -   Marian Paige Murdock
Alameda - June 30, 1917
Jane -   Billy - Marianne - Suzanne

Jim Rattray - m. Margaret Temple
    Greig   (daughter)

Arnold Rattray - m. Jeanette Edwards
    Mary - Everett - David

CONTENTS

Certain fictionalized liberties have been taken to move the story. Some non-family names were changed. All facts and dates are as accurate as possible. JRM

The house in Ross, summer of 1924. Visiting McRitchie
cousins, Greig and Steele, playing on steps with
Billy and Jane Rattray.

PART ONE

In the Beginning

UMMER OF 1924 WAS hot and dry but that didn't detract from their pleasure about the new house. They moved in, finally, on August 11, carrying the wind chimes. There was no garden, none at all, just tan and matted grass, smashed down close to the bungalow by the paraphernalia of building, standing tall and untrampled out to the unmarked boundaries of the lot and beyond. That was merely a challenge to Marian. Already, in the back of the little red leather book in which she wrote sayings that touched her, she had started a section labeled *Our Garden— August 1924,* and had sketched a general plan for the planting that would take place as quickly as possible.

In the first ten days, mostly on weekends, she and Bill put in 300 feet of bender board, delineating the pathways, the drive, and the future gardens and lawns. They also put trellis work on the front of the house and a small fence across the driveway. They discovered that the soil was uncompromisingly bad – rocky hard clay. It would be a miracle if anything grew but Marian was undaunted.

Once the board was staked and curved into place, gravel was ordered for the paths and driveway. After Bill spread it, they turned their attention to digging holes for plants, adding good soil, and putting in roses, Scotch broom and acacia (the last two, they came to regret!) as well as hollyhock and zinnia for quick bright color. It began to look a bit less bleak and closer to the image Marian carried in her heart.

During the previous spring, Marian and Bill, with the two children in tow, daily walked the block between where they were living and where the dream was taking form, to check on the progress being made on their home.

With Marian carrying baby Billy and cautioning little Jane to watch her step, she and Bill checked the foundations, the framing. As the weeks passed and the building progressed, they paced and measured the floors, mentally placing furniture.

"Janie, this'll be your room. And where that door is will someday be a sleeping porch. And," continued Marian, stepping between the studs of the unfinished wall, "this'll be the baby's."

They loved it and were happy those evenings and weekends, watching the dream become reality, overjoyed when they finally moved into the house that August.

The warmth and dryness were welcome after the wet fall and winter which left two feet of water standing for weeks in the basement of the rented house. It is impossible, Marian found, to create warmth in a place that is harboring, under the floor, the makings of a swimming pool.

Those months before the move were hard for Marian in many ways. Bill, working for an insurance company, was often on the road for adjustment claims, sometimes away for days at a time. Besides, the children seemed to be constantly sick. Jane brought whooping cough home from a birthday party in the spring and Billy nearly died when he caught it. Marian had weaned him at six months and now went back to nursing him around the clock as he whooped up all nourishment. Years later, Jane would remember her mother, hollow-eyed and gaunt, standing at the kitchen sink, drinking gallons of water and taking heaping spoons of powdered malted-milk, the retching baby in her arms. Marian lost fifteen pounds during those weeks but the baby, she was proud to tell, didn't lose an ounce!

Billy had his first birthday early in November of that bad year and Jane reached five just before Christmas. They caught one cold after another, passing it back and forth. The dampness didn't help. Jane, little chest heaving, suffered bouts of asthma. On those sleepless nights, the coal-oil stove was placed in her bedroom with a pan of boiling water containing benzoin, bubbling on top. The steam, with its sweet vanilla-scented aroma, seemed to help. Janie liked it much better than the punks that were sometimes burned. They had an acrid smell that made her feel worse. And the mustard plasters that Marian often put on her daughter's chest made Jane sob both from the smell and the burning heat.

All in all, it was not a good time; rain, colds, raspy dispositions, and Bill fighting – or failing to fight – his problems.

Yet as the days lengthened and warmth came back into the sunshine, they looked toward the new house and its promise of better things.

Before the move, to improve the health outlook for the next winter, Marian, on the doctor's advise, decided to have Jane's inflamed tonsils removed. Her friend, Ruth Rowland, who lived in Alameda, was planning the same procedure for her son, Clem, so they decided to do it together.

Billy was left next door with Susan and Marian bundled Jane over to Ruth's the evening before the scheduled operations.

When they reached the doctor's office, Clem, being a bit older, was given the dubious honor of going in first. He accepted the ether cone without a whimper and his tonsils were out in no time. Jane was a different matter. Without knowing what was about to happen, she hung back and hid behind her mother.

"Come on, Janie, walk!" That didn't work so Marian scooped her up and carried her in to the room with its table and bright lights and the waiting doctor and nurse. From then on, it was frantic. Jane would not let go of her mother. When pried loose, she refused to sit on the table to be properly robed for the ordeal. Her cries intensified with each passing moment and her little body became a whirlwind of flying arms and legs.

The nurse struggled to hold her down while the doctor tried to get the ether cone over her nose.

"Mommy, Mommy she screamed.

"Wait! Stop! There must be a better way." Marian reached toward Janie just as the ether took effect and her thrashing body went limp. Marian turned away, heart pounding. The doctor proceeded to snip out the offending tonsils and adenoids. That part was over in minutes, but the terrible beginning haunted both Marian and Janie for years. And it didn't seem to improve the little girl's health to any measurable degree.

She healed quickly, however, after the first few days of refusing to speak or eat anything but ice cream. Back home again, under Marian's direction preparations for the big move progressed daily.

Finally, the rented place was empty and clean and the new home held their modest belongings. There was a wonderful smell of fresh paint and drying plaster. The house, though tiny, seemed big to Bill and Marian, big enough to hold all four of them and their entire future.

The bungalow stood half way up the slope of a grassy hill on an elm lined street. The road was narrow and built with a crown so water would run off to the wide dirt areas on either side. At the corner, an elm thicket grew and through it, diagonally, ran a shortcut to Bolinas Avenue, like an airy tunnel with the branches meeting over head.

There were three modest houses on the other side of Glenwood Avenue, and up the hill on the corner of Fernhill, stood a big vacation place built before the turn of the century. Standing in their yard and looking toward the big house, Marian and Bill could see in the distance Marin's landmark, the sleeping Indian princess, Mount Tamalpais. Across the street, above the

From the side lot, looking up the hill. In the distance, Mount Tamalpais can be faintly glimpsed.

roofs and through the branches of the elms, they could spot an intimate friendly hill, Baldy, close enough to climb if they were so inclined. In fact, during house parties at Ben Brae years before, they had done so many times.

Nothing grew around the house except grass that first hot summer, high dry tan grass, up the hill to the big house and down to the thicket. It seemed spacious and open but Marian's father, looking at the place after the house was underway said, "Your property line is right there." He pointed. "That's where the driveway will be. Not an inch to spare when someone builds on the lot next door. Terrible."

Marian looked for the little markers, hidden in the grass, and saw what he meant. It was just an illusion that there was space to spare. Before she could react to his pronouncement he went on almost as though thinking to himself, "Well, I'll buy the lot for you. As a buffer. Just promise you won't try to plant it."

Marian nodded acknowledgment while planning in her mind how to get Bill to accept an additional gift from his father-in-law. It wouldn't be easy.

Another part of her mind was saying, *Damn, if you were going to be so generous, why didn't you do it sooner, before the foundation was poured so we could've moved the house into the center of the two lots. We're close on the other side, too.*

"Thanks, Dad," she said, smiling. "That's really wonderful of you. Bill will be thrilled."

Oh, yes, he'll be thrilled all right! It had been touchy all along every time Marian's father opened his pocket to help them over yet another hurdle.

This would be more salt in the wounded ego.

George had bought the lot for them – and now a second one – and had made ("It's just a loan") the down payment on the $4500 mortgage. They would, Marian prayed, be able to handle the monthly payments for the next 30 years. But they could never pay her father back. He wouldn't allow it and that rankled Bill.

Marian had been handling their finances since the beginning, keeping strict accounting in a series of small notebooks. She was good with figures and excellent on planning and projections. The only challenge was to get Bill's paycheck before he cashed it and spent too much in drinking. There was no margin for such expenditures in her notebook. Now, taking on the house payments, allocation was particularly critical and she would have to be even more vigilant. It didn't seem strange to her to be managing the money. She had still been in high school when she relieved her mother of the household accounts – managing the shopping, disbursement of funds to the help, payment of various bills – accepting the monthly allowance from her father for such things. Bill, on the other hand, had lived at home until he and Marian married, and had merely contributed a small amount to the Rattray household without any knowledge of its disposition. Now he gave his total check to Marian, except on those occasions when he didn't get it home intact.

It was decades before they openly talked about his drinking and what havoc it caused in their lives. It was easier for Bill to resent anything George did for them and Marian knew telling him of this second lot would be touchy and she didn't look forward to breaking the news.

In the years just prior to America entering the Great War in 1917, Marian was still living at the three-story family home in Alameda at 1809 San Antonio Avenue and attending the University of California in Berkeley. She was an attractive young woman, tall and slim, with a direct glance from her green eyes. "They're too small and close together," she always remarked if someone happened to mention their color or brightness. Her face was strong with a determined set to her jaw. Her hair, dark blonde with a slight curl, she wore up on her head in an arrangement that always let wisps slip out. "Too fine and really no color at all, just *hair* hair," was her assessment. But her nose, almost too small for her face, she liked because it wasn't her mother's prominent Fuller nose; it came from her father's side of the family and was short and straight. Marian walked with a free stride that drove her sister, Rill, to distraction.

"Short steps, Marnie. You don't look the least a lady the way you gallop about." Rill, on the other hand, was every bit the fashion-plate, her full-bosomed small-waisted figure lending itself to elegant dress, and her nature eminently suited to the frills, fuss and foolishness of "proper" society. Unlike Marian, she was willing to mince about in the tiny steps enforced by hobble-skirts. Marian didn't think her older sister had any depth or even a very good brain, but she kept her opinion to herself, something Rill never did.

Eighteen-Ought-Nine, the Murdock family home in Alameda, early 1900's.

Sunday evenings, in those gentle times, young people gathered at the gracious homes of their friends' parents for simple pleasures; popcorn, charades, sing-alongs, lemonade, taffy-pulls.

Marian came back from one such evening and said, "There was a fellow at Edwina's tonight who could really play the piano. He came with Deek and has the rosiest cheeks and curly reddish hair. Played *Alexander's Ragtime Band* like I've never heard it and ragged all the other songs, too. He's fun. His name is Bill, Bill Rattray."

"Never heard of the Rattrays. Funny name," said Rill in a looking-down-her-nose voice. "They can't be anybody."

"I don't care. Deek brought him. And he seems nice."

Bill lived on Benton Street just blocks away from Eighteen-Ought-Nine, the family name for the home on San Antonio Avenue. He was out of

Marian Paige Murdock
at 18 years of age.

Perce Murdock and his bride, Catherine
Warfield, August 1912

Marian with Bill Rattray, Deek Larkin and Edwina Moyes,
in Auburn where Bill was playing a piano engagement
with a dance band, summer 1914.

Marian Paige Murdock,
during her college
years, 1915

school and working for an insurance company and it wasn't long before he supplanted all the other swains in Marian's life. Especially Frank Spring whose half-sister, Catherine, was Marian's older brother Perce's wife. The two couples had spent many evenings together, dancing in San Francisco, rollicking at Tate's at the Beach, even, sometimes driving to California Park in Marin County. Frank and Perce taught both Marian and Catherine to drive their respective cars, a big Franklin and a Cadillac, to change tires should the need arise, to understand the nature of the beasts, a rare accomplishment indeed for women then.

There was something about Bill, however. Maybe his talent on the piano, or his smile, or high coloring. Perhaps his sense of humor. But suddenly Marian thought Frank was a dandy, his shoes too pointed, his manner too polished, and gave a definite and final "No" to his frequent proposals.

Another casualty of Bill's arrival was Charlie Baldwin, the brother of Pauline Baldwin, Marian's young school teacher friend who used the Murdock home as headquarters for several years. Charlie was a gentle soul, serious, and much in love with Marian. She treated him with sisterly joshing but until Bill appeared on the scene he didn't give up hope. And even after Bill's arrival, he was in a position, as Polly's brother, to maintain a close and special friendship with the Murdocks, especially Marian, for the rest of his life.

Marian Paige Murdock, 15 months old, April 1895.

Marian had been a "surprise" baby, born to Susan and George at the family home in mid-January 1894 nearly fourteen years after Charles Percy and his 13-month-older twin siblings, Hamilton and Laurilla. Marian's parents were unique and by the strength of their personalities molded her life without even trying, often because she went in a contrary direction.

Susan Letitia Fuller was born in Hancock, New Hampshire, December 1, 1857 and had an older sister and a younger brother. She was tall, plain and intelligent with a quiet sense of humor and, before migrating to San Francisco, graduated from college. She numbered among her ancestors several of whom she spoke with pride. Christy Duncan was one she often mentioned. There was a vague connection with William Bradford, first governor of Massachusetts, and a stronger tie to Timothy Paige and Thomas

Susan Letitia Fuller before her marriage, 1879.

George Hamilton Murdock, a young man sought after in San Francisco society, 1876.

Fuller, two young men who bore arms in the Revolutionary War. This qualified her as a Daughter of the American Revolution, a title she wore with gracious pleasure.

George Hamilton Murdock was born in Boston, Massachusetts, August 24, 1847, and came to California at the age of seven with his older brother and sister. They sailed with their mother from New York in 1855, crossed the Isthmus of Panama on the new railroad, then sailed up the coast to San Francisco where they were joined by George's father, Albert Hamilton Murdock. The family spent a decade in Humboldt County, followed by some time in Nevada, before George, by then a handsome young man, took up residence in San Francisco. He was welcomed into the brilliant society of the day. Why he, a veritable peacock of a man with a proud head of blonde curls and a full moustache, china blue eyes, and a pink and white complexion, picked a brown wren like Susan to marry was something she never understood.

Although Susan was only 37 at the birth of her fourth child, she favored a heart condition from that time on and lived the life of a much older woman. George was ten years his wife's senior, a dignified and aloof presence who found little to say and less to do with his rambunctious young daughter.

Laurilla Murdock kneels beside her five year old sister, Marian.

Marian, as she grew, found beloved father-figures in her older brothers, Tone and Perce, and, if not a substitute mother, at least a female adversary in her imperial sister, Rill.

Whenever she was noisy or boisterous or wanted to do something daring, she was shhh-ed and reminded to "Remember your mother's heart."

But the "boys" spoiled her and she reciprocated by polishing their many tennis trophies every Saturday before going off to play, tagging after them whenever possible and doing whatever else they asked of their little sister, "Buster, the kid." They taught her to play blackjack and she learned her number combinations so well in getting to the point where she could best them that it stood her in good stead for the rest of her life.

Marian was twelve, and a tomboy, when the earthquake struck in the early hours of April 18, 1906. At 5:15 AM the house began to shake. Noise of falling bricks, rattling window-weights within the walls, crashing dishes, windows and bric-a-brac, and the grinding of the earth itself, was deafening and terrifying. Marian reached Susan and George's room first, then, Rill, screaming, sprinted the length of the hall, and her brothers clattered down from the third floor, all seeking the reassurance of being close. Years later, Tone and Perce always asked, "When did we put on our trousers?" They'd gone to bed in usual nakedness and their next conscious memory was racing down the second floor hallway, properly clad.

They gathered in the quivering rattling room. George said in his deep cultured voice, "Good-bye, children. Good-bye, Susan. This is the end of the world, the very end."

Marian Murdock at about the time of the 1906 earthquake, 12 years old.

"Shush, George," Susan answered calmly. "You'll frighten Marian." Marian, however, was least upset of the lot. Rill, on the other hand, was in a state of hysteria. Tone and Perce were exhilarated.

How could so much happen in less than a minute? Time has an elastic quality and can be stretched to great lengths in an emergency until it seems to stand entirely still. Finally, the world settled down, a few late falling bricks punctuating the sudden silence. Yet that wasn't the end: During the entire day minor rumbles from the disturbed earth sent loosened plaster and bricks crashing down.

Susan was undaunted by such things. A mere earthquake couldn't stand in the way of a conventional meal for her family. She told them all to dress and get downstairs. Then, properly attired, she went to check on Lim, their Chinese cook. She found him standing in the kitchen, gazing impassively at the big old French range whose chimney had collapsed.

"Can't use, Missy," he murmured sadly. "What do?"

"Why, Lim," Susan replied brightly. "We'll just have use the kerosene Perfection heater in the dining room to prepare breakfast. I think scrambled eggs, and whatever else you can find. We must eat a substantial meal to be ready to cope."

Every step on the dining room rug left an imprint in the soot. That chimney had fallen *in* (others throughout the house had fallen *out*) bringing the soot of winter and all the blackened bricks crashing down into the room.

Right after the ingenious breakfast which they ate, much to Susan's annoyance, wherever they could sit without soot rather than properly around the table, Marian took advantage of the general confusion to grab her beloved roller skates and slip out. She skated several blocks to where she could look across the Bay and see San Francisco. A pall of smoke covered it, and occasionally towering flames shot up. San Francisco was burning! Marian skated home as fast as she could and, out of breath, said to her parents, "The City is burning . It's all on fire!"

"Susan," said George sternly, "you must forbid Marian to play with those children next door. They're nothing but rumor-mongers and they're teaching Marian to lie." Having abolished the possibility of a fire by his proclamation, George strode from the room.

It was not his nature to rescind the order when the fire proved reality rather than rumor, and the children next door continued to be suspect in his mind, slightly to blame in some way for the entire tragedy and Marian was forbidden their company.

When Tone, Rill and Perce settled down to married life in their thirties and began producing sons with their spouses, Marian, in college in the beginning and then married to Bill and, eventually, pregnant herself, was a perfect baby-sitter. She adored all her little nephews; Tone and Bess's Bobby and Geordie, Perce and Catherine's Steve and Dickie and even Rill and Oscar's Otis.

Otis always had a tantrum when left with Marian. Once when she scolded him for his behavior, he immediately ceased wailing, looked up at her with tears still flooding his big brown eyes and said, "But it makes Mommy feel good when I cry."

Marian knew this was absolutely true. She could hear Rill saying, "Poor Otie, he loves me so much, it breaks his little heart when I leave him!"

Otis continued to please his mother by howling when she left, and Marian, amused, watched his well-planned performance.

Marian understood her sister's almost neurotic need for love and reassurance from her young son. It stemmed from the tragedy surrounding the birth of their second son when Otis was barely two. Rill had an uneventful pregnancy marred only by the memory of the long painful struggle she'd endured at Otis's birth. When the time came to deliver, she was installed in the hospital in case of trouble which the doctor feared.

He was correct in his assessment but the family was left in agony, wondering if he was equally as correct in his action. After the labor had been underway for long painful unproductive hours, Rill was put under anesthesia and the doctor used high forceps to pull the baby into the world. All concerned were left to wonder how things might have turned out if those forceps hadn't been used, if instead a section had been performed.

The baby was a big beautiful boy but he didn't have a chance. His neck had been broken. When Rill returned to consciousness, Oscar bent over her and said, "It was a little boy. He didn't make it. I'm so sorry." Rill became hysterical, screaming and screaming. Oscar sobbed, too. Nothing in either of their lives had prepared them for such a loss, such a tragedy.

The baby was named Nicholas Andressen Schlesinger. He was buried in a tiny casket in an unmarked grave with only his weeping father on hand. He was never spoken of again by either of his parents..

Marian visited Rill in the hospital to express her sympathy the day after it happened. Rill put her hand up. "No, Marian. I don't want to talk about it. I can't. I won't. Never again." Even though Marian felt it wrong not to openly grieve and let family share the pain, there was nothing she could do to change the way things were. Except sympathize with her sister and understand why she doted on Otis, and go to the house with Oscar to remove all traces of preparation for the baby they'd never bring home.

Before her last year at the university, Marian realized she'd do better spending it at Mills College in Oakland. The courses she needed to complete her home economics major were available there, and it was an easier commute. She talked Edwina into switching, too, so they could share the ride in Edwina's electric car.

Those were happy days. Marian loved learning and the scientific

Marian on a Key boat trip on
the Bay, 1912

Edwina Moyes electric car that
transported them to and from Mills
College, 1916.

Marian and Bill on an
outing in Marin County,
1913.

Marian in her daring swim
suit from Jantzen, 1916.

aspect of nutrition was something in which she found an abiding interest. It all made such sense.

The nights and weekends were happy, too. With Deek and Bill, the two girls enjoyed outings to the beach, boat trips on the Bay, excursions up Mount Tamalpais, hiking and riding the "crookedest railroad in the world," and evenings around the piano. Somehow they managed to hold the mess in Europe at bay. It seemed so far away.

One day as they were getting ready to go to the beach, Marian said to Edwina, "This bathing outfit has to go! I can't swim in all this material, bloomers and skirts and sleeves! It's impossible."

"So what can you do instead?"

"I can go over to the factory at Jantzen's in San Francisco and ask them to make me a suit like Bill's, only sew up that funny second hole under the arm. It would be great. I'll go tomorrow."

The people at Jantzen's were more than a bit surprised when a tall attractive young lady walked in the front office and asked to speak to someone who could adapt a swimsuit to her specifications.

"You mean you want to appear on the beach in one of our men's swimming suits?"

"Yes," Marian replied, looking at them levelly out of her green eyes. "That's what I mean to do."

"Well, it's your business. I guess we can do what you want. I'll have to get one of the ladies to measure you so we know what size to use. Just stitch up that second hole, you say? Strange!"

Within two weeks, Marian had her revolutionary outfit and was ready to appear in public. It actually matched Bill's in color. He thought it great, though somewhat intimidating, to have such a daring female as a companion.

Their first outing caused a few raised eyebrows but beyond that, many young women were taken with the idea of dressing more comfortably and appropriately for forays into the water. They could hardly wait to ask Marian where she had gotten her startling attire.

"From Jantzen's," she replied. "They made it to order for me." Marian never again put on the voluminous bloomers and long sleeved blouses she'd been saddled with up to this point. And she became a strong swimmer, doing the Australian crawl long before other women where getting totally immersed in water.

After a couple of years of keeping company, it was understood that marriage was in their future. Bill always said later that they'd been engaged for two years; Marian said it was only six weeks. They were often that far apart in perceptions.

Early on, however, Bill started bringing Marian to the family home for dinner once a week. Even with the older children married, it was a boisterous group. Bill had three brothers, Alec, older, Jim and Arnold, the baby, and two sisters, Bella, the oldest, and Charlotte, between Alec and Bill. The first three children had been born in Scotland before James Rattray left Dundee for California. A year later he sent for Ellen Greig and the children. Bill was born in Oakland in 1892, Jim and Arnold at yearly intervals after the move to Alameda when Bill was a baby.

The birthing of Arnold became a favorite family story. And no wonder! It happened one late stormy afternoon. Only five feet tall and "great with child," Ellen Greig was home with little Willie and baby Jimmy. The family doctor, making his rounds by horse and buggy, found himself on Benton Street. Knowing that his patient's time was near, he stopped in front of the Rattray's home. At the sound of his knock, Ellen waddled to the door which she opened, stepping behind it with a small cry of surprise. The cry was not at seeing the doctor but because the baby was suddenly and completely arriving! The doctor did what needed to be done right there on the floor, then carried mother and son to the closest bed. Here James and the older children found them happily resting when they arrived home.

Bella married Ernest McRitchie in 1912 and produced two boys, Greig and Steele, Charlotte married another quiet Scot, James Panton, and they, too, had a son, Ronnie, and, in time, three more children, two girls to challenge Jane's spot as princess of the clan. Alec was courting a quiet German girl, Bertha Enderlee and handsome Jim was planning to marry Margaret Temple.

The senior Rattrays, with ears attuned to their own deep Scottish burrs, found Marian's speech both strange and amusing. She spoke like her parents who were born and raised in New England. Susan, especially, had quite an accent, most noticeable in the dropping of "r" in many words and the placing of it on the end of others.

"So, Marrrian, what did you do yesterday?" James would ask, knowing full well the answer since the question was by now a ritual.

"I 'ioned' my clothes," she'd answer to great laughter. She never understood why they thought her speech so funny or why they didn't realize she could hardly understand Ellen Greig's spoken word. Or why their laughter felt to her somehow both depreciating and embarrassing.

The amusement at her speech particularly irritated Marian since her use of English was more polished than the Rattrays. This was understandable;

both her parents were well educated, both read extensively and were avid members of a Shakespeare club with others who enjoyed readings of the bard's plays. By the time Marian began talking, her older siblings, too, were shining examples correctly spoken English.

When she was sure she and Bill were going to spend the rest of their lives together, she undertook a pruning and sprucing of his speech. First to go were his colorful swear words. "Bill!" she would say with a withering look whenever one slipped out. Gradually, they disappeared from his vocabulary, substituted, when necessary, with a resounding "Damn!" which Marian didn't mind. In fact, she used that expletive herself when the occasion arose.

More subtle pronunciations were corrected, too. "It's 'gen-u-*win*' not 'gen-u-*wine*'," she'd say, "'*hiss*-terical', not '*hy*-sterical', '*hill*-arious', not '*high*-larious'. And please say 'ahnt' not 'ant' for Aunt Charlotte." Bill

Bill and Marian, 1913.

accepted her directions, grew to excel in his manner of speaking and, even, in the final years of his life, delighted in catching TV newscasters in errors of usage and pronunciation.

Bill and Marian were married on June 30, 1917 three weeks after her graduation from Mill's, at a wedding kept simple by the Great War and Susan's delicate heart. The next spring, Marian was pregnant and the flu epidemic was in full swing, people dying by the thousands. Bill planned to enter the army – to join his younger brothers Arnold and Jim, and his older brother Alec – but an attack of the flu left him seriously underweight and no candidate for war. Besides, his imminent fatherhood would keep him from going "over there."

The war to end all wars ceased on the eleventh hour of the eleventh day of the eleventh month of 1918. One month and four days later Jane Paige Rattray made her appearance.

As time for delivery drew near, Marian and Bill moved to San Francisco to live with Aunt Charlotte, George's sister, so that arrival at the designated hospital would be easier. Getting across the Bay from Alameda was impossible at certain hours; this seemed the sensible way. Mt. Zion was the hospital being used by Dr. Ran Sharpstein for his maternity patients. Many hospital beds were filled with flu patients, the turn-over horrendous. Even with the war's end this greatest scourge was still claiming more victims than had been killed in France.

The last day of her pregnancy, Marian walked the hilly streets of San Francisco, down the steep curves of Lombard Avenue pausing to rest on a bench at each turn. When it finally seemed that she might really be in labor, she walked, heavily, the few blocks to Charlotte's home. Two hours later, with a nervous husband at her side and a far from calm driver at the wheel, she was whisked to the hospital in a taxicab.

Marian was in her glory producing the baby. It was as though having babies was what she'd been born to do. She loved her little daughter and spent Christmas 1918 happily holding court in the hospital.

She shared a room with a large Jewish lady whose son, delivered by Caesarean section, she never forgot. Plucked as he was from the womb without the usual painful journey, he was pink and white with blond hair sculpted to his perfect head. *Nicholas could have looked like that,* Marian thought with a pang. He was a large baby resembling a Michaelangelo angel and he totally delighted and astounded his proud parents.

No more so than Janie astounded and delighted her family. Imagine! A girl! Five nephews on Marian's side, three on Bill's and now, the first female of the generation.

They went back to their small apartment in Alameda when Jane was eleven days old. She was a good baby and Marian took great delight in the new role of motherhood.

Alameda was built on an island, totally flat. When the bay tide went out, mud was exposed for a quarter mile. A canal had been deepened between Alameda and Oakland and traffic crossed on two bridges. The town was laid out in regular squares with wide sidewalks. All her life, Marian had found those sidewalks perfect for skating. Now she discovered them perfect for pushing a baby in a perambulator which Marian did both morning and afternoon, unless it was raining.

Marian, with her daughter, Jane Paige Rattray, six weeks old.

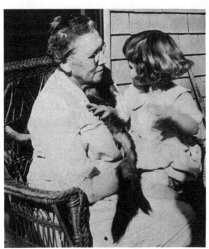

Jane with grandmother Susan Murdock, at the apartment in Alameda

Jane, 2 years old, pedaling her auto on Alameda's level sidewalks.

Their apartment was two blocks from Eighteen-Ought-Nine so the morning walk usually ended with a visit to Susan who loved to fuss over her first granddaughter. Afternoons, Marian walked to the next corner to visit Ruth Rowland, whose son, Clem, of tonsillectomy fame, was six months older than Jane. Ruth was a divorceé at a time when such a status was totally risque, and she lived in the middle flat of a huge house. Other days, Marian would walk several more blocks to Edwina Larkin's house. It was at Edwina's, years before, that Marian had met Bill. Deek Larkin, who had brought Bill to the gathering, was now Edwina's husband and they had a tiny redheaded daughter, Madeline, eight months younger than Jane but bigger, almost from the start.

The three young mothers often traded baby care when the need arose. It was a pleasant arrangement. Growing out of childhood friendships, the closeness between Ruth, Marian and Edwina was greater than that between most sisters. They were friends for seven decades but no time was more rewarding or enjoyable than those years when each had a new baby.

Another little girl came into the Rattray clan when Jane was six months old. James and Lottie Panton presented their son Ronnie with a little sister, named Ellen Greig for her maternal grandmother. Benton Street was added to Marian's daily walk several times a week and the mothers enjoyed chatting about their daughters' accomplishments.

Marian loved routine. Evenings after nursing Janie, she made a habit of taking a few moments while rocking in the old mahogany chair, to review the day's events in her mind, plan the next day, and sing a lullaby to her little girl. One evening Bill stood at the doorway for a moment listening.

"Please, Marian, I know you mean well, but don't sing to her. You'll ruin her ear."

Marian stopped in mid-note. "What do you mean?"

"I hate to say this but you sing off-key. You'll ruin her ear," he repeated. Marian knew he was serious. She didn't believe her voice could have such a drastic effect, but she never sang to her little daughter again.

Jane was christened when she was eighteen months old. Marian was busy organizing the event and the gathering to follow it at McRitchie's. At the last moment, she asked Ruth Rowland to take Jane to have her hair trimmed. Oh, how she rued that request! Ruth took Janie to the same barber who cut her son Clem's hair. Every trace of curl was clipped off Jane's head, and the bangs became almost non-existant. Ruth was so

A Rattray family gathering at McRitchie's home. (back row) Ellen Greig Rattray with her namesake granddaughter, Ellen Greig Panton, James Rattray, Bertha Enderlee Rattray, (front row) Alec Rattray with Ronnie Panton, Lottie Rattray Panton, Greig and Steele McRitchie.

Ellen Greig Panton with her cousin on Jane's christening day. This is the terrible haircut that made Marian weep.

Ellen and Jane with Greig and Steele McRitchie, and Ronnie Panton.

Marian and Bill with their daughter, Jane Paige Rattray on her christening day

horrified with the results, she stopped and bought a magnificent christening bonnet to hide the disaster before taking Jane home. Marian cried when she saw her daughter!

The ceremony was impressive, none the less, and the family gathering afterwards full of high spirits. Jane's hair grew out but over a decade passed before it showed any sign of curling again.

Living room at Ben Brae, 1906.

View of Ben Brae., 1905

Before the turn of the century, it was fashionable for East Bay and San Francisco families to journey by train and boat to Marin County, being met at stations along the way by livery wagons and buggies from the hotels. Several summers, the Murdocks spent lazy days vacationing at Mountain View Inn, which was located between Ross and Kentfield on a hill with a magnificent view of Mount Tamalpais. From there, George and Susan took short trips by buggy looking at property to buy. They located a lot that seemed appropriate and George purchased it.

In 1905, Tone and Perce designed and supervised the building of a summer home for their parents on the lot George had bought in San Anselmo. It was a simple house, with a wide porch across the front. Windchimes hung where the breeze could constantly keep the little glass pieces tinkling. There was a large living-room with a dining area at the west end where tall windows looked out to a vacant lot. A door led to a short hall, the kitchen on one side, the bathroom, opposite, and straight ahead, the back porch. The other door from the living room opened, first, to a steep stairwell, then beyond to a small bedroom which, oddly, also had a door into the kitchen. The stairwell led to the huge attic area with a big dormer window and room for half a dozen brass beds.

In succeeding summers, notched rails were added to the porch, another dormer window was put in the front face of the steep attic roof, and an open air sleeping porch was constructed over a garage on the east side of the house off the stairwell .

The floors, that first year, were wide pine planks, stained dark and highly glossed. Over the fireplace mantle, in the middle of the north wall, a large four-pronged buck was mounted, his bright glass eyes surveying the room noncommittally. None of the Murdock men were hunters: The deer was added for atmosphere.

Years later, when Janie was barely one, she pointed to the head and said, "Moo!" Her delighted parents felt this a sign of great intelligence, to transfer the sight of a cow in a book to the deer on the wall. However, they were quick to point out to her that it wasn't a cow, wasn't even bovine.

"It's a deer. The head of a dead buck." Jane buried her face on her

Ben Brae, when George and Susan moved from Alameda.

mother's shoulder and burst into tears.

The summer after the 1906 earthquake, the Murdock family spent several months at Ben Brae. Much of the permanent planting of the garden was done. A stone wall, made from rocks left over from repairing earthquake damage to the buildings of the nearby theological seminary and generously given to neighbors willing to haul them away, was constructed across the front line. A fragrant mock orange and a pittasporum were planted just behind it. On the west line, with much ceremony, Marian helped her brothers move a small redwood into a prepared hole. She felt proud and fiercely possessive of the young tree. Apple, apricot, figs and a black walnut were planted in the big backyard. A row of artichokes were placed near the back door.

Many vacations and college house parties were held there. Finally, in the early 1920s, George decided to cut back on his responsibilities at his office, going in only once a week, and sell the family home in Alameda. It was much too big for them now that all the children were out on their own. Lim, the Chinese cook, had left several years after the earthquake, housekeepers and maids were difficult to train and keep. Susan, physically, found the task of running the three-story old place far beyond her energy.

So, with a feeling of vacation-like freedom, they moved everything to San Anselmo. The only tug was leaving their close friends and all the members of the Shakespeare Club who had met monthly for years to do readings of his plays. That was hard to give up. On the other hand, it was a relief not to have to keep on doing it. They were, after all, getting on in years, Susan already in her late fifties and George ten years older. It would be good to take life a bit easier.

With the departure of her parents from Alameda, and the scattering of her siblings' families all over the Bay Area, Marian decided they, too, should move to the country. After several scouting weekend visits at Ben Brae, the home in San Anselmo, Marian and Bill were able to locate a little place on the corner of Melville and Austin avenues, just a block up hill from George and Susan.

The telephone rang one afternoon while Marian was still at the apartment in Alameda. Jane was down for her nap and Marian was trying to get some packing done.

"Marian, it's Bella. Terrible news. Sit down."

"What is it?"

"Little Ellen. She's in the hospital. She's dying."

"Oh, my God," Marian cried. "What happened?"

"She was out in the backyard. Got into some ant poison. She swallowed it. Lottie found her. She's not going to make it." Bella was crying.

"Oh, my God," Marian said again, in a whisper. "I'll go over."

Word came soon that Ellen had died. Marian wept as she dressed Jane, her heart breaking for Lottie and Jim. She left Jane with Ruth Rowland and went to the Panton's where she efficiently kept the tea kettle going and the teapot full for the people who were gathering to offer support and sympathy to the distraught parents. The afternoon was long and dreadful, the evening even worse. Marian finally went back to the apartment, picking up Jane at Ruth's on the way. As she hugged the sleepy little girl she felt overwhelmed with agony for Lottie and Jim. "Oh, God," she whispered again. This time it was a prayer.

The packing went on albeit subdued. There was a pall over everything Marian thought or did. But, as always, she did what had to be done and eventually was able to say good-bye to her friends and family. Taking leave of Lottie was the most difficult. Lottie, however, was coping beautifully, putting all her attention and energy into the pregnancy that seemed to sustain her through Ellen's tragic death.

Easter Sunday at Ben Brae. Susan, Jane and Marian in Easter bonnets, 1921.

So Marian and Bill crossed the Bay to Marin, back near her parents. It wasn't any need of their support or help that caused Marian to make the move. In fact, she felt that both Susan and George were dependent on her youth and strength for many things and she was glad to bring herself close enough to be of daily use once again. It was wonderful, too, when holidays came to be right at hand.

The house they rented was just a flat, small and sunny (when the sun shone, drafty and gray when it didn't). It was up a long steep flight of cement stairs from the road. After a miscarriage when Janie was two, Marian started nudging Bill to think about moving some place without those awful stairs. With another pregnancy underway, she renewed her efforts to get off the hill.

Before Billy's birth in November 1922, a newly built house right next door to Ben Brae was available for renting and they moved down the hill. The house was built with a basement, partially below ground level. Whenever it rained, which was often both winters they lived there, the basement flooded. This created a rank dampness that pervaded their bones. But to be right next door to George and Susan was worth it. For Easter that year, James and Ellen Rattray came from Alameda to spend the day and meet little Billy, an occasion which made up for weeks of water in the basement.

The Murdock women: Marian, Bess, Susan Catherine and Rill, Summer 1923.

Ellen and James Rattray, Susan and George Murdock holding baby Billy and Jane, Easter, 1923.

Summers were better. Billy rolled, crawled and played on the front porch, growing up with Chummy, an Airedale-mix with limited brain-power. Chummy loved the baby even though once, when he refused to eat a wooden block, Billy bit his ear with four sharp teeth! Summers, too, the entire clan gathered at Ben Brae for family celebrations and the Rattrays were right at hand.

While still living on Melville, Marian met Ethel Landon whose home was on Austin Avenue two doors up the hill. Ethel and Warren had a daughter, Betty, just Jane's age. The two families became close friends. In fact, holding the Landon's six-month old baby daughter, Florence, strengthened Marian's resolve to have another child as soon as possible.

Out of this friendship came another blessing: The Coterie. Ethel had been in San Anselmo all her life. Her parents, the Buoicks, still lived on a low knoll in the middle of a block of land, directly across the street from Ben Brae, at the foot of Seminary Hill, bordered by Austin, Waverley and Bolinas Avenues. Ethel began including Marian in the monthly luncheons she and her lifelong friends took turns hosting. Wanting something with more substance and meaning than mere socializing, they decided to form a permanent core group of twelve and dedicate themselves to a cause. Thus The Coterie came into being. It lasted for decades and the friends' lives were enriched and warmly intertwined. Marian had taken her turn at hostessing the group in the rented house, sharing her frustration with the winter's problems as well as her excitement over the new place.

Now they were making the move. It was only a block away but in that distance crossed Bolinas Avenue, the street that marked the line between San Anselmo and Ross. This was significant. San Anselmo was a nice place, elm lined streets and circling hills. But Ross was "exclusive." Even in those days, property values were appreciably higher once you crossed the town boundary.

Such things were of little importance to Bill and Marian when they finally took possession of their home. When everything was moved and in place, they stopped at Ben Brae to tell Susan and George. They stood on the wide porch, awkwardly saying good-bye as though they were going more than a short walk away.

"Bill, get the step-stool. I have a housewarming gift for you. I think you'll like it," said Susan.

"Put it here," she continued when he returned to the porch with the little ladder. "Now, take down the wind chimes. They're yours, for your brand new home."

Bill removed the chimes, causing the little rectangles of painted glass to move and tinkle.

"Mother, this is wonderful!" Marian took the fragile musical mobile from Bill. "I've always loved them. Thank you." So carrying the chimes and accompanied by their light melodious sound, the four Rattrays walked home.

Their small bungalow was built just as larger attic/basement roomy homes were going out of vogue and before anyone had figured where to store the things that used to go in the attic or basement. One of the three small bedrooms didn't even have a closet!

The house sat facing the street with three large windows across the front of the living room. A roofless porch had five steps leading from the driveway, a solid shingled banister on either side of the stairs and across the front wall. From an awning support above the banisters, the wind chimes found their new home. Opposite the stairs, a door flanked by two windows opened onto the porch from the living room, and on the right hand wall was the window from the front bedroom.

In the living room, on the north wall directly opposite the front door, was centered a brick fireplace, on the right wall a wide opening to the dining room where a swinging door led to the kitchen. A built-in cabinet with glass doors above and solid wooden doors below, filled that wall. Then came a French door to the hall. Three bedrooms, the kitchen, a closet (for the bedroom without one) and the bathroom opened off the hall, also a broom closet and, across the width of the hall right by the French door, a linen closet with individual doors for each shelf that opened down in an amazingly inconvenient way. Marian called them "flops" and hated them.

The little closetless bedroom also had a French door but, on this first summer, it was usually kept shut since the sleeping porch it was to open on had yet to be built. That was scheduled, along with a garage and a roof on the front porch, for the following year.

The kitchen had two windows over the sink on the north wall, a tall cooler, with screened louvered openings to the outside, a door to a porch with washtubs and the outside door to the tiny square of a porch, where another five wooden steps led down to the path from the front yard. Also in the kitchen was an icebox, a coil hot-water heater, a gas cooking stove and the large Arcola, a coal burning stove which heated water that went to radiators in each room providing gentle warmth.

Their furniture, being sparse, made the house look roomier but Marian had plans and desires for many new items. She was careful, however, not to push for them nor to mention anything in front of her parents. She'd get what she needed somehow and keep Bill happy, or at least unbruised, while she did it. Marian had long before assumed control of their finances so it was up to her to make the decisions as to what to spend for what. She spread their resources as far as they could possibly go and unless Bill "slipped" the budget worked well.

On the top of Seminary Hill, stood the chapel of the San Francisco Theological Seminary. Like the other buildings on the campus, Montgomery and Stewart Halls, it was built in the manner of a Scottish castle on the banks of Loch Lommond, from sandstone mined locally. High on the hill, it dominated the countryside. Each hour the chapel bells played the Westminister Chimes notes, then tolled the time in deep resonant tones. There was a magic to living where you could hear the bells. On special occasions and on holidays, hymns were played. People all over the valley set their clocks, led their lives, and marked their passing by the tolling of the bells.

It was wonderful, Marian thought, as she counted the measured notes to eight o'clock on a Sunday morning, to awaken in the four-poster bed beside Bill, to hear Billy in his room shaking the sides of his crib, to know that Jane was dreaming in her room – either awake or asleep. She was a dreamy child, quiet. *I thought I had all the answers when Janie came along,* Marian mused. *I'd seen mistakes made with my nephews so with her, I corrected them. At least, that's what I thought until I tried my great theories with Billy. Turned out, Jane was the reason everything went so well, NOT my wonderful parenting skills. She is so easy. Billy is a different matter. Is he more like his daddy? Or is it just plain maleness?*

Marian rolled on her side to gaze at Bill, relaxed in sleep. *Does he look thirty-one? What does thirty-one look like?* His hair was darker than when they'd met twelve years earlier but somehow he still seemed a redhead because of his high color, the freckles and the copper hairs on his arms.

He looks so vulnerable, so innocent asleep. I wonder why he drinks, sometimes? I wish he didn't. Do I make him do it?

An imperious yell from Billy cut into her reverie and caused Bill to grunt. He turned to reach for her just as she slipped out of bed.

Marian closed the bedroom door behind her and knotted the cord to the robe around her waist.

"I'm coming," she called to her son as she peeked into Jane's room. She could see an inert lump under the covers and decided to tend to Billy first, as always.

He was standing in the far corner of the metal crib, shaking the side and crying with gusto. His face was flushed, his golden hair a damp halo. The moment he saw his mother the sound stopped, just a left-over hiccup or two. With an angelic smile, he reached out his arms to be lifted from his prison.

Marian snuggled his warm little body and felt the again the flood of love that always overwhelmed her when she held him. *What a miracle! What a perfect family! Sweet Jane, and this dear boy!*

"Morning, Billy-kins. Let's get you dressed."

At two, Billy was a beautiful child, more flamboyant in coloring than his sister, definitely more assertive by nature. He had what his parents referred to as a "red-headed temper" which flared up whenever he was frustrated or crossed. He used it with great effect against Jane until she went off to start kindergarten. Then, the first morning she was gone, something went wrong in his playing. He opened his mouth and howled,

"Mommy, her took my toy!"

Bad mistake! Had Jane figured it out, she could have gotten away with anything from then on. Even valid complaints wouldn't have been believed. But she wasn't a devious or designing child and went on taking the brunt of his tattling for years, making only small rebuttals, usually just dissolving in tears when things went wrong.

One tradition that Marian, who was strong on family rituals, started when her daughter was tiny, commemorated Jane's December birthday. It was a visit to the City of Paris in San Francisco just as soon as the huge Christmas tree was magically installed in the three-story rotunda of that elegant department store.

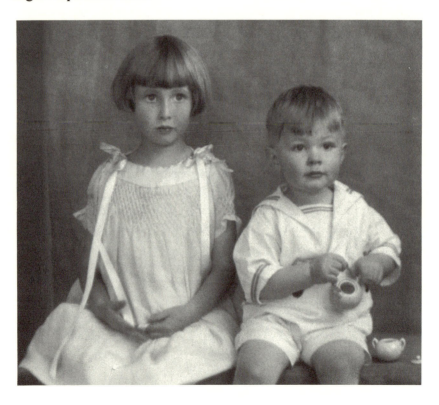

Jane Paige Rattray and William Murdock Rattray, Christmas portrait, 1924

The first year, little Jane, just over one, dressed in a pale pink woolen coat and matching bonnet, stared wide-eyed at the overpowering sight of so many sparkling ornaments and colored lights. She then burst into tears, burying her face on her mother's shoulder. Marian had to leave the building before Jane would look up.

Succeeding years, however, found her excited by the sight and filled with anticipation weeks in advance of the big event.

By the time Jane was seven in 1925, she was an old hand at the excursion. That was the first year Billy was included in the outing. At three, he was deemed old enough by Marian to take part. Perhaps she overestimated his staying power.

Up early and dressed in their best, all three walked down Bolinas Avenue from the little house on Glenwood to the station where they boarded the Northwestern Pacific electric train for a 30-minute ride which, stopping at all the villages on the way – Kentfield, Escalle, Larkspur, Baltimore Park, Corte Madera, Alto, Almonte – whisked them south to Sausalito.

Here, hustled along by the crowd, they walked to the waiting ferry boat. What a thrill the children had gazing in awe through the big glass window in the middle of the boat at the engine, big brass pistons, cylinders and walking beams, pumping and gliding, up and down, propelling the boat through the water.

From the Ferry Building, they took a streetcar up Market Street to Grant Avenue, then walked the last few blocks to the City of Paris. Before entering, they stopped outside to gaze at the special animated corner window which each year depicted an elaborate Christmas scene and drew large crowds of admirers.

Then inside, up the elevator to the mezzanine, where they worked their way to the bannister so the children to look down, straight ahead, and up to the high high ceiling, at the marvelously decorated tree. What astounding overwhelming brilliance to their young eyes!

The next treat was to continue by elevator to the dining room on the fourth floor where Marian treated them to a light lunch, elegantly served.

Marian was proud of her two well-behaved children who, awed by their surroundings, were their shining best.

In the middle of dessert on his maiden trip, Billy, whose eyes were drooping, pushed his still half full crystal ice cream dish on its silver plate, off to one side.

"I want my little bed," he murmured and put his head down on the snowy white tablecloth, instantly sound asleep.

Marian paid the bill, hoisted his inert body to her shoulder and led the way down to the street. That was one day when she splurged and took a taxi back to the Ferry Building.

Billy slept peacefully while they waited nearly a half hour for the next boat, while Marian carried him aboard, throughout the 30-minute ferry ride, and halfway to Ross on the train. He woke up cross that he'd missed so much.

"I want my ice-cream," he said loudly, glaring at his mother.

Jane was five and a half when she started kindergarten, already tall for her age and thin. Her dark blond hair was fine and straight, cut in the short bob of the day with bangs almost to her eyebrows. Her eyes, dark blue like her father's, were large and somehow sad. In fact, her whole demeanor was one of diffidence that made Marian want to shake her. *From where does she get it? Certainly not from my side of the family!*

Certainly not. George was vain as a peacock, Susan serene, Rill, proud to a fault, Tone and Perce as self-assured as possible without being conceited, and Marian, herself, filled with utmost confidence in her capabilities. *Where, then, does Jane get this insecurity? And what can I do to help her, give her some spunk?* Marian didn't have a clue.

Perhaps it was hereditary. Perhaps not. Marian, taught by her brothers to be as capable and efficient as any man, was startled when she found Bill totally unprepared to pound a nail or use a screwdriver. Early in their courtship, when she began visiting the Rattrays she discovered the reason for his inability.

Bill was a child prodigy, able to play the piano at an early age with great mastery. He was six years old when he first played in public. Marian was shown a picture in the family album, under which was written in a fine hand, "Willie, 6, ready for first concert." The picture showed a solemn faced little boy, hair in corkscrew curls almost touching the wide lace collar of his dark velvet suit. He looked angelic and scared to death.

Marian realized that, "Don't let Willie do it" whether "it" be hammer, paint, swing a baseball bat or shovel in the dirt, was the cry of the family during all his growing years. Keep Willie away from anything that might hurt his hands and his astounding ability to use those fingers on the keyboard. No wonder he grew up inept at carpentry! Never had such an activity been expected of him.

Since, however, he was now an insurance adjuster and not a concert pianist, since he only played for small gatherings and not professionally, Marian thought it was about time he learned to help with the little odds and ends that needed doing about the house and yard. And learn he did, although

Marian always wanted to grab the tool out of his hand and attack the problem herself, feeling she could do it better and faster. Probably she could, but Bill was more precise and painstaking: She went for the "effect." He became an excellent paperhanger and meticulous painter. And much later, even raised with pride beautiful tuberous begonias, getting his hands muddy, his finger-nails dirty and enjoying a heady feeling of creating something, making a difference, however small.

During those first summer months, weekends were spent in the garden bringing Marian's plan to life. Bill learned to shovel and hoe, bend garden board, spread gravel and plant roses.

For their seventh wedding anniversary on June 30, the year they moved, Bill had given Marian two plants, an escallonia and a cotoneaster, which she had nourished and nurtured, awaiting the day of their planting. Susan gave them a rose bush, an acacia tree and Scottish broom, all in large pots, on the same occasion. Their first weekend in the house, six weeks after the anniversary, they dug holes in the spots Marian designated and, with ceremony, placed the gifts in the ground.

By mid-October they managed to dig a trench through the rocky north side of the yard. Leaving openings for the walk along the north and the driveway in the center, Bill laboriously continued the trench across the front

Jane and Billy in backyard, before sleeping porch added, 1925

line. He was getting pretty adept with the pick and shovel and managed to keep ahead of Marian who spaded good soil into the bottom of the trench, then, lovingly, lowered small privet hedge plants into place. They looked sparse and spindly the first few years but in time provided a nice barrier.

Three Finnish hawthorns, each nearly seven feet tall, with tiny branches about six inches long, were planted close to the house to eventually shade the front windows. However, by the next spring as the little branches reached out, Marian could see they would do more than shade the house, they'd block vision entirely! So she had Bill perform the first, but by no means

The second lot that Marian promised not to cultivate, planted with wild flowers, 1925.

last, "move that tree" feat. One was shifted to the north line, another to the south line, leaving only the one by the porch in its original position.

The following year, a square box of a garage, flat-roofed and shingled, was built at the end of the drive, ten feet beyond the new roofless sleeping porch. Three locust trees were put in along the driveway, edging what was taking shape as the rose and fruit tree garden. Marian felt a twinge of guilt working here. Her father, when he bought this second lot for them, had told her to leave it unplanted. But she and Bill couldn't; it had become part of the total plan in the back of little red leather book.

Late on Saturday and Sunday afternoons, Bill made a habit of quitting whether Marian was ready to stop or not. After cleaning up, he sat at the Steinway and played for an hour or so – Chopin, Grieg, Lizst, liquid melodies. It was one of the few times he played just for his own pleasure. But others enjoyed the music, too. From wherever she was, Jane crept close, to sit silently, listening for however long her father played. Marian usually busied about and then went to the kitchen to start dinner, which, no matter what, had to be on the table by six PM. Even Billy kept the peace, pushing his little cars quietly across the floor, or out in the gravel where he made intricate roads.

After supper on Saturdays, Marian lit the hot-water heater to bathe the children. As the months passed and the evenings became colder, she also started a fire in the living room fireplace. Then the two clean damp children, wrapped in towels, raced down the hall to be rubbed dry in front of the blaze. On such occasions, Marian wound the Victrola and placed a fresh bamboo needle in the head. As the thick record, usually *March of the Wooden Soldiers*, started spinning, she carefully dropped the needle into place. When the marching music began, Jane and Billy, naked, ran in a wide circle around the rug, arms swinging. "Tippy-toe," Marian called and they both, laughing, raised up on their toes to continue the march. "Other way," she directed, and bumping into each other, giggling, they reversed their direction. Sometimes Marian rewound the phonograph and played the record two or three times before they stopped to get into their night clothes and settle down for her to read them a bedtime story. These were happy evenings and Bill looked on with amused tolerance.

Saturday nights, too, Bill and Marian's friends, Doris and George Mayer, often walked over from their home several up-and-down-hill blocks away. George was a brilliant man who engaged Bill in verbal battles. No matter which side of an issue either took, the debate was heated and erudite. Doris was a quiet womanly person with a surprisingly raunchy sense of humor. She became Marian's friend on a deeper level than anyone else. Perhaps, because Doris had no children, her relationship with Marian was not diluted by the demands of motherhood and they could share their total selves.

The foursome played card games, often jettisoned in favor of the current argument between George and Bill, or records on the Victrola. Jane and Billy were allowed to come in to say "Good night" and get a hug, which they enjoyed since it postponed bedtime for a bit. The couples bought their first crystal radio kits together and George managed to talk Bill through putting his in working order. Oh, what a thrill to wiggle that hair-like wire against the crystal and actually hear voices or music on the earphones! They were able to pull in faraway places – Cleveland, once, they thought. It seemed completely magical, such a distance!

On Monday mornings Madame Calame walked the two and a half blocks from her home in San Anselmo and marched into the house just as the eight o'clock chimes finished their count.

"Good morning. And how are you?" she'd ask as she removed her shapeless coat and tied an apron around her waist. "Are we ready to get started?" Marian always was, having lit the hot water heater, sorted the laundry and gotten the breakfast dishes out of the way.

"Yes, Madame Calame, all set and ready for you." Theirs was a strange relationship – not the mistress of the house and a woman who came in to do the laundry, more like an older countess condescending to help an inept niece! And Marian was far from inept. There were very few people in the world who kept Marian on edge: Madame Calame was one of them. For all the Mondays and Tuesdays they spent together, Marian toed the line, providing what was needed and staying, as much as possible, out of sight.

The two metal wash tubs were filled with hot water, soap was added to one and the white clothes dropped in. A scrubbing on the washboard took care of any soiled spots. Then, hand-wrung, the cleaned clothes were tossed into the clear water, the next load of colored clothes put in the soapy tub. After being swished around in the rinse water, again the items were hand-wrung and dropped into the laundry basket. Out on the little porch, screwed to a tall post, was a pulley clothesline. Here, Madame Calame hung the clothes with wooden pins, in her definite and meticulous way. This was repeated through the colored clothes and finally the dark things, Bill's socks, Billy's outdoor coveralls, dust rags and throw rugs. It took the whole morning to get all washed, and longer to get them hung. Unless it was an unusually warm day, Marian was the one who brought the dry clothes in, and hung the last load out on the line. When it rained, an expanding wooden rack was used and the house resembled a Chinese laundry for days as the heat from the Arcola slowly dried the draped clothing and other articles.

Tuesday mornings, Madame Calame came back to attack the pile of ironing. She worked all morning, making wry comments to Marian whenever she happened into range, which was as seldom as possible. Marian concerned herself with getting Janie off to school, straightening the bedrooms, tending Billy. Working in the kitchen, while Madame Calame held forth, was not to Marian's liking since the ironing board was built into a closet on the wall by the icebox and formed a barricade across the center of the room when down, trapping her as a captive audience.

Actually, Madame Calame was a fount of information and except for the cutting edge of her remarks, an interesting storyteller. She also worked a couple of days a week for Susan which was one of the reasons Marian was reluctant to be too familiar with her; she didn't want words repeated to her mother, not with the twist Madame Calame could give them!

The milkman came daily, delivering two quart bottles of milk. He came whistling down the path to the back door, knocked and walked in, and placed them in the icebox, picking up the empty bottles. It was Jane's chore, and pleasure, to drop the little ladle down into the hourglass like top to trap the cream, and then to pour it carefully into a pitcher for use on their cereal.

The iceman carried blocks of ice, usually 10 pounds, to the icebox in response to a sign in the front window. If they'd forgotten the sign, Jane was sent to flag down the truck. She then had the treat of ice chips picked off by the iceman just for her!

Two things happened in the mid-twenties that delighted Marian. The first was the coming of the flapper era – hair was bobbed, skirts shortened, bosoms flattened, and everything became much less formal. All this fit Marian's personality to a tee. She was the first in her circle to have her hair cut. Bill wasn't sure he liked it but to Marian it looked smart and modern, held a fingerwave well and was a breeze to care for.

The second thing was in a way even more liberating. George bought an automobile, a 1924 Chevrolet, black, with four doors and isinglass curtains that snapped into place on sturdy grommets. George had never learned to drive an automobile, didn't want to, but since Frank Spring and Perce had taken care of her early training in automotive arts, the car was put into Marian's possession with the understanding that she would chauffeur her parents wherever they needed to go. She thought it a wonderful arrangement since they seldom wanted to be driven anywhere. Marian kept the car in their new garage. She was able to take Janie to school, pick her up, even go shopping for the few things that weren't delivered and still be able to attend to her parents needs when they asked.

Once she was stopped in downtown San Anselmo by a policeman who was not amused to see little Billy sitting on his mother's lap as she drove down the street.

"Sorry, lady, that's totally illegal. You can't hold a baby in your lap when you're driving."

"Why not?" Marian asked. "He's safer here than loose on the seat."

"Yeah, but it's still against the law."

"I'll remember that, but I'll have to drive home this way." She left him scratching his head. But after that she figured out a way to tie Billy in the seat beside her.

Once Marian concocted a contraption to keep Billy safely harnessed, she began organizing picnics for the family and for friends, especially Ruth Hansen, one of the Coterie, who had two boys, Harold Junior, Jane's age, and Graham, a bit younger than Billy. Ruth also drove a big car. She sometimes picked up Ethel Landon and her girls, too.

Marian had located a little sandy beach near China Camp in San

Rafael. Way out in the country, it was reached by a twisting road that hugged the bay. The big advantage was that the beach, though small, was only steps from the road. When picnicking with six young children, this is a true plus. The ladies usually went in the late morning, let the children play and paddle, ate lunch and then packed up and went home for naps.

One slightly foggy July Saturday, Marian talked Bill into coming to her favorite spot. Off they went, bag and baggage, Billy and Jane bouncing on the back seat, he straining his harness to the utmost. Marian was a perfect commissary officer: Picnics were her specialty. She could produce fantastic lunches, well-balanced and appetizing, and serve them with a flourish. This day was no exception: cold chicken, carrot sticks, fixings for sandwiches, cookies and fruit juice.

Though overcast, the weather was warm. Bill played with the children in the shallow water, then lay on the course sand, contentedly watching them. Neither he nor Marian gave a thought to the sun, dimmed as it was by the high fog. They should have paid attention.

Almost before they reached home, blisters were appearing on Bill's feet, his shins, his shoulders. By Monday, when time to work came around, getting into his city clothes was almost impossible. The pain of that outing lasted for weeks and changed Bill's outlook about the joys of picnicking on the beach. It was years before he made that mistake again.

The first summer they had the car, Billy was two, Jane six, and after poring over brochures, Bill and Marian decided to go to Castle Hot Springs in the Sierra foothills for vacation.

Bill's oldest brother, Alec and his gentle wife, Bertha, were invited to come over from San Francisco and spend the two weeks in the house. This suited everyone – gave Bill and Marian knowledge that place would be cared for, the garden watered, and it moved Alec and Bertha away from the city's summer fog for a sunny respite.

Finally it was time to leave, the car was packed with Billy in front on a pillow, strapped between his parents and Jane on the back seat, in space left by suitcases and boxes. They drove all afternoon and stopped overnight in Auburn, staying in a big two-story hotel with a wide veranda across the front. Their corner room was on the second floor with tall windows overlooking the roof of the veranda and, on the long side, down to a vacant lot next door. A crib for Billy and a cot for Jane had been provided.

In the middle of the night, the clanging of bells and shriek of sirens woke the children and Marian. Both children began to cry. Marian could smell smoke, hear the crackling of flames and see the orange reflection of fire on the ceiling of their room.

"Wake up, Bill," she said, shaking him. "There's a fire!"

Bill opened his eyes, reached up his hand to feel the wall behind him. "Not even warm yet," he said, rolling over.

"Damn! Do something!"

"What, for instance?" he asked, not moving.

Marian ran to the window and looked out. Pandemonium. Fire engines, firemen shouting, hauling hoses, volunteers running about. And in the middle of the vacant lot, a blazing haystack. *Nothing but a bloody blazing haystack!* Marian turned from the window in disgust.

Within minutes, the flames were doused, the fire dying. Marian, disappointed that there was no need to roust Bill out of his annoyingly unconcerned sleep, reassured the children, and, with a withering look at her husband's unperturbed form, allowed them both to climb into bed with her for the rest of the night, hoping they'd bother Bill. They didn't and she had a hard time sleeping.

Cousin Jamie Panton and Billy on the porch at Castle Hot Springs, 1925.

Jane and Billy on the step of their cabin, Castle Hot Springs, 1925.

Castle Hot Springs was a jumble of cabins, spread around under the branches of tall trees, oak, pine, and occasional cedar, reached by dusty dirt paths and roads. There was a dining hall that also served as a recreation room, with an upright piano in the corner where Bill and a woman who rolled her eyes at him, played duets of the latest dance music for the rest of the guests after dinner, pounding out *Dinah, Sweet Georgia Brown* and *Sometimes I'm*

Happy with a rousing beat. Adjacent to the dining room, down a dirt walk, was a covered swimming pool, with a sulfur smell to the warm water. Farther down the hill was the ice house. Here Horace, a tall slim cowboy-type handyman, worked, stacking perishables by the large blocks of ice, bringing watermelon and other delights to the dining hall. Horace also gave the children rides on the bed of the truck, and in the evenings, while Bill was playing the piano, tried to entice Marian to go for a drive. She flirted with him but never climbed into the truck.

Bill's sister, Lottie, with her husband, Jim Panton, and their children, Ronnie, Jamie, and little Betty Ann, were also vacationing there. They had seen the Pantons only at holidays since leaving Alameda and this was a happy reunion. The older cousins had fun romping together. Jim taught Ronnie to swim the side-stoke he'd learned in Scotland. Marian almost succeeded in teaching Jane the crawl and everyone was on guard to keep Jamie and Billy from leaping into the pool.

Two more summer vacations were enjoyed by Bill and Marian, Billy and Jane. In 1926, they drove to Donner Lake in the Sierra. Almost there, Marian had Bill stop the car at the side of the road by a bank of snow. Jane was looking quite green as she always did in the mountains.

Marian ready to make snow cream for Billy, Jane, and other children above Donner Lake, 1926.

"This'll fix you up, Janie. Come on. Get out and carry this up on the snow." She handed Jane a bag, and rummaging around dropped some bowls and spoons into it. Then, hauling Billy, and handing Bill another sack to carry, she led the way up the snow.

"Here's a good spot." She sat Billy down on a piece of canvas, then scraped the top layer of snow away in a small circle in front of her. Digging a hole, she poured milk from a can into it, then, from another bag she took juicy peaches, skinned and sliced them into the hole, added sugar from a jar and mixing it all with snow in the hole, she filled a bowl for each of them.

"How's that?"

"Good, Mommy." Jane spooned it into her mouth, smiling at her mother. She was feeling much better now. The sun was warm, the snow melting through her clothes was cooling. The view was spectacular. Huge granite rocks, rising out of the leftover snow and tall pine trees wherever she looked, faintly but pungently scenting the air.

Soon the impromptu ice-cream (or snow-cream) feast was finished, everything packed and put back in the car and off they went on the last miles before reaching Donner Lake.

They had a cabin, one large room, with screened windows to keep out the bugs and shutters to protect against the chill of the nights. Meals were announced by the cook clanging the iron triangle with a metal rod, producing a penetrating sound that roused even Jane out of bed in the morning. Food was hearty and abundant.

Mornings were spent at the beach, romping in the cool water of the lake, after lunch was a quiet time, then hiking or horseback riding until dinner. There was an outdoor dance platform with a Victrola and records. All the children happily learned the Charleston by watching the grown-ups dance to *Yes, Sir, That's My Baby*, and they performed each evening before being trundled off to their cabins. Some nights there were bonfires and singing. It was a small resort, low scale and friendly. They spent two lovely summers there, ten days each year. Both years, Enid and Carlos Hildebrand who lived across the valley in Ross with their sons, Kenny and Don, who were older than Jane, and Levant and Florence Brown from the big house up the hill, with their children, young Levant, and Sheri, who was just Jane's age but twice her size, were also there. This made it comfortable for the children. Neither Jane nor Billy was good at making new friends which irritated Marian. Enid was a large woman with a ready smile and a matter-of-fact attitude. She and Marian became close during vacation and carried the friendship into their everyday Ross life. Next to Doris, Enid was Marian's closest friend.

The summer of 1927 was their last vacation for a long time. They went to Silver Lake, also in the Sierra, even more casual than Donner and, an important factor, comparatively inexpensive. Here the accommodations were more 'tent' than 'cabin' and there were fewer guests. But the setting was beautiful - same tall pines, mammoth granite boulders, scratchy chartreuse moss on branches blown from the trees.

Jane's hair was cut in a boyish bob that summer and in her navy blue short pants that Marian had made and shirts, she looked like Billy's big brother. Her favorite pastime was to ride with the cowboys in the late afternoon when they went to corral the cows. The pasture, under snow and water in the winter, was cracked and dry, and as the horses trotted along, hundreds of tiny frogs leaped out of the way. Most of them made it.

Jane and Billy on edge of Silver Lake, 1927.

Jane on horseback before he ran away with her, Silver Lake, 1927.

One night, coming back from a run, Jane took a shortcut. When the horse sensed his closeness to the barn, he bolted across a field. Unfortunately, it was where the clotheslines were strung and before Jane could duck her head, a wire struck her across the throat, knocking her back in the saddle.

She continued on to the barn, turned in the horse, and tears streaming down her face, hurried to the tent.

"Good heaven's, what happened?"

Janie couldn't speak but somehow managed to convey to Marian about the horse, the wire, the pain. The red line across her neck was mute evidence of the injury. It was days before she could swallow without wincing, and even longer before she could make a sound. But to everyone's surprise, Janie was ready to go riding the next afternoon!

"Can you believe it?" Marian asked Bill. "She's usually such a crybaby, and here she is, can't even talk, but up on that horse again." She shook her head in surprise and pleasure.

"Maybe she's more like you than you think," Bill answered. He was proud of his daughter and delighted when Marian seemed to share his feelings. So often she criticized Jane and, Bill felt, indulged Billy.

The summer couldn't have been more special even if they had known it was the end of an era. In spite of Jane's injury, a few bee stings, several sunburns, and a tummyache or two, it was relatively free of trauma. Bill and Marian had a fine time with a minimum of tension between them. To add a fitting climax to the season, a family gathering was planned at Ben Brae to celebrate Rill's and Tone's forty-seventh birthday the end of July. Marian, just home from Silver Lake and full of energy, threw herself into the preparations with her usual gusto.

Only Perce was unable to come. He and his boys, Steve and Dickie, had a trip planned for that weekend which he couldn't cancel. The entire family felt disappointment. Perce was everyone's favorite and his dynamic presence would be missed. He kept people laughing. All except Rill. He always teased her (he had for over forty years) and the best part of it, for the rest of the family, was that Rill didn't know she was being teased. He drove her to distraction as everyone laughed harder and louder. Perce was unmer-

Twins birthday, Ben Brae: Front: cousins Otis Schlesinger, Bob and Geordie Murdock, Jane and Billy Rattray. Back: Tone, Marian, Bill, George, Susan, Rill and Oscar.

Susan and George flank the twins, Rill and Tone, at their birthday party, July 1927.

ciful, verbally bantering his poor big sister until he finally tired of the game, hoping always that she'd catch on and laugh with the rest of them. This year Rill was safe. Perce wouldn't be around.

Tone and Bess with their two arrived just minutes after Rill, Oscar and Otis drove up.

"Look at Otis," Bess exclaimed. "He's nearly a year younger than Bobby and he's a head taller. Come on, Bobby!" she said to her son. "Shame on you. You can't let that happen. Grow!"

"Sure, Mom," answered Bob with a laugh as he threw a mock punch at Otis, who ducked.

"Hey, look," he said. "Here comes Uncle Bill and the kids. Wouldn't you know they'd be last to arrive. They have to walk two whole blocks!"

Marian had been at Ben Brae since early morning getting everything ready. It was a simple gathering, just a baker's dozen of family members. Marian planned potato salad, fried chicken, corn on the cob and, of course, a huge decorated sheet cake. Susan had ordered it from Keintz Bakery and Marian picked it up on her way over. Madame Calame was there even before Marian and by the time everyone arrived, all was in readiness. The afternoon went quickly. The boys climbed the black walnut tree in the backyard and taunted Jane and Billy from their lofty perches.

Soon time ran out and the automobiles were loaded up for their trips back to the East Bay. The boisterous good-byes lasted until the final car rounded the corner and disappeared from sight.

Less than a month later Marian greeted Bill , as he came home from work, with news.

"We have a letter from Charlie Baldwin, Bill. He wants to come visit us next weekend."

"Great. Been years since we've seen him. What time?"

"The four o'clock train, Friday."

And so it was that Charlie came back into their lives. It had been a long time. In fact, Marian hadn't seen him since the day they met in San Francisco seven years before when Janie was 18 months old. Thinking back on it now, the whole scene – every word – sprang into clarity from the deep recess where she'd shoved it.

They'd met by prearrangement, that long-gone day, on the sidewalk above the entrance to the Stockton Street tunnel. Charlie had insisted, with uncharacteristic determination, that he must see her. Marian couldn't image why, but for old times sake and thinking of her dear friend, his sister, Polly, she'd agreed to his plan.

It was a sunny day but the wind was brisk and cool. Wearing a navy wool peplum dress, her blond hair peeking out from the brim of the round hat perched on her head, she faced him.

"Hello, Charlie. What's this all about?"

"You're looking great. Motherhood becomes you."

"And?" Marian prodded.

"And – I'm concerned. I've heard Bill's drinking quite a bit. Too much, too often."

"Oh, Charlie. It's not that bad. Usually." She shrugged and made a moué. "Anyhow, what can I do about it?"

"Leave him. Marry me."

"Oh, Charlie," she said again, this time shaking her head and smiling at him. "No. No before, no now."

He took her hand. "Why 'no'? I could understand before. You wanted a baby. I can't give you babies but I can be a good father to Janie. And I've always loved you. You know that. And you do love me 'like a brother' you once said. But it could become more." He looked so earnest, so determined, it was difficult to tell him it just wouldn't work. She couldn't even imagine being married to Charlie.

"Dear old friend!" Compassion clouding her eyes, she reached to gently touch his face. "I do love you. And you're sweet to care and be so concerned. But I can't leave Bill. He's my husband. We'll work it out. And besides," she said raising her chin against what she imagined his reaction would be, "I want another baby. I don't want Janie to be an only child."

Charlie shook his head as if to clear the words away and smiled to hide his disappointment. They talked awhile longer, not saying much, and parted then with a hug and a friendly kiss.

Now Charlie was coming to spend the weekend, to see Jane and meet Billy. Where would he sleep? Lately, Bill had been using the extra bed in Billy's room. Well, she could move one bed into Janie's room for Billy and give Charlie Billy's room. Bill would have to share her bed. He'd enjoy that. More than she would, Marian thought with a little grimace. Funny, now that she had her two babies she really didn't want anything to do with Bill, physically. She knew that was very difficult for him but she couldn't help it.

Bill walked down to the station to meet the train and escort Charlie home. They had always gotten along well; Bill had sensed no threat in Charlie and, of course, he knew nothing of the long-ago meeting above the Stockton Street tunnel. Probably wouldn't have worried about it had he known.

Later, after supper they sat and caught up with each other's lives. Janie, who recognized a friend, climbed onto Charlie's knee and settled back with contentment. Billy clung to Marian and glowered through his long eyelashes at the man he saw as a stranger and perhaps even an enemy.

Saturday, they worked in the garden until Bill and Charlie went in to listen to the football game. It was a relaxed and happy weekend. Charlie left on the noon train Sunday without ever speaking to Marian out of Bill's hearing. Evidentially, what he saw reassured him that Marian was happy and well. He said he'd come again and everyone, even Billy, hugged and kissed him good-bye.

Marian began feeling sick just a few weeks later and figured she'd picked up a bug somewhere. Then one morning, early, when her stomach turned over and the room spun around she groaned aloud. "Oh, no, it can't be. I'm not!" But she knew beyond doubt that she was pregnant, dating from the weekend of Charlie's visit when Bill had shared her bed.

Once she'd adjusted to the fact, her overwhelming love of having babies filled her heart. However, she continued to be wretchedly sick, much worse than ever before. It was impossible to keep anything down. She forced herself to try, knowing that nutrition was doubly important now that she was, as they said, "eating for two."

She waited for Bill to notice her sudden boltings to the bathroom. When he didn't, she finally told him.

"Bill, guess what? We're going to have another baby. Isn't that nice?" She smiled at him, brightly.

He looked stunned. "Why? No, when? Are you sure? Oh, God!"

He sat without moving. She continued, "I think it'll be about June. I haven't been to a doctor yet but I'm sure. Harry's not doing obstetrics any more. He was so great when I had Billy. I have to find someone soon. I've never felt so sick."

When she finished talking, he got up without a word and left the room. Soon she heard the front door close. He didn't come home until much later that night, long after she'd cried herself to sleep. He slipped in beside her, looking at her face softened in repose and touched by moonlight. *Oh, God,* he whispered to himself. *How can I handle this? What am I going to do? She's been crying. I hate it when she cries. When I tell her to stop, she says, "When I stop crying, that's when you should start to worry. It'll mean I no longer care." But what can I do? What should I do?*

What he did was drink more than usual, coming home later evenings after work, spending more money foolishly at a time when every penny should be put away for the coming expenses. Because he couldn't face the responsibility of another child, he turned his back on the two he had and their mother – his very sick and pregnant wife. He hated himself for what he was doing yet couldn't bring himself to stop.

The distance between them grew. He moved back into Billy's room the night after he'd learned of the pregnancy. Always a quiet man, he became almost nonverbal during the infrequent times when he was around. Marian was no help. She was too sick to make any effort toward bridging the gap that stretched between them. In fact, she was so angered by his actions that whenever their paths crossed, she lashed out at him. He quickly left the room, refusing a confrontation.

Marian's anger slowly faded. Each day was spent trying to drag through the simplest acts; feeding the children, getting Jane to and from school, keeping up with the laundry and housework, both of which were cut to the minimum. As the holidays approached, Billy had his fifth birthday, then Jane her ninth. Marian was determined to have a happy Christmas and to bring Bill back into the family circle. She stopped confronting him with all the things she thought he was doing wrong. Instead, she matter-of-factly included him in her plans and quietly told him what she expected. It worked. Christmas, in spite of her nonstop nausea and lack of energy, was everything Marian wanted it to be. Bill was home and sober. They went to church, St. John's Episcopal across from the grammar school near the Ross Common. It was a far cry from Marian's Unitarian roots but somehow very sustaining. The children received the gifts they most desired. The weather was clear, cold and crisp.

Perhaps I'll live through this, after all, Marian thought as she climbed into bed that night. *Thank you, God.*

The months dragged on. Marian became huge. "Look. This baby is a perfect ledge to set the telephone on! In fact, a dinner plate, fully loaded, could balance here."

The baby was due the middle of June. Early in May two things happened. Somewhere, somehow Marian picked up a staph infection which Dr. DeLancy was worried about. The second discovery was even more disturbing. Because of her size, the doctor ordered X-rays taken. He returned to his office after viewing them.

"Well, it doesn't look too good," he said. Then added, with total lack of sensitivity. "We can definitely see two heads in the picture – but I only pick up one heartbeat on the stethoscope. Don't know what to think."

"What are you telling me?" demanded Marian. "That I have a two-headed baby? Or twins but only one's alive? What?"

"I really don't know what to think. We'll just have to wait and see. I'm more worried about that infection. It could be serious."

Marian sat, stunned, trying to grasp what she'd just been told. Her clearest feeling was one of anger at the doctor, not a "shoot the messenger if the news is bad" reaction, but anger that he could be so unaware of the impact of his words, so unfeeling in the way he presented the situation.

"Make an appointment for next week," Dr. DeLancy said, dismissing her. She rose and waddled out to the nurse's desk.

"Next week," she said numbly.

Marian found it almost impossible to slide behind the wheel of the car. *Guess I'll have to be driven from now on*, she thought, superimposing the ordinary on the other thoughts racing through her mind. *I won't mention this to anyone. It'll have to turn out all right. If it doesn't, that's soon enough to face it.*

Two weeks later, her waterbag broke and pains started. Bill was at work, Billy napping, Jane at school. Marian picked up the phone.

"Enid, I need help. The baby's coming." Enid, her dear friend from Donner Lake days, best of all, had an automobile she could drive. "Can you come, right now?"

"I'll be there."

What to do about the children? Mazie MacDonald, in a new house two lots up the hill, was closest. She was weeks overdue with her fourth child but she could handle the situation.

Another call and Mazie, holding four year old Robbie's hand, appeared at the door. "Don't you worry, now. I'll be here when Billy wakes up and when Janie walks home. Then we'll decide."

Enid arrived. They helped Marian into the car and Enid drove off to Cottage Hospital in San Rafael, just minutes away.

"I'll go back to the house and relieve Mazie and stay until Bill gets home. Wish we could reach him, but don't you worry. Just have that baby." Enid squeezed Marian's hand as she was wheeled away.

There were several white-coated men around her bed. Dr. DeLancy had arrived and was explaining the facts to them as though Marian weren't there and deeply involved in the situation.

"We have a problem or two here," he said. Describing the X-rays, he continued. "So it could be a difficult delivery. And I have reason to believe her heart can't stand a long labor. But there's that staph infection. Can't do a section, she'd die of blood poisoning. The prognosis isn't too good."

At this point, Marian sat up, grimacing. "Get out!" she shouted, "Just go away. I won't have you around. I won't have this baby if you're in the delivery room. Go!" A pain rocked her and she fell back on the pillow with a groan.

Dr. DeLancy took a step toward her. "No! I mean it. Don't touch me. Don't even look at me. Get out. NOW!" Another groan.

"What's going on here?" Dr. Harry Hund, the genial and efficient doctor who had delivered Billy five years earlier, recognizing Marian's voice, stepped into the room.

"Oh, Harry! Tell this idiot to get out of here. I don't know or care about protocol. Just get rid of him and take over. Please!" Harry looked at DeLancy who shrugged and walked out of the room.

Harry took a quick glance at the nurse's chart, placed his hands on Marian's belly, felt the sharp contraction that arched her back.

"Get her into delivery. I'll meet you there."

"Yes, Dr. Hund," said the nurse, moving swiftly and efficiently into the breach. "Let's go have this baby."

"Yes!" replied Marian as another pain grabbed her middle in a vise.

Five minutes later, in the bright lights of the delivery room, Harry looked up. "The baby's breech. But you're doing fine. You can handle it, Marian. Now, push. Deep breathe. Again!"

As the pain took over, Marian threw all her strength into pushing and was rewarded by the sight of a red and wiggling baby in Harry's big gentle hands. "It's a girl, Marian. A perfect little girl." He passed the baby to the waiting nurse.

"I'm not done," Marian panted. "I don't feel finished. Oh, God!"

"Well, guess what?" Harry's deep voice sounded amused and calm. "You aren't through! There's another one, breech, too. It won't be long. Don't worry. You're fine. The baby's fine. Here we go!"

Marian gave herself over to the pain and pushed beyond where she'd ever gone before. "I forgot it hurt like this! No more! I can't stand any more!"

"You don't have to. She's here, another girl!" Harry's voice was exultant. "A beauty! Two babies in ten minutes. I call that a miracle! You did well, Marian, really a good job."

"I had to," Marian whispered, smiling faintly. "I had to show that idiot DeLancy what a fool he is."

The babies were named Suzanne Leticia and Marianne Laurilla.

Bill and Marian with the twins, six weeks old, July 1928.

They weighed 5 pounds 11 ounces and 6 pounds 4 ounces. In spite of being three weeks early, neither of them classified as premature since both were over five pounds.

Having wrapped Marianne in a blue blanket with a border of white rabbits, and Suzanne in a plain pink one, the nurses dubbed them "Bunny" and "Pinky". And thus they were known for several months. Finally Marian put her foot down.

"From now on they'll be called by their proper names, Marianne and Suzanne, by all of you. Even you, Billy. No more Bunny and Pinky around here. Understand?"

Bill, to his surprise, was thrilled with the babies. He arrived at the hospital each evening, sober and smiling. He brought Janie to see her little sisters. She felt an almost guilty responsibility for them. "I wished for a little sister on turkey wishbones twice. And I won, both times. That's why!"

She was both proud of her feat and stunned by her power.

Billy was not as happy about the newcomers as his sister or his father. He saw them, rightly, as usurpers of the place he'd held in the family all the years of his life.

Indeed, two babies made a difference in the household. Marian's smug assumption that if the baby was a girl she'd share Jane's room, or if a boy he'd bunk with Billy, was shot down. It was soon apparent, whatever the final room arrangement, they had to be separated for the present by as much distance as possible or they'd continually wake each other up. For the first three months, Marian nursed one and gave the other a bottle at alternate feedings. The babies thrived but she was thin and exhausted.

"You'll have to wean them. Put 'em both on bottles," Harry informed her. "Let Bill feed them sometimes. Let Jane. Sleep all night for a change. The infection DeLancy was so big on is all cleared up. But you're way down, for you. Be good to yourself."

Mazie MacDonald had gone into the hospital two days later than Marian. After a long and strenuous labor, she'd brought forth her first daughter, a ten-pound black haired colleen.

When the babies were three weeks old, Mazie carried Jean-Marie down the hill. The twins were lying, pink and bald, dainty and tiny, on the big double four-poster bed. Mazie gently placed Jean-Marie between them. With her mop of black curls, black brows and eyelashes, and weighing nearly twice as much, Jean-Marie looked months older. Actually, she was. The twins were three weeks early; Jean-Marie, a month late. It showed.

Jane's first duty when she arrived home from school was to fold the pile of diapers in the middle of her bed. And what a pile it was! It took about an hour to transform the jumbled heap of squares into several neat piles of triangles. Luckily, summer vacation started and the diapers could be folded as soon as they were taken from the line.

Madame Calame no longer came to do the laundry but Marian organized the chore with efficiency, doing small loads as soon as possible, never letting it get ahead of her. She used Jane's help in many ways. Jane loved being able to dress one of the babies while Marian did the other. Suzanne was the more placid of the two and, in a sense, became Janie's baby. Marianne

Both sets of grandparents celebrate the twin's first birthday. James Rattray with Ellen, holding Marianne, George Murdock and Susan, holding Suzanne.
(above) The Rattray family on the same occasion, May 1929.

showed flashes of temper, was harder to handle. Because of this, she was a challenge to her mother. Marian did love a challenge!

The weekend closest to the twin's first birthday, all four grandparents came to celebrate the day. George and Susan walked over the two blocks from Ben Brae as they often did. James and Ellen made the trip from Alameda, crossing the Bay on two ferry boats, first from the mole to the Ferry Building in San Francisco, then on a second boat to Sausalito. There they boarded an electric train to Bolinas Avenue where Marian met them in the automobile. On this great occasion, the little guests of honor were outfitted in ruffles and bows and looked like angels.

Marian and Bill were proud showing off the babies. Jane was happy with the gathering but Billy glowered most of the day. All this fussing over two little girls was more than he could stand.

Marianne was startlingly beautiful. Her hair was a halo of silver blond ringlets that seemed to give off its own light, her eyes, full of mischief, were sky blue, and her cheeks so rosy she looked almost feverish. Added to this was her agility. She was constantly in motion and full of laughter at her own antics!

Suzanne, too, was a darling baby. She was, however, slightly overshadowed by her twin. Her hair was strawberry blond, but straight. Her eyes were deeper blue, but didn't give off sparks, her round cheeks were pink, not flaming. Her smile was sweet and gentle. And she was content to sit, to crawl, frustrated in her attempts at walking.

In spite of the healthy happy babies, things were not all sunny. One day, as Marian was cleaning the top shelf of the cooler, an act she didn't perform often, her hand found a bottle. Pulling it out she saw it was a pint of whiskey, still sealed. "Stupid man," she said aloud and instinctively moved to the sink where she twisted the cap off and poured it down the drain. "There! You won't drink that!" Just then Bill walked into the kitchen.

"What are you doing?" he asked in irritation, reaching for the now-empty bottle.

"What's it look like? I dumped it out. You have no right to spend our money on such stuff."

Anger flared in Bill's eyes. He spotted her wedding and engagement rings on the window sill above the sink where she placed them while cleaning and quickly picked them up.

"What kind of a wife are you? Doing that?"

"Better than you deserve," Marian said. "If you drink…"

Bill turned and went to the back door. Standing on the little porch, looking over the vacant lot next door, he raised his arm and hurled the rings into space. With a cry of disbelief, Marian spun on her heel and left the room.

Now I've done it, Bill thought. *That was a stupid move. I've just made her madder.* Sheepishly he went down the back stairs and out into the tan grass on the rocky slope next door. Carefully eying the distance from the porch, he dropped to his knees and began looking for the rings.

Within a sort time he located both and brushing off his pants, headed home. Marian didn't look up from where she was sitting in the bedroom. He walked over and held out his hand, the rings in the palm.

"Sorry," he said softly. She picked up the rings and slipped them on her finger, with a slight acknowledgment of her head. With typical inability to discuss their feelings, that was that. They just went on.

The month after the twins turned one, Marian and Bill rented the house for the summer and moved down to Ben Brae to stay with Susan and George. It was a tremendous job, getting all the personal items out of the house but worth it since vacation rentals were prodigiously high.

Under the now tall redwood tree that Marian had helped plant when she was twelve, Jane and Billy built the whole kingdom of OZ that summer. Billy insisted that all his precious little automobiles were appropriate additions, and the two made a maze of roads. Using the head of a hammer and a bit of water, they smoothed the dirt to a sheen, just the right width for the cars. Jane landscaped the surrounding terrain with rocks and pebbles and tiny living plants. This was one of the closest times the two had ever shared and

At Ben Brae, the twins in Billy's red wagon, Summer, 1929.

they played long hours without any bickering, each allowing the other to do what they did best. Forty years later, on the last afternoon of his life, wracked and weakened with cancer, regressed in his mind to a happier place, Billy spoke, in a youngster's voice, of the kingdom they built. Jane realized he was *there,* a red-headed six year old, enjoying a carefree time long gone. Somehow it eased her heart.

This was the summer little Marianne began to climb. Suzanne was content to sit and smile at the world but Marianne wanted to look down on it. Getting up on chairs and tables was easy. Reaching the top of the piano took longer but was not impossible! She couldn't get down from her high perches, however, and would yell, "Mommy, Mommy, Mommy!" until rescued.

She never fell. Learning to walk, her wiry agile body seemed perfectly balanced. Suzanne had a more difficult time, suddenly plopping down on her well-padded bottom, with a surprised look on her face, after two or three tottering steps.

One afternoon, Jane started out to pull them around the block in Billy's red wagon. Halfway there, Suzanne leaned over the side and lost her balance, tumbling out. Jane was horrified at the blood on her little sister's face. Picking her up, she ran to the closest house.

"Come in, come in," the woman who answered the door said, leading the way to the kitchen sink. A cloth with cold water was used to wipe Suzanne's face, disclosing a small cut on her lip which soon stopped bleeding.

"Isn't this one of the Rattray twins?" the lady asked.

With a shock of panic, Jane remembered Marianne, sitting in the wagon in the street.

"Thank you, thank you," she said to the woman, and grabbing Suzanne, rushed out, afraid of what she'd find. But Marianne was happily and safely ensconced, surveying the world with pleasure.

Jane reversed her direction and returned home, both babies happy, but one, to her shame, wet and bloody.

This was the summer, too, the Graf Zeppelin, Germany's mammoth airship, made her round-the-world tour. Papers were full of her progress from the time she left Lakehurst, New Jersey, starting the race on United States soil as requested by William Randolph Hearst, who put up the quarter million it would cost, across the Atlantic to Frankfort, for the beginning of the German race, over Europe, Siberia, Asia, to Tokyo, Japan. Next stop would be San Francisco. Actually, it wasn't a stop. It was more of a fly-by. The ship was scheduled to dock at Mines Field, Los Angeles.

Marian read all she could find on the event. "I think we should take the children to see the Graf," she said to Bill.

"Where? How could you get close enough? They wouldn't be able to see a thing."

"We could drive up Corte Madera grade and see from there."

"It'd be too crowded, and too far away. They'd never see it."

"What do you mean? It's as long as two city blocks and as tall as a twenty-story building. *Not see it?* They aren't blind?"

"So where do you think you can park the car on the top of the grade?"

"I'll make dinner reservations at Tam O'Shanter Inn. We can sit and see and eat, too."

"It'll never work. But go ahead. Do what you want."

So Marian made all the arrangements. She hired a young neighbor to come in to help Susan with the twins. They were, she agreed, too young to enjoy the event. Billy and Jane were excited. Bill condescended to accompany them, hoping, Marian was sure, to see it turn out as dismally as he predicted.

She drove. They started mid-afternoon on a warm August day going through Kentfield, Larkspur and Corte Madera, and on up the narrow twisting, curving road. There were a few more cars than usual, but nothing as dire as Bill imagined. Marian found a place to park at the inn on the crest of the hill. Their table was ready and located by one of the wide windows that overlooked the valley down to the Bay at Sausalito and across to San Francisco. It was perfect.

As they finished eating and the sun began to drop, someone spotted a silver silhouette in the bright sky. The zeppelin came right at them, an amazing sight, then swung in a slow lazy arc toward the Berkeley hills and Oakland. It was visible for quite awhile, much to the smug delight of Marian, the excited joy of the children, and the grudging pleasure of Bill.

When they went out to the automobile, the horns, sirens and whistles of a multitude of boats could be faintly heard. As the children piled into the car, Marian grinned at Bill and he had the grace to smile back.

Later, Billy and Jane were both bouncing with excitement as they told George and Susan of the wonders they'd seen. Marian was glad she'd made the effort.

That was the last summer the three generations would spend together. Some homing instinct within George and Susan caused them to turn their thoughts and hearts back to Alameda. Ben Brae was put on the market and sold quickly. A big comfortable two room and bath suite in a boarding house, directly across the street from the old Rattray home and conveniently near Tone and Bess on Benton Avenue, was rented by George. They moved "home" just a few blocks from where they'd started.

Here they were close to the few friends who had survived the years the Murdocks had been in San Anselmo - the Maurers, the Coburns. They were happy, and pleased with the ease of living where all meals were provided, where other gentile older people were being served as befitted their stations in life.

The last big celebration in San Anselmo before Ben Brae was placed on the market, was an elegant family party to commemorate George and Susan's golden wedding anniversary.

September 10, 1929, dawned clear and warm. Marian and Susan, with the efficient help of Madame Calame, had been working for days to prepare for the gathering. People started arriving before noon, driving, most of them from the East Bay. Rill and Oscar came, bringing Oscar's sisters, "Auntie" Grace and Letia, as well as Otis. Tone and Bess, with

Bobbie and Georgie, arrived soon thereafter. Then, in the baby blue Packard, Perce, who had divorced Catherine in 1925, with his sons, Steve and Dickie, turned in the driveway with a flourish. Added to the six Rattrays and the honorees, the group became quite noisy as cousins greeted cousins and siblings shouted salutations.

Tables were set in the dining room, lavish platters of food on one, bowls of punch on the other, smaller one. Both were covered with white linen tablecloths with large bouquets of yellow and rust chrysanthemums in crystal vases. The grandchildren were stopped in their tracks by the glory and stood, fidgeting, waiting permission to fill a plate with goodies and get a glass of punch.

Susan and George Murdock
on their golden wedding day,
September 10, 1929

Later, sitting comfortably in the garden, Marian said, "Well, how does it feel to be married such a long time, to have started all this?" Her sweeping arm encompassed the children who were racing around.

"It's all wonderful," answered Susan.

"Tell us again how Dad proposed."

"Well," said Susan with a smile. "We were rowing on Lake Merritt. It was a warm day and George took off his coat. I almost changed my mind. His shoulders, without the beautifully tailored jacket, weren't as broad as my brother Matt's. I was used to the massive Fuller builds and I hadn't known George was so slight! Anyhow, it really didn't matter, all you children got the Fuller breadth!" she chuckled.

"So, he leaned forward and popped the question. When I said 'Yes' he reached into this coat pocket and pulled out an envelope which he handed me. 'This is your engagement present. I picked it up yesterday.' I opened the envelope, unwrapped the black tissue paper and found a shiny silver fifty-cent piece. 'It was just minted in San Francisco. They didn't make many. Keep it to commemorate this day.' So I did. I still have it. And it's still wrapped in the same black tissue paper tucked in the same envelope."

"Why, Dad, that was romantic," said Rill.

"And *cheap*," laughed Perce. "Didn't you think it was cheap, Mother? A fifty cent engagement gift?"

"Not at all. Besides, it's worth lots by now."

They talked and reminisced while the children played. The drivers kept track of time. It was a long ride home.

With many hugs and kisses and jostling among the cousins, the party broke up right after the cake, cut with ceremony, was consumed. It was the end of an era, the last gathering at Ben Brae but no one mentioned that fact.

Back in their Ross home right after the golden wedding celebration, and before George and Susan's big move took place, Bill and Marian found life good. His position with Fireman's Fund insurance company seemed solid and he even received a small raise, a landmark one that boosted his salary to $100 a month which Marian entered with pride in her accounts book. She was feeling fine, full of energy and ambition.

Jane in the sixth grade picture, Ross School, Fall 1929.

Janie, nearly eleven, entered sixth grade, a good student and a happy learner. She was freckled faced, her straight hair still cut in a bang across her brow, taller and thinner than most of the children in her class. Every time Marian looked at her oldest daughter she said, "Stand up straight. Hold your shoulders back." She even thought of inventing a garment that would force Jane into alignment, but until she did, she used her constant reminders instead. Jane tried but somehow she always seemed to be slouching with her head forward and her chin down.

Billy was a second grader that fall. His golden hair had darkened but still curled. He had hazel brown eyes fringed with long lashes and, like Jane, freckles across his nose. He loved little cars and his erector set, and bedeviling Jane. He could still make her cry.

The twins were running around, getting into everything. Marianne began to display quite a temper when crossed, but most of the time she was in rollicking good humor.

When the annual Big Game was held between Stanford University and University of California, it became a family radio event. Jane chose to stand with her mother and root for Cal, Marian's alma mater. Bill, who hadn't attended college, picked Stanford. In honor of the day, Jane dressed Suzanne in a yellow dress with a blue sweater, Cal's colors, and Marianne was dressed in white with a bright red sweater, honoring Stanford.

Bill, Marian and Jane crowded around the radio to listen. When Stanford made their first touchdown, Bill grabbed Marianne off the floor where she was playing and held her, giggling, over his head. "Hurrah, for us, Marianne! Yea, Red and White!"

A tying touchdown by Cal brought Marian to her feet with Suzanne in her arms, a few minutes later.

"Come on, Bears," she shouted. "Go, Blue and Gold!"

So it went, all afternoon. Billy was on his dad's rooting section, Jane shouted with Marian and waltzed around the room holding Suzanne in her arms whenever Cal pulled ahead. Unhappily, for the Bears, and for Marian and Jane, Stanford won the game. But the lines were drawn, the sides chosen. Jane was forevermore a Cal fan, Billy chose Stanford. The twins were dressed as mascots until they were old enough to revolt.

Periodically, without warning or reason, Bill "slipped," as Marian referred in her mind to his drinking. When he didn't arrive home on time for dinner, Marian sat down at six o'clock sharp to eat with the children, keeping up a cheerful façade, as much for her own sake as theirs. Later, after they were bedded down, she finished the dishes and sat on the chesterfield, staring over its back out the front window to the street up which he would eventually walk. She hated this wasted time but was unable to use it. She hated her tears. *I'd rather be mad, angry, furious, than to feel so helpless and hurt. Get mad!* she told herself. But the tears continued.

One night, long after Jane should have been asleep, Marian looked up to see her standing in the doorway, tears in her eyes, too.

"It's all right, Janie. Come here," Marian reached out her arms and Jane clung to her. "It's really all right. Daddy's just late and I'm being silly.

He'll be home soon. Let's get you back to bed now. I'll rub your back. Okay?"

Jane nodded and headed to her room. Marian sat in the dark on the edge of the bed, rubbing the skinny body until Jane relaxed into sleep. Marian gave up her vigil for Bill and went to bed, too.

In the morning the tears were forgotten and usually for a few weeks everything was normal.

Whenever Jane heard her mother crying, she connected it with her father's absence. It made her unhappy and many times she crept out to sit with Marian, hoping that would help.

With Bill's raise of a few months back, making things a bit easier on the money-management front, Marian looked at Bill critically and announced, "You absolutely have to buy a new hat. The one you're wearing is a disgrace. Stop and buy one today."

Since it was easier in the long run to carry out directions from his wife as soon as possible, Bill did just that. He purchased a dark gray Stetson with a lighter gray band. He consigned his old hat to the trash and took off for the ferry building feeling debonair and well-dressed.

On the boat, because the day was clear, Bill went out on the upper deck to see the Marin hills come ever closer. Suddenly, a brisk gust of wind lifted the new hat off his head and gave it wings. As it wafted down to the water where it bobbed a few moments before disappearing, Bill said to himself, *That does it! No more hats for me.*

When he told Marian, she realized it would be no use to argue that wearing a hat was fashionable, everyone wore one, or any other reasonable fact she could present. Bill was through with them, almost as though the wind blowing his brand new hat away was a God-given sanction for his going bareheaded forever. He never bought or wore another hat as long as he lived.

These fall afternoons when she got home from school, Jane loved to strap on her roller skates and take off down the road to San Anselmo. There were smooth sidewalks around Montgomery Chapel on the corner of Richmond and Bolinas where it was easy to skate but after a few minutes, she took off on the street again and skated several blocks before reaching another smooth cement sidewalk.

Her destination was the far end of San Anselmo Avenue where she could roll right up to a small open-fronted hut and order a hot dog prepared right before her eyes. Delicious! Both hot dog and the roll were sliced open and placed on the buttered grill. Then pickle relish, chopped onions, mustard and ketchup were spread on the roll. The whole thing was wrapped in a piece of waxed paper and a paper napkin. Holding it, warm in her hand, Jane skated toward home, munching happily in the crisp autumnal air. Never had a nickel bought so much pleasure! It didn't seem to spoil her appetite, perhaps even whetted it. When she removed the skates, her feet tingled from the vibration on the macadam roadway. She envied her mother having miles of Alameda's flat sidewalks to skate to her heart's content during all her growing years.

Suzanne and Marianne,
Christmas 1929.

Nineteen twenty nine was a comparatively happy holiday season. Bill managed to come straight home from work most nights so none of the gift money went for drink. Marian stopped holding her breath around train time and prepared for the big celebration. On Christmas day, after church, they drove on the Richmond-San Rafael ferry over to visit, first Rill, Oscar and Otis in Piedmont, then George and Susan at the boarding house, to end up with the Rattray clan at Ernest and Bella's Alameda home.

It was particularly rewarding to Marian to see her parents so content in their new surroundings. The rooms were big and flooded with sunshine. The few pieces of furniture they had kept fit well and made the place their own.

"I'm glad we made the move, Marian," George said. He looked natty as always, immaculately dressed, his white hair still thick, his posture still arrogant. "It's good to be back."

"But we do miss seeing you and the children," Susan added, pulling Jane close for a hug. They stayed as long as they could in the sunny rooms before leaving for the next phase of their Christmas celebration at the McRitchie's.

The phone rang, just over two weeks later. It was Tone's wife, Bess, who lived across the street from the boarding house.

"Marian, your dad's gone. Heart attack."

It was a total shock. He seemed so well. No one had ever suspected his heart would give him trouble, that was Susan's province. Marian told Bess she'd drive over as soon as she could find someone to care for the children.

On her way a short frantic time later, Marian found herself thinking back to the illness her father had eight years before. They'd still been living in the rented house next door to Ben Brae. George was 75 then. It had been a long damp winter. Finally his vulnerable lungs had fallen prey to pneumonia. A dedicated nurse cared for him around the clock, snatching a few brief hours off, and Susan seldom left his bedside.

One dismal morning the doctor came out of the bedroom after his daily visit and said to Susan, "He's nearing the end. You better notify the rest of the family."

When the call to George's deathbed went out, Rill, Tone, and Perce left their children in care of convenient relatives or hired helpers and, with husband and wives, hurried to Bill and Marian's house to crowd in and wait the inevitable. They took turns cutting through the fence to the other house to stand by his bedside. Days stretched on, George slowly weakening with each one until he no longer recognized any of them.

And then came the message they were dreading. The nurse called over that the end was near. They all hurried next door. Susan's long vigil at his bedside made her look older and sicker than George. Bess slipped her hand over his wrist. The nurse, on the opposite side of the bed, also had her fingers on his pulse. His four children crowded close, their spouses behind them. Bess and the nurse suddenly looked at each other. The significant silence of the last suspended breath went on and on. Too long. Bess gently let go of the wrist she'd been holding. The nurse, seeing confirmation in Bess's eyes, turned to Susan and nodded.

George was dead. His tired heart had ceased beating, his painful breathing had stopped. Bess reached to draw the sheet up.

Then, in the hushed silence of the room, broken only by Rill's sobbing, George took several short quick gasps, then a normal breath. He opened his clear blue eyes for the first time in days and looked at each of them with recognition. In a firm voice, softened with awe and tinged with regret, he said clearly, "It was beautiful, very beautiful. But I missed my turn. Now I have to wait."

With that he settled his head on the smooth pillow and dropped into quiet sleep. He recovered rapidly. When he was entirely well, they questioned him about the experience that had touched them so profoundly. He remembered nothing.

But now his time had come and Marian was driving to Alameda to face the reality of his death. Somehow, having gone though the previous time, having said good-bye, having heard his sorrow at coming back from wherever he'd been for those few moments, made it easier to face his real departure.

Susan was in a state when Marian arrived. Bess, using her expertise once again as a trained nurse, was a tower of strength and had already taken care of the immediate concerns. The two younger women helped Susan calm down and make a few decisions. She wanted to leave the boarding house right away. Bess said she'd take her across the street to her home for awhile. Then, as soon as possible, they'd find another place for her to live.

By the time Marian left for Ross late that evening, Susan had been moved, temporarily, to Bess and Tone's, arrangements for the funeral had been made, furniture tagged for distribution among Tone, Perce, Rill and Marian, notice given that Susan would be out of the boarding house by the end of the month, and several new options had been mentioned. Marian and Bess were an unbeatable combination when it came to accomplishing the impossible. Two weeks later, to everyone's satisfaction, Susan moved into a furnished apartment on the second floor of a new building that boasted elevator service. Mrs. Gee, a large capable woman, was hired to come in days and take care of everything.

No sooner had the crisis of George's sudden death been dealt with than a new challenge arose. In the middle of January, Marian suddenly developed abdominal pains. When they didn't go away but instead intensified, she began to worry.

Again she turned to Enid. "I'm not feeling the least bit well. In fact, I've never felt worse," she said on the phone. "Can you come over?"

"Of course. I'll be right there."

Like all of Marian's close friends, Enid knew Marian would never call for help unless the situation was desperate.

She arrived to find Marian doubled up on the bed, her face white and shining with sweat, her body burning with fever. Jane was standing in the doorway looking scared. The younger children were playing in their rooms.

"Enid, it's awful," Marian said. "I need a doctor. I can't move, the pain's so bad. Oh, God!"

"You need an ambulance," Enid replied, heading for the telephone.

Enid sponged Marian's face, smoothed her hair. "We're going to get your mommy to the hospital and make her better," Enid told Jane. "You go now and get the twins ready for bed. Tell Billy, too."

"But we haven't had dinner yet."

"We'll take care of that after the ambulance comes. Go now."

In spite of her pain, Marian managed to laugh when the two men carrying the stretcher to which she was strapped couldn't navigate the sharp turns from the bedroom to the hall to the dining room.

"Tip me sideways," she said. "Or stand the darned thing upright. Just get me out of here!"

Sideways worked. With the wide-eyed children watching, the stretcher was carried to the waiting ambulance. After it drove off, Enid set about getting a simple supper for them, although Jane couldn't eat.

An hour later, Bill arrived home. The children had been put to bed but only the twins were sleeping.

"Bill, Marian's in the hospital. You better go right away. I phoned Carlos and told him I'll stay here tonight, so don't worry about the kids. Just go. Phone me when you can."

"You're great, Enid. Thanks." He slammed the door and she heard the car pull out of the driveway.

That night changed everything for a long long time. Marian was rushed into emergency surgery where the doctors worked feverishly to try to save her. In their haste, they cut through muscles, not taking time to spread them out of the way. They found a ruptured fallopian tube. Peritonitis had set in. The situation was desperate. Even after the doctors had done everything they could, they gave her so little chance to live they didn't bother to stitch up the hasty incisions. They just put a drainage tube into place and bandaged her temporarily.

Marian became conscious of voices, hushed male voices. She had no idea where she was, or who they were. It was very light even though her eyes were closed. She thought she must be in bed although she couldn't feel her body. She strained to listen.

"It's too bad. I understand she has four children, two of them just babies. Really tragic."

"Sad case. There's really no hope that I can see. We can't clean up such a massive infection."

"I'm surprised she's hung on this long."

Hey, they're talking about me! They think I'm dying! This is like that idiot DeLancy when the twins were born. I will NOT die. I can't.

It was too much an effort to open her eyes and see who was talking. *In a little while. I'll rest now.*

The next time Marian heard voices she was able to raise her eyelids. The room was white and blindingly bright. She couldn't see anyone nor could she make sense of the voices so she let her eyes shut again and drifted away.

For over a week, Marian floated in and out of consciousness, never coming fully alert, not knowing where she was or what was going on. Bill was unable to cope with seeing her, white and still, or deal with the doctors' dire prognosis. He saw her the night she was rushed into surgery, wept at the side of her bed when she was wheeled back into the room. He felt the doctor's hand on his shoulder.

"I'm sorry. We did all we could. It doesn't look good." The doctor patted his back, "I can't offer you much hope. Too massive an infection. It'll take a miracle."

Bill nodded and bowed his head. The doctor left the room.

It was more than he could bear, more than he could face. As the days went by, he wasn't able to take over at home, either. He tried to work but instead slipped into a bar for "just one drink." When he left, hours later, he headed home. Once there, he went right to bed with barely a nod to whichever friend or relative was caring for the children.

Family rallied around, seeking temporary solutions for the children, forced to act without Bill who was never available. Enid found a reputable woman in Winship Park, just a few blocks away to care for the twins in her home and they were moved there where they stayed two months. Jane walked over to see them but it was too upsetting for all three of them to be together in those strange circumstances so she didn't go back.

Billy, to his horror, was allotted to Rill, in Piedmont, across the Bay. He was packed up and hustled away, protesting. He fought her silently every step of the way. Enrolled in school within walking distance, he was dressed each morning by Rill, in a shirt and tie, flannel shorts, and a jacket, topped by a scarf and a beret, clothes she'd tenderly saved since Otis was a pampered youngster. Kissed good-bye by his aunt, who stood and waved until he turned the corner, Billy walked away, little back ramrod straight, murder in his heart.

Once out of her sight, he stopped, took off the tie, the scarf, the beret and, no matter what the weather, the hated jacket. He rolled them up, stuffed them into a thick hedge. There was nothing he could do about the short pants except march the rest of the way to school fighting tears of humiliation. On the way home, he retrieved the articles of clothing he'd shed, but he could never find the courage to tell his overpowering aunt that he didn't like the way she made him dress, that it wasn't the way the other boys looked and he felt miserable. The months he was boarded there had an indelible and bruising effect upon him.

Jane, as all this began to happen, was allowed a special visit to the hospital, where she stood, looking at her mother, tears running down her face. Marian opened her eyes, focused on her daughter and said, softly, "Don't worry, Janie. I'll be all right." She tried to raise her hand to touch Jane's face but couldn't. "Be good. Be a big help."

After that meeting, which Enid had arranged, Jane was taken to Alameda to stay with her grandmother, Susan, in the apartment she'd moved into after George's death.

Jane was enrolled in Haight School, within walking distance of the apartment. She even had time to dash home for lunch which Mrs. Gee prepared and all three of them sat down to eat together.

The elevator was of particular interest to Jane and she loved being able to make it work, taking many unnecessary trips from basement to roof.

A music appreciation course held throughout the school on Friday afternoons was something else that thrilled her. Although Jane had missed half the semester, she picked up, during reviews, knowledge of most of the earlier music. Fifty composers and their best known pieces were presented in the classrooms with the teachers playing records on the phonographs, supplemented by facts about the composers themselves. Jane, who had heard some of the pieces played by her father, loved this hour of the week above all others. It erased homesickness, worry about her mother, missing her father and the twins, even her tormenter, Billy.

Another especially happy time for Jane was after supper when she and her granny talked. Then, just before bed, Susan would make them each a cup of hot Ovaltine. She was trying to put a bit of weight on Janie, and was delighted to have found something nourishing that she enjoyed.

Susan had never recovered from the feeding problem she had caring for Jane when Billy was born. She had insisted, at the first breakfast, that Jane eat the cream-of-wheat mush in her bowl. Jane took one small spoonful, gagged and spit it out. Susan, in an uncharacteristic display of authority, said, "You have to eat it. You'll sit here until you do."

After twenty minutes of watching the little girl crying quietly into her mush bowl, Susan said, "All right, go now, without any breakfast. I'll warm the mush up for lunch and you'll be hungry enough to eat."

She underestimated her granddaughter. At both lunch and dinner, Jane sat in rigid silence, lips firmly closed, refusing to put the slimy stuff in her mouth.

Afraid of starving the already skinny child, Susan capitulated and prepared macaroni and cheese with a bowl of applesauce. Jane smiled and ate two helpings of each. Neither ever forgot the battle of wills although, until nearly the end, they never mentioned it to each other nor to anyone else. It was a sad secret between them.

Marian defied all predictions of the medical profession and gradually became stronger. She demanded daily reports on each of the children which Enid tried to keep the hospital supplied with. She wondered about Bill's absence but somehow couldn't ask anyone why he didn't come. She was afraid to know.

When word got to him that she was better, he braced himself to visit. Luckily, Marian was still too weak to do anything but smile at him, which he took as a sign of forgiveness. They never spoke of the days he was missing or how he'd let her down. They just went on.

Five weeks after she was admitted, Marian was released from the hospital. Perce, without a word to her, had paid the sizable bill. It made her sad to have to accept his money but there was nothing she could do but bless him for being who he was. She was given a list of things she couldn't do; drive, pick up anything heavier than a feather, bathe, walk, bend, stand on her feet for any length of time, on and on.

With these restrictions, although it broke her heart, she realized she couldn't see the twins, not until she could pick them up, hold them close to her. Nor could she stay alone in the house even though Bill would be around, hopefully, nights. So it was decided that he would drive her over to Alameda where she would stay with Susan and Jane. Mrs. Gee could expand her care to one more!

Several days following the joyful reunion of the three generations, Jane woke up feeling rotten. Within hours it was obvious she had measles. Her temperature soared, the rash spread over her whole body. The Murphy bed in the living room was made up for her by Mrs. Gee, the curtains in the room pulled to protect her eyes. No sooner had Jane been settled down than Susan had severe pains in her chest. The doctor was summoned. His diagnosis – a mild heart attack. Bed rest was prescribed. Mrs. Gee tucked her in and pulled the shades in that room, too.

This left Marian, who was supposed to spend most of her time lying down being waited on by Jane and Susan, as the only one without a bed! She had to stretch out on the chesterfield in the darkened living room to rest, or sit in the breakfast room with Mrs. Gee. Gradually, because she couldn't sit around and do nothing, Marian took over the simple care of her daughter and her mother, leaving Mrs. Gee to do the shopping, cooking and tidying up.

As Jane felt better, Marian read *Mrs. Wiggs and the Cabbage Patch* to her. Sometimes as she drifted off to sleep, Janie imagined a continuation of the story happening in the vacant lot next door. Later, she was unable to figure out what was in the story and what was in her fevered mind.

Getting back on her feet and taking charge of things again did Marian a world of good. She began to look around to figure what had to happen so she could go home to Ross and gather up her children.

First, Susan had to move again, to a boarding house where all her needs would be taken care of. That problem solved itself easily. Mrs. Beasley's wonderful old home on the corner of Benton and Central had a second floor room and bath, with a little rooftop porch, available. Bess checked it out, declared it perfect and paid for a month on the spot. Jane wanted to stay at Haight School until vacation in June especially to take part in the school-wide music test to be given to all the children from fourth grade up, in the auditorium. Jane was sure she'd do well. She didn't want to miss a chance to shine at something she loved. Bella was approached to see if she would take Jane in. She was thrilled to do so.

Billy, on the other hand, could hardly wait to get away from Piedmont and his aunt even though it meant a new school for a few weeks. It was agreed that he, and all his belongings (Rill even tucked in the clothes she'd been forcing him to wear, thinking he'd be thrilled!) would be picked up in the car that Bill was driving to Alameda to get Marian.

So it was, in early April, Marian kissed Jane good-bye at Bella's, hugged Billy as she climbed into the car, waved to her mother on her rooftop porch at Mrs. Beasley's, and, with Bill driving, set off for Marin County.

They went to the house first, to get things ready for the twins, and then, having phoned to say they were on the way, drove the few blocks to pick them up.

Two months is a long time in the lives of babies as young as the little girls. When they saw their mother, father and brother, they looked confused and shy. Then Suzanne began to smile, and holding out her arms, ran toward her mother. Marianne first turned away as though it was too much to look at, then turned back. Seeing the loving her sister was getting, she, too, ran to be hugged. Marian was weeping. So many times she had feared she'd never see her babies again, never hold them close to her. Now she was, and her happiness soared beyond containment.

All the paraphernalia of caring for the girls these months had to be loaded in the car, then Bill carried them, one on each hip, to the waiting car-seats for the short ride home. Billy watched the entire proceedings with suspicion and a scowl, but remembering the clothes he'd worn at Rill's he managed to smile. He, too, was home again. Only Jane was outside the family circle and she, they thought, would be back at the Ross house again in a few short weeks.

It didn't work out that way. Four years would pass before they'd all live on Glenwood Avenue again, four long painful wonderful years.

The house on Estates Drive, Oakland, 1930.

PART TWO

The Years Away

ON'T FORGET THE wind chimes," Jane said to her mother on the telephone. "Please. I've missed them. Mom, can't I come home first, before we move?"

"That would be silly. You'd just have to turn around and go back. No, we'll do it this way." Marian said good-bye, put the earpiece back in its bracket on the side of the phone and shook her head. *All this has happened too fast, and it's so good it scares me,* Marian thought. *Imagine Bill being asked, at a substantial raise in pay, to go over and run dad's insurance business in the same building where both Tone and Perce work. I can't believe it!* Charles Percy Murdock had the whole top floor of the Realty Syndicate Building in Oakland for his million dollar real estate business. Hamilton Murdock ran a thriving architectural concern on a lower floor and between them was George Hamilton Murdock's insurance company, which Bill was going to manage. Young Bob, Tone's older son, even ran the elevator when not in classes at the University of California in Berkeley. The family practically owned the building.

It was wonderful. Everyone was doing well. Nineteen thirty had started out badly with George's sudden death and Marian's near-fatal illness, but the outlook now was good. In spite of the market crash in 1929, things seemed solid here.

A marvelous house on Estates Drive in the Oakland/Piedmont hills was leased for two years and the Ross home put up for rent. In record time Marian organized the move, boxing and tagging every item, writing on the tag where it should be put in the big new place. The last thing she packed, remembering Jane's plea, was the wind chimes. Finding a sturdy hat-box, she made a bed of crushed tissue paper and gently collapsed the chimes into place, separating the little pieces of glass with paper so they wouldn't bang together. "This I'll take myself," she said. But she still labeled it: WIND CHIMES THIS SIDE

UP JANE'S ROOM in crisp black lettering.

This was the first move they'd ever made with movers and a van. She and Bill waited with the children in the car, loaded with the most precious items, until the big truck pulled away. Then they took off for the Richmond ferry and the drive to the Piedmont hills, hoping to be there before the van arrived. It was an exciting move, a move *up* – to a bigger house, a better job. To be all together again after nearly six months! No wonder Marian's heart was light. She felt well physically, too. Each day she regained some of the strength and energy that had been her hallmark since childhood.

Bill, although he would never have said so, had different feelings. The offer of a position managing George's office was welcome financially, but it was more responsibility than he liked. And under the noses of his brothers-in-law. He didn't enjoy being in charge, making decisions that effected other people. Change made him uncomfortable rather than challenged. He prayed things would go as well as Marian was sure they would but he had his doubts.

Ernest and Bella drove Jane from Alameda to arrive just after her family, the logistics all settled by phone calls. With her collected belongings piled around her, Jane crowded into the back seat and could hardly contain her excitement. Months had passed since she'd seen her baby sisters, her little brother, and her father and ten weeks since bidding her mother good-bye when Marian returned to Ross. What a long *long* Spring this had been. And now school was out, summer was starting, and they were to be a family again! Jane smiled happily to herself.

The road they were to live on, Estates Drive, was similar to the roads in Ross. It was cut on the side of a hill and, like them, had no curbs, sidewalks or gutters, just a slight crown, flanked with dirt and space to walk on the down side. Their house, on nearly two acres of wooded terrain, about a quarter mile off Moraga Boulevard, was invisible from the road. A steep driveway led to a wide graveled yard. To the left, dropping sharply from the road to the house, was a rough lawn, mostly wild grasses and dandelions, under dozens of oak trees. There were undeveloped lots on either side, the one on the left, a steep ravine clogged with wild blackberries and hardy native shrubs. The closest neighbor was barely visible on the other side of the ravine.

Four buildings clustered around the yard – the two-story stucco main house, a small cottage, and two garages, one to serve each dwelling. Behind the cottage, the heavily wooded lot dropped off steeply to railroad tracks far below. Actually, Marian and Bill didn't know of the existence of the train when they moved in. Later they found it was the Oakland-Antioch line, lightly used, and certainly no threat to their welfare, except for one brief moment and then it was only in Bill's mind.

Marian was feeding the twins their breakfasts on the second morning in the house. Bill was in Oakland, checking out his new responsibilities, Billy and Jane were unpacking toys on sun porch floor. Suzanne and Marianne were in the tiny breakfast nook off the kitchen which had windows looking out to the ravine and on to the porch that ran across the back of the house. They were sitting in their high chairs, spooning scrambled eggs toward their mouths. Marian, cleaning up dishes from earlier breakfasts, looked at them with a smile on her face.

The smile froze as she saw a large black hand reach through a lower pane of glass in the window. She hadn't even noticed the pane was missing! Now the hand was turning the latch. Marian picked up a knife and walked toward the breakfast nook where she could see a man as large as the size of the hand indicated.

"Stop!"she said firmly, grasping the knife. The man pulled his hand back as though it had been burned.

"Oh, ma'am," he said in a deep voice. "Sorry. Didn't know anyone moved in here. We've been dropping off the train and hiking up the hill to sleep days, till the next train."

"Well, you can't do that anymore."

"Realize that, ma'am. I'll pass the word. You won't be bothered again." He nodded his head. Marian looked at him, met his steady eyes and responded to the slight smile on his black face. She made a quick and typical decision. "Come on in and have some breakfast before you go."

He walked to the back door which she opened and, hat in hand, crowded in at the table opposite the twins who looked at him with friendly amazement having never seen anyone as big or as black. He ate the meal Marian quickly prepared and then, with dignity he stood up.

"Thank you, ma'am. That was mighty kind of you. I'll see that you don't get disturbed again." With a broad smile, he went out the door, jamming his battered hat on his head, and disappeared around the cottage and down the steep hill.

Bill was horrified when she told him of the incident that evening. "You could have been killed, raped! Good Lord , Marian, what were you thinking, letting a person like that in the house?"

"Well, if he wanted to break in, I couldn't have kept him out, not even with a knife in my hand." She chuckled. "Besides, he looked like a good man, just down on his luck. I decided it was better to have him on my side than against me. We actually had a nice breakfast. I'm just sorry Billy and Jane were playing in the front room and didn't get to see him."

"Do you think he'll tell the other bums not to come up the hill any more? You might not be so lucky next time. When I think of the chance you took! You and the kids could all be dead!"

"But we aren't," Marian said. "We're fine. We'll be fine. Yes, he'll pass the word not to come here. And we'll replace that pane of glass right away. And keep the windows and doors locked, just in case. For awhile, anyway." She smiled at him. "Don't worry."

The square stucco flat-roofed house was placed close to the west line of the lot where it dropped off toward the ravine. This meant the although the entrance was on ground level on the southeast corner, the northwest corner had room for a good sized basement under the kitchen.

The small entrance hall opened on the left to the living room, with a fireplace in the center of the front wall, windows overlooking the ravine straight ahead and on the right, the dining room which in turn had French doors to a sun room, with windows on three sides, that jutted out from the house on the edge of the ravine. From the dining room, a swinging door led to the kitchen, another door on the right to the hall off which there were two bedrooms, a bathroom and the stairs to the upper story. The second floor only covered the back half of the house. From the landing, the stairs separated, the left set leading to a large bedroom, the right set to a smaller bedroom and a large bathroom. Between the bathroom and the big bedroom was a strange area, perhaps planned as a dressing room. It had three wide steep stairs and French doors that opened to the roof. This was to be Jane's room, and in the doorway she hung the wind chimes. Beyond, a 12 by 12 foot wooden platform was placed on the tar and gravel for protection, making a little spot for sunbathing. Around the entire roof was a three-foot balustrade which made Marian feel safer should the children forget her instructions and leave the platform. They couldn't *accidentally* fall off and she thought they were smart enough not to deliberately climb up and jump. It was a nice house. Four bedrooms, two baths, basement with a furnace and washtubs. Big dining room, large kitchen with stove, refrigerator, windows that looked west over Oakland and to San Francisco, across the Bay. And all the space and privacy one could wish.

The first Sunday they were in the house, Marian and Bill had just finished unpacking books and placing them on the built-in bookcases when she said, "I need to talk to you about something serious."

"What?"

"Something awful. I don't know what, but it's been bothering me ever since I came back to Ross last month."

"What?" Bill sounded slightly annoyed at her rambling. It wasn't like Marian. "Something happened while I was in Alameda, or earlier, when I was in the hospital. Something awful. Doris and Enid won't talk to me. Neither of them. Not at all. We aren't friends anymore. What happened Bill? What did you do?"

Bill looked at her, stunned. "Do? I didn't do anything. You must be wrong or crazy!"

"No, I'm not. I tried over and over to talk to them. And they wouldn't. Said they couldn't talk about it. Both of them. I want to know what it's all about. This is the worst thing that's ever happened to me, my two best dearest friends! What did you do?"

"Nothing," he repeated. "I can't imagine what they're upset about. It'll probably all blow over, whatever it is."

"No, it won't. Not the way they sounded. So final. Both of them. So through with me. They don't want to talk, or see me. I know you did something terrible. You must have."

"I tell you I didn't. And that's the end of it." He put a last book on the shelf and walked out of the room.

No matter how many times Marian tried to talk about the subject, he wouldn't say a word so she figured he didn't remember what had happened and couldn't tell her, and gave up asking. She never learned what had caused the break with Enid and Doris. Even forty years later when their paths crossed again, first with Enid, later with Doris, and after great effort the rifts were healed, none of the parties concerned would discuss the reason behind the ugly breach. Marian died not knowing why she was rejected for four long decades by two people so dear to her.

Summer weather in the Piedmont hills was quite different than it had been across the Bay in Ross. Situated as they were, looking down on Oakland, across the water to San Francisco, and to the west where a piece of the Pacific was visible, they could see the fog bank that rolled in the Golden Gate to spread out in the evening. They saw it hanging there in the morning, retreating by midday, and sneaking back in again toward sunset. Often, it climbed right up the hill and obliterated their view. This kept their days cooler than they were used to, and conditions were just right to create winds whenever the fog was coming or going, which was most of the time. Ross was in a valley, protected from the fog, usually untouched by the winds, keeping the climate much warmer.

Billy and Jane, however, treated the long days like any other vacation they had ever had. To one side of their garage, they again created a kingdom, this one nameless, but filled with rivers, lakes, bridges, roads, mountains and landscaped with tiny trees, bushes, rocks, and gravel. Billy's beloved cars travelled smooth roads and took daring trips on hairpin turns and steep danger-fraught grades.

Tiring of that, one day they decided to cut the grass. The lawn was on too much of a slant and too many oaks grew there to make it practical to push the ancient mower around but they tried. Of course, the blades didn't faze the dandelions which sprang upright instantly, untouched. They ended up using kitchen shears for the task.

Taking turns, switching from right hand to left, even resting and enjoying a glass of lemonade, they both raised blisters on their hands before every single wiry stem on the large slope was severed. What a feeling of accomplishment it gave them as they raked all the prickly oak leaves and dandelions into piles and tossed them into the ravine!

The twin enjoyed the summer, too. They'd had their second birthday just before leaving Ross, and were able to run around the flat area of the yard, playing made-up games. Marian had a sandbox set next to the front step and here they built their version of Billy and Jane's village. Theirs wasn't permanent, however, suffering constant demolition and rebuilding. But that was the fun.

One early evening long before sunset, Marian and Bill took the children in the car to a house on the other end of Estates Drive, across Moraga Boulevard several blocks. In spite of their questions, Marian didn't tell them where they were going or why . "Wait and see," she said with a smile. "It's a surprise, one you'll love."

They reached a modest house and Marian turned in the driveway. A woman came to the gate.

"Mr. Rattray?" she asked as Bill got out of the car. He nodded and herded the children toward the gate. "I'm Mrs. Donovan. Come on out back," the woman said. "We're all ready for you. The children get to choose."

She led the way to a large pen on the lawn in the corner of the backyard. Inside, rolling and romping, was a tangled mass of puppies. All four children let out squeals of delight and ran to kneel by the pen and poke their fingers through the wire to reach the scrambling pups.

"Their mother is an Irish terrier, a darling dog. I've put her in the house but you can see her later. Their daddy, unfortunately, was a traveling man, so we can't sell these pups for what we usually ask. That's why I advertised that they were available for so little."

"Can we really have one?" Jane asked looking at Marian.

"Yes. Decide which one you want."

There were six puppies in the pen but only two came nibbling and shoving each other against the children fingers. One was russet with wiry hair, the other, slightly smaller, was tan with a smoother coat. Both were fat and sturdy with bright black eyes, perky ears, sharp little teeth and eager pink tongues.

"I want the tan one," Jane said.

"I want the other one," Billy said. "Mommy! " he whined.

"Watch that tone of voice. Work it out, you two. Take your time. This is a serious decision."

The bigger of the pups, the reddish one, came to sit in front of Jane. "Look, he likes me!" she said, captivated. "You're right, Billy. I want him, too. Okay?"

"Yeah. Let's get this one." So it was decided, with the help of the puppy. They proudly took him home.

"Can we call him 'Sandy' like Little Orphan Annie's dog. He looks sort of like him," Jane suggested. There was no argument.

Sandy became a member of the family immediately. But before the end of the week, his fat little legs carried him up the steep driveway when none of his young masters was watching. There one of the infrequent cars that traveled on their road struck and killed him.

The gloom that settled on the Rattrays was palpable.

Suzanne and Marianne with puppy Tippy, Summer, 1930.

Several nights later, there was a knock on the door. It was the lady who had sold them Sandy. "We heard what happened and knew the kids would be heartbroken so we've brought you his brother as a gift. Would they like him?"

She opened her sweater and there was the little tan puppy Jane had originally wanted. There was no doubt of his welcome. This time a more formal name was chosen by Marian, Tipperary, in honor of his Irish heritage. Tippy was never let out of their sight by Jane and Billy and quickly grew to be their beloved companion.

Bill went off to work every weekday, and most evenings he was home for dinner. Marian, except for the unresolved pain of losing her two dearest friends for unknown reasons, was relatively relaxed, not even harping too much on the evenings Bill arrived home late and worse for wear. She, somewhat erroneously, felt he was safe where he was, working near the brothers who had always made everything right for her. She refused to face what was obviously developing into a problem. She managed to keep busy organizing the house, planning meals, shopping, caring for the children, keeping in touch with her mother in Alameda, Rill in lower Piedmont. She was once again on the right side of the Bay to contact Ruth Rowland or Edwina Larkin and did so often, trying to see them at least once a month.

Billy, Jane and Alan Martin,
Summer 1930.

Another constant visitor that summer was Barbara Martin Murdock, Perce's second wife, with her young son, Alan, who was Jane's age. Barbara and Perce had married in 1925 after a torrid courtship. Where Perce's first wife, Catherine, had been classically beautiful, lovelier by far than her famous cousin, Wallis Warfield Simpson, Barbara was the essence of pretty, the personification of Flapper, with dark bobbed curls, bright blue eyes, pert features, dimples and a flirty smile. She was short and almost too shapely for the times. And she had a robust spirit of fun. All the children adored her.

Steve and Dickie, who lived with Perce during the summer of the divorce on the seventh floor of the elegant Hotel Oakland, found a wonderful ally in their soon-to-be stepmother. Often, as they left the elevator, Barbara would remove her elegant high-heeled pumps and race the two boys down the long carpeted seventh-floor hallway, shrieking as the eight-year-old and twelve-year-old beat her to the door. It was years before the enchanted boys realized she had allowed them the victory! Barbara knew how to wrap males of any age around her little finger which was one attribute she shared with Catherine. And she certainly proved, with her charm, bubbling personality and wit, that Perce had a discerning gift for spotting beautiful women. He had, as brother Tone pointed out more than once, "an eye for the ladies" and he had, twice, married the loveliest the Bay Area had to offer!

Barbara and Marian became close friends that summer. She was nearer Marian's age than Catherine had been years ago when Marian and Frank had double-dated with Perce and his glamorous wife. Then Catherine had been the mentor, the older (and richer), more worldly and sophisticated sister and Marian the eager, though fiercely independent, learner.

"You'll never know the temptations of being a beautiful woman, Marian," she once said, without any conceit, "It's truly difficult. I find it hard to resist sometimes." This inability to resist had been, in fact, what led to the divorce in 1925. And why Steve and Dickie were awarded to Perce (who, as soon as possible, enrolled them in Montezuma School for Boys in the mountains above Los Gatos.)

And now Marian was becoming acquainted with her new sister-in-law. They enjoyed each other's company, found they had much to share. It didn't fill the hole left by Enid and Doris, that was too wrenching a vacancy, but it helped alleviate the loneliness and added color to her days.

For the first time since she ran Eighteen-Ought-Nine for her ailing mother years before, Marian was in a position to have full-time help. She probably would never had thought of it had there not been a cottage on the property which she figured she could fill with someone who would be willing to work for the rent.

To this end, she advertised and was delighted when the first answer brought Mrs. Dennis into her life. After a letter and a phone call, the two met over a cup of tea to settle the details. Mrs. Dennis (she was never called by any other name) was a widow with two young boys, Nathan and Gail, fourteen and fifteen years old. She was a motherly type, comfortable in big aprons and prone to baking cookies. She loved the twins at sight and seemed to understand both Billy's and Jane's needs. As soon as she learned of Marian's illness and the children's separation from each other, their parents and their home for so many months, her heart went out to them, and to Marian who had nearly lost her life.

Mrs. Dennis poured her healing love on the entire family and they lapped it up. She even had a special affinity for Bill. Her late husband, she admitted once, had been a drinking man and she knew the strain such action puts on a family, especially the wife. Marian found it difficult to discuss Bill's drinking. She never wanted to admit there was a problem. Or, more truthfully, she refused to be diminished by it. Therefore she rose above it, weaving the family's life around and over the situation, becoming ever stronger as manager and decision maker, leaving Bill with less and less of a voice, less of a role to play, in the family. He was, however, bringing home better money than ever and what he spent on drinking he used from the portion Marian meted out to him. She was even able to put aside a little each payday, secretly, for the nebulous future.

So it was that the summer drew to a close and school had to be faced. Billy was no problem. He entered the elementary school in Montclair, a village down on the flat. A bus picked him up and delivered him back to the corner of Moraga and Estates Drive. Luckily, he caught the bus on their side of busy Moraga Boulevard early in its route and rode to the perimeter of the area before circling back to the school. He was a third grader and soon found that his months at school in Piedmont and weeks at Ross, the spring before, placed him ahead of his classmates at the new school.

Jane was a different matter. Ross School had gone from kindergarten through eighth grade, as did Haight School in Alameda. But now, suddenly, instead of becoming a hot-shot seventh grader she had to enroll in a seventh-eighth-ninth grade junior high school as the smallest frog in a big puddle.

Marian drove her, that first day, down to Oakland, where she was thrown into a large city school with alien halls, rushing strangers, scary schedules, unknown teachers and an atmosphere entirely foreign to her previous school experiences.

"Bill, you should have seen her," Marian said to him that evening. "I felt like a monster leaving her there. It just didn't seem right. So many children and they were all big and noisy and looked tough and, well, they weren't Ross caliber, not at all like her friends there. "Anyhow, I couldn't stand it so I went to the office and explained where we live and told them how hard it would be to get her down here and asked what they could suggest."

"If I know schools," said Bill, "they had nothing to offer."

"On the contrary, they had a wonderful suggestion – Piedmont Junior High School, right down Moraga about a half a mile! They even gave me an inter-district transfer and I went right to Piedmont on my way home and got Jane all signed up and that's where she'll go tomorrow! When I picked her up this afternoon, we drove there to show her. We went in and saw the office and her home room. She feels much better. I know she was overwhelmed by the other place. It would have been an awful commute. I couldn't have taken her and picked her up and she'd have had to transfer twice!"

Bill's nod of approval ended the conversation. He was glad Jane wouldn't have to struggle with an overwhelming situation. He felt he was in over his head at work and didn't like it one bit. Unfortunately, he couldn't discuss this with Marian. Too much of the pressure came from Perce and Tone and their expectations of his managerial ability. There really was very little work to do but every situation called for a decision which he postponed making. It was getting worse all the time, like being on a runaway train heading for certain destruction and powerless to stop or get off. Many days he rode the bus down to the heart of Oakland, walked to the Reality Syndicate Building, took the elevator to the third floor, hoping Bob Murdock wouldn't be running it, and went in to sit at his desk. After a few minutes of shuffling papers around, he'd get up and leave.

"Have to get some cigarettes," he'd say to the receptionist, and down to the lobby he'd go. The outer lobby of the Syndicate Building, separated from the inner lobby by imposing glass doors, had a cigar counter along the north wall. It was run by a pleasant bespectacled little man called Doc, and his unlikely partner, Lou, who must have come from Flatbush. The stand sold all manner of sundries – tobacco, soft drinks, papers and periodicals, sandwiches and hot coffee.

Lou was happy to shoot dice by the hour and Bill Rattray was the man most likely to keep him company. Their dice rolling sessions took place several times a day for thirty or forty minutes each time. While such a course of action did nothing for Bill's business, it at least gave him relaxation, fresh air and some release from his worries. The other outlet for Bill was the speakeasy, located, when he first started working there, on the 4th floor and, later, in a back room on the second. Nephew Bob, running the elevator, sadly watched his favorite young uncle make many trips to the hidden "den of iniquity," wishing he could somehow reach out a helping hand but knowing there was nothing he could do or say.

Not all days were bad. And life went on. Thanksgiving that year, Bill and Marian took the children again to Alameda to the old family home on Benton Street, stopping en route for a short visit with Rill, Oscar and Otis Schlesinger. Billy was definitely uncomfortable to be back in the house where he had spent so many miserable hours and didn't leave his mother's side for a moment.

Once in Alameda, they parked in front of the Benton Street home but before going in, all walked to the corner to spend a few minutes with Susan in her room at Mrs. Beasley's. She hadn't seen the twins for nearly a year and was amazed at their growth and development. And even Jane seemed to have matured in the months since June. Mrs. Beasley was preparing a traditional dinner for her "guests" and there was a festive air and holiday aromas permeating the place. Susan seemed content with her lot and they left with light hearts and a promise to see her before Christmas when Marian was planning a triple birthday celebration.

That was a special Thanksgiving . There was much to be thankful for and as always when the Rattray clan gathered it was noisy and high spirited. For a group of individually near-silent Scots, the sound level was remarkably high when they were together. And their laughter was hearty to the point of being boisterous. The children added to the general din by shouting and shrieking as they chased each other around the house.

Ellen Greig was in her usual chair by the fire, tinier than ever, her once-red hair now pinned up a white puff, her Scottish burr still terrorizing her oldest granddaughter who never knew how to respond. Jane didn't understand a word Ellen said and always felt stupid when her cousins laughed at her. They, living nearby, had the advantage of seeing Granny often and were able to make sense of her words. Besides, she didn't grill them with a series of seemingly unintelligible questions the way she did Jane.

The twins were too little to be forced into conversation with Ellen and Billy steered a wide berth, but this "Go say 'Hello' to your grandmother," that Marian (who should have remembered her early days at the Rattrays and spared Jane) insisted on, upset her daughter many holidays of her young life. Years later, Jane was to read Bobby Burn's poetry and realize that she wasn't dumb; her grandmother was speaking what was basically a foreign language. The important words were definitely *not* English and none of them sounded familiar. But reading *Oh wad some power the giftie gie us, To see oursels as others see us! It wad frae monie a blunder free us...* brought to Jane's mind the tiny rocking figure of her long-ago grandmother and she was surprised at the warmth she felt.

That day when Bill and Marian entered with their four children, James and Lottie Panton were there with Ronnie, Jamie, Betty Ann and Tot, Ernest and Bella McRitchie with Greig and Steele, and Alec Rattray with his wife, Bertha. The family circle was incomplete only because Jim Rattray and Margaret with their tiny red-headed daughter, little Greig, were still living in

Japan and Arnold, the youngest, had settled at East Hampton, Long Island, with his wife Jeanette Edwards and their three, Everett, Mary and David.

Marian, Lottie, Bella and Bertha bustled about in the big old-fashioned kitchen separated from the dining room by a large pantry. The cousins noisily renewed their friendship and raced out into the backyard to see the recalcitrant parrot who lived in a shed in the far corner. He was a bright green bird with a baleful gleam in his yellow eyes and a vocabulary that matched his nasty disposition. The bigger boys teased him. He in turn frightened the little ones with his raucous utterings and they ran screaming into the house to get underfoot and be shooed away again.

The house was old, big, and dark. There was a fire blazing in the fireplace next to which Ellen Greig rocked, surveying the romping grandkids with detached amusement. In an alcove on the opposite wall stood an ancient upright piano. Bill, having learned to play on it years before, opened the piano bench, dug out some old music and sat down to play. Soon Alec took his violin from its battered case and joined him. Greig McRitchie and Ronnie Panton, both budding musicians in their mid-teens that year, came to stand by their uncles, Greig finding particular glee in their rustiness. He was big and clumsy with a thatch of dark red hair and a wide infectious grin that matched his enthusiasm for life. Ronnie was as tall, sandy-haired with bright blue eyes like Granny Rattray, and much quieter. Steele McRitchie, younger than the other two, was bigger, heavier, slower, and all brown – hair, eyes, skin. He didn't have the musical interest or talent of his brother and his cousin but he joined Jane in being a good audience.

One holiday, Ronnie and Greig presented Bill with the music to George Gershwin's Rhapsody in Blue. He amazed his young nephews by playing it through on sight with almost no noticeable mistakes although he said he dropped enough notes to make a whole new piece!

Jane always drew close when her father played, doubly so when Ronnie and Greig were at hand. She adored her older male cousins. They were the best part of the holidays during all her growing years and this one was no exception. They made her feel important.

Finally, Marian and the other women had the table set, the turkey on the platter, gravy made, vegetables and potatoes heaped in bowls, and called everyone to eat. Twenty strong, counting the twins who sat in high chairs, and Tot who was elevated on phone books and pillows, they crowded around the expanded table. James Rattray had passed the carving duties to his son-in-law, Jim Panton, who quietly and efficiently attacked the huge bird while Marian and Lottie took care of the plates for their little ones. When all was ready, Ernest McRitchie rose to his feet and pompously intoned the Thanksgiving grace, while the cousins looked at each other from lowered lids, and slyly smiled. From then until the last bite of pumpkin pie was tucked away in uncomfortably full stomachs, the clan enjoyed themselves with normal friction and problems subdued. And it was nice at Thanksgiving to know that within a month they'd all be together again at McRitchie's for Christmas.

On Susan's birthday December 1, she would be 73. Marian would be 37 on January 16. Marian decided the coincidence of the numbers was reason enough for a double party with one cake, the candles counting out both ages depending on which side it was observed from.

Jane would be 12 on December 15 and couldn't be left out, so a second cake would be added to the festivities. They set the date for the Saturday closest to Jane's birthday and asked the Schlesingers and Perce and Barbara, with Alan, to join them.

It was one of those perfect California winter days, clear and crisp, shining with a special polish. Perce drove over to Alameda to pick up his mother and they all arrived in the early afternoon. Too cold to be outside in spite of the sun, the grown-ups gathered in the living room where the decorated Christmas tree already stood while the children played in the sun room. Dinner was early, served just as the sun set and the lights below twinkled on. When the cakes were carried in by Barbara and Rill, everyone sang to the celebrants, laughing as they said the three names all in a row. Susan faced the cake where the grouping of seven and three candles read "73" and Marian opposite her saw three and seven candles making her "37." Jane's cake had twelve candles plus one to grow on.

The party was a great success. At the end, in a flurry of good-byes, Marianne was dragged forward to follow Suzanne's lead and kiss each aunt and uncle. She balked when reaching Perce and Marian had to push her forward for the little peck she planted on his face. This was her least favorite part of family get-togethers. In fact, she hated it with all the passion of her two-and-a-half year old heart.

A few nights later, the family drove to the elegant homes in upper Piedmont to join a parade of slow moving cars looking at the gorgeous outdoor Christmas trees lavishly lit and decorated. It was like a fairyland, each one seeming to surpass all previous trees in glory, some starkly silver and white, spotlighted and shimmering icily, others warmly multicolored and more traditional. Even the twins, up past their normal bedtime, were enchanted and Billy, too, watched in wide-eyed wonder.

Christmas came and went in a flurry of visiting and gift giving, wrapped in a special magic. Marian was delighted to have a bit more leeway in spending and made wise choices for the children, mostly practical items of clothing but each a little unique and personal. As 1930 ended, she breathed a sigh of thankfulness. She'd made it! The family was together, the children were healthy. The new year was bound to be good to them.

The phone rang early in the morning on a cold foggy day just after Marian's birthday. Pulling on her robe and shuffling her feet into slippers, Marian hurried to the hallway to answer it.

"Hello," she said. "Barbara, what is it? WHAT! Oh, no!" Her voice broke in a deep sob. "No, no, it can't be. Oh, my God! Perce, not Perce! Barbara, what can I do? Who's with you?" She listened for a moment, looking with unseeing eyes at Bill, Jane and Billy who had come from their beds to stand by her, drawn by the unusual pain in her voice.

"Does Mother know?" she asked. "I'll call Bess. She can tell Tone and they can go to Mother together. I'll let Rill know, too. Then, I'll be over. Hold on, dear."

Marian hung up just as another sob broke. Tears were already streaming down her face.

"Perce is dead," she said. "Dead. Someone found him up on that lot, the one where he was going to build their home." Her usually strong voice quavered. "They say he committed suicide." She raised her chin. "I don't believe it! He was underneath the Packard, on a blanket, with his head near the exhaust. The engine was still running! Somebody did it. Perce wouldn't commit suicide."

Marian turned to the children, put her arms out to them and said, gently, "Go get dressed now and we'll have breakfast. Bill, call Mrs. Dennis. I'm going to need her."

It was a long disjointed sad day. After breakfast Billy and Jane went off to school. Marian felt normalcy was the best treatment for children in the face of tragedy. The twins were left with Mrs. Dennis. Marian and Bill drove to Barbara's after first making the difficult and heartbreaking phone calls to the rest of the family. Marian, her eyes shiny with unshed tears, was a tower of strength the whole long day, only breaking down when she reached her bedroom that night.

Perce had always been her beloved, more than an older brother, closer than a father, dearer than a friend, more human than a god. His death tore at her heart with a pain that was physical and mortal. As she put her head down on the pillow, she didn't want to wake again. She gave herself up to crying, barely conscious of Bill's hands on her shoulders trying to comfort her.

This was not the futile weeping of a wife awaiting her husband's return that Bill had often heard in irritation. Here was the raw expression of an unbearable anguish. Bill felt totally useless, unable to do a single thing to help her. But he sat there on the edge of the bed, pressing her shoulders, rubbing her back, while the coldness of the January night crept into the room. Marian's rending sobs gradually subsided into exhaustion and she slept. Only then did he stand up, undress and slip in beside her, moving close for mutual warmth and comfort.

Jane, that first day on the way to school, walked past a newsstand and was surprised to see the headlines, CP MURDOCK SUICIDE and RICH REALTOR FOUND SLAIN, both papers using two-inch type to scream the news. She hadn't realized her Uncle Perce was a personage of such importance. She had never been related to anyone whose name appeared in headlines for all the world to see and considering the message, she was reduced to tears by the sight.

The whole day had an unreal aura to it. Jane kept finding her mind shifting away from the classroom to remember the sadness that had come into their lives over a telephone line in the gray dawn. Uncle Perce had always been her favorite with his craggy face and gentle smile. She loved riding in his powder blue Packard with the red leather seats. She loved his laugh, the hunch of his wide shoulders, the way he talked to her as though she were grown-up and interesting. And now he was dead. She thought about his sons, her cousins Steve and Dickie, and was sad for their loss.

When Grandfather George died just a year ago, Jane had felt a sorrow but not much deeper than when he and her grandmother had moved away from Marin making it impossible to see him as often as she used to. She didn't cry then but now, sitting in class, the loss in her heart made tears well in her eyes. She turned to concentrate on the teacher's voice, to focus on her face, absorb the words to push all other thoughts from her mind. It worked but the day was long and her heart was heavy.

The next few weeks were difficult on many levels. Suicide officially was declared the reason for the death but Marian was steadfast in her denial of such a possibility. Barbara, too, felt that foul play on the part of one of the many who had lost millions in the crash of C.P. Murdock's real estate empire, was a more likely act. There was much to substantiate her feelings, and Marian's, but it was labeled suicide and nothing could be done to change that on the records

Susan crumbled under this new loss. It had been just a year since

George's death. Though that was sudden and a blow, she had rallied and built a new life for herself, first in the apartment, then at Mrs. Beasley's. She had changed the pattern and gone on. But now, there was no pattern to change, nothing new to build. Her son, her precious vibrant wonderful son, was dead and something in her died, too. A light had gone out. Even remembering all the years of his life didn't help. She could see him as a curly haired baby, quickly catching up with the twins, then running circles around them, always bright and joyful. She could see him with his tennis racquet, hot and grinning in victory. She could see him, a cavalier father, with Steve and Dickie clinging to his arms, his legs, all laughing with the zest of life Perce imparted. She could see him quietly picking up tabs, writing checks, making wrongs right for all of them. She could see him a million ways in her mind but that didn't help the pain. If anything, it made it worse. How could such a light be extinguished? And how could anyone say he killed himself? How could she bear to think he had been driven to such an awful final act? How could he – who had always reached out to each of them, been there whatever the trouble, fixed any problem – go alone and silent into such terrible blackness? The weight of that crushed her. She would never forgive herself the negligence of not noticing, not ferreting out the problems that led him to his death.

Susan didn't realize that nothing she could have done as a mother would have penetrated the business shield Perce held between himself and his family. From that world, he only shared the good parts, the pieces that impacted on their lives. But Susan didn't know that and since she was unable to talk about her personal feelings with even Marian or Rill, or her daughters-in-law, no one could lift the burden of guilt she imposed upon herself.

Business at the Realty Syndicate Building came to a complete halt on the floors where the Murdock name was on the door. Perce's real estate enterprise was under investigation, barred from any transactions, declared bankrupt with all books and records confiscated.

Tone had long since given up in his architectural firm, closed the office and found a much smaller job with the county of Alameda, designing what few buildings they could justify expending money to construct.

And Bill, at George Hamilton Murdock's insurance office, signed a few papers and just drifted away, leaving the capable secretary to deal with whatever was left, hoping that Susan would still have something from her husband's lifelong endeavors.

With his father and uncles gone, one of them dead under very public and scandalous conditions, Bob had no reason to travel so far just to run the elevator, and quit his job. There was the taint of disgrace, of suicide, of failure that none of them wanted to be connected with. The great high days of success and glory were gone and so were the three businesses started by Murdock men so many years ago.

Marian realized they had another year and a half on their house lease and no way to pay the monthly charges. Bill was looking for work, along with thousands of others. The renters in the Ross house were delinquent, too. The situation was desperate and it was up to her to fix it. First, Mrs. Dennis was called in for a serious talk.

"I can't afford to let you have the cottage in return for what you can do for us, Mrs. Dennis, "Marian said. "I'm sorry. If you can find employment somewhere else, maybe nearby, you can still live in the cottage and pay a reasonable rent."

"I understand, Mrs. Rattray. I'll start looking right away." That underway, Marian talked to Rill and Oscar. He was a mechanical engineer with a good firm. They owned their home. Marian figured if they were willing to totally discombobulate themselves and rent it, they could move in with her and put their new-found rent money toward the lease on the Estates Drive place. It was a lot to ask of a sister who wasn't known for her selflessness but Marian was desperate. It would be a tight squeeze both financially and physically but surprisingly, Rill and Oscar were more than willing.

"It's the least we can do," said Oscar who had seldom been in a position to help members of his wife's family. Rill assumed her Lady Bountiful persona and treated the entire situation like a beneficent adventure.

Their home, in a choice part of Piedmont was able to bring a fine rental and, furnished, was snapped up in record time. So the Schlesingers moved to Estates Drive. Otis took the small upstairs bedroom, his parents the larger one. Jane was shifted, from the funny little room that opened on to the roof, to the sleeping porch. She took her beloved wind chimes with her. Billy was crowded into the twin's room much to his disgust. Marian and Bill had the front bedroom downstairs. It wasn't ideal but it worked.

Luckily, in spite of all the people seeking employment, Mrs. Dennis found a place right away where she could care for a home and a family.

"I hate not being with you and the children," she said to Marian when reporting her luck. "But at least I'll still live here and be able to see you. And in emergencies, I can help out."

Spring finally came. Bill was taken back at Fireman's Fund, where he'd been an insurance adjuster before his foray to Oakland the year before, at a decrease in salary and a lower position. That was all right with him. The less responsibility the better, as far as he was concerned.

Marian, in the meantime, had answered an ad for kitchen help at Highland Hospital's cafeteria. She accepted the job with her eye on quickly moving up to manager. With her energy, efficiency and education, her days peeling vegetables and serving on the line were brief. She, became assistant manager in a short time, with, of course, an increase in pay. Things were definitely looking better.

Then one morning at work, she realized that what she thought was a normal monthly period was much more. It had been going on for well over a week but instead of decreasing it was getting heavier by the hour. Finally she had to leave the floor; she was hemorrhaging. With the help of a kitchen aide, she was able to get to the emergency room.

As an employee of the hospital, she was given quick attention and put to bed. A phone call to Rill alerted her to the situation. Mrs. Dennis would be commandeered when she came in from work and put in charge of the household, and hopefully would be able to take a few days off from her job to help out. That's as far as Marian could plan. She was waiting for the results from a conference of doctors who had attended her, taken her history, and were plotting her treatment.

An hour later they came back into her room. "We have to stop the bleeding," one said. "Now, we have several options, but what we'd like to do, because it's non-invasive, quick and painless, is a radium pack after a dilation and curettage. In your case, we think it would be much more appropriate than a hysterectomy."

Marian listened, looking from face to face. After her problems with Dr. Delancy, she had a wariness of the medical profession but the four men standing around her bed seemed concerned and trustworthy. She nodded.

The tall dark-haired doctor was evidently the spokesman because he continued. "You must understand. This is a very new procedure. But it's given excellent results with no bad side-effects. You'll have to stay here overnight, maybe two nights at the most." Marian nodded again.

"We'll start right away. Any questions?" Marian could think of a hundred but could voice none. "It's settled then. I'll send a nurse in."

The procedure went quickly and the doctors were pleased. Marian was quite chipper when Bill, with Jane in hand, came to visit that evening. "I'll be home tomorrow, don't worry," she said. "How's everything going?"

"Fine," they answered in unison, then laughed. Bill continued. "That Mrs. Dennis is something else. She even had Rill out of her negligee and taking her turn at the sink happily. That's amazing!" Bill was more than slightly irritated by Rill's "lady of the manor" airs and pleased when someone shook her into menial labor, however fleetingly.

"And the twins are okay, too. They're glad to see Mrs. Dennis again. So am I. She's nice and makes us all mind, even Billy!" Jane added. This visit to the hospital erased the apprehension Jane had been feeling. The last experience she'd had with her mother's hospitalization was the frightening memory that preceded the long separation of the previous year. Now Marian was sitting up in bed looking cheerful and healthy. Marian had hoped, when she asked Bill to bring Jane, that it would accomplish just what it did. Jane chatted happily, telling her mother all about her day at school and what was going on at home. It hardly seemed possible that Marian had been gone such a short time!

She came home the next day, but didn't go back to work yet on the doctors' orders. As time went on, she tried to tell herself she was okay but she knew she wasn't.

"Bill, there's something wrong. I feel weird inside. I can't explain the feeling. It's just there."

"You better go back to the doctor. It's been nearly two weeks. You should be better."

"I'll go tomorrow."

Bill looked at her. She was drawn and pale, her usually buoyant spirit missing. Her hair was limp, her eyes dull. A shiver of apprehension shot through him. *I should have noticed how badly she looks. Lord, I hope it's nothing serious.*

The next afternoon, Marian was resting in her hospital room. She'd checked in that morning and swiftly undergone a major examination under light anesthesia. The doctors had seemed quite concerned and had moved with speed. Now, one of them appeared by the side of her bed. She pulled herself into a sitting position.

"Well, Mrs. R," said Dr. Torrance, the tall dark spokesman of the team. "We found the trouble. You were right. There was a small hitch in the procedure."

"What do you mean?" Marian asked.

"Well, Mrs. R," he repeated. "I don't know how it happened but one of the packings was left in."

"Left in? You mean, inside me? In my uterus?" Marian's voice was incredulous, her eyes flashing. "What does that mean?"

"Nothing serious, now that we've removed it. Really, everything is all right, I assure you."

"But wasn't the packing full of radium? Wasn't it supposed to be taken out in a very short time? Seems to me you said it was a *very short* procedure. That's why there'd be no side effects. Now what? Will I glow in the dark? Will my hair fall out?"

"No, no, the radium itself was removed right on schedule. Just a little packing was overlooked. Probably no radium connected with it at all."

"Probably? Can you be more specific."

"Not really. It's been disposed of. Very odoriferous. Actually putrid. That was what you smelled. Unfortunate. But no harm done."

"No harm? Except it's been inside me for two weeks and heaven only knows what might happen, might still happen. You don't really know, do you?" Marian didn't wait for an answer. "And I should be well by now. But I'm not. I came in because I was feeling worse every day." Marian was glaring at him. All her previous animosity toward the medical profession was bursting forth. "DAMN!"

"Now, Mrs. R," he said soothingly, "You'll be all right. I'll check back in the morning. Then I'm sure you'll be able to go home." He gave her a weak smile and slipped out the door.

Marian lay back on her bed to consider her situation and options. *I wish Perce were here. He'd know what to do. He could tell me. Should I sue? Heck no, that wouldn't change anything. I guess I'll just consider myself lucky to be alive and go on.*

And that's what she did. But she didn't go back to work at the cafeteria. Instead she gave notice and blamed it on her health. She could have taken more sick time. However, she didn't want to run the risk of seeing Dr. Torrance. She just wanted to stay home and get her strength back, hoping that he was correct in saying there should be no problems now that everything was cleaned out. That better be the case or she would raise a commotion the like of which they'd never seen!

Summer came, their second at Estates Drive. Billy and Jane went down the hill to Montclair where they attended a community daily vacation bible school. There was less bible than arts and crafts. Jane learned how to make elaborate crepe paper skirts for a doll to sit on the bed and she wove several sturdy baskets. Billy's accomplishments were mostly lumpy clay bowls and bookends. They did learn several Psalms by heart and heard many of the stories from both the Old and New Testaments and sang familiar hymns. But the highlight, in their minds, was the daily showing of *Felix the Cat* cartoons which they both loved.

At Parents' Night to close the session, Jane's work received blue ribbons, Billy's bright green honorable mentions. Jane refrained from pointing out to her proud little brother that every single offering in the whole school sported a ribbon of some color!

Tippy was a year old. The children gave him a birthday party which he did his best to destroy. But his canned dog food cake was a big hit and they got the candle off before he ate it! Marian, who stood by to light the candle and lead the rendition of the birthday song, smiled as she watched the children romping with the pup.

Tippy was filling out, a medium sized dog, with a coat of soft curly blond hair, intelligent brown eyes, ears that stood up straight and tipped over just a bit at the top. He was displaying a happy disposition, a great heart and fine intelligence, altogether a satisfactory pet. Marian was pleased with him and the children thought he was wonderful.

The twins at Estates Drive, 1931.

Suzanne in buggy with Marianne pushing, three years old, Summer 1931.

Marian took a moment to sit and watch, an indulgence that was difficult to allow herself. She *should* be doing something productive. But look at them! Marianne and Suzanne were three years old, no longer babies. They loved swinging on the swing Bill had tied to the branches of a sturdy oak, or taking turns pushing each other in a large doll buggy and riding on their tricycles.

Billy, too, was growing up. He seemed happier this summer, less threatened by the twins, less likely to torment Jane and even able to tolerate his Aunt Rill's overtures of affection. But Jane! That was where the big change had taken place. She was still tall and skinny but the contours of her body were subtly shifting. Most amazing of all, her straight hair was developing a curl! *If only she would stand up straight,* Marian thought

Her mind drifted to their situation and Bill. Hard to realize they'd known each other nearly twenty years, been married fourteen. It didn't seem possible. Yet so much had happened. The four babies, now growing up, the little house in Ross that seemed so far away. Would they ever be able to get it back? Her father's death, her terrible operation and just recently, the radium scare. Perce's death – she wouldn't, couldn't call it a suicide. And Bill. What about Bill?

He's my husband, father of my children. And he has so many great qualities – a good sharp mind, a wonderful sense of humor. He's as silly as a clown sometimes and makes us all hysterical. And his music! He can play the piano better than anyone I know, almost better than anyone I've ever heard. I like how he treats women. He's not fresh or demeaning. He respects them and gives them credit for being intelligent and capable. I like the way he looks, too. He's still so slim and stands so straight. There's such a spring in his step. And his smile is wonderful! I think Billy looks most like him, except for his eyes. Bill's are deep blue, Billy's hazel. Then, slowly her mind shifted to a part she didn't want to face.

Why does Bill drink? It messes everything up. No matter how long he goes without drinking, it's always hanging over me. If he's a minute late, I begin to wonder. Life would be so simple if it weren't for that. And if we had more money! How will we ever get through this time? He's working, Rill and Oscar are helping, the lease will be up the end of next April and we'll be able to get out of here. They'll move back to their home and we'll go to their cabin in Woodacre. At least we'll be back in Marin and can figure a plan from there. I will get our house back. I will raise the children in Ross. I will have a happy life. We will be a happy family.

Marian brought her attention back to the playing children and the romping dog. Then she rose from the wicker chair on the cement area by the front door and went into the house to see what Rill was doing and to discuss dinner with her.

Rill was sitting on the chaise in their big sun-flooded bedroom, reading.

"Any special requests for dinner? I'm planning a tuna casserole and I have a bunch of carrots. Bread pudding for dessert. I made it this morning."

"That sounds fine, Marian. We don't eat much, as you know," Rill answered. She reached for another bonbon from the fancy box at her elbow, not seeing the incongruity of her act. It made Marian smile.

"I was just thinking of the place in Woodacre, Rill." Marian sat down on the edge of the bed. "And Jane. Are you sure you want to have her with you until the end of school? It'll be about six weeks. And she can come over to Marin weekends."

"It will be fine, I'm sure. We'll have a grand time. She's such a nice child! I can do a lot for her."

"What's the cabin like?" asked Marian, not wanting to discuss what Rill thought she could do for Jane. Her daughter, Marian knew, could resist or withstand any unwanted improvement.

"Rustic, very crude actually. On the side of a hill. The kitchen is underneath part of the living room in the back. You go down outside stone steps to get to it. Oscar put running water in the sink but it just drains to the ground out back. Ockie also put in electricity last year. He's so handy! There's an open sleeping porch down wooden steps on the other side of the living room. And an outhouse up a trail. The builders dug out a place off the road where you can park the car. Rustic for sure."

Marian could hardly imagine her elegant sister roughing it in such a place, but she also knew that it would have artistic touches wherever Rill could put them. But an outdoor privy, that seemed a bit much! The children would have a great adventure.

"We'll stay there through the summer. It'll be like camping. And I'm sure we'll find something in Ross by autumn. Or get our place back. I really appreciate all you and Oscar have done to help us out. We couldn't have made it without you."

"Well, you are family," said Rill with a nod like a benediction.

Autumn came and school started for Billy and Jane. She was in the eighth grade but there would be no graduation from elementary school coming up at the end of the year as there would have been in Ross. Jane was now a middle sized frog in the big puddle but comfortable and quite at home. She was a good student unless she had to speak before class. Answering questions, reciting, doing anything that brought attention to herself was paralyzing to her. But her ability to write made all other assignments easy. Even math was simple. That talent she inherited from both her parents. She could draw and paint, too, had a fine sense of design. Rill took credit for any talent Jane had along these lines, pointing to her own framed artworks as proof.

"It runs in the family," she said. "Except for you, Marian. Tone has lots of talent, too. His oil landscapes of Marin and the Bay are fine. I do watercolors," she said with a touch of pride. "Jane will be able to paint, too.

You'll see." Rill nodded as though it were an accomplished fact, made true by her words.

With the holidays and the new year, specters of the previous year hovered over everyone. "It was just a year ago…" filled each heart. A year ago that Perce had laughed and joked at the double birthday party, a year ago that they'd been together at Christmas, a year since his tragic death, a year since Marian's radium treatment, a year since the world had changed.

"Change," Marian often said, quoting an unknown source, "is the only constant thing in life." And she could cope with it better than most. Her eye was firmly on the coming spring and what it would bring – out from under the lease, back to Marin, a good change!

But before spring, several changes, not good ones, took place. First, Ellen Greig, Bill's mother, became ill. The doctor prescribed a stringent diet, hoping it would help. James, who was working in Berkeley, took a longer lunch period than usual and came by streetcar from there to Alameda so that he could prepare and serve lunch. Then he sat with her to help her eat every bite. It made her happy to have him at her side, and the food tasted better being shared with him. If he didn't come home, she wouldn't touch a thing.

In spite of James's careful ministrations, Ellen did not improve, getting smaller and smaller, weaker and weaker, sicker and sicker. There was nothing that could be done. Within six weeks she was gone. Bella notified Bill. The family gathered together at the old homestead on Benton Street to comfort James and each other.

Marian went with Bill, leaving the children under Rill's supervision. She felt they were too young to be exposed to the sad aftermath of death. At breakfast she said, "Daddy and I are going to Alameda. Your Granny Rattray died and we need to be with the rest of the family. Come right home from school and be good for Aunt Rill. Jane, you help with the younger ones."

"All right," answered Jane. "I'm sorry, Daddy." She walked around the table to give him a self-conscious hug. He smiled at her. "Thanks," he said, giving her a small hug back.

The saddest part was still to come. James, who in his devotion to is wife, had prepared and eaten the food prescribed for Ellen during the last month of her life, was found to be suffering from an illness, exacerbated by a diet diametrically opposed to his condition. It was too late to save him and he was gone within weeks of Ellen.

Although it was probably what he wanted, this second death shattered the family and left them reeling. It was almost more than they could bear. Jim and Arnold were too far away to come for either service. All the details fell to sons-in-law Jim Panton and Ernest McRitchie who were right at hand. Alec, across the Bay in San Francisco, was not close enough to help with the arrangements and Bill, although near, wasn't constitutionally able to take part in preparations. He could only silently grieve.

But they were stoic Scots. They did what had to be done, consoled each other as much as they could and went on.

The move to Woodacre was accomplished at the end of April. Mrs. Dennis had moved out in mid-month, the Schlesingers were ready to go the minute their place was vacated by the renters, and Marian had everything organized to be put into storage or travel with them to the cabin.

Jane stayed with Rill and Oscar so that, once again, she could finish out the school year without interruption. She was able to walk to school or take a short streetcar ride and wasn't the least disturbed by staying with her aunt, uncle and cousin. Rill might try to knot scarves around her neck, tuck a fancy handkerchief into her pocket, but she couldn't make any drastic changes in Jane's attire as she had in Billy's two years before and Jane found her aunt's duchess mannerisms amusing.

She loved her room. It was on the second story, a glassed-in porch that looked down on the overgrown back garden. At thirteen, with poetic yearnings in her adolescent heart, Jane spent many evening hours gazing at the moon-touched white roses climbing below her and dreamed dreams tinged with a yearning she couldn't understand.

Weekends she headed for Woodacre as soon as school was out. The trip was made on two streetcars, two ferryboats, an electric train and, finally, a small train powered by an oil-burning steam engine! And, unless connections were perfect, Jane spent over three hours en route, quite a journey for a lone young lady her age.

As the Oakland-San Francisco ferryboat eased into the slip at the Ferry Building, Jane could see the boat for Sausalito still in its slot. She shouldered her way to the front of the boat and was one of the first to run down the wide gangplank. Instead of going through to the waiting rooms with the crush of debarkees, she turned right and dashed down the passageway to where she could see passengers boarding the ferryboat she wanted. *What a break!* she thought as she ran. *I'm saving 30 minutes.*

Jane hoped her father was on the boat. They were supposed to connect at the Ferry Building but sometimes he wasn't there. He'd been on hand the first Friday that she'd made the trip, and since then she'd done it alone twice. After today there were only two more weeks and school would be over. She'd move to Woodacre and be with the family again.

She found her dad on the front upper deck, his curly hair blowing in the slight May breeze. He was easy to spot, tall and the only man in sight not wearing a hat. She went to stand beside him and he put his arm around her shoulders with a welcoming smile. They stood silently as the boat pulled out of the slip and headed toward Sausalito.

"Beautiful," he said.

"Yes," Jane answered, her eyes sweeping the sparkling waters of the bay, the hills ahead still sheened with green from the late spring rains. Sea gulls circled and squawked. The sky was pale blue with clouds over Mount Tamalpais. First the bastion of Alcatraz, then the wooded greenness of Angel Island slipped by on their right. Numerous sailboats dotted the water. Sausalito, getting ever larger as the boat pulled closer, looked clean and washed, houses in a multitude of pastel shades climbing the steep hill.

"I think that's what the Mediterranean, the French Riviera, must look like," Jane said. "All those colorful buildings clinging to the side of a mountain. What do you think?"

"Could be. I don't know, I've never been there. This is about the biggest trip I've ever taken," Bill answered with a chuckle. Truthfully, he had never been out of California. Never gone to Los Angeles, even. He had travelled by train as far north as Eureka when he was settling claims for Fireman's Fund eight or ten years ago but he was right. Crossing the Bay on a ferryboat was the extent of his journeying!

Jane laughed with her father. "I hope I go to Europe someday. Maybe Spain. Or England. Scotland, for sure. Wouldn't that be great? I'd love to hear bagpipes played better than Uncle Ernest does at Christmas. He is awful, isn't he? I mean, they don't sound that terrible, do they?"

Bill snorted. "No. Ernest isn't the best player. But it's a hard instrument to master. I never could. Not enough wind I guess. Or enough patience to practice. Piano is much easier. I never had any trouble with that, not even when I was a little boy."

"I love to hear you play," Jane said shyly. She wasn't used to giving compliments to her parents. It seemed sort of forward to her, somewhat embarrassing.

"Good." Bill replied. The dock was coming closer. Funny how it seemed that the boat was standing still and the land approaching them! They turned to hurry down the stairs to rush off with the rest of the commuters. They headed for the electric train whose sign proclaimed its final destination as Manor. There were other cars behind signs for Willits, San Rafael via Greenbrae, and Mill Valley. The commuters quickly sorted themselves out and climbed on the car they wanted.

Jane slipped into a window seat and settled down beside her father, who quickly unfolded his newspaper to read. Thirty minutes later, after stops along the way, plus losing one car in San Anselmo that went on to San Rafael, they reached Manor. Here they left the electric train and walked down the cement platform to where a puffing steam engine with a baggage car and three passenger cars awaited them.

This was the most exciting part of the ride for Jane. To get to the other side of White's Hill, which separated central Marin County from wilder West Marin, the train went over a high trestle and through a long tunnel. Woodacre was the first stop on the other side of the mountain. There Bill and his daughter left the train. They stood and watched as the engine whistled and belched off toward San Geronimo, Lagunitas, Forest Knolls, Samuel Taylor Park, Tocaloma and finally Point Reyes Station.

Woodacre was in a valley. The station stood in the middle of the flat land. Behind them was the mountain they'd just tunneled through, ahead an opening to a wider valley down which the train was now disappearing in a puff of smoke. To their right rose a grassy hill, one lower shoulder of White's Hill. To their left, and ahead diagonally, was a ridge covered with tall redwood trees that gave way to a rocky hillside with oaks and manzanita and tan summer grass by the time it reached across from where they stood.

It was toward this hill that Bill and Jane headed. Woodacre roads were narrow and full of ruts and rocks. They crossed a bridge under which ran an almost dry creek. Willows grew along the banks. Then they headed up a steeper road that circled around the side of the hill, climbing as it went. Finally they came abreast of the summer home of Trube Scott, Rill's best friend from Piedmont. The Rattrays had been introduced to her while still in Piedmont since she was to be their closest neighbor and had a telephone they could use if an emergency arose. Jane looked down on the large house. It was still shuttered; their neighbors weren't on hand this weekend.

The Schlesinger cabin couldn't be seen from the road, just the cut that had been made for parking. The car was sitting there, big rocks shoved under the front wheels to keep it from rolling down to the creek far below. Tippy heard their voices and came racing toward them, tail wagging and ears back against his head in happiness. He was followed by Billy and the twins. Marian waited at the open door, smiling her welcome.

"Look at us, Jane," Marianne called. "Do we look different? We're four years old now!"

"Gosh, I'm sorry I missed your birthday," Jane answered giving her little sister a hug and reaching out to Suzanne with a pat. "Yes, you do look different, both of you. Bigger. Older." Marianne grinned with pleasure as they ran down the stone steps.

The cabin was built on the side of the hill. Steep stone steps, gouged out of the hillside, led from the road. To the left, where the steps continued down to the kitchen, Oscar had started to make a patio under an oak tree that spread its branches over the house. There Marian had set a wicker table and several garden chairs. And there, many days, she served a picnic lunch.

The one big room, with paned windows all across the back and continuing part way up the left wall stopping just short of the little cast iron stove, was light and airy. The windows were on notched runners that Oscar had made and could be opened by sliding one over the other, opening up half to the great outdoors. Here Marian had hung the wind chimes where constant drafts kept them tinkling softly. Exposed rafters and knotty pine walls gave the place an informal rustic atmosphere. Rill had furnished it for comfort and utility with touches of her usual flair. Four beds, against the side walls, were covered with bright spreads and piled with pillows. There were low bookcases under the back windows, filled with National Geographics and other light reading. Chairs were old and comfortable. Oriental rugs added an elegant touch to the plank floor.

Billy with Tippy, Woodacre,
May 1932.

Marianne on the hillside,
Woodacre, May 1932

The twins' cribs had been placed along the wall near the side door to the sleeping porch. Marian felt more comfortable with the little ones close by at night. The temperature dropped before dawn and the sleeping porch was open to the elements. She wanted to be able to cover them up if the need arose in the chill of the night.

Billy slept on the porch the weekends Jane was there to keep him company. Otherwise, he took one of the beds in the main room with the rest of the family.

Jane went right to the sleeping porch to dump her suitcase on the bed she had claimed weeks before. Then she ran up the rocky path to the outhouse. It faced away from the cabin and had no door. Tippy thought it was a game when his playmates went in there. He stood outside, front legs stretched out, rump and wagging tail high, barking at them to come play! Jane found it embarrassing, imagining that their far-flung neighbors knew why he was making such a commotion. She always tried to sneak out there without the dog in noisy attendance but seldom made it.

The evening meal, served at six sharp as always, was light and wholesome. They crowded in at the table in the tiny eating space separated from the kitchen by a high narrow counter. In the back wall above the table was a small door that opened on to the bare hillside under the house. Here Oscar had built a wide deep shelf for storage. Later that summer, Bill supervised the concocting of a batch of root beer which they bottled and "put down" to age. One extremely hot day, the bottles, even in that cool sheltered environment, started exploding. It was a wet and noisy mess. Only a few bottles escaped to be enjoyed as planned by their makers.

That weekend the children clambered around the hillside, spending some time down at the bottom of their lot where a shaded creek made pools under the oak and willow trees that lined its banks. Nowhere was it deep enough to cause a hazard so they played happily, making small dams and searching for salamanders and water skaters.

Sunday afternoon, just before she was due to pack up for her trip back to Piedmont, Jane said, "Mom, I don't feel well." Marian placed her hand on Jane's forehead and could tell from the feverish warmth that Jane was not just procrastinating. She was sick. "Okay, let's get you to bed up here in the living room. I'll give you an aspirin and later some soup. You'll be all right. But I'll go down to the store and call Rill that you won't be back for awhile."

What Marian had hoped was an isolated simple cold turned out to be a full-fledged flu bug that almost instantly attacked the other three children. The living room began to resemble a hospital ward. To add to the discomfort, it started to rain for the first time since they'd been there. They discovered that the roof leaked copiously. Marian scrounged around for buckets, pans, bowls, whatever she could find, to place on the rafters under the leaks. It was a dismal time. Bill drove the car down to the station where he parked it for the day. In the unlikely case of an emergency, Marian would have to hike down in the rain to fetch it but that was the best solution they could think of to keep Bill relatively dry as he commuted to work.

And so May 1932 ended. June first was Bill's birthday. When he came home, after parking the car in its spot, he beckoned to Marian to come down to the kitchen. She looked at the four little bodies inert in their beds and went to join him.

"Well, I got a great birthday present," Bill said as he sat down at the table across from her. "I got fired! Would you believe it?"

"I guess I'll have to," Marian replied calmly. "What else can happen, I wonder? Sick kids, leaking roof, no job! It can only get better!"

As she spoke, there was a loud crash. Braving the rain, they went out the door, up the stairs and across the front of the house. There was no car where it belonged. Their eyes followed a track that disappeared in the bushes beyond the outhouse and there they saw the back end of the automobile which had nosed into a tree with a scrunching impact.

"Well, it didn't take long to find out what else could happen," said Marian. They looked at each other and started to laugh. "This is it!" said Marian, clutching Bill. "Now it has to get better! Happy birthday!"

"Thanks," replied Bill returning her hug and shaking rain from his face. "Let's get inside before we drown."

The evening was spent in reviewing their options, planning their future and periodically reverting to the uncontrollable laughter that the situation evoked in them. It was an unforgettable birthday and one of the best times they'd had in their marriage. To find that they could hit such a dismal low and laugh together about it, albeit hysterically, gave them strength to face the situation honestly which is something they weren't always able to do. Marian didn't even ask if Bill had placed rocks under the car's front wheels. At this point it didn't matter. Nor did the reason, if there was one, that he lost the job have any relevance. This was where they were and they'd just have to go on from here. Bill had two more weeks to wind things up so two more checks would be coming in which would help.

"You do remember, don't you," Marian asked, "that I put away a little every week when we were doing well? It's not much but we have it. Only we aren't going to use it unless the children are starving! No, I mean it. Don't plan on it bridging the gap. That's not why I saved it. It's for moving to Ross and getting our house back."

"Do you really think that'll ever happen, that we'll get the house back?

It's not likely."

"Maybe it's not likely. But it WILL happen. And that's what the savings are for. First, to move out of this place before the rain." She looked at the water streaming down the kitchen windows and laughed. "Well, before the winter rain! And the cold. Can you imagine going to the bathroom when the temperature is freezing? Even Tippy wouldn't bother chasing us and barking. No, this is very temporary. I'm thankful to be here, especially now that we have this latest problem. But just remember, there is no extra money, no cushion, nothing except what you earn. We can't be stuck here – and we might be if we touched the savings."

Bill looked at her and wondered where she got her strength and her assurance. He wished that he could draw on it. Most of the time, however, it made him feel diminished, almost assaulted. Not tonight, though. His job would soon be gone but he'd find something else. And he agreed, what Marian had been able to save while they were in Oakland should remain inviolate.

They would make all the right moves and perhaps Marian's dream would come true.

First, as soon as the rain stopped and the hillside dried out a bit, they'd arrange to have the car towed back up to the road. It would be quite a job but Bob, the hulking young man at the garage, loved a challenge and wouldn't charge too much. The question was, would the car still run? "We'll worry about that when we know," Marian said. "And in the meantime, pray it will."

Next, Bill would make contacts in San Anselmo and Ross, looking for jobs. They had several ideas. Perhaps organist at St. John's Episcopal Church. And there was a dancing school where he might be able to play the piano for classes. It was exciting to think about using his musical talent to earn money. Since his days of playing the theater organ for silent movies years before, and his stint with a dance band in Auburn the summer of 1914, Bill hadn't done that. Even both the church and the dancing classes, if they turned out, would hardly be enough to live on but it would be a start.

The next morning the sun was shining brilliantly on a clean-washed world. The air was fresh and warm. Although the ground was still soggy between the rocks, the children were begging to go out and play. Since none still had a fever, Marian said they could. "But stay dry. Don't play in the water, don't go down to the creek. And don't go near the car. It might move."

Jane stayed in the house. She was still pale and Marian knew she was worried about having missed so much school. It didn't look as if she'd make it back before vacation started next week.

"We'll write a letter to the school and tell them you're over here and sick. They'll send your records to the high school for next fall. It'll be all right,

Janie. You were doing so well, I don't think missing these days'll matter much. Sorry about the dance, though. That would've been fun."

Jane smiled wanly. She wasn't sure. The thought of a big junior high school dance had been upsetting her. Marian was making a lovely dress, almost finished, from material Rill had gotten from Trube Scott, apricot organza with a large border along one side of embroidered flowers in several shades of blue. Marian planned to use the material so that the full skirt would have the flowers around the bottom. She would nip it in at the waist with a smooth bodice and then a fold of the embroidered material as a stand-up ruffle around the top. Now it wouldn't be put together since there was no place to wear it. To Jane's relief, her mother folded the pieces with a sigh and placed them carefully, protected by tissue paper, in a box.

"Someday," she told Jane, "we'll get this out and whip up a lovely gown for you." *That'll be the day!* Jane thought. She was still more than a little apprehensive of the social scene and couldn't imagine whirling around in a gorgeous gown in the arms of some strange boy.

Three days later, Bob came and winched the car out of the gully. It was, amazingly, undamaged, just scratched and dented. With a bit of coaxing, the engine turned over and took hold with a gratifying roar. "Praying helps," said Marian. "Thank you, God."

Oscar, having been notified of the multitude of leaks during the rain storm, arranged for two young men to come repair the roof. They amused the twins and upset Tippy but finished the job and life went on.

Billy spent one more week at school, being bussed there from the station. He was enjoying the country school and once again had found himself ahead of the class when he transferred before the end of the term. Next September he'd be a fifth grader but now the long wonderful days of summer vacation stretched ahead.

Early mornings were foggy. Through the quiet came the muffled sound of bleating goats, the sharp tinkle of their bells, the crowing of roosters. These were morning sounds that had been missing in the Oakland hills and the fog seemed different, too. Closer, wispy and slightly eerie, slipping through the branches of the oak trees and trailing off, moving in silence. And then, as the sun rose, melting away except for little pockets in the creases of the gullies.

Jane and Billy left their warm beds in the chilly post-dawn to start those wonderful vacation days as early as possible. They dressed and pulled on sweaters, took turns at the outhouse accompanied by the bouncing barking dog. "Wake up the world, you dummy!" scolded Jane, trying to hush him.

It never worked and by the time they got to the kitchen, Marian would be there, with the twins, ready to feed everyone and eager to dispense her enthusiasm and plans for the day. They were working on the patio Oscar had started. Jane discovered she had a talent for rock work and somehow could fit them into place better than anyone else in the family. Billy was good at digging out the bank to fill in where Jane was building a retaining wall to enlarge the area. They were a good team and the work was like an extension of their play kingdoms of earlier summers.

Mid morning they took a break and all four, after a snack, walked down to follow the creek to the lower road. Here, in the shade, a box was nailed to a tree for the milkman to place their milk, two quarts each day but Saturday when he left four.

One day, to their horror, a dead doe was lying just off the trail. The twins wouldn't even walk past her and went, skittering, back to the cabin. Billy and Jane bravely continued on their mission and picked up the milk before racing home. Marian reported the carcass to the authorities and in due time they came and removed it.

Some days they'd eat lunch on the patio and then pile in the car to drive to Samuel Taylor Park to play in the bigger creek there. Other days, Marian would pack a picnic and they'd go early to their favorite spot on Papermill Creek, to the right just after crossing the last bridge before the entrance to the park. Here, a deep water hole with a large flat rock rising in the middle, provided for water play, and a shady beach allowed Marian to spread a cloth and set out the picnic.

The twins paddled in the shallow water. Billy and Jane swam out to the rock. Marian leaned back against a tree and read while she watched the children. Suddenly, the tranquility was shattered as Jane screamed in panic.

"Help!" she yelled. "There's a monster in the water." She pulled her legs up under her chin in case it leapt out and grabbed her toes. "It's big and ugly and scaly!"

Billy peered into the clear water. "It's only a lobster 'bout a foot long. Oh, look, there're two, no, three!" Jane shuddered and pulled herself into a closer ball.

"It's a crayfish – a crawdad," Marian said. "Water makes it look bigger than it is. Probably only four or five inches long." That didn't reassure Jane who knew, lacking the ability to dive, that she would have to put her feet down into the water, right into their claws, to get off the rock and paddle safely to the shore.

Billy immediately belly flopped into the water and headed for the beach leaving Jane in a ball of agony on the rock. When the water settled, she gazed again into its depths and saw two of the three crayfish, lying in wait for her feet, she was sure.

"Come on, Jane. Slide off the rock and swim," Marian said.

"I can't," cried Jane. "Of course you can. And you will. Unless you want to spend the rest of your life sitting on that rock!" *Come on, daughter. You may as well learn right now that there's no way OUT but THROUGH. Take a chance. Shove off!*

Jane looked pleadingly at her mother who smiled back with warm encouragement.

"They're more afraid of you than you are of them, believe me. Come," she said gently.

Finally, Jane shivered, took a deep breathe, crouched with her toes just touching the water and let her body fall forward until she could give a little shove with her feet and be waterborne. She swam the few yards to the beach as though a host of huge crayfish where snapping at her heels. She emerged victorious with a little grin on her face.

"Good girl!" said Marian, throwing her a towel. The rest of the afternoon was uneventful. Jane stayed in the shallow water or on the beach beside her mother.

Marian allowed the children almost total freedom that summer within the parameters she'd set forth at the beginning. They were to stay together or at least in pairs, no solitary excursions. And they were to come back promptly at mealtime. This was easy to do since a penetrating whistle from the firehouse echoed across the entire valley at noon and again at 5 PM, an unmistakable signal to for the little Rattrays to head home.

Those hot summer days, filled with simple adventures, childish games and sibling companionship even had an unforgettable special smell; sun on rocks, sage, bay from the creek, dust, heat – an indescribable mix, changing with the temperature, the time of day, shifting makeup with the location, turning damp and heavy along the little stream, shimmering on the hillside amid the rocks and shrubs where lizards scrambled, wet and salt-tinged in the early mornings.

Most of the time, the children hiked and poked about. There was a huge smooth rock just below the road not far from the cabin that they loved to climb. They could only get on from the road side where they had located footholds but the fun was sliding off the downside, too steep and smooth to clamber up, but an exciting exit!

One day, as they all ran down the rough road toward their rock, Suzanne tripped and pitched forward to crash face down. Jane raced back to pick her up, horrified at the blood pouring off her chin. Holding Sue in her arms, she ran toward the cabin, calling to her mother.

Marian met her and carried the sobbing child to the kitchen. She could see that Suzanne's teeth had cut completely through below her lower lip.

"This'll have to be stitched. I'll take her to the doctor's." Marian pressed a wet compress to Sue's mouth, tied it in place with a dish towel and made her way toward the car.

"Get my purse for me, Janie. And take care of Billy and Marianne. I'll be back as soon as I can. Don't worry she'll be all right."

As Marian drove off, Suzanne on the seat beside her, Jane went to herd the other two children back to the cabin. They'd missed the whole excitement and were full of questions which Jane answered as they made their way home.

Suddenly the world was a dangerous place to Jane and she wanted the little ones safely inside. Marian returned in a couple of hours, Suzanne proudly wearing a bandage over the seven stitches it took to close the hole. For several days she was the object of all their attention much to her delight.

Saturday evenings Marian brought a galvanized wash tub into the living room, heated a kettle of boiling water and carried it up from the kitchen, dragged the hose in, mixed the water in the tub until it was just warm and then started bathing the children. Twins first, while another kettle was heating. Then Billy, then Jane. A final kettle of hot water and Bill climbed into the tub, sitting down with his knees pulled up to his chin. He soaped thoroughly, Marian poured rinse water over him. Then she held out a towel so he could stand up and get out.

Only he couldn't! He was wedged in, the corrugation on the sides of the tub working against him. Marian grabbed his hands and pulled. No action. She soaped his back. Nothing! She began to laugh. Bill began to fume.

"Okay, kids. We're going to tip the tub over. The water will run through the cracks between the planks. Then we can pull the tub off Daddy. I hope! All of you, come help."

Billy and Jane each grabbed a handle, the twins put their little hands on the edge to push.

"One, two, three, pull." Marian gave a huge shove to the back. "Again. Harder!" Another couple of tries and the tub was upended, water pouring out and spreading across the floor before seeping through the cracks between the boards and escaping to the dirt below.

Bill was still wedged in but with the children pulling back on the tub and Marian tugging on his arms, he finally popped out! Taking a cue from their mother's laughter, the children all thought it was funny. Bill, however, was not amused. He quickly wrapped his dignity in a towel and retreated to a dry corner to put on his clothes. By the time he was dry and dressed he, too, could see the humor and laughed as he grabbed a broom to sweep the remaining puddles down the cracks.

Summer ended. Labor Day came. Marian planned and executed a final picnic at the creek. Jane wouldn't swim out to the rock even when Billy reported no visible crawdads. Bill enjoyed the outing. He'd been writing letters, making appointments and taking the train over to San Anselmo and San Francisco to seek employment, so a day of relaxation was welcome. He didn't like asking for work although he enjoyed talking to people. Often, he spent an hour or so chatting with someone without ever mentioning that he was looking for a job!

But he did find a small opening, more like a crack. He was to start playing the organ at St. John's Episcopal Church in Ross the middle of September. His monthly stipend of $40 wouldn't go far but it was a beginning. He continued his search in San Francisco but the church was the only firm offer. For this commitment, and because the cabin was no place to spend a winter, it was imperative that they find a house to rent on the other side of White's Hill.

Marian was determined to get her family back to Ross. In fact, she was formulating plans to reclaim their little house There was an agency she'd heard of to help people who wanted to regain homes repossessed during these years of depression. She was definitely going to push Bill into taking some action. But that would need more time than they had before the winter weather made living in the cabin, even with a repaired roof, impractical. The first thing to do was find a place they could move into right away.

All of this was churning about in Marian's head when the two older children started back to school. Billy's was easy, same school, same classmates, same bus, same routine. Jane, however, faced a traumatic new experience. First, long ride over the hill on a big school bus to the east end of San Rafael to attend a new high school. This would be a strange place for her, filled with strange teachers, strange classmates, strange routine. Her stomach was tied in knots for days beforehand and she was almost physically ill by the time she boarded the bus the first morning. It was difficult enough to make the switch to high school in the company of supportive friends. Jane didn't know a single soul. She was painfully shy, too. It would be months before she felt comfortable in this new environment.

Marian agonized over her oldest daughter. She, who had attended one grammar school and one high school, from first grade through twelfth, with the same classmates, had seen Jane uprooted from Ross to Alameda, from there to Oakland for a desperate day, then Piedmont, and now this move to the biggest school yet. And at a time when so many changes were taking place in her body and her emotions that she didn't understand herself at all. Marian's heart went out to her although she could only vaguely imagine what Jane was suffering never having been afraid of any new situation in her life.

Jane in San Rafael High School uniform,
Fall 1932.

The matter of the school uniform made it even more difficult. Jane had to wear a middy blouse, a tie knotted just so, a pleated navy blue skirt at a prescribed two inches below the knee, long stockings and oxfords. Nothing that Marian purchased fit her tall slim daughter except the triangular black tie! Rayon stockings were the only ones Marian could afford and they hung in folds around Jane's knees after she'd worn them for a few minutes! The garter belt to hold up the stockings almost slipped off her hips. Marian tried to take the blouses in along the side seams so they would fit better, and added an extra pleat or two to the skirt to make it hug Jane's waist, but there was nothing she could do to make the stockings, cheap as they had to be, cling to those long thin legs! None of this made Jane feel any better about herself.

"Stand up straight. You'll be fine," Marian said as she pulled and jerked and smoothed the clothes into place. But Jane couldn't stand up straight. She felt too tall and too skinny.

The one thing that saved her spirit was the delight she discovered in the journalism class. Her teacher realized that Jane could write anything as long as she didn't need to go strange places or ask direct questions. Mrs. Thompson assigned her all sorts of stories that she could write from quiet research or expand with her imagination. As her work began appearing in the school paper, even carrying bylines, Jane developed a confidence in herself that she'd never before had. This spilled over into the rest of her school life and she began, slowly, to make friends.

After school activities were out since she had to ride the bus to Woodacre but even here she had a friend, Helen Grimm, a tall (taller than Jane!) brunette with a quiet sense of humor and the added bonus of two brothers. Artie was younger, still in the school Billy attended. The other, Don, was a sophomore. To Jane's eyes, he was perfect. Tall, quiet and shy with the same type of humor as his sister. And handsome! He had brown hair, brown eyes, a hesitant smile that lit his face with warmth and a tolerance for Helen's friends that allowed Jane into the magical circle. He was her first big crush and certainly the very first one she'd ever been able to speak to.

When they got off the bus after school, she often walked with them to their big home at the base of the mountain. Although she and Helen usually took a snack into her room, it was enough for Jane to be able to say a word or two to Don on the walk, and to mumble good-bye when she departed.

One afternoon, Billy brought a note home from school from the teacher requesting that Marian come in for a conference the next day. She arrived with the twins who stayed on the playground.

The teacher greeted Marian at the door. "Come in. Have a seat." She smiled graciously. "Billy is doing fine. Really, he's a smart young man. But I was wondering. You signed up for him to have daily milk and he's never brought any money to me. Did you change your mind?"

"Not at all. In fact, I've sent a quarter with him every time he's brought a note home for it." Marian looked puzzled. "I'll check into it and let you know." They chatted for a few moments more. Then Marian left to collect the children. Billy had skipped the bus knowing that his mother was coming to the school to provide a ride home.

"Billy," Marian said as she started the car. "What's going on with your milk money?"

"What?"

"The quarter I give you to pay for milk. Have you been getting milk?"

"No."

"How come?"

"Teacher says I haven't paid for it."

"But the quarters. What have you done with all the quarters?" Billy hung his head and didn't answer. Marian realized this was a situation that called for eye-contact and pulled the car over to the side of the road where she stopped, turning off the engine.

"Look at me, son. Where are the quarters?"

He looked up briefly. "In my drawer. At home."

"Why?"

"Because I like them," Billy whispered. "I like money."

"But that's not your money. We gave it to you for milk because we want you to have milk every day at school. You'll have to give back all those quarters. And then you'll have to take money to school for milk for the rest of the year, all at once, in advance. I'll figure it out. Do you understand?"

"Yes," he whispered again. "Okay." Marian started the car and they drove the rest of the way home.

"If you want money, your own money, to save in your drawer," she said as they arrived, "we'll have to figure out jobs you can do to earn it. But you can't just take it. That's stealing. And I know you don't want to steal. What extra work can you think of that you'd like to do to get some money?"

"I don't know," Billy mumbled. Then he looked up with a grin. "Maybe I could give Tippy a bath and brush his coat every night so he's not all full of burrs. Would that be a good job?"

"That sounds great. You've helped us bathe Tippy so you know how. And you're big enough to manage him. Yes, that would be good. And a nightly brushing would be wonderful."

"Can I start right away?"

"Sure. Just bring me all the quarters first. And I'll write a note and send money in an envelope to your teacher explaining everything."

"You mean you'll tell her I stole the quarters?"

"Yes," said Marian. "You did, and she has a right to know. But she won't do anything to you. We'll take care of any punishment after I've talked to your father." Billy looked so crestfallen Marian was sorry she'd mentioned talking to Bill. But she didn't feel it was right not to consult him on such matters, even if he always went along with her decisions in the end. It had to be a mutual agreement. Or at least look like one!

But Billy! What to do with a little boy who liked money so much he wanted to hide it in his bureau drawer along with his socks and underpants? She guessed the important thing was to teach him he had to earn it and could never ever just take it, to help him see the mistake he'd made in diverting his milk money to his own secret cache. And to allow him a chance to honestly earn a bit of money that would be truly his own.

Billy never stole again. But he continued to like money. When he started a savings account years later, that money was always inviolate; he never counted it as spendable! And during World War II, he actually hoarded a drawer full of zinc pennies just because he liked the sight of so many coins piling up and rattling about.

Marian spent many days when the older two were in school visiting friends on the other side of the hill. She renewed her connection with the Coterie and monthly attended their luncheon meetings. Here she had a perfect forum to talk about her need for a place to rent. Ruth Hansen, Ethel Landon, Mabel Crisp, Ada Fusselman, Clara Worsley, Ruby Krell, Geneva Coddington and the others were all women with their fingers firmly on the pulse of the community. Between them, a wide cross-section was covered.

At the October luncheon, Ruth Hansen said, "Marian, I have a line on a house on Shady Lane in Ross. It's been empty for awhile and the owner's anxious to get it rented. Could be cheap. Here's his name and telephone number." She handed Marian a slip of paper.

"Thanks, Ruth. This is great. Clara, can I use your phone?" Granted permission, Marian went into the hall to make the call. When she returned, her face was beaming. "Sounds good! He'll meet me at there at three this afternoon. How's that for progress?"

The house was opposite St. Anselm's Catholic Church, the fourth place from Bolinas Avenue. It was two story, brown shingle, with a wide porch across the front and down the south side. Square white posts went from the bannister to the roof. The stairs were placed diagonally on the southwest corner. The top story had a steep roof with a single window in the center of the front wall and a dormer window on the south side. It was an old house,

The rented house on Shady Lane, Ross, November 1932.

the windows were tall and narrow, the wooden front door was halfway down the porch on the south side.

Marian stood looking at it, waiting for the landlord, Mr. Krause, to arrive. The twins ran down the level driveway to the flat backyard.

"Mommy, come here!" Marianne called. "Come see this."

Marian walked to the back, noticing that the porch was glassed in across the end and part way up the side, almost to the front door. *That'll make a nice protected sitting place,* she thought. *Great spot for the wind chimes.* Jutting out from the back of the house was a screened porch. Above that, she could see a window similar to the one on the front. In the yard was a whirligig clothes drier and in the corner, a ramshackle garage. There was no planting, no semblance of a garden, just a few weeds, a shrub or two and a lot of dead grass. The ground looked wet although it hadn't rained recently. *Not a good sign,* Marian said to herself. *Water probably stands here when there's a storm. No drainage at all. I wonder where the closest creek is? Hopefully not right through here!*

A car turned into the drive behind Marian's.

"Come, girls. Let's go out front." They came running and all three met Mr. Krause as he climbed out of his automobile.

"Hello. You want to see the house? Is a good house for a family. You have a family, yah?" He smiled expansively at Marian and the twins.

"Yes, we have four children."

"Good, good. Come. We look."

They followed him up the flight of stairs and down the side porch to the door which he unlocked, stepping aside so Marian and the little girls could enter first .

A musty long-closed smell met them, not unpleasant to Marian. It reminded her of the attic at Ben Brae when they first opened the house after a long winter away, and nostalgia swept over her. She looked around. Not prepossessing, so far. A small entry, with doors on either side, gave way straight ahead to a narrow hall.

Mr. Krause reached around Marian to open both doors. The room on the left had two windows, both opening on the wrap-around porch, one in the front wall, one on the side wall. The room on the right was bigger, with dark paneled wainscotting below a plate rail, above which was dark maroon wall covering. This gave a heavy air to the room, only slightly relieved by the two windows, one to the porch, the other to the back.

They stepped into this room. There was a door into the kitchen and near it, a jutting protrusion that turned out to be a pantry entered from the kitchen. *That'll have to go*, Marian thought. *Takes too much off this room.* The kitchen had a pair of tall windows on the north wall and another two flanking the door to a large screened back porch, as big again as the kitchen. Linoleum with a geometric pattern covered the floor and a big gas cooking stove stood on spindly legs against one wall, with the sink and drain board under the windows. There were built-in cupboards on the wall between the living room door and the pantry. Marian opened the door and peered into the latter. *Yes, we can remove most of this. We could never fill it with what we have!* It didn't surprise her that she was already making plans in her head. If the rent was affordable, she was willing to move in tomorrow without even looking upstairs. It was in Ross, it would definitely be a roof over their heads. Hopefully, the roof didn't leak, and the gas stove standing in the living room would keep them adequately warm in that room, at least.

Marian opened the door to the screened porch. The floor seemed to slant slightly but she didn't think that mattered. It was a large room, cool on this autumn afternoon, and there were cupboards and shelves on the solid wall, and close to the kitchen door, washtubs.

Next, they trooped back through the kitchen and out the hall door to peer into the small bathroom. *Not fancy but everything necessary is here,* Marian thought. *Nice bathtub. Bill will be happy. That corrugated iron washtub didn't please him!*

Another waft of nostalgic air hit Marian as the door to the second story was opened by Mr. Krause. The twins led the way up the narrow twisting stairway. Pushing open another door, they found themselves in a wide hallway. Off this opened three rooms, all with slanted ceilings that sloped to walls barely five and a half feet high. Each room had a tall narrow window, and a closet door into the unfinished portion of the attic where framework had been put up to hold a clothing rod and a high shelf.

Marian could imagine the four children up here. But the narrow wooden stairway with its sharp turn didn't please her. It would be a disaster in case of fire. *We'll have a drill right away and I'll teach them to climb out on the roof, should the need arise,* Marian thought.

"So how much do you want for rent?" Marian asked when they were again downstairs. "We'd be willing to do painting and repairs for something off. I think you said that would be agreeable."

"I have to talk to your husband, Mrs. Rattray," Mr. Krause replied.

"Well, tell me what you have in mind so I can tell him."

"No, I deal with your husband."

"That's ridiculous. You can deal with both of us, starting with me because I'm standing here and I want to take a report to him tonight."

Mr. Krause looked uncomfortable. Marian wasn't behaving as he thought a woman should, acting as though she could make decisions and understand contracts! He didn't know how to take a female who looked him right in the eye and wanted to talk about money. Then she smiled at him and said, "How much?" Very matter-of-fact and business-like.

After a moment of indecision, he smiled back and answered, "Tell your husband fifty dollars. And if he wants to do some work each month, only twenty-five. Will that be all right with him, do you think?"

"It's all right with me! Of course it'll be all right with him." Marian grinned. It was what she hoped for, prayed for! Back to Ross, where their home was, where her heart was, where her children belonged.

Thank God for the cache! Marian put all her plans into effect and almost before they knew it, they were moved into the house on Shady Lane. Their furniture was delivered from storage. They were all excited to see the things they'd almost forgotten. Bill's beloved Steinway was given a place of honor in the living room and he often sat and played the music he was most familiar with to everyone's enjoyment This was the husband and father they loved, the gentle happy man who made jokes and showed up on time for dinner. But how long would he stay that way?

Billy was the one most out of joint about the move. He had to transfer back to Ross School. He'd been in second grade when he was uprooted to go to Piedmont, now he was returning as a fifth grader and he knew it would be harder than the country school where he'd been ahead of the rest of the class. However, he remembered many of his classmates so it wasn't as bad as he'd feared. And he could walk to school; that was an improvement.

Jane stayed at San Rafael High School although Ross was in a different district than Woodacre. In time she'd probably transfer but not right away. For now, she'd ride an electric train from Bolinas Avenue to San Anselmo, then on to San Rafael where she'd have several blocks to walk to the school. She found the trip enjoyable, better than the crowded noisy school bus that had grumbled over the mountain each day. She's miss her friendship with Helen and her brothers. Even though they were still in the same school, since Jane was no longer a bus rider, they now moved in different worlds. Getting together would be difficult, almost impossible, in spite of good intentions.

It was a shorter walk from the house to Bolinas station than it had been from the cabin to the bus stop, and much easier. And once on board, the ride was quicker, smoother and quieter. Almost immediately after Jane chose a seat, the train pulled into San Anselmo. Here the conductor opened the car door, stuck his head in and called out in a singsong voice, "Change cars for Yolanda, Lansdale, Pastori, Fairfax and Manor. This car goes to San Rafael." It was a chant that she'd hear in her head long after the efficient electric trains were replaced by belching diesel busses. Soon she began recognizing the regular passengers, and smiling at them, but no other high school students rode the train. That didn't bother Jane a bit. She enjoyed the time alone to think about what was going on at school, what was going on in her head, what was going on at home. Sometimes she read assignments, or scanned papers she'd written. It was a pleasant productive time. The short walk from the depot was fine, too, unless it was pouring rain.

In the afternoons, Jane often walked past the depot to the heart of San Rafael, about three blocks, to wander through J.C. Penneys or Woolworths, looking at things she'd like to buy but didn't have money for. Once in awhile she bought a needed pair of rayon stockings with the fifty cents Marian had given her.

The twins made the move from Woodacre to Ross with very little dislocation. The flat unimproved backyard was a great place to dig, pull their wagon and build things. They amused themselves and Marian kept a casual eye on them while working around the house and garden.

Bill was involved with the church, playing the organ at two Sunday services, being at choir practice midweek, and picking up some extra money performing at weddings. He enjoyed the challenge of the organ and St. John's had a fine instrument. He was still hoping for a job somewhere. How long they could live on forty dollars a month he didn't know.

Marian was the one to whom the move meant the most. For one thing, it was a step toward the realization of her dream. For another, she was back where her friends were. The Coterie, as a group, and its members, individually, enlivened her days, leading her to discover new and exciting pursuits that would change and enrich her life for years.

Thanksgiving came. For the first time they wouldn't be going to the East Bay to be with the Rattray clan. That was more than their limited resources would stretch to accommodate. Marian managed a small turkey, potatoes, and carrots. She baked an apple pie the day before with apples off Ruth Hansen's tree. When the turkey was nearly ready, Billy and Jane set the table in the living room with all their best tableware and a bowl holding autumn leaves as a centerpiece. Bill mashed the potatoes while Marian made gravy. They sat down as a family. Marian lit the candles and said a Thanksgiving grace. It was a festive meal and they all enjoyed its simplicity.

It began to rain the following week. By Jane's fourteenth birthday, mid-December, Marian found that her hunch about the lack of drainage in the yard was true. The whole front area was under water. Luckily, the driveway was a bit higher than the rest of the front yard. It was possible to get from the lowest stair to it without stepping in their unwanted pond. Spots in the backyard were boggy, too. The creek was almost a block away, but for some reason there was no way for the water that collected in their yard to run off.

The tall elm trees that lined Shady Lane, so bright with yellow leaves when they moved from Woodacre a month before, now stood stark and bare. The days were gray and damp, the nights cold. Only the front room and the kitchen had any warmth. Climbing from a cozy bed in the morning was torture. But it was still paradise compared to what conditions would have been in the cabin with all its cracks, open rooms and exposed stairs, not to mention the outhouse!

Marian was bothered about their financial situation as Christmas approached.

"How are we going to get anything for the children?" Marian asked. "Even fill their stockings?"

"Maybe we aren't," Bill answered. "Maybe we can't."

"The stockings, at least, we have to do. An orange, an apple, I'll find things that'll work. And I'm making some clothes they don't know about. I have yarn and time to knit a cap for Billy." Marian tried to sound positive. "But it won't be much. We'll be lucky if I can pull together a dinner of any sort! Too bad we can't get over to McRitchie's. Then at least it'd seem like Christmas. Maybe we should try to do that. What do you think?"

"Whatever you want," he said. "If you can swing it, fine."

Marian concentrated on finishing dresses for the girls, knitting the cap for Billy, and accumulating enough to fill the stockings. She also set aside, by really skimping, enough money to make the trip to Alameda. The sun came out, the yard was less soggy, life seemed brighter.

Christmas Eve morning there was a knock on the door. Marianne ran to answer it with her mother and siblings following. Standing on the porch were two well-dressed ladies. One of them was holding a huge wicker basket, gaily tied with ribbons and bows, out of which poked packages, one obviously a loaf of French bread.

"From the Ladies' Auxiliary at St. John's. We thought you could use it," said the taller lady with a smile. "Here." She held it out to Marian. "A turkey. Fixings. Little gifts for the children."

"Oh, no," said Marian. "There's some mistake. We're fine."

"Please, for the children. Take it." She pushed it toward Marian who reluctantly took hold of the handle. "There. Enjoy. Merry Christmas!"

Both ladies smiled and backed away.

"Thank you," Marian forced herself to say. "Thank you."

With the children clustering about her, Marian made her way into the living room. "Damn," she said, tears glinting in her eyes. "We're not a charity case. We don't need their basket. We don't, we don't."

The children were bewildered by their mother's angry outburst and intrigued by the bulging basket.

"Can we open it?" asked Jane.

"No. No, don't touch it! I have to decide what to do." Marian knew it was unreasonable to be so furious about a gesture of goodwill, to be so unaccepting of the bounty of these Christian ladies. But she wanted to destroy the basket, hurl it away. Or give it to someone who needed it, someone who was poor. In spite of their lack of money, Marian had not felt poor, certainly not a charity case, even on the moment she looked out the door and realized they were on a list of needy families. That was a shock, totally demoralizing. Her pride was threatened.

"Go play on the porch," she said to the children. "I'll call you for lunch in a bit." She smiled at their worried faces. "Everything's okay. Shoo!"

Bill couldn't understand her being upset. He thought it was nice of the church to reach out to them with food and something to make the children's Christmas a little better.

"I think it's great. You said yourself we don't have enough for them."

"But I didn't want to be visited by two do-gooders from the church! We're not destitute, for God's sake! It makes me sick." She had, however, unpacked the basket. The turkey was in the refrigerator. The gifts hidden until morning and the rest of the things were put away. "I hate it! The whole thing! We're not poor."

As they all dressed up, in the fanciest warmest clothes they had, to attend the midnight candlelight service at St. John's, Marian was still fighting her anger. *How dare they? How dare they give* me *charity?* She held her head even higher as she walked into the church with the four children, looking like a proud Ross matron, not like one of St. John's "cases," meeting every glance with a serene and level gaze. The twins, bright-eyed after a long nap, followed their mother into the pew, sliding over to make room for Billy and Jane. Bill, on the organ bench, saw them enter and almost immediately eased into Jane's favorite Christmas hymn, *O Holy Night.* Jane smiled her thanks in his direction, warmed by his recognition and the melody of the lovely old song.

It was a short beautiful service. At the end, all lights were extinguished except the candle flame on the altar. From it, tapers were lighted and passed, pew by pew, to the individual candles each person held. Then, as the organ swelled into the triumphant notes of *Hark the Herald Angel Sings* they filed out into the frosty night. Standing there, candlelight sparkling in their eyes, calling "Merry Christmas" to friends, they experienced a magical moment. Truly the message of Christmas was in every heart. Marian felt the last vestige of her anger slip away. But memory of the incident lasted, changing forever the way she was able to categorize people as "rich" or "poor," and making her more sensitive to the feelings of the "poor" when they were on the receiving end of largess. They would not necessarily be pleased or grateful!

Bill joined them at the automobile and they drove the few blocks home. It took only minutes for the children to hang their stockings from the plate rail flanking the heater in the living room. Then they were off to bed, with the proverbial visions of whatever dancing in their heads.

It wasn't a lavish Christmas but the children enjoyed themselves and spending the afternoon at McRitchie's with all their cousins was fun. Jane thought Greig McRitchie and Ronnie Panton were wonderful and sat close enough to hear their every word, mostly about music. She could only listen and smile, but she did a lot of that and it made her Christmas a happy one.

The younger children romped with their cousins and tried to show surprise when Uncle Ernest played Santa clumsily with his Scottish burr intact, a dead giveaway for even the youngest child.

The new year, 1933, came and with it stronger hopes and dreams for Marian. *We need a way to have more cash. I'm tired of skimping and I want to get high above that Christmas-basket list at the church,* she told herself. Although her anger had gone, she was still aware of the impact of the incident and the nakedness of spirit it caused in her. She refused to ever let it happen again. Always retrospective on birthdays, Marian felt a vague uneasiness on this, her thirty-ninth. Perhaps because the next one would be her fortieth. It made her wonder if she had come anywhere near the mark she'd set for herself back in her college days when her dreams were nebulous and nascent but certainly filled with joy and prosperity.

Marian was sitting in the living room on this mid-January evening, darning socks from her mending basket. Jane was at the kitchen table working on a school project. Marian could see her bent head through the open doorway and smiled at the deep concentration. Billy and the twins were already upstairs in their beds and Bill was out. He'd been home earlier for her birthday dinner but was now at choir practice at the church.

Looking back, Marian realized that in the beginning, it had all been a rosy indefinite vision, almost a fairy tale (which wasn't like her in the least), with none of the nittering details of daily living to dim the luster: She and Bill would marry, have children, buy a house, be happy ever after, sharing, dancing, having lovely discussions, laughing together. No problems.

Her romantic dreams had been replaced by a prosaic existence, rocked by Bill's periodic "slips." After each of these, she re-evaluated their situation and always decided, imperfect though it was, there were enough positive attributes to keep it going. Besides, what was her alternative? She knew she had yearnings that would never be met, great areas of herself that she'd never share but that, she guessed, was the way things were for most people.

One thing she knew, they needed more income. It was up to her to figure how to get it.

Jane spent a great deal of the winter and into early spring being sick. The doctor knew it was some sort of recurring infection but couldn't pinpoint the cause or the source.

"I just don't know," he said to Marian after one of Jane's bouts with fever, congestion, sore throat, aches. "Something is definitely making her repeatedly sick. I'd think it was bad tonsils, except you said hers were removed years ago. She's awfully thin, too. We'll have to do something."

"Yes, Dr. Hensler. Besides, she hates to miss school. But better weather is coming. Maybe she won't be sick again."

"We can hope."

"And pray," Marian added.

Weeks went by and it seemed Jane might be all right. Marian put her mind to their financial situation. She heard, again through Ruth Hansen at a Coterie meeting, that Ross Grammar School was hoping to start a hot lunch program. This seemed to Marian a heaven-sent opportunity, right up her alley. She made an appointment to see Leitha Jenkins, the principal and outlined her credentials, her experience and her plans. Mrs. Jenkins was impressed and arranged to have Marian put a pilot program into effect right after Easter vacation. If it was successful, Marian would be placed in charge of the cafeteria, serving simple hot lunches daily during the next school year. With Easter looming on the horizon, Marian started right in – planning menus, developing shopping guides, figuring costs. It was work she enjoyed.

In the weeks before Easter, Bill, Marian and Jane were all involved in pre-confirmation classes at St. John's. With Bill being the organist and the family attending services, Marian felt it important to belong to the church It was an emotional moment when they took part in the confirmation ceremony that season.

Jane, especially, found comfort and faith in the words and prayers, and soon became active in the Youth Group. Marian, raised in the Unitarian Church, was slower to embrace the theology although she had a firm and abiding faith in God. Bill, true to his nature, didn't discuss how he felt about joining the Episcopal church. His family had been Presbyterians but religion hadn't played a large role in their life and Bill had seldom been to church as a child.

They were, however, a united family when attending that Easter service and the message was more meaningful than ever before. Jane concocted an Easter bonnet from a pale yellow straw hat that Marian had. She bent and folded the wide brim and tucked pastel silk flowers in appropriate places, with pink tulle to tie it together. The result was remarkable and Jane wore it proudly, worrying only that the unwelcome rain would ruin it.

No damage was done and the rain stopped before the McRitchies with Alec and Bertha arrived after church.

"The Lord is risen!" Ernest boomed as he climbed out of the car.

"He is risen indeed!" everyone replied as expected of them. The Easter gathering was in session.

After church on Easter, Greig, and Bella McRitchie, Jane, Ernest McRitchie behind Marian, Bertha Rattray, Steel McRitchie, Marianne and Suzanne, Billy and Bill, 1933

The next day, Marian went into action early. When the cafeteria opened at noon, the entire student body and staff lined up to be served. She was ready and the program was off to a propitious start.

The twins, not quite five, accompanied Marian to work each morning, played quietly and then ate with the children. Billy was slightly embarrassed to have his mother on the premises. He solved that by ignoring her for the first few weeks. Once the shock to his 10-year old system wore off, he could be nonchalant, even a bit proud about her presence, especially since his friends thought she was okay.

An added bonus during the whole spring was that Marian could bring home each day whatever was left over, which, in spite of weekly signups and careful planning, was adequate for their dinners. This made an enormous difference in the available cash, Marian found.

Since moving from Woodacre nearly six months before they had needed to match the rental amount with an equal expenditure of time and material in improving the house. It was difficult to come up with enough money to get the necessary paint, wallpaper and other supplies. The salary from the school, plus the extra food which cut down on buying dinners, made all the difference.

Bill, too, was expanding his earning base. He had several piano pupils and often was hired to play at weddings, not just at St. John's. At this time, he followed the example of his older brothers and joined the Masons, taking his degrees at the lodge in San Rafael, where, in short order, he became their official pianist/organist. This gave him wider exposure and in turn led to additional jobs that actually paid. He knew he wasn't earning enough to satisfy Marian's dreams but he was trying.

Jane continued to have bouts of recurring illness and missed an alarming amount of school. Dr. Hensler was baffled and wanted extensive tests and observations done which meant hospitalization. This presented a whole new set of financial problems for Marian to cope with.

Talking with Amy Yerington, a longtime member of St. John's and a soprano in the choir, who had been their neighbor on Glenwood Avenue, Marian received a great piece of information.

"You know, the church has several endowed beds at St. Luke's Hospital in San Francisco. They're for situations like this. You should look into it."

"How do I start?" asked Marian who felt this was quite different from Christmas basket charity. "Who do I call?"

Armed with the proper names and requirements, Marian gathered all the necessary papers and the doctor's reports and presented them to the church committee for consideration. Jane's case was approved. She would be admitted as soon as school closed for the summer.

Before June, Marianne developed an infected gland at the angle of her jaw. Dr. Hensler told Marian that it needed to be surgically removed. The church committee was agreeable to adding Marianne to the agenda so in early June Marian drove her oldest and youngest daughters to St. Luke's Hospital. It was a quiet trip; both girls were apprehensive and their mother's admonitions and instructions fell on deaf ears.

Marianne took one look at the crib in Jane's room and balked. Insulted by being treated like a baby, she loudly resisted all attempts to put her to bed. No one had explained what was happening, and going to bed in a strange crib in the late afternoon was not to her liking!.

"What time will they come for her in the morning?" Marian asked. "What time should I be back?"

"Actually, Mrs. Rattray, there's no reason for you to try to get here before we take the baby to surgery. She'll be sleepy and it's so early. Just be sure you're here when she comes back up to the room. About ten o'clock, I'd say," replied the nurse with a bright smile.

So Marian saw that both girls were settled in and then kissed them good night. Jane was subdued but all right. Marianne, in spite of being with her big sister, was upset with her strange surroundings and fumed for a long while before finally falling to sleep.

In the early morning, when the orderlies came to prepare her for the trip to the operating room, Marianne displayed every facet of her volatile temperament, kicking, screaming, fighting, lunging, alternately flaying her arms and legs and clinging to the bars of the crib. Her voice reached a crescendo of terror. It took several strong orderlies to pry her loose and strap her to a gurney. Jane was in tears before her shrieking little sister was wheeled from the room.

Marianne's ordeal was over on schedule. Even straight from the operating room, still under anesthesia, her cheeks were rosy, her hair a golden halo, and her eyes, when she finally opened them, blazing blue. Only the white dressing on her jaw near her left ear gave testament to what had happened. Marian returned just before they wheeled the little girl back into the room and was standing beside the crib when Marianne regained consciousness.

"Mommy," she said, "I want to go home. Now!"

"It won't be long. Right after lunch. Okay?" Marianne sat up in bed and held out her arms. She wanted out of the detested crib. Marian lifted her and went to sit in a chair. They spent the time, with the hospital routine surging around them, talking about what they'd do when Jane was able to come home. After a bit of lunch and a final checkup, the intern declared Marianne fit for travel .

Left alone, Jane settled down to the quiet routine of hospital life. Tests were run every day, searching for the source of the infection, the cause of her recurrent problems. Week after week, the tests were negative. Scratch tests on her arms of every substance known to man were run. Nothing. House dust, cat dander, dog hair, mold, mildew, on and on. Still nothing. Marian tried to visit at least once a week, and Aunt Bertha, Alec's wife, who lived in San Francisco took the streetcar to the hospital as often as she could. Aside from those infrequent visitors, and the constant testing, Jane found nothing to do but read books from the extensive library and sleep.

One day when the sun was shining, Jane was taken, in her bed, up to the roof garden. It was beautiful, a rare July day when the summer fog had not rolled in. There were large trees in huge tubs around the perimeter of the decked area. In these tubs lay a clue to Jane's problem. A soft wind was blowing gently. Jane breathed deeply of the air, savoring its freshness. Within minutes she began to choke, wheeze and feel feverish.

"Nurse," she called. "I'm getting sick." The nurse took one look and whisked her back to the room.

One of the interns, hearing of the incident, went up to the roof and searched for a reason for Jane's reaction to the great outdoors. He found it in the tubs. Not the flowers, but wild blooming grass that hadn't been pulled, heads of ripe seeds nodding in the breeze.

The following week, new serums were procured from the east coast of all the grasses that grow in California, some of them specific to Marin County. Jane's arms were "scratched" in double rows to test her reaction to 32 grasses. After so many weeks of negative tests, this was definitely on the verge of over-kill.

Within minutes both her arms turned red around the scratches, then began to swell and itch. Soon her entire body was in the throes of a gigantic attack. Wheezing, sneezing, almost unable to breathe through her swollen nose and constricted throat, Jane was in serious danger.

The entire staff assigned to her case, rallied around She was given injections to counteract the effect of the serums, and adrenaline. Gradually, the spasms decreased, her breathing became less labored. The crisis was over.

Nevertheless, it was a breakthrough. At least part of her problem had been located. But the cause of the recurring fevers was still elusive. In the fifth week of her hospitalization, the results of tests on samples from her sinuses and throat showed two areas of infection: the roots of her tonsils not completely removed in the operation when she was five, and the sinuses in her cheekbones. The doctors contacted Marian with their findings and the treatment they suggested.

"We feel we should go in and remove the rudiments of the tonsils. And also open and scrape the sinuses to clean them out. That should do it. It's not a bad procedure. She'll be able to go home about a week later."

"That's good news," Marian replied. "What about the allergies to grasses? What can be done for that?"

"We'll send complete reports to your doctor. He can do some immunization that will help. She should be better and once we get rid of this infection, there'll be a big improvement in her general health."

"So when will you do the operation?"

"We'll set it up as soon as possible. Tomorrow or the next day."

"Good."

Everything went off as planned and after the packings in the sinuses were removed and the throat healed, Jane was released from the hospital, seven weeks from the day she entered. She was delighted to be home. The world seemed bright and enormous. Marian was relieved, glad to have all her chicks under one roof, and no longer assailed with guilt about her infrequent visits. Maybe now Jane would gain some weight and make it through next winter without the problems that had plagued her for so long.

Jane after her summer in St. Luke's Hospital, 1933.

Suzanne and Marianne, ready for kindergarten, September 1933.

During this spring and summer other exciting things were developing. Marian would look back on mid-1933 as the beginning of coming into her own true self: Involvement in the fledging Marin Musical Chest, discovering the Ross Valley Players, formation of the Gabby Girls, volunteering for various services with the American Red Cross, putting into motion paperwork to reclaim the Glenwood Avenue home.

Maude Faye Symington, a flamboyant retired opera diva, had a dream. Its intent was to bring "the greatest music in the world to the greatest number of people at the lowest possible price."

For this she started the Marin Musical Chest in 1932, lining up friends and acquaintances to sweep it into action. She and her husband, Captain Powers Symington, maintained a summer home, High Hat, in Kentfield which became the first headquarters for the fledgling organization.

Both Bill and Marian became involved, he on the artistic council to screen performers, she as one of the "captains" of the corps of 200 workers soliciting membership. This was the heart of the plan.

Everyone in the county would be offered an opportunity to join. One dollar was requested but larger offerings could be given and would be happily accepted and smaller amounts, too, if necessary. Then, when the concerts were presented, the membership card plus 25 cents, took care of admission. Without a membership card, the price was $3.00.

It was a revolutionary concept. The money collected for the memberships would be used to secure the artists. Marin Musical Chest would always be solvent, never spend money in advance. Maude was sure that in spite of, or maybe because of, hard times, people would be eager to join and have an opportunity to hear the greatest artists in the world perform for a small fee, right here in Marin, without the long and difficult trip to San Francisco. She was right. Thousands of the "little" people Maude so believed in, became members and made her dream blossom.

Attending all the organizational meetings and being privy to the plans, Marian and Bill gradually grew into important positions becoming, among other things, concert managers. Bill was overwhelmed by the responsibility, Marian relished the chance to get her teeth into something challenging.

By the time Jane came home from the hospital and the school term started in September, the Marin Musical Chest was forging ahead and the Rattrays were deeply involved.

The cafeteria, too, was blossoming. Marian was busier than she'd ever been. Luckily, Suzanne and Marianne were now in kindergarten so her

Kindergarten picture, Ross School, 1933.

mornings were free to pursue duties for the cafeteria without having to keep an eye on them. She was beautifully organized and happy that she was making a success of her project.

Another bonus of being at the school was meeting the mothers of Billy's buddies. Two became her close friends. Both lived on Shady Lane, on opposite sides of the street a block nearer the school than the Rattrays.

First, she met Beth Lloyd, a tiny still-pretty lady, whose son, Rick, was Billy's almost-best friend. Beth and her husband, Gene, were involved with the Ross Valley Players. In fact, he was president of the decade old group. Beth was in charge of costuming for each production. As friendship grew with Beth, Marian found herself being drawn into the world of behind-the-scenes activities. And she brought Bill along to be involved with the musical side of the productions. This opened a whole new slice of life to them, exciting and rewarding, which lasted for almost a decade.

The second friend Marian made was Hazel Pitman. Her son, Davey, was Billy's other almost-best buddy, and with Rick Lloyd, they formed a terrifying trio. Hazel and Marian had a rare and deep affinity right from the start. As their friendship developed, it came close to filling the void left by Doris four years before.

Here, again, was a woman with whom Marian could share her most secret thoughts and feel perfectly safe. Hazel was short, almost stocky, with sparkling brown eyes that could flash with anger, soften with compassion or dance with amusement. She was efficient in the same manner as Marian and they worked together like salt and pepper, adding spice and pizazz to everything they tackled in tandem. Her husband, Eric, was tall, slim, with chiseled features and a small neat moustache. He worked for PG&E and had a quick mind and sharp tongue. He and Bill hit it off, much to their wives' delight. Once again, there was a couple to spend time with in the spot vacated by Doris and George. Eric and Hazel had a daughter, Betty, two years younger than Jane. It was a long time before this age difference lost its importance. When they met, Betty was in grammar school, Jane in the different world of high school. Jane went on to college. Betty entered the "real world" after high school. Suddenly, she was the one out ahead. Eventually they were on the same plane. Their friendship became special, but that was years down the road.

One late summer evening when Marian and Bill were sitting at home, she said, "Look here. An article in the paper about FDR's New Deal."

"What's our great president Franklin D. doing now?" asked Bill with a sneer in his voice.

"Says a Home Owners Loan Act has been put into effect to help people get their homes back," said Marian, ignoring his tone. "We should look into it."

"Why? It'd never work. The house is gone. You should realize that." Bill rattled the part of the paper he was reading and looked back at the page in front of him.

"But it's for people just like us. That's its purpose," Marian said. "We have to check it out."

Bill knew that tone of voice. "Go ahead if you want. It won't do any good, I can tell you that." This time he didn't even look up from the newspaper which exasperated Marian. *Why can't we ever discuss anything? Why does it just have to be flat-out impossible if I suggest we try something?*

"Well, I will. I'll look into it." Marian had the last word which didn't bother Bill a bit but made her feel better. The next day she went to the bank that had carried their mortgage and explained the situation to the president. It wasn't that he was discouraging, he just didn't know much about the new act. Nevertheless, he was more than willing to investigate the possibilities for her and took down all the information he could think of that might be relevant.

It was two weeks before he called.

"Mrs. Rattray, I have some forms. If you drop in we can fill them out and then you can get your husband's signature and we'll be able to start this business." Marian told herself he sounded encouraging and positive.

"I'll be there right away," she said and set about getting ready for the short drive to San Anselmo. So it was, in the middle of summer, 1933, Marian took the first positive step toward reclaiming their home, using, as did thousands of others, a brand new act that had just been put into effect.

"Bill," she said that night, "I want you to listen. Here are the preliminary papers, our request for consideration. You need to sign them. What they'll do is rewrite our original loan, at five percent interest, with 15 years to repay it."

"What about our delinquent taxes and stuff like that? How are we going to handle that? We can't do it."

"Everything will be consolidated with the principal. We won't have to come up with any big amount. I think, if it goes through, we can handle it. Don't you?" Marian looked at Bill, hoping he'd discuss the situation.

"I don't see how," he answered, "but I'll sign the papers." His tone of voice implied, *to shut you up and get you off my back,* Marian thought, *Why do I hear those words in my head? Maybe I'm being too sensitive.* At any rate, he wasn't about to engage in a conversation on the subject so she folded the signed papers and put them in the envelope for return to the bank. Then she put the matter out of her mind, knowing how slowly official governmental business takes place.

One afternoon, Hazel Pitman dropped in. She had never learned to drive and was walking back from San Anselmo with a small bag of groceries. She found Marian sitting in the sun on the porch, her mending basket on the floor beside her chair, carefully and efficiently darning one of Bill's socks.

"That's what I should be doing," Hazel remarked. "I never take the time to sit down and get at my darning until the kids or Eric yell that they're totally sockless."

"Bring it over here some day," Marian answered. "We'll do it together. We can talk as we darn and then have a pot of tea and cookies or something."

"Sounds like a plan," said Hazel with a smile. "Maybe we can ask some others to join us."

"That'd be great." Marian folded the finished sock with its mate and dropped the darning ball into the basket. "I like the idea. But maybe evenings would be better. Everyone's so busy nowadays. We could meet here. Bill's always out on Tuesdays, Glad's ballet classes. What do you think?"

"Beautiful," Hazel replied with enthusiasm. "Who should we ask?"

"Ruth Hansen, for sure," said Marian. "And a couple of other Coterie members I think you know. Adele Higgins, Clara Worsley?"

"Fine. I'll call Ruth. You phone the others. We can get more names from them if we want later. Next Tuesday, here, seven o'clock, okay?" Marian nodded and Hazel picked up her groceries and headed home.

It was a fine get-together and the beginning of a four-decade tradition. Additional women were invited to join the group: Daisy Hollingsworth, Hortense Styles, Mabel Seimer, Mary Donnelly, Serena Robinson. Later they started meeting at other homes, rotating alphabetically. It was the husbands to gave them their name - Gabby Girls - saying they got together to "darn and to damn." That was an unfair assessment. They were a supportive group and did very little damning! But they did do a lot of talking. Often when Marian stepped out of the room to start the water heating for tea, she heard the many voices and wondered who was listening!

They were uniquely wonderful at solving each others problems. Their different personalities and areas of expertise made them a formidable unbeatable group. Nothing was too big to be tackled or too small to be considered. If one of them needed help, a solution, or an answer, it would be provided. They cheered each other through child-rearing traumas and accomplishments, swapped horror stories of teenage behavior, supported each other through erring spouses and death, staged weddings, made baby clothes for the eventual grandchildren, exchanged patterns and recipes, laughed a lot, talked a lot and cried together when things were really tragic. Through the years they were more than friends, closer than sisters. And they got the darning and mending done each week from mid-1933 until the 1970's!

The Marin Musical Chest's first concert was scheduled for January 3, 1934, at the Fairfax Pavilion. Nelson Edy, an up-and-coming but relatively unknown young baritone, was signed to be the soloist. Bill and Marian had been working for months setting up the concert. For the first time, they had to meet the challenge of getting the programs designed and printed, the publicity, through Kitty Oppenheimer, out to newspapers, the hall itself reserved and ready, with lighting, piano, props, ushers, setup, clean-up, ticket-takers, all the multitudinous details organized and coordinated. Surprisingly, Bill enjoyed it. He and Marian mapped the entire procedure, plotted every move, plugged every hole, scanned every detail. They were working in the dark since neither had ever been in charge of a concert before but they worked well together, bolstering each other and refining their concept of how a concert should be.

Maude Symington, with the Captain, was to meet Nelson Edy at the San Francisco airport and keep him at Top Hat until concert time. The countdown was complete. Bill and Marian went early to the Pavilion and found everything in order. People, membership cards and quarters in hand, began to stream in. Excitement mounted. Nelson arrived backstage, exuding health and enthusiasm. Maude swept through, nodding and waving to everyone, and stepped on stage to made her welcoming remarks. She was loudly applauded. And then Nelson Edy came forward and the concert began.

Marian was enchanted. "Isn't he wonderful, Bill?" she asked. Then realizing how little she knew about voices rephrased her question.

"He is wonderful, isn't he, Bill."

"He certainly is," Bill answered.

Before intermission, Nelson strode off stage and came to Marian. "I hate to be a bother," he said, " but I have an awful stomach ache. Do you think you could find me a cup of peppermint tea? And a place to lie down? Intermission's coming up soon."

"Of course, no problem," she said, looking around, hoping to see a tea kettle, a hot plate, peppermint, a cup, a comfortable bed, all things that had never crossed her mind as necessary to provide! Where, how to find what she needed?

Adele Higgins, who had been pressed into service as an usher, appeared at Marian's side.

"Need me for anything, Marian?" she asked.

"Do I ever! Can you call home and have Syd bring a pot of peppermint tea over right now? With a cup. And a pillow and blanket." Adele didn't bat an eye, just went to the phone to ask her husband to fill the strange order. Since the Higgins lived only a short distance from the Pavilion, it was faster service than one would get in most restaurants.

In the meantime, Marian, not finding a bed anywhere backstage, cleared off a high narrow table and offered it to Nelson when he returned.. With an accepting smile, he took off his jacket which he placed under his head, and stretched out his long body with a thankful sigh.

Soon Sydney arrived with the blanket, pillow and steaming pot of tea. Nelson sat up and slipped the tea, then lay back down with the pillow under his head, his feet hanging off the other end. Marian tucked the blanket around him.

"There," she said. "Anything else?"

He grinned at her. "Yes, there is. I've had this before. It's the way I handle nerves. I just get a stomach ache and gas. It helps if someone takes pity on me and does me the great service of rubbing my stomach. Could you do that?" His smile grew wider. "We don't have much time."

Startled but game (after all, she was concert manager and needed to do everything necessary to keep the star functioning happily), Marian stepped close to the table and folded the blanket back.

"This certainly will be something to tell my grandchildren," she said as she capably massaged his stomach. Adele and Sydney, laughing, left the room. "I'll send Bill, if we see him, to relieve you!" said Adele over her shoulder as she disappeared.

Too soon, intermission was over. "Thank you so much, Nurse," Nelson said, getting off the table and putting on his jacket. "I feel much better." He gave her a hug.

"You're welcome," replied Marian. "Glad to help."

There were over 2,000 people in the audience that night and they were wildly enthusiastic about the huge friendly young man with the magical voice. Most had never heard his name. None had ever before heard him sing. They took him to their hearts with the pride of discovery. Nelson Edy became, in one evening, Marin County's own!

Just before leaving home for the concert that afternoon, Marian realized neither of them had remembered to provide a cash box so Bill collected all the money at the gate during intermission, using a sturdy shoe box tied with heavy string.

"This is better," said Marian. "It doesn't look like it's full of money."

They carried the shoe box home with them, and after counting the money, shoved it under their bed until they could deposit the "gate" at the bank Monday morning. The system worked so well, they used the shoe box for all the years of collecting the money and hiding it over the weekend.

Nelson Edy was the opening attraction offered by the Musical Chest for the next two years. The newly constructed outdoor theater at Forest Meadows on the grounds of Dominican College in San Rafael, was the scene of the later concerts. Over 6,000 were in attendance on August 25, 1935, for Nelson's second appearance in the county. After the concert, there was a near riot as excited fans swarmed around, clamoring to touch him. Marian, Bill and the security guards joined forces to get him into the limousine and safely away from their adoration.

Marin Musical Chest concert at Forest Meadows,
Dominican College, San Rafael, 1935.

By now, his success with Jeanette MacDonald in a series of musicals had made him a well-known star but those who attended that first concert at the Fairfax Pavilion in January 1934, always felt that they had discovered him, almost *invented* him. And Marian found it difficult over the years, sitting in darkened theaters with his bigger than life figure emoting and singing on the screen, to realize that she had actually rubbed his stomach to relieve gas pains! It was a memory she treasured.

In May 1934, Marianne and Suzanne had their sixth birthday. Because Marian was at the cafeteria until after lunch, their celebration took place at home in the early afternoon with just a couple of little friends to make it a special, with cake, ice cream and lemonade.

The next day, Marian took the twins, with Billy and Jane, to Muir Beach for a picnic. Bill declined to go. His experiences with the sun over the years were not happy ones. Marian had to watch all four children closely, too. Their skins were more likely to burn and freckle than to tan, but none of the girls were as red-headed as their father. Only Billy had that distinction.

Marian watched the twins race the froth on the hard sand, trying not to get touched by the water. Billy and Jane had wandered down the beach looking for treasures and she could just hear their voices and laughter. It was pleasant lying in the warm sunshine. *We've come a long way,* she thought.

And we're going farther. We'll get the house back soon, I'm sure, although Bill's so negative I could scream. He's certainly no help!

"Come on, girls," Marian called. "Let's walk down the beach and find Jane and Billy. It's time to head home."

Trip to Muir Beach on twin's sixth birthday, May 1934.

She was right about the house. With unbelievable slowness, the paperwork was crawling through channels. Problems were being unraveled. It was happening! As the school year drew to a close, they were able to give notice to Mr. Krause. They'd be out of the house by mid-August. That would be the last month they'd pay rent. Marian thanked him for all the help he'd given them during the years they'd been his tenants.

Permission to start papering and painting the Glenwood Avenue house was granted. The move, at long last, was under way. The children cooperated by packing all their belongings except what they needed for daily living. To Jane, it was really exciting. She had the clearest memories of living there and she'd been away the longest.

Months before, she'd walked up Fernhill and down Glenwood to stand and stare at the place that was so important to her mother. It looked deserted and slightly shabby. Grass had grown high in the area between the untrimmed front hedge and the road. A sign was posted on the telephone pole warning that action would be taken if the grass weren't cut back. She wondered if they were responsible and was willing, in spite of hay fever, to pull every blade by hand! Removing that grass was the first thing Marian had Bill take care of when they were allowed to work around the place.

The twins were too young to remember their first eighteen months in the house. Billy didn't care one way or the other. The only difference would be the hill he'd have to bike up and being a couple of blocks farther away from Davey Pitman and Rick Lloyd.

Bill, now that the miracle was actually happening, became enthusiastic about recovering the house, almost as though he'd instigated and executed the move. Marian didn't care if he took all the credit: She was going home! That was what mattered.

*Glenwood Avenue home, 1927, before sleeping
porch was roofed and enclosed.*

PART THREE

Back Home Again

UMMER OF 1934 WAS hot and dry but that just added to the pleasure of getting back into their home. They moved in, finally, on August 15. Jane carried the wind chimes this time and hung them from a hook on the porch before even going into the house. The garden was neglected but the trees, planted a decade before, had survived the Rattrays' four-year absence and were appreciably taller, providing slender strips of welcome shade.

A moving van was hired to get their belongings the few blocks from Shady Lane to Glenwood Avenue. There was no other way to do it. Even Marian acknowledged that she and Bill couldn't, alone, move the stove, refrigerator, washing machine or the piano, so they might as well have all the furniture professionally transported from one place to the other.

Billy and Jane were to share a room until the sleeping porch could be glassed in for one of them. However, Billy chose to take up residence there immediately rather than share space with Jane. She was delighted, irritated only by the fact that he had to walk through her room to get to and from his. The twins had the other back bedroom, Bill and Marian the front one that had been theirs in the beginning. All the rooms were freshly painted and papered in the weeks before the move. The twin's was done in white paper with dime-sized red dots, Jane's in a floral pattern, and the other in a clean crisp blue and white plaid.

Bill was the paperhanger with Marian giving help and advice. Both the plaid and the polka dots almost caused his eyes to cross.

"Next time I get a vote on the wallpaper patterns or you get a new paperhanger," he said to Marian. She laughed and replied, "That'll teach you to ignore me in the planning stages!"

"I never think you're asking my advice," said Bill in a rare disclosure of his feelings. "You always seem so sure of what you're doing. It doesn't seem necessary to put my two-cents worth in." He shrugged and smiled at her. "Or even possible. But with wallpaper patterns, from now on I'll decide."

Marian was startled. She always told herself she wanted to have discussions with Bill and now he was practically saying it was her fault they didn't. He wasn't accusing her, or blaming her. He was matter-of-factly saying she allowed no room for his opinions in her already-made-up mind! *Is that true?* she thought. *Am I that overpowering? Do I take decisions away from him all the time? God, I hope not*!

For the next few weeks, Marian spent spare moments going back in her mind over the things that had happened, especially in reclaiming the house. She thought of all the times she'd come to him and said, "Now, Bill, listen to this. This is what we have to do. Okay?" and then, receiving a noncommittal shrug or nod from him, had gone on and done whatever it was. Always telling herself how she wished he'd *discuss* the issue. But never giving him an opportunity. *I'll try to do better,* she told herself. *But I can't take it when he's negative. He'll have to be more positive about the outcome of things or there can't be a discussion! Well, there must be a compromise, a happy middle ground and I'll find it.*

Marian was amazed at how content she was to be back in the little gray home on Glenwood Avenue even though it was less elegant than the house in the Oakland hills and much smaller than the one on Shady Lane. It made a deep difference in her feelings, gave her a sense of belonging that was totally missing in the leased place, the borrowed cabin, the rented house. Being here reconnected her little family's roots to their tiny corner of the universe and set her beside her own treasured hearthstone. This was the first, the only, place that was truly theirs and even though it would be fifteen years before they owned it, free and clear, it was an overwhelming wonder to be back for which she thanked God, FDR, and her own indomitable perseverance. And Bill for not standing in her way.

Over the years, from the time Marian was in high school, she had kept in touch with Pauline Baldwin DuBois, following her as she traveled with her West Point graduate Army officer husband to bases throughout the world. Whenever they were scheduled for a new assignment, Polly carefully packed all the valuable family silverware and sent it, registered mail, to Marian to hold until they were settled at the new post. This had been happening for nearly two decades. Other than that, receiving a scrawled note with a Christmas portrait of the three DuBois sons, sometimes clustered around their mother, was Marian's only contact with her longtime friend.

The shipment of silverware had arrived just as the Rattrays moved into the Shady Lane place. This time it wouldn't be necessary to mail it to the next address. Colonel "Buddy" DuBois was to be commanding officer at Fort Baker, on the Marin shore of the Bay just inside the Golden Gate.

Marian was delighted. Their friendship went back a long way. She was still in high school when Pauline, then a neophyte teacher, had come to live with the Murdocks at Eighteen-Ought-Nine in Alameda. Pauline was betrothed to a handsome young man at West Point. She and Buddy wrote frequently for the years he was at the Academy but hadn't seen each other since the meeting that led to their engagement. Marian supported and cajoled Polly through her pre-nuptial misgivings when Buddy graduated in 1912 and headed for California, a virtual stranger, to claim his bride.

When Marian met Buddy for the first time, she was overwhelmed by the emotion that swept through her entire being. He was handsome, erect, with chiseled features and a commanding presence. But more than that his warm brown eyes seemed to see right into her heart. And every word he said echoed something she had thought all her life.

Why did I talk Polly into going through with this wedding? she wondered. *I could be totally happy with this man. And he with me. But it can never be. We can't even explore the wonder of it!*

Marian continued to support her friend and steer her toward the simple wedding that would take place as soon as possible. She tried not to meet Buddy's eyes or have any moments alone with him. The one time they found themselves with no one else around Buddy said, "This is all wrong. I don't even know Polly. What are we doing?"

Marian looked at him and lied. "You're doing the right thing. You'll be fine. Polly's the one for you. I know her; she'll be a perfect army wife."

"Marian, look at me. Remember these words by Tennyson? It's how I feel." His voice deepened. "*The shackles of an old love straitened him. His honor, rooted in dishonor stood, and faith, unfaithful, kept him falsely true.'* Does that make any sense? The world's greatest oxymoron. I'm committed to do this."

Marian nodded. "It makes as much sense as the way I feel." There were tears glinting in her eyes. She looked away, turned away, and heard a deep sigh as Buddy left the room. She couldn't understand how so much feeling could spring from so little contact. It had come full blown, and now was ending, aborted, before it began. Another phrase from Tennyson sprang to her mind and stabbed her heart: *There must be now no passage of love betwixt us twain hencefoward evermore.*

That was all that happened.

The wedding took place. The young couple went away. Marian met Bill, graduated from college, got married. A war was fought. Babies were born. The silverware and photographs arrived periodically, showing Polly with white hair while still in her twenties. Marian seldom thought of Buddy, and when she did, it was only fondly as Polly's husband, nothing more. The words, the feelings which surfaced before that long-ago wedding had slipped into oblivion under layers of ordinary living. And now, two decades later, Pauline, Buddy and Marian were coming face to face.

So, at the depth of their most desperate times, just before the Christmas of the charity basket from the church, Marian packed her four children in the old car along with the box holding the silverware and drove over Corte Madera grade, through Sausalito, around the point and down to Fort Baker. The buildings and two-story cream-colored wooden homes, all roofed with deep red shingles, faced the road that circled the green grass parade square. The commanding officer's quarters, slightly larger than the rest, was dead-center on the back leg of the road, with its rear to the towering hill and its face toward the Bay.

Marian pulled to the side of the road and switched off the engine.

"All right, children," she said taking a deep breath. "Let's go meet my dear old friends and their boys."

"What are their names?" asked Jane.

"Well, my friends are Colonel and Mrs. DuBois. That's what you'll call them. And the oldest boy is Bill, the middle one is Ted and the youngest is Johnny. You remember them from the Christmas pictures, don't you? We get one every year."

"Sort of," Jane replied as her mother reached to open the door so she could get out and help the younger ones in the backseat. Marian picked up the heavy package. As they walked up the straight path to the front steps, two boys raced around the corner of the house and stopped short at the sight of the visitors. While the children stared at each other, Marian rang the bell.

A sharply dressed enlisted man answered the door.

"Yes, ma'm," he said. "Mrs. DuBois is expecting you." He held the door open, taking the package from her, and Marian stepped into the hall, followed by the children, just as Polly appeared.

"Marian! I can't believe it! After all these years! And here are your children." She smiled at Jane, Billy and the twins, calling each by name. "Come in, come in. Back here. Buddy's at his office. He'll be here as soon as he knows you've arrived. Didn't want to waste time waiting! You know Buddy. No, actually you don't. He's terrible!" Polly laughed. "Uses his time so wisely it drives me crazy. He has a built-in clock in his head. Down to a millionth of a second! Here, sit down. Alfred, bring the lemonade and cookies. There!" Polly sat down with a wide grin, embracing all of them with a glance. The DuBois boys crowded into the sun room and introductions were made amid giggles and shy looks. Into this melee of seven youngsters vying to establish a pecking order, strode a compelling figure, arrogantly erect, totally crisp and pressed, Colonel Buddy DuBois – commanding officer, husband, father. Each person in the room reacted to his presence. Alfred, busy serving lemonade and cookies, sprang to attention momentarily, then went on with his duties. Bill, Ted and Johnny stopped jostling each other and stood straight. The Rattray children became even more subdued. Polly smiled and waved. Marian, with her heart leaping unexpectedly into her throat, stood up and faced him.

"Hello, Buddy," she said. "How are you?"

"Marian." He looked right at her, into her, and the twenty years vanished. "You're looking well." He turned to the children, breaking the tension between them. *Oh, Lord,* Marian thought, *I shouldn't have come. I should've mailed the silverware. Calm down, be still. Maybe it's all your imagination.* His glance met hers again and she knew her imagination had nothing to do with it.

When the lemonade was gone, Buddy marched them out the door into the backyard. Pointing to the hill towering above them, he said, "See right up there where those bushes are? That's where the road to the bridge they're going to build will come out of a tunnel."

"Really?" asked Jane. "Are they *really* going to build a bridge across the Golden Gate? When? Soon?" Marian silently blessed her daughter for being interested and asking questions. It gave her a chance to gather her scrambled thoughts and quiet her racing heart.

As Buddy talked to the children and answered Jane's and Billy's questions, Marian took the twins' hands and walked back toward the house. Polly joined her and they went into the sun room. It was easy and natural to talk to her old friend, almost as though they'd never been apart.

Marian laughed, "Oh, it's good to see you, Polly. And your hair! I knew from the photos but it's so beautiful and becoming."

"I can't take any credit for going white at an early age. It runs in the family. But I do like it, so thank you! You're looking great. All over those hospital things you had a few years back?"

"Absolutely. I've never felt better. Never."

"And Bill? How is it with Bill? Charlie's been a good little brother and written me about Bill's drinking. But I haven't heard from him for awhile. What's going on?" Pauline paused for breath and waited.

"Everything's fine, really fine," Marian glibly replied. "No," she continued more quietly. "It's better but it's not fine. Okay, maybe. How are things with you and Buddy?" she countered, reluctant to discuss any problems in her marriage even with Pauline. It was too soon; they'd just re-met.

"Wonderful!" said Polly with a laugh. "He's impossible to live with and he thinks I'm crazy. Other than that, we're a perfect couple. Once in awhile we even talk to each other. Most of the time, we happily coexist and lead totally separate lives. It's easy with the boys. They make so much noise, no one else can get a word in anyhow. And Buddy's so busy. The Army's his life. I'm surprised he took off to come over to see you today. You should be honored! I don't know when he's been home in the daytime."

"Well, it is great to see you. We'll have to do this often. And you come up to Ross. We really have so much to catch up on."

That afternoon, two years ago, had ended without Marian and Buddy coming face-to-face again. During the intervening months, Marian had driven down with the children to see Polly on several afternoons when she knew Buddy would be busy elsewhere. It had worked out well, she thought.

Now they were back in the Glenwood Avenue house. They had just received a formal invitation, with Polly's handwritten scrawl saying, *Please come!*, to a Command Tea being given at the residence of the commanding officer, at Fort Baker.

Bill had never met the DuBoises but he, through Marian, had kept track of their lives. "Do you want to go?" Marian asked him. "It's on Sunday afternoon, just before Labor Day."

"If you do," Bill answered.

"Okay. I'll answer that we'll be there." Marian wasn't sure she wanted to go but there was no turning back without making too big a deal of it. *Nothing, but nothing, has ever happened between us, not a word, not a touch. I'm just being silly. It'll be fun. Bill will like them both. There's nothing to worry about.*

It was a swank, formal affair, the ladies wearing flowered gowns, large hats and white gloves and most of the men in military dress attire. Pauline was in her element, definitely the commander's wife, the colonel's lady, no hat on her shining silver hair.

The guests moved through the polished rooms of the large house and floated through the sun room to the back lawn where table and chairs had been set. It was a clear warm September day. The punch and champagne, the hors d'oeuvres, the tiny cakes, all were excellent. Marian introduced Bill to Pauline and Buddy. Polite words were said. They moved on. Everything was all right

Marian was relieved and chatted happily with Bill as they stood in the yard. Her eyes turned to the hill above them and she pointed out to Bill the road that was taking form high above. "We'll have to remember to tell Jane. She's really interested in what's going on. The first time we came down here, Buddy told us that a road was going in up there. It was hard to believe, it seemed so far away."

"Another few years and they may have a bridge." He gazed up at the hill. "Sure was slow getting started. At least the tower on this end is finished." Bill remarked. "It's a huge job. Things'll never be the same once it's done, you'll see," he said almost gloomily.

"Oh, it'll be wonderful to just zip over to the City," Marian said. "Imagine, no more sitting in line waiting for the next ferryboat!"

"It'll wreck the county. Too many people, too much traffic. Wait and see."

"Bill, you're such a pessimist! Let's have fun while we're here." Marian headed over to where Pauline was holding court. Bill followed her and they were soon drawn into the light chatter. Luckily, Bill didn't express any doomsday thoughts.

Home again, they reported to Jane that, yes, on the way back they'd driven as close as they could to the bridge and the North Tower was standing proud and tall, all 746 feet of it, a structure of boggling dimensions, waiting for the beleaguered South Tower in San Francisco to catch up to it. Jane questioned them at length and extracted a promise to go see for herself next time they went down that way.

Jane had spent a busy summer getting ready for yet another school switch. After two years at San Rafael High School, she was enrolling as a junior at Tamalpais High in southern Marin. To make it easier to face the new school, in early summer Jane contacted Aloha Jones, a friend she'd made during a brief attendance at a San Anselmo grammar school near Ben Brae. They'd been in the same second grade class and before Aloha could visit Jane after school, her beautiful mother came to check Marian, the house, speech patterns and the "standards" in force. Luckily, they passed on all counts and Marie allowed her daughter to see her new friend!

Jane and Aloha had been close buddies back then and had no trouble reestablishing their friendship. This made the move to Tam much easier on Jane. Aloha was firmly established in a group of girls and Jane was taken into the fold. The gang had a nucleus of four girls when Aloha introduced Jane. The "leader" was Dottie Rossi, a vivacious brunette, who, like her younger sister, Buddy, was a talented acrobatic dancer. The girls frequently performed on stage in gorgeous satin costumes lovingly stitched by their mother. This talent was important in the role the group played at school. They used it as a starting point for skits and plays and this set them apart and made them special without having to battle for a place in the sun.

Getting to school was part of the fun. Northwestern Pacific ran *The*

Special, a five-car electric train, from Manor, north of Fairfax, to the school in Mill Valley. Dot and her sister, Buddy, were among those who boarded at the first station. It fell to them to each grab and save double seats for their friends. Aloha got on at Lansdale, Jane at Bolinas Avenue, and then, just before the train entered Alto tunnel, under Corte Madera grade, Helena MacKall and Carol Pixley boarded and made their way to the reserved seat. Those were the regulars. Others came and went but these five were constant faithful components of the group. Buoyed up by her new-found friends, Jane made the transition to Tam with a minimum of trauma.

She felt, however, that each of them was prettier and more talented than she was. Aloha Jones was the daughter of Benjamin Bufano, the famous San Francisco sculptor. She had his olive skin. Her hazel eyes were enormous, her brown hair curly, her figure short and curvaceous. Added to this, her sense of humor was delightful, her laugh hearty and her zest for life, supreme. Helena MacKall was almost as tall as Jane. When school started, she was just home from a long vacation and her golden tan filled Jane with envy. Helena's eyes were gray-blue, her hair dark blond and wavy, her manner often humorously depreciating, especially of herself. Carol Pixley was truly blond with sharp features and the sweetest manner Jane had ever run across. Then there was Dot's vivacious Italian beauty and dancing ability.

No wonder Jane felt a bit overshadowed by them! Her self-image was murky at best. Marian hadn't helped when, sensing Jane's lack of confidence in facing a new school, wrapped up one of their mother-daughter discussions by saying, "You may not be pretty. But you have naturally curly hair and a nice disposition. That counts for lots." It wasn't what Jane needed to hear. Marian, who came from a background with a vain father and conceited sister, was determined to keep her children realistically humble about their physical attributes. She more than succeeded!

However, as Jane developed her artistic and journalistic talents at school she began to shine in her own quiet way. At any rate, she was part of the popular Rossi Gang and as such, she was safe and happy. Part of her happiness was the more relaxed dress code at Tam which allowed bobby sox instead of stockings. Freedom from the detested garter belt filled her with little prayers of thankfulness!

Billy was in seventh grade that Fall. He was still buddies with Rick Lloyd and Dave Pitman and they spent most of their free time together. Two years before, right after Billy received a secondhand bicycle, he was able to get a route delivering a daily newspaper, the *San Rafael Independent*, throughout Ross. He was thrilled at the chance to earn real money. The route was

Tamalpais High School: Jane…
Carol Pixley….Aloha Jones …
Dottie Rossi… 1935.

difficult, up and down steep hills, on narrow crowned roads, with long driveways curving up to many homes. And everyone wanted the paper by the front door! Tippy learned the route by heart and ran ahead of Billy. Marian was glad that the dog went with him. His coat was such a light tan, he was more visible than the boy on the bike and his sturdy little body served as a warning flag.

Billy was a good student, quick in math, but he had a tendency to hide things away instead of facing them, like term papers and book reviews. Marian often questioned him and found that he was on the edge of being delinquent with some assignment. She quickly organized him and put a strict schedule into effect. This almost kept him up to date. But with the route, time with his friends, hours at school, and the demands of daily living, in spite of his mother's prodding, he still managed to thwart her plans and fall behind with his assignments and projects.

Marianne and Suzanne were big first graders, walking the mile to and from school unless it was pouring rain. Then Marian drove down to fetch them. They were both quick in learning to read and Marianne displayed her parents' talent with numbers. Without trying she was at the head of the class. Whatever the subject, Marianne was finished first and her work was perfect. The reward for this was inexplicable to her. Since she completed assignments in record time, she then doodled or daydreamed in class. "You're being lazy, Marianne. Look how hard Suzanne is working! Why don't you work like she does? Read another story. Stay busy. Instead you waste time!" This is what she heard.

It seemed a strange attitude! She had no desire to do twice as much work as anyone else just because she was faster and better at it than they were. So she learned to hide the fact that she was finished until the rest of the class caught up to her. She was never challenged, instead, to go beyond or sideways down an interesting path. Her first grade teacher did introduce the class to birds, however, and Marianne pursued this on her own for the rest of her life with great satisfaction.

People often said to Marian, "The twins don't look alike but I don't know which is which."

"Oh, that's easy. Just think 'Sue, straight.' Marianne's the one with curly hair."

What this did to Suzanne's self-esteem was terrible. She had the impression that curls were to be prized and she was somehow less than her twin without them. When Marian finally realized the damage done with her careless words, she made an appointment at the beauty parlor for Suzanne to have a permanent. It was not an unqualified success. Sue's hair was so fine it didn't hold a curl well. Even on her best days, when it looked almost like Marianne's, Susan always knew in her heart, no matter what, that her hair was really straight and it, and she, were somehow inferior! It took her years to overcome the impact of this thinking.

They had only been back in the house a short time when one of Bill's many feelers paid off and he obtained a position with a good company in San Francisco using his considerable experience and talent as an insurance adjustor. He was also playing for Gladys Kenny Hodgson's ballet classes several evenings each week, had a few piano students, and, of course, St. John's organ work. For the first time since everything collapsed after Perce's death, the Rattrays were solvent. Marian decided that running the cafeteria at Ross took more time and energy than she wanted to expend and, after locating a replacement agreeable to the school, gave her notice.

"It's been wonderful working here," she said to Mrs. Jenkins on her last day. "I've enjoyed the children. And the teachers. Thank you."

"We've certainly benefited by having you here, such good meals! Thank *you!*" replied Lethia.

During the summer, rehearsals for the September production of the Ross Valley Players next offering, *The World We Live In*, were underway. Tom and Anne Kent, members of the founding family of Kentfield, made a portion of their estate available for development into an outdoor theater. With a steep wooded hill as a backdrop, a large dirt "stage" was leveled and smoothed. Seating for the audience was plotted. A sturdy frame, almost a small house, was constructed, with canvas walls and roof, like a huge tent. Electricity, tables, shelves, mirrors, benches and chairs were added. This was to serve as dressing rooms and by the time the enormous cast was ready to rehearse on the spot, it was finished, all done by members' volunteer labor. Eric Pitman supervised the electrical work and provided the wiring needed for the lighting the entire hillside. He also helped Bill with the loudspeaker system that would carry music that Bill had assembled on records.

Marian, Hazel Pitman, Adele Higgins, Ruth Hansen and Hortense Styles were among the workers who helped Beth Lloyd with the costuming. The children were all pressed into service as extras. There were plenty of parts for them to play. *The World We Live In* was an imaginative allegory with insects as all the characters, acting out human foibles, quirks and feelings. Somehow, transferred to bugs, human traits were humorous.

To make two dozen children look like two hundred ants, the director had them winding up and down the hill in a continuous line, back and forth, until they were breathless with the exertion. Their parts didn't call for emoting but endurance was essential.

Making the costumes for beetles, ants, and other insects stretched the women's talents to the utmost. They succeeded, if a bit surrealistically. Finally, dress rehearsal with enough horrors to make everyone feel the real thing would be wonderful.

"Isn't that what they say?" Marian asked Beth as they watched still another muddle on stage. "A bad dress rehearsal means a good opening night? And since we're only doing one night, we can't miss."

"I hope you're right, Marian," Beth answered in her soft sweet voice. "But it really doesn't look too good."

Beth need not have worried. The play, on a warm wonderful night in late September, seemed perfect. The only glitches were so amusing the audience thought they were part of the script! From the biggest beetle to the tiniest ant, the cast performed beautifully and enthusiasm ran rampant. All the months of hard work paid off.

"Why aren't we doing it again tomorrow night?" Marian asked. "It's over too soon."

And so it was. But no provision had been made for a second performance. Everything was disconnected, dismantled, packed up, and taken away. Or stacked, to be picked up the next morning.

Bill and Marian, clutching records and a pile of costumes, drove the children home. Jane was put in charge of getting her exhausted siblings to bed. Bill and Marian were going to the cast party at one of the big homes near St. John's.

The affair was in full swing when they walked in, everyone exhilarated by the success of the play. Hortense Styles rushed up to Bill and grabbed his hand.

"Come, you darling," she said. "They have a gorgeous piano and tons of new sheet music, *Blue Moon, Beer Barrel Polka, Stars Fell on Alabama,* lots more. We want you to play." Marian braced herself for Bill's refusal. He never performed at parties. That was giving away his livelihood, he always said when she complained about his adamant refusals. Marian's eyebrows rose in surprise as she looked at Bill. He smiled sweetly at Hortense, squeezed her hand and said, "Lead on, McDuff!" Marian knew he was totally sober, yet here he was suddenly behaving like the young man she'd met so many years before, sitting at the piano with laughing friends clustered around him with obvious enjoyment. She looked at Bill with an assessing eye. He was a good-looking man, still slim. His hair was darker with a sprinkle of gray at the temples. And his hairline had receded giving him a "noble brow." Now, with excitement shining on his laughing face, he was joking and smiling and having a wonderful time.

It must be Hortense! I certainly don't get that response from him! Marian thought with amusement as she moved away from the piano to join a group around a lavishly loaded table. She spent the rest of the night talking with Philip Greer whose wife, Virginia had been part of the costuming group. Philip was tall, dark, quiet with a sweet smile and soft brown eyes. He and Marian found many points of mutual concern to discuss and she was impressed with his knowledge and humor.

"This has been fun. I don't know when I've had such stimulating conversation, Philip."

"Neither do I," he replied. "Good talk is a very special thing. We'll have to do it again." He smiled as Marian walked away in search of Bill who was taking a break from the piano. She found him sitting with Hortense and several others, deep in animated discussion of recent movies.

"I think Shirley Temple is darling," Hortense was saying. "She's so natural, I can't believe it. Only five years old and able to act like that!"

"She's all right but I liked *It happened One Night* more. That was funny and clever. I really don't enjoy seeing little girls being cute," said Hortense's handsome husband, Francis. "I get enough of that around the house, with Betsy and Martha Lou!" Everyone laughed. Knowing the Styles' daughters, they agreed with him.

"Oh, but weren't all our kids wonderful tonight in the play? Such busy little ants!" said Marian sitting down on the arm of the chesterfield. "Does anyone know what time it is?"

"It's nearly five o'clock," someone answered. This elicited a number of groans.

"I had no idea it was so late. Or is it early? We better be going." The party dissolved into happy good-byes as everyone thanked the hosts and headed home.

Marian found herself replaying the conversation with Philip in the days that followed. *I think it's because there's something of Buddy about him. And we talked so much. I've never said so many things to anyone, certainly not to Buddy. Hardly even to Bill in all these years.* Marian enjoyed her memory of that evening, not just because of Philip but for the lighthearted happy person Bill had seemed. She had almost forgotten he could be that charming and debonair. *It must be the job in the City and being back in the house. Maybe it's because I've stopped harping on him!*

She didn't realize what a profound effect that night, and talking so deeply with Philip, would have on her life. Even had she known, she would probably have done nothing differently. There was a part of her, awakened by a long-ago glance from Buddy, that craved a kind of sharing she hadn't found in marriage or motherhood or with any of her friends, male or female. It wasn't a sexual thing; more it was a sense of being known completely and accepted, even challenged, for her own inner self.

Back in 1912, had she and Buddy met under different circumstances, she knew they could have been all things to each other. But since that was totally impossible from the beginning, she had given up hope of ever experiencing the kind of sharing of *self* she longed for. Until those special hours she and Philip talked, that is. Then she found herself being more and more stimulated, more and more willing to risk thoughts she'd hardly formulated even to herself.

As his words came back to her, it was like balm to her heart, like rain falling on parched land, echoing and adding new dimensions to her thoughts. That they were both married didn't enter into it at this point. This was an intellectual pursuit. No spouse could complain about *conversations*. There was no harm in that. Besides, Marian told herself, she probably wouldn't see Philip again until the next Ross Valley Players production. And that was a year away. By then, all would be forgotten.

Two days later there was an envelope in the post office box addressed to Marian. She opened it and found a note signed by Philip.

> **Marian, I've been reading a book, *Seven Gothic Tales,* by Isak Dinesen (you know - Baroness Blixen – we touched on her life). I think you'd enjoy this book. Besides, I'd like to find out what you think of it – and of her, after reading this new work. I need to talk with you again. How can we arrange it? Drop me a line at my business address – it's on the envelope – and tell me what you think.**
>
> **Sincerely, Philip**

Several days went by before Marian could get to the library to ask for the book. Another week passed in reading it. All that time she was wondering if she'd answer Philip's note, and if she did, what she'd say. She finally penned a short missive, fighting a wave of guilt. It was the use of the business address, she knew. But remembering his wife, Virginia, and tales she's heard about her irrational jealousy, it was understandable that Philip chose to do so.

> **Dear Philip, Yes, I enjoyed the book. Yes, I would like to discuss it with you. No, I don't know how we can arrange it. I think we**

should just leave it to chance. It's a small world and we will meet
again sometime, somewhere. Yours, Marian

With the note posted, Marian went on with life as usual. She found it gratifying to be home all day, not having to run the cafeteria which had consumed many hours. And with the twins in school until 2:30, she was truly free for the first time since the beginning months of her marriage. It was like being blessed with at-home daily vacations!

Days started early. Marian was in the kitchen by seven while the rest of the family were juggling turns at the bathroom. They went in order of their departure. Bill was first. To eat and walk down to catch his 7:30 train to San Francisco, he had to be out of the house by 7:15. Jane was next. She had until 7:45 to make *The Special* at 8 sharp. Then came the twins who usually sat at the dining room table together for their oatmeal and toast, orange juice and hot chocolate. They had to be at school by 9 AM so left the house at 8:30. Billy had to be there at nine, too, but on his bike he could make it in half the time, so he left at 8:45. Marian felt like a short order cook on most mornings. They certainly ate in quick shifts! It was great on days Marian made pancakes instead of hot mush. Each person was just in time for an individual order.

Once Billy left the house, Marian sat down in the blessed silence with a pot of tea and her share of whatever she'd cooked. She planned her day as she munched toast, making lists of what to do, where to go, what to buy, the menu for dinner. Then, with maximum efficiency she did the dishes, made the beds except Jane's and Billy's, who did their own. Housekeeping was something for Marian to get through so she'd be free to do other more enjoyable things. She kept the house tidy but didn't like deep cleaning. She'd much rather garden; the results were showier and lasted longer.

Marian was a good basic cook. She served nourishing meals but she wouldn't spend more than 30 minutes on preparation! Of course, roasts, turkeys, some casseroles, stews and soups often had to cook longer but she put them in to be ready on time. Dinner was scheduled for the table by 6 PM sharp. All the children knew they had to be on hand. Whoever was setting the table that week better be there in plenty of time to get the job done correctly. Centerpiece fresh and attractive, place mats, napkins, silverware in proper alignment, butter plates, glasses, cups and saucers for the adults, butter in its dish with a special knife, milk in a pitcher ("Get that bottle [later 'carton'] off the table this minute! *Never* put the container on the table!"). Marian was adamant on that.

As the chimes tolled six, the children sat down, some of them breathless from hurrying and still damp from hasty washing. Marian brought the steaming plates to the table, usually serving them up in the kitchen. Meat, vegetables and starch, dietetically balanced. Second glass of milk, bread and butter only after the plates were clean. Dessert. And talk! Usually it was friendly with jokes and laughter. Billy teased Jane lightly, in fun. But sometimes a child became defiant or siblings began to squabble. At such moments Marian said in a firm voice, "Leave the table. We don't have that tone of voice at dinner."

The child being sent away usually made a statement by slamming the French door into the hall with such force that a pane of glass cracked or shattered! After several replacements of broken panes, Marian had Bill remove the door from its hinges and store it in the basement. They got along perfectly without it but it did spoil the children's self-expression.

Some summer evenings, when it was time for Bill's train from the City to arrive, Marianne and Suzanne walked down Bolinas Avenue to the station to meet him. Marianne, who really loved her father, enjoyed this ritual. Suzanne was often reluctant to go, but went anyhow since her twin was not allowed to make the trip by herself.

Sometimes the little girls walked all the way down and their father wasn't on the train Other times, he arrived home before they expected. One night he came in just before six and sat down in his chair at the table. Jane's stomach lurched as she recognized his condition. Marian's face hardened. He smiled fatuously at them and reached to hug Suzanne when she walked by. As his arm went around her shoulders to pull her closer, Suzanne bent her head and bit his thumb.

"Ouch!" yelled Bill releasing her.

Suzanne ran from the room. "She doesn't like it when you've been drinking," Marian said.

"Drinking? I haven't been drinking!" answered Bill, getting unsteadily to his feet. "Why do you say that?"

"Don't make it any worse. Sit down. Dinner's ready."

"No. No, I'm not hungry." He left the room and Marian heard the bedroom door close.

"Jane, go get Sue. Bring her back. She's probably sorry she hurt her daddy." Jane found her little sister sitting on the edge of her bed. "Come eat dinner. He's gone to his room."

"I don't like him."

"I know. But you probably shouldn't bite. That's what animals do, not little girls. Come now." Jane understood her sister's action. She loved her father but the moment she saw the strangely out-of-focus person he became when he drank, the love was replaced with a sinking feeling. *How can he be that way? He's like two different people and I only love one of them. Why does he have to do it?* It was a question she couldn't answer. None of them could.

For weeks, sometimes months, at a time, everything was on even keel. It all depended upon Bill. The whole atmosphere of the home, the behavior of each member of the family was influenced by him. Billy showed the least reaction to his father's fluctuating personality: He just became quieter. Marian had, from the early days of her marriage, assumed more and more responsibility and authority. This put her in charge of setting family rules and dispensing parental discipline. To the children this meant she was the one to look to, or steer clear of, depending on their deeds and desires. Bill, even in sobriety, had a small role to play. His music, his intelligence and his wit were his contributions.

Marianne, starting almost at birth, reacted with stubbornness against authority. This put her at odds with her mother from day one. And caused her to champion, as her awareness grew, the person she viewed as a victim of the tyranny she hated in Marian – her father.

Suzanne by nature was more compliant so there was less friction and conflict expressed in her relationship with her mother. She, however, was hostile toward her father whenever he had been drinking as evidenced by the bite she gave him when he tried to hug her.

Jane, being older, had a decade of experience beyond the twins. Through this she had developed an empathy for her mother and a cynicism about her father. She still remembered the nights when the twins were tiny babies and she heard her mother crying. She had crept out to sit beside Marian and had allied herself with her mother then. Although Marian no longer wept when Bill was late coming home, Jane's alliance was still with her and, therefore, against her father whenever he drank.

Bill was not a violent man. Drinking didn't make him ugly. He never raised his voice, or a hand. Yet just by setting foot in the house when he'd been drinking, he cast a pall over everyone and everything, changing the atmosphere in a subtle and destructive manner which was unfortunate since otherwise it was a happy place filled with good music, good food, good books, good conversation and good humor.

Marian ruled with a light touch, and added as many treats as she possibly could. She still loved moving meals outdoors. On hot summer afternoons she often called Hazel Pitman.

"What are you planning for dinner?'

"Oh, probably something light. What's up?"

"I thought maybe we could meet up at the picnic grounds and eat there." Marian liked the area beyond the end of Lagunitas Avenue in Ross where the town had a rustic park on the creek that flowed from Phoenix Lake. At the picnic area, the stream had been slightly dammed to make a little pond where the children could play with wooden boats, rocks and sticks and manage to get thoroughly wet. Scattered about were heavy tables and benches and, off to one side, a stone and log open-sided cabin.

"Marian, you're on! I have a cake and makings for a big salad. I'll bring hot-dogs and fixings for our family. How about you?"

"I'll do hot-dogs, too, so my four won't get the 'I want what Davey and Betty have' whine. And a watermelon? Come any time you want so the kids can play and cool off. We'll eat at six sharp."

So through hot afternoons and warm evenings the two families shared outdoor meals several times a week, reluctantly giving them up as the leaves began to turn and weather became crisper.

School was going along well. Especially for Jane even though French was a frightening challenge. She had taken two years of the language at San Rafael High from Miss Roselli, a young Italian teacher whose French accent left something to be desired. Now Jane was faced with Mr. Juch, an authentic Frenchman who, with his third year students, tolerated no English in class. Jane, who had never heard French spoken except slowly with an Italian accent, was lost.

Mr. Juch took pity on her. "For you, Mam'selle Rattray, I just told the class to open their books to page 32 and read the first paragraph." With these constant asides in English, Jane was able to stumble through. Her spoken French offended his ear. "*Non, non!* Speak, *s'il vous plaît*, in English. Translate the sentence. Your French, *c'est intolerable*"

Luckily for her, Mr. Juch was sick on the day of their big year-end examination so it was cancelled. Everyone received their current grade as the final one. Jane passed the course which she probably wouldn't have if subjected to an examination totally in that inexplicable language.

Her happiest class was journalism. She wrote a special weekly column on fashion. For that, she designed a heading and added a big "Y" to the middle of her name. Soon she was signing everything that way and became Jane-with-a-Y, Jayne, instead of plain Jane.

One day after she'd turned in a particularly smooth column, Mr. Waterman, the journalism teacher and advisor for the student newspaper, received a call from Mr. Chirone, the man who headed the print shop. "I can't print this column 'Fashions by Jayne'. Sorry."

"Why? What's wrong with it, Al?"

"It's not original. She copied it from somewhere and is passing it off as her own. That won't do," he answered.

"I think you're wrong. I'll call her in and ask her about it. But I'm sure she wrote it herself. That's the way she writes, believe me," said Mr. Waterman with a touch of pride in his student.

When Jane came into class a short time later, he pulled her aside.

"Just had a call from the print shop. Mr. Chirone doesn't think you wrote your column. He doesn't want to print it. Thinks you copied it from some fancy magazine and there's a law against that."

"I didn't. I wrote it myself. Honest!" Jane replied. Then she grinned. "How great!"

Her teacher smiled back at her. "Yes, it is. Mr. Chirone is quite a critic after all these years. I'll tell him to go ahead and run it. And, Jane, congratulations! It's a good piece."

The only class that terrified her was Oral Expression. The year was spent in giving short talks in front of the class. Before each one, Jane became almost physically ill. But the worst day of all was at the end of the semester when each student had to give a ten minute speech. They were called in alphabetical order so Jane had days and days to wait before facing her ordeal.

If the speech came up short by even a second, a whole new one would have to be prepared and presented so Jane had given a friend the last paragraph of her talk with instructions to signal her if she were short, holding up a finger for each second she lacked. She then intended to repeat, for emphasis, the powerful closing paragraph, which ran five whole seconds! Jane had timed her speech over and over and it ran beyond the required ten minutes by a safe margin unless she left something out.

The dreaded day came. In a paralysis of fear Jane rose and moved woodenly to the front of the room. Her throat was parched, her eyes glazed. "Fellow students," she began, "I'm talking today about Will Durant. He is a New York educator/author who ten years ago, when he was 40, wrote an ambitious book, *The Story of Philosophy*. I want to tell you about this book." Jane had written and memorized a coherent, interesting treatise of Durant's work. She held her classmates' attention, partly because her fear was so palatable that they were either rooting for her or looking for her to break down completely. When, after an eternity, she reached the final paragraph, she looked toward her friend in the back row. Three fingers were raised. She'd be three seconds short of ten minutes when she reached the end of the paragraph. Jane took a deep breath.

"For emphasis," she said, "because it's so important, I want to repeat that last passage." Another deep breath, and she launched into the final paragraph, slowly, savoring it, sounding for the first time since she started the speech, in control and not terrified. Then she said, "Thank you," and returned, self-consciously, to her seat. The teacher nodded in her direction, signifying that Jane had fulfilled the time element and thereby passed the course. Detailed grading would come later. But the biggest hurdle of her high school career was behind her and Jane felt weak with relief.

As Marian had mentioned in her note to Philip, it's a small world and they would meet again somehow, somewhere. They did, strangely enough in a shopping area that neither of them normally frequented.

"Marian!" he called. She turned at the sound of her name.

"Philip, how nice!" They stood grinning at each other.

"Come. Let's get a cup of coffee. Or tea, if you'd rather." He steered her toward a nearby shop, and led her to a table. "There. Now, tell me what you've been doing, what you've been thinking, how you've been feeling. How *are* you, my dear friend?" He smiled. She smiled back.

The waitress came to the table and he ordered a pot of tea.

"I can't think of a thing to say," said Marian, laughing. "All the things I've wanted to share with you and I can't remember a single word!"

"It'll come. Take your time. Forget I asked all those questions. Here, you pour."

Marian busied herself with the teapot and their cups.

"How are you?" she asked.

"I'm overwhelmed with how glad I am to be sitting here with you," he answered soberly. "Truly, I didn't know how much I wanted this. You don't have to say anything. Just sit there and smile at me."

"That's easy. Don't ask me *not* to smile!" Marian sipped her tea contentedly.

"Is there any problem with me writing to you? I mean, do you pick up the mail yourself?"

"Yes. I'm the one who goes to the post office every day. No one else is likely to."

"Then, can I write to you? Will you answer?"

Marian felt her heart pounding. "Yes," she said, softly, "Yes." Then her smile faded and she sat up taller. "No! Philip, what are we thinking? I'm a married woman with four children. You have a wife, a son and a daughter. We're middle-aged, not high school kids. And we're sitting here holding hands and grinning at each other." She shook her head. "Even letters aren't a possibility. You know that." Her smile was tinged with sadness.

"Marian, listen to me. That night we talked I took a crash course in Marian Rattray. I learned *you*. I know you. I want to give you something you've never had. I want to be a shoulder you can lean on. I want to *cherish* you. You're right. We're both married. But we're not middle-aged. What are you, 39, 40? That's young! I don't want to do anything that would upset our lives. Bill and Virginia don't deserve that. And certainly the kids don't. But you need someone somewhere to take care of your dreams, to *hear* you, to tell you how wonderful you are, to support you. You've done it on your own all your life. You become strong, too strong. Forgive me for saying so but you're losing a very precious part of yourself. You're getting *hard!*" Philip, his face serious, his eyes reflecting concern, reached for her hands which were tightly clasped and wrapped his around them. "Trust me. I won't hurt you. I won't ask anything you can't freely give. I won't put our lives in jeopardy. Okay?"

Marian relaxed her hands so that they were lying in his. Then she pulled them away and picked up her cup. The tea was cold but she sipped it anyway, not noticing.

"I may not answer if you write," she said softly. "But I can't stop you." She looked up at him with a smile beginning in her eyes. "And I won't throw anything away unopened."

"Good," he replied. "Just know that I'm here. To take care of you, the secret private you that no one else has any claim on. Okay?" Marian nodded in, for her, a tentative way. She wasn't sure. She only knew she couldn't shut the door on what he was offering.

So it began. Marian opened his letters and read them in the car before driving home. Often they contained references to a book, a quote by an author. When they did, she picked up the original work and read it, going before and beyond what he'd written. Sometimes she copied excerpts into her little red leather book, the one she'd started in 1915 before her marriage, her children, her home. It was interesting for her to reread the earlier excerpts and see what had seemed important to her so long ago, to see the things she'd outgrown, the ideals she still cherished.

Philip's third letter started with a new salutation.

> **Mily, That's what I'm going to call you. It means "Marian I love you." I can hardly wait to say it to you. Mily, Mily! It has a nice sound, don't you think? How about dreaming up a name for me? I'll be looking for your answer. Your P.**

Days passed before Marian started an answering note to Philip. Then she tore it up and rewrote it several times. Finally it said:

> **You asked for a name. I've come up with one. I hope you don't think it's silly. There is something of a fairy tale in this connection of ours and, although you're not in shining amour, you are a knight**

who rescued a part of me that was definitely locked in a dungeon. So I dub you "Kim" – my Knight in Mufti!. . .

He replied with delight. After that many entries in the book were to Mily from Kim, little poignant sentences that displayed an amazing depth of feeling and understanding. Months went by. Everyday life for Marian was unaffected. But underneath, for the first time ever, was a safety net of love and concern. As Kim had written, "a part of you is the center of my every day." So she felt about him. Everything was easier. She was more tolerant of Bill, gentler with the children, more outgoing with her friends, more available with her feelings. In fact, she became more *aware* of her feelings and, conversely, more aware of the feelings of others. As the first year back in the house drew to a close, Marian was happier than she'd ever been.

She also found an additional outlet for her energy. The American Red Cross chapter in San Rafael held summer swimming classes at the local high school. In April, she approached the office with an offer to organize and conduct the classes, with her friend Beth Kaufman as instructor. The executive director was happy to turn the project over to Marian.

Publicity brought a record number of signups which Marian divided into a spectrum of half-hour classes, starting with brand new total nonswimmers and progressing to the stringent lifesaving classes. Students from the latter were used as aides in the earlier classes to gain experience. So from mid-June through the end of August, Marian and Beth spent their mornings at the pool, while over 100 children learned to handle themselves in the water. Proficiency certificates were given out at the end of each ten-day session, children moving up the ladder as rapidly as they could.

Both Marian and Beth registered their children in the program. Beth's son and daughter were little water-babies and did well. The twins were resistant and couldn't – wouldn't – learn to float. Jane had learned to swim many years before but refused to put her face in the water which restricted her progress. She could do a face-out-of-water crawl, float, tread water and jump in the shallow end. But beyond that, she would not go! She was too grown up to be with the little beginners who were developing the skills she didn't have, so she dropped out and spent her mornings at home. Billy picked up the rudiments quickly and used the summer to become proficient.

Weekends starting the first summer back on Glenwood Avenue were spent in the garden, where Marian organized the children into work parties to accomplish what she wanted. If only she could make things grow faster! There were household chores, too, which she meted out daily.

One morning as Jane slowly came awake she planned her morning. *I'll clean the stove and oven, and bake a cake, then wash the kitchen floor.*

While she was happily contemplating her tasks, all as a surprise to her mother, her door burst open and Marian strode into the room, clapping her hands.

"Come on, lazybones. Get up! I want you to clean the stove and oven for me. Then, bake a cake and wash the kitchen floor while the cake's cooling. Let's go!"

Jane, her gift shriveled into an expected, no, *demanded*, chore, by her mother's words, rolled to face the wall, and pulled the covers over her head. Even though her mother seemed somewhat less overpowering lately, it was impossible to *give* her anything. It didn't help to say, "I was planning to do just that to surprise you." Jane groaned and struggled out of bed, her day spoiled.

Sunday summer dinners were special. Often Aloha Jones joined Jane. She thought the entire clan wonderful and laughed so hard she could hardly eat. This spurred the punsters to greater heights and made everyone perform to their utmost. Bill often played the piano while Marian and the girls prepared the meal which put everyone in a festive mood.

So many questions had to be answered or substantiated during any dinner conversations that a small table was placed under the dining room windows to keep within arms reach the big *Webster's International Dictionary*, the new *Lincoln Library of Essential Information* and an atlas. Hardly a meal went by without one, or all three, books being consulted to prove a point and settle an argument.

"But, Dad," Jane was saying. "Of course Lake Superior is bigger than San Francisco Bay. Each of the Great Lakes is bigger especially Lake Superior is. It's the biggest of all."

"Yeah, Dad," Billy chimed in. "I bet the Great Lakes all poured together would cover the whole state of California!"

"You're crazy," scoffed Bill. "San Francisco Bay is bigger than the biggest Great Lake."

"Stop arguing, Billy," said Marian. "Get the atlas. Twins, sit down! Billy, get it."

Billy brought the book back to his place and opened it, quickly locating the map of United States. "Look," he said pointing to the large blue shapes of the Great Lakes. "Look at that, Dad. See them. Now look over here." Billy's finger moved to the coast of California and paused opposite the tiny blue area of San Francisco Bay. "See? It's almost invisible at this scale." Billy turned the book toward his father.

Bill looked and realized he was wrong. But he couldn't accept that.

"Damn book lies!" he stated to hoots of laughter from his children. "Can't trust anything these days!" He was laughing, too. But in his heart,

San Francisco Bay was still bigger than Lake Superior. It always would be.

Another evening, after a spirited discussion on the conjugation of irregular verbs, Billy said, "All right, Jane. How do you conjugate "poodle?"

"Poodle's not a verb, stupid. It's a noun. You can't conjugate nouns."

"Sure, you can. Try."

"I know," said Bill with a grin. "How about poodle, piddle, puddle?"

"Not bad, Dad," admitted Jane as the rest laughed. "Quite irregular, I'd say. Two nouns and a verb! But it sounds good! You win the prize."

"What's the prize?"

"There isn't one. But you win it anyhow."

Aloha tried to get a forkful to her mouth and failed again as the Rattrays went off on another grammatical tangent.

"What about "noodle?" Or "needle?" Noodle, needle, nuddle?" asked Billy, laughing.

"That really doesn't make any sense. Give it up."

Marianne looked at her father and said, "Make a camel face. Please?" She smiled at him.

"A camel face at the dinner table? Wouldn't that spoil your appetite?" Bill asked. Marianne looked toward her mother to see if it was all right. Marian was smiling so Marianne swung back to her father. "Oh, yes, do it!"

No one could ever figure out how Bill could transform his pleasant regular features into a blubber-lipped grimace that truly resembled a camel. The sight of it caused them all to break into loud cheers of appreciation. Aloha, who had never seen the act before, nearly fell off her chair.

When the laughter died down, Susan said, "Now do the dime trick."

"That old thing?" asked Bill. "No one wants to see that."

"Oh, yes, we do!" Jane said, and the others chimed in.

"Well," said Bill, rolling up his sleeve and reaching into his pocket for a coin. Putting his forearm, palm up, on the table, he placed the dime just above his wrist. Then, flexing his powerful fingers as through striking a piano key, he caused the dime to flip into the air. His appreciative audience applauded.

"Oh, I can do that," said Billy. "Here, loan me your dime." Billy set it up just as his father had but no amount of straining could budge the dime.

Jane had an advantage over the other three children. She was old enough to accompany her father to the San Francisco Symphony concerts. He purchased a pair of tickets whenever the soloist was a pianist he admired and took Jane with him. She treasured this time with her father and enjoyed the playing of Jose Iturbi, Sergei Rachmaninoff, Vladamir Horowitz. She liked her father's comments, too. Iturbi he found to be "flashy." Rachmaninoff was summed up as "lugubrious." Horowitz received Bill's highest praise. He was "not bad."

"You play as well as he does," she always maintained no matter who the soloist was. Bill pooh-hooed her remark but was secretly pleased. He even practiced and played some of the pieces later in response to Jane's requests.

Bill tried giving piano lessons to his children but wasn't successful. Impatient at best with ineptitude, he jumped unmercifully on their blunders.

"Read the notes!" he'd say. "No, no! That's not what it says! What's the matter with you?"

Only Marianne showed any talent. The other three were reduced to varying degrees of tearfulness and were finally deemed impossible to teach by their father who, to them, was an impossible teacher.

Jane often observed her father sitting in his chair on the evenings he was home with a piano score in his left hand. His other hand would be tapping out the notes on the arm of the chair.

"Can you hear that in your head?" she asked. "Does it sound like music?"

"Of course," Bill answered. "It's easier to read than words. There are 26 letters and only eight notes." To him, that was a logical reply. To Jane it made no sense.

"Yes, but – do you hear music?"

"Of course," he repeated unable to understand why she even asked a question with such an obvious answer.

Jane felt her father was a musical genius to be able to read music and hear it in his head. Such ability was beyond her ken. She was sure her cousins, Ronnie Panton and Greig McRitchie, could also perform what, to her, was a magical task. It was another reason to admire them.

Starting way back when Jane was a baby, Marian and Bill had gone to Summer Home Park on the Russian River whenever they could. For years, it hadn't been a possibility. Now they decided to reward themselves with a short stay at Villa Valleau, the summer home owned by Tone and Bess Murdock's family. It was a wonderful two-story house designed by Tone for his new mother-in-law years before. One feature of the property was Bottle Springs where a natural clear cold spring came out of a small hollow in a shady bank providing sensational drinking water. The family had long ago built a concrete basin into which the water flowed. Maidenhair and woodwardia ferns surrounded the watering hole. There were rustic benches against the banks on either side making it a great place to rest and enjoy nature on the challenging walk back up the wooded canyon from the River. Once Jane discovered a small water snake happily residing in the cistern. Billy removed it to a safe distance up the creek but it was days before Jane would drink from the bottomless bottle embedded in the side of the basin.

Summer Home Park was unique on the River. It was off the beaten path served only by a narrow dead-end dirt road. Even the Northwestern Pacific railroad trains stopped across the River at Hilton, a long hot walk away. Bill, like most of the other fathers, came up from the City by train for the weekend. The children loved being there. Twice a day, accompanied by Marian, they trudged down the dirt roads and crossed the bridge to reach the sandy beach where they could play in the placid water.

Evenings after supper people strolled down from their homes scattered throughout the two redwood covered canyons to the country store for delicious ice cream. It was a nightly treat that Marian promised the children, a reward for perfect behavior. Marian enjoyed visiting with the other ladies while keeping a casual eye on her children. Very few men were on hand. Most of them worked in the City all week and only joined their families for the weekends.

There was informal dancing on a square wooden platform to records played on a portable Victrola by the college-age group – tan lean young men and laughing self-assured long-legged girls. Most had been coming to Summer Home Park for all the vacations of their lives so they knew each other well. Jane, an awkward skinny sixteen and a half year old outsider, could only stand yearningly on the fringes, longing to dance but having no entry into the clique.

The songs she heard those evenings forever made her feel sad and lonely. *Stairway to the Stars, When I Grow Too Old To Dream,* or *Red Sails in the Sunset* could bring tears to her eyes. Even such spirited ones as *The Music Goes Round and Round, Goody* Goody and *Lookie, Lookie Lookie, Here Comes Cookie* were capable of causing a lump to her throat.

Marian, too, heard the music and found the words of *When I Grow To Old To Dream* unbearably poignant. They brought Philip to mind and the inevitable sadness of their situation. A year later she was to write the lyrics in her little red book, followed by a small notation, *Good-bye, Mily – Kim.* She shivered with premonition on that warm September evening in 1935.

Bill arrived on the train late in the afternoon on Friday of Labor Day weekend to help them pack up for the drive home Monday afternoon. This was the end of the more than just summer. The Northwestern Pacific was discontinuing service entirely in November. The trains that ran back to Santa Rosa and on down to the ferry boats in Sausalito would be the last ever, ending six decades of faithful runs. And on the day after Labor Day, the bridge across the River that gave access to the beach, would be, as always, removed and stored for the winter. Summer Home Park went into annual hibernation, this time sadder because the trains wouldn't return next year for the commuting fathers to ride. The rest of the River suffered worse

Billy and the twins at
Summer Home Park, 1935.

deprivation since resorts were more dependent on tourist trade than Summer Home Park, which was, as its name said, made up of the summer homes of permanent residents, passed on, in many cases, from generation to generation .

Back in Ross, the children started school the next morning. Jane was a senior at Tam. With the horrors of Oral Expression and the incomprehensions of French behind her, Jane had nothing to fear in her last high school year. Billy, too, was at the top of the heap – an eighth grader – one of the "big kids," with all the rights, privileges and responsibilities such a position entailed. He was up to the task though Marian kept a careful eye on his assignments to see that he didn't come up short at the last minute.

Spurred on by the summer accomplishments of her friends, Jane had Marian drive her down to the police office at Ross where she asked Chief Joe Regoni for a permit so she could learn to handle an automobile.

"Fine," said Joe. "You're old enough, aren't you?"

"I was sixteen last December," Jane replied.

"Well, that certainly does it!" replied Joe, rummaging through his desk for a packet of forms. He torn one off the pad and filled it out. Handing it to Jane he said, "Now, take your mom or dad wherever they need to go, get a lot of practice time. Then come back and I'll give you your permanent driver's license."

"Thank you, Chief Regoni," said Jane, proudly clutching the piece of paper.

"Yes, thanks, Joe. We'll see you soon," Marian said as they left the office and walked to the car. "Want to drive?" she asked Jane.

"Oh, no. I don't know how. You need to teach me on Bolinas Avenue where it's flat and straight and there aren't many cars."

"Okay," laughed Marian. "We'll take it in easy stages. First you can learn to shift for me when I tell you." They climbed into the car and Marian explained the gear shift. "Now," she said turning on the ignition, "when I say 'shift' you put it in gear."

Jane managed to locate the right slot and when Marian took her foot off the clutch the car moved slowly backwards. Jane was elated.

"Now, "said Marian, applying the brake. "Do you think you can find low gear? Remember where it is? Remember the box, it's through the middle and up to the left corner. Try it."

And so it went. Marian talked Jane through the various gears and eventually they reached home, lesson one completed. Within days she was sitting behind the wheel on Bolinas Avenue, doing everything.

One trip out with her father riding shotgun was enough for Jane! He wasn't as calm as Marian and had a tendency to suck in his breathe through his teeth or shout "Watch out!" which unnerved her completely, especially since there was seldom anything within range to cause his reaction. Jane declined to drive him anywhere but was happy to take her mother wherever she needed to go. Over the months she developed more and more confidence.

Once again the holidays were upon them. Marian chose to spend Thanksgiving in Ross, just the six of them. Billy was glad. The *San Rafael Independent* went overboard with advertising supplements on Thanksgiving and he could only do half his route at a time, and even then his bag was overloaded when he started out and it took longer to deliver because he couldn't throw the papers. He had to carry each up to the door!

There was no paper on Christmas. As they took off for the East Bay right after church with Marian driving, she remarked to Bill on their improved situation.

"Remember three years ago when we had to scrounge change to make the trip? And that big basket the church ladies brought? That was a terrible Christmas!"

"It wasn't too bad," Bill answered. "But you're right, things are better. You got the house back. I didn't think it was possible."

"I know you didn't. You certainly weren't any help. But I had to," Marian replied. "It was something I just had to do." She glanced briefly at his profile as if to gauge his mood. "Now I want us to work on plans to get all the children through college. I think it's important."

"Well, good luck," said Bill with a snort. "That's about impossible."

"Nothing's impossible," Marian snapped, irritated by his negative response. Marianne, sitting between them, looked up at the sharpness of her mother's voice. Marian sensed her daughter's concern and softened her tone. "Really," she said, "all things are possible with the help of God and a lot of work on our part. I read somewhere that nothing's impossible to a willing heart. And I certainly have that!" She laughed lightly and said, "Merry Christmas. We're doing fine and the kids will get to college." Bill stared straight ahead not seeing the smile Marian tossed his way.

The children in the back seat began to sing carols and kept it up until they reached Rill and Oscar's home in Piedmont. Bill refrained from asking them to stop.

A short visit there and they were off to Alameda to meet the entire clan at McRitchie's.

"Do you think Uncle Ernest will be Santa Claus again?" Suzanne asked, her voice tinged with a snicker.

"I hope not," said Jane. "He's so awful at it!"

"Corny!" agreed Billy.

Marian laughed. "Now you kids be kind if he does his act. It means a lot to him. He's been Santa for all the years since I've been in the family. I remember the first Christmas Jane saw him. She was only a year old and burst into tears."

"What else is new?" jeered Billy. "Jane always cries about everything! Always has."

"I do not!" said Jane indignantly.

"Do to!"

"Stop it, this minute!" said Marian. Billy silently mouthed the words at Jane who turned away, refusing to be bated into proving him right by crying in frustration. He had always been able to get under her skin and make her cry. But not this time. She was seventeen, too grown-up to be bothered by a thirteen year old brother!

Ernest did his "Ho ho, here comes Santa" routine. The children tried to be politely interested, aware of their mother's warning glance. Ronnie and Greig stood with the adults and didn't even pretend. After the presents, dinner was served. The parents, with Alec and Bertha, sat at the dining room table. Jane, Ronnie, Greig and Steele had a card table in the living room. The big cousins teased Jane unmercifully but this wasn't like her little brother. She enjoyed their attention, however they displayed it. The rest of the children were banished to the sun porch where they could misbehave without being seen.

On the way home they stopped at Mrs. Beasley's to climb the stairs to Susan's little room. In spite of the December weather, the twins and Billy immediately went out on the tiny porch. "Look, there's Uncle Tone's house. Are we going to see them, too?"

"Yes, we can run in for a minute," Marian answered not noticing Bill's pained expression. He just wanted to get home. It had already been a long day, starting with the eight o'clock service at St. John's. More visiting now didn't please him a bit. Yet, if Marian said they'd go, that's what they'd do. No use to argue.

A hour later, all visits ended in hugs and best wishes, they were on their way. This time Suzanne was in the front between her parents and the other three were soon asleep in the back. Bill was thankful they weren't singing carols.

Spring came and Marian had plans to build a fish pond in the uphill corner of the front yard and then replant the lawn down to the driveway. She marked the perimeters for the hole Bill and Billy would dig, brought home loads of rocks in the trunk of the car, along with sand and cement.

For several Sundays after church they changed into grubby clothes and went to work. Jane arranged the big granite rocks around the edge of the hole. Then it was lined with fine chicken wire and the concrete, mixed in the wheelbarrow, was poured. Smoothed into a deep oval, it was worked up over the base of the surrounding rocks and between them, to form a watertight edge. Marian and the twins planted iris bulbs behind the pond, and then shrubs between them and the hedge to eventually block the sight of the road. Finally all was finished, the cement cured, and the pond was filled with water from the hose.

They hadn't provided any way to drain water from the pond. Marian hoped the necessity would never arise. Fish were obtained to eat mosquito larvae, snails were added to take care of algae, and finally, tubs of water lilies were sunk to the bottom. Marian was pleased and satisfied. Now she turned her energies to replanting the old lawn. This took another two Sundays. The last day they rented a roller to smooth the prepared ground. All was in readiness.

One afternoon after Jane arrived home from school, she was using

Twins sitting by completed pond, 1936.

the shovel to dig around the edges of the future lawn to make a bed for perennials when a tall dark haired young man walked into the yard, carrying a brief case.

"Hello, ma'm," he said to Jane with a smile. "My name's Tom Regan. I'm selling subscriptions to *Sunset Magazine*. Are you familiar with it? May I show you a copy?"

Jane nodded and he pulled a magazine from the brief case. Handing it to Jane, he took the shovel from her hands.

"It's very nice," said Jane leafing through it, "but my mother's the one to order things and she's not home right now."

"Well, I can wait." Tom smiled again, white teeth flashing in a tanned face, bright blue eyes laughing. Jane thought he was the handsomest person she'd ever seen. So Irish looking! "Do you want this dug up?" he asked, turning a shovelful of dirt before Jane could answer.

"That's all right," Jane stammered. "Please don't bother. It's ready to be planted."

"No trouble," said Tom, continuing to dig. "This is fun. I don't have a chance to do much of this in the City." Jane stood by helplessly, mesmerized by his looks, his smile, unable to say, "Stop! No, don't dig any more." *Oh, my goodness, what'll Dad say? He spent so much time rolling this to get it ready!*

Finally she stepped closer and said, "No more, please." Tom looked at her in surprise.

"Why not?" he asked.

"Well," said Jane, "because it's already been rolled so we can seed it next weekend and my father won't be happy if you dig up any more of it."

"Oops," said Tom, sheepishly. "That's no way to make a good impression, is it?" He grabbed a rake to smooth out the humps he'd made, then tried to stamp them flat with his feet. "Think this'll work?" he asked with a laugh. "Maybe he won't notice."

"Yes, he will," said Jane. "But he'll be nice. So will my mother, only she probably won't take a magazine now." Jane was teasing and she laughed to see the disappointment on Tom's face. "Why don't you go away now and come back tomorrow afternoon. I'll try to fix it up. Okay?"

"Sure," replied Tommy, his smile breaking through. "I'll be back. I'm working over there." He pointed toward San Anselmo. "A couple of blocks away. I'll come back here when I'm through. I want to see you again, even if your mom doesn't take a subscription." He picked up the briefcase, slipped the magazine back in, said good-bye and walked out of the yard. Jane watched him go. He turned around to wave and smile.

Wow, thought Jane. *That's the best looking guy I've ever laid eyes on. And he wants to see me again! Oh, glory be!* She was still trying to smooth out and stamp down the results of Tommy's shovel work when Marian drove in. She thought the whole story was amusing and helped Jane hide the last traces of the unwanted digging before Bill arrived home.

Tommy came back the next afternoon. Marian subscribed to *Sunset* and invited him to dinner. Jane was in heaven. Bill was sober and charming. He shrugged off the faux pas of the unwanted digging with a laugh. Tom joined them the following weekend for the seeding of the lawn and returned for many weekends that spring, always helping with whatever garden chores Marian had lined up. Then he and Jane hiked up Baldy or went to a movie or just sat and talked, grinning at each other. He stayed until after dinner, catching the last train at 10 PM. That hour, after the family had gone to bed, was special. It was the first time Jane had been seriously kissed and she found it a heady experience.

At school, she went about in a daze. Luckily, she was in a place where she didn't need to use her mind too much; most serious work had already been completed and she could almost coast until graduation. Marian watched her young daughter and made time to talk to her about "setting limits" and "saving herself." This was the latest in a series of conversations they'd been having all Jane's life and it reassured them both.

Billy was having his moment of glory, too. He was the *Independent Journal's* Paper Boy of the Year, with his picture and an article in the publication. Most of his customers were pleased at his honor and tipped him lavishly when he next had to collect for the paper. This he loved. Having his picture in the paper was something, but to get money of his own, that was wonderful! He worked even harder to give good service for the newspaper and for the people on his route.

Billy, Independent Journal's
Paper Boy of the
Year, 1936.

Jane and Helena MacKall on the last
day of high school, June 1936.

Jane graduated in June, a memorable event marred by a misunderstanding with Tommy that ended their story-book first love and left her with a broken heart and no date for the Senior Prom. What happened, she never knew but the sun had gone from her life. For once her brother was right, everything made her cry!

Billy, too, graduated and would be ready for high school come September. The twins viewed these milestone ceremonies with envy. They had completed second grade and the many years stretching ahead of them before getting out of Ross School made that event seem improbable, graduating from high school impossible! Marianne continued to be a quick student but never did anything beyond the requirements. She felt that getting by easily and remaining first in the class was enough. There was no point, in her mind, to doing more of the same. Suzanne had a harder time but she kept up with Marianne, although it was a struggle.

The Ross Valley Payers had chosen an ambition work to present on August 20 and 21. This time they wouldn't make the mistake of having only one performance. *Peer Gynt*, based on the music of Edvard Grieg, the Norwegian composer, had a huge cast and a strong story line. Bill was in charge of the music which delighted him since Grieg was one of his favorite composers. Again Eric Pitman was chief electrician. He and Bill synchronized the lighting and the music in a wonderful way. For *Morning,* as the hidden loud speakers, placed high on the hill, began to play the plaintive melody, pink lights placed behind trees at the crest, came on. Then gradually, as the music soared, more and more light was added until the entire hill was as bright as day. The first time the cast saw and heard this, they broke into spontaneous applause. It was spectacular.

Gladys Kenny Hodgson's ballet classes were to do all the dancing. The twins and many other Gabby Girls' daughters were her pupils so were part of the production. Their big number was as trolls, imps and witches in the *Hall of the Mountain King*. Both daughters of Hortense Styles, who was doing makeup, were imps, along with the twins and Patty Hansen. Martha Lou Styles had a real part, too, as the Ugly Brat, which her parents felt was inspired casting. Hortense also played Peer Gynt's mother, Aase, with one big scene. As Aase lay dying and praying for her son's return, in a small open-faced cabin built into the side of the mountain, her anguished cry, "Oh, Lord my God, why doesn't he come? It's late and I grow exceedingly cold," brought shivers to the audience.

Marian helped with the costumes once again, with Hazel, Ruth, Serena, and the others, including Virginia Greer, Philip's wife. It was a strange sensation to sit across the table from Virginia, knowing what she did about her. Philip never talked against Virginia but the things he so appreciated in Marian gave her a hint of what was lacking in Virginia. Somehow she couldn't address Virginia directly but she included her, generally, in her remarks to the others.

After the second successful performance of *Peer Gynt*, which by all accounts was the best play they'd ever done topping even *Night Over Taos*, the previous year's stark drama, the cast and crew held another party. Marian was both anxious and excited at the thought of going. She and Philip had written often but had seen each other infrequently since that first party two years ago. It was a strange relationship. On one level, deep below the surface in a sort of magical fairy tale, it was intense and overwhelming. On the other level, their day-by-day existence, it was remote and almost negligible. Marian felt supported and comforted by the *idea* of Philip's love but most of the time that was it. Now they would meet again, face to face. Could they talk without betraying the submerged love that sustained them? Could they be casual and almost cool in their demeanor? That was what caused the anxiety in Marian's heart. Bill probably would be too involved to notice anything. He was not a suspicious person anyhow. But Virginia was irrationally jealous, often driven to violent outbursts about nothing, as they had all seen over the years. Marian knew that Mily and Kim could not make the briefest appearance at the party. That would be difficult, perhaps impossible. *No. Nothing's impossible* Marian told herself sternly. *Not even carrying off this meeting*

After depositing the children at the house, Marian and Bill arrived at the party which was already in full swing. Once again, as if on cue, Hortense materialized to drag Bill off to the piano. This was a routine by now and Bill was a willing hostage. He seemed to enjoy playing for this group of creative people. This time Christine Harrison was on hand to help lead him to the piano. Marian watched them go off and smiled at their exuberance. Then she stood just inside the door, head high, bright color on her cheeks and a quiver in her heart, her eyes scanning the crowded rooms. In a moment she spotted Philip's tall body, his brown head bent, deep in conversation with someone. She headed in the opposite direction to join a group discussing the wonders of the play.

During the whole long evening, Marian met Philip's glance only once and that with such a jolt she knew they dared not exchange even casual words. It was strained and difficult. Marian was relieved when Bill signaled that he wanted to go home.

"You seem awfully quiet tonight," he remarked as she started the car and maneuvered out of the driveway.

Marian was startled by his observation. It wasn't like him to notice. Hortense and Christine were certainly sharpening his awareness. "I'm tired," she replied.

"I don't doubt it. Me too," said Bill with a chuckle. "Good thing we didn't try to do the play for three nights. We'd all be dead!"

They drove the rest of the way in silence, each in their own thoughts.

Marian, her mind in a turmoil, wasn't surprised by the note from Philip she received two days later.

He wrote:

> **Mily, Do you feel the immensity of what we are struggling against? When we are in the same room, I feel the waves of our love beating back and forth between us, restless, full of longing. I should think everyone could sense it even when we don't look at each other or say a single word. I'm so conscious of your presence, I can hear what's in your heart as you must hear the thunder of my feelings shouting at**

you in the silence! I have to see you. Meet me in the parking lot at 3 PM
Wednesday.   Kim

Marian knew this was one meeting she couldn't ignore. It had to be faced. She spotted his car as she drove in and parked some distance away. He saw her and started toward her car at a run. Almost instantly, he opened the door and slipped in beside her. He reached for her hands and they clung to each other.

"Mily, Mily," he said. "Thank God you came." He smiled and leaned to kiss her softly. "We have to do something. Saturday night was hell."

"I know, my dearest Kim." Marian answered. She wasn't smiling. "But what we have to do isn't what you want."

"What do you mean?" Philip looked concerned. "You know what I want? We have to be together."

"And we can't be. Never." Marian pulled her hands away. She reached to gently touch his face. "What we must do is *nothing*. I can't bear another night like Saturday. We can't even be in the same room together ever again."

"No. NO! We need more, not less! I love you, Mily. These two years of writing to you, thinking about you, dreaming of you, hoping, planning!" Philip shook his head. "No, I can't live without you. I need to live *with* you."

"You promised in the beginning you wouldn't ask anything I couldn't give, you wouldn't upset our lives. Now you want to." Marian was close to tears. "I've been thinking and thinking since Saturday. Up until then, what we had, what we were doing, seemed all right. It was enough. Then all of a sudden Saturday you were across the room from me. I wanted to run and throw myself in your arms. But I knew that would be the end of the world. I could almost see the shocked looks on everyone's face, on Bill's and Virginia's, and all our friends, how they'd look. I knew that we were in an impossible situation. That we'd put ourselves there. And I knew we had to get out."

Now she was crying. Philip reached again for her hands. She clung to him as though she were drowning. "You see, Kim. Nothing stands still, nothing stays the same. Without even knowing it, we've moved a long way from where we started. We can't go back. And we can't go any farther."

"And you think we can just stop? Stop loving each other?"

"No. I'll always love you. I can't help that. But I can help what I do about it. I can control my actions." Marian sat up straighter, lifted her chin almost defiantly. "This has all been a beautiful dream. It's not real. To make it real would ruin too many lives, even our own. We couldn't build happiness on other people's tears."

"But what will we do? How can we stop thinking and feeling and sharing?" There was pain in Philip's voice. "How?"

"I don't know," Marian whispered. "I only know we could talk for hours and nothing would change my mind. You know I'm right. We haven't done anything *wrong* so far. Just our notes – oh, how I'll miss those notes! And talking, when we could. I'll miss that, too. Your words have been so important to me. And to tell you things! Anything, everything. But, Kim, you know we can't stay where we are. And we can't go forward. I won't go forward. Saturday at the party, I was scared. I couldn't even look at you. I didn't trust myself."

"Oh, Mily!" There was agony in his voice. He drew her into his arms and pressed her head to his shoulder. "Oh, Mily," he whispered. "I may die."

"No. You won't," said Marian. "Forget about us as a couple. Later, remember us as we've been. When you can without it hurting." Their embrace was desperate. "Go now." She was sobbing. "Go, quickly."

"I can't say good-bye." He raised her face and gently kissed her lips, tasting the salt of her tears. Marian pulled herself back, out of his arms, away from his touch.

"Good-by, Kim," she said with a catch in her voice. Echoing in her head she heard the words, *When I grow to old to dream, this kiss will live in my heart.* "Kiss me, my sweet, and then let us part," she whispered, hardly realizing she was quoting.

"Good-bye, Mily, my love." Philip opened the door and slipped out. Marian dropped her head to the steering wheel and sobbed. It was over. He was gone.

No one noticed that she was quieter than usual that evening. Or that there was less spark in her voice in the days that followed. With tremendous effort she refused to let herself think about Philip or their parting. What was she losing anyhow? Just the thought of him, just the knowledge of his sustaining love for her, just a dream. Nothing in her daily life was changed in any way. So she busied herself getting the children's clothes ready for the opening of school. She concentrated all her energies on caring for them, on preparing meals, seeing friends, planning the immediate future. She listened to their voices, answered their questions, smiled and laughed.

In time it became second nature and when she happened to read the entries in the red book, it was like reading beloved well-remembered fiction. Marian moved on.

Billy was now the one who raced out of the house to run the length of Bolinas Avenue to catch *The Special* to Tamalpais High School every morning. Jane entered Marin Junior College in Kentfield. She walked home the two miles each afternoon but in the mornings she was lucky enough to be part of a car pool. Jack Beine, a tall young sophomore, picked up a neighbor of Jane's and she asked for Jane to be included. This worked out well and lasted most of the years she attended Marin Junior College.

The twins were now third graders and in school until three-thirty each afternoon. This gave Marian so much time she looked around for new things to occupy her energy. Fund raising seemed to be her forte. Both the American Red Cross and the Marin Musical Chest used her talents and each year she organized her friends, starting with Hazel Pitman and Ruth Hansen, into efficient teams and raised more and more money.

Marian kept the family busy, too. One evening sitting at the dinner table she remarked to Bill, "Look at that! I never really noticed how stupid that is, but it certainly is."

"What? What's stupid?" Bill turned to look behind him where she was staring.

"The little wall that sticks out on both sides between this room and the living room, where the opening is. It's so we could put double French doors in between the two rooms but that would be even stupider. See?"

Everyone was looking at the opening.

"It would be much better if the opening went all the way to the outside wall on that side," she pointed, "and as far as the radiator over there." She nodded toward the other wall. "Wouldn't it?" she asked Bill.

"What do you want me to do? Knock it down?" Bill had a touch of sarcasm in his tone. "The whole ceiling will collapse!"

"No, it's not a bearing wall. And besides you'd only take the walls out up to the top of the opening, just to make the opening wider, about two feet on each side." Marian could already see it in her mind. "It wouldn't be hard to do."

Bill left his place at the table and went to the back porch, returning in a minute with a hammer and a chisel. To Marian's astonishment, he said, "Here goes!"

"I want to help," said Billy jumping to his father's side.

"Go get another hammer," Bill said, putting the chisel at the edge of the facing and whacking it. A few hard blows and the nails holding the facing made a screeching noise. Billy brought a second hammer, another chisel and worked below his father. Soon the first board was loose. They pried it off and put it, exposed nails down, on the living room floor.

"Why don't you your finish dinner before you do any more?" Marian suggested.

"Nope," he answered. "We're not going to lollygag around eating when there's a project to be done." Bill moved to the other side of the opening and attacked that board. Marian couldn't tell if he was being sarcastic to make her uncomfortable or had undergone a complete character change in the last few weeks! She decided it didn't matter: The job was underway. Removing the facings and the moldings was the easy part, quickly accomplished before Marian and the girls finished dinner and removed the plates from the table.

"Whoa!" said Marian. "Take a break. We have to get organized here." Bill and Billy looked at her. "Those boards will all be used again so the old nails should be removed. Billy, you can do that. Then they should be stacked outside where they won't be in the way. The next step will be a messy one. We have to chop the plaster and lathe off, back to where we want the opening to start. We need to move everything and cover it up, roll up the rugs, shove the table back. . ."

"Think I will finish dinner and have a cup of coffee," said Bill, putting down the hammer and sitting at his place. Jane went to the kitchen and returned with dessert and coffee. She brought dessert for Billy, too, and a glass of milk.

"Thank you, Bill, for starting like that," said Marian. "You surprised me! We can really tackle it tomorrow."

The job took longer to finish than Marian hoped. At times it looked like an impossible task. Young Billy proved himself more than a carpenter. He had a knack for improvisational design which, in an undertaking like this, proved invaluable. Marian was delighted to have such a talented capable worker on her team. She directed him well! Ten years later he removed the front door wall and made the porch part of the living room. Twenty years later, between marriages, he remodeled the garage into a bachelor pad. Other times, he constructed closets, paneled the fireplace wall, and with his engineer buddies, moved the Arcola heater and its attic storage tank to an out-of-way corner in the kitchen. He had strength and vision, and the ability, to exceed his mother's plans. She couldn't have asked for more. Neither could Bill! He was off the hook for big jobs now that Billy took over.

They were still working on enlarging the opening one chilly Saturday when Bill decided to quit early and take a hot bath. Marian was out winter-proofing the garden for the freezing weather. On the fishpond she discovered a thick covering of ice. *Bill will never believe this,* she thought. *I better take a piece in and show him how thick it is.* It was difficult to break through the ice but she finally had a large sheet in her hands. She rushed in the house, clutching her treasure. She found Bill in the bathroom, sitting in a steamy tub of water.

"Look," she said, gleefully, "Ice!" As Bill turned toward her, she, with a diabolic grin, slapped the sheet of ice against his back. For a stunned moment, he didn't feel it. Then he reacted with alacrity, leaping from the tub, and lunging toward her. Marian retreated, laughing.

"Stop, Bill! You're naked! Don't come out here, remember the children," she said, running down the hall. He kept on chasing her but she had a good lead.

"You started this," he said. "I'll get you!"

Marian bolted out the front door into the freezing air of the winter day. She stopped and turned to face him, still laughing. "Come on! Dare you! Come get me!"

Bill looked down at his nakedness. Already the frigid air was chilling him more than the ice down his back had. "You win, for now. But just you wait." He sprinted back to the bathroom, stepped into the tub, turned on the faucet to run more hot water, and finally, sank happily into the welcome warmth. *Should put a lock on this door. I can't trust that woman!* He was smiling.

Christmas came. The job was finished and the rooms seemed much more spacious with an extra four feet added to the opening between them. Marian decided to have two trees this year, small ones, placed on little tables, flanking the fireplace. Billy was in charge, for the first time, of stringing the lights, all blue and green. Then the girls hung the large round blue or green ornaments. Finally, Bill, the only one with enough patience, took charge of the tinsel which he placed, one careful strand at a time. The results, although a break with tradition, pleased everyone.

After the holidays, for some reason the happy mood was shattered. Bill started coming home late, obviously stopping for a few drinks on the way. Marian's face settled into strained hard lines, the children became edgy. One evening, just before dinner, Marian said, "This is ridiculous! Jane, take the car and go to Meager's. See if your father's there."

Jane looked stricken. She hated driving down to San Anselmo's bar, located across the street from the train station, a convenient stopping place for the commuting men. Walking in, eyes searching for her father, gave her a pain in the pit of her stomach.

"Do I have to?" she asked.

"Of course! It'll only take a minute. Then we can all eat dinner."

Jane drove the old Chevrolet and parked right in front of Meager's. Taking a deep breathe, she pushed the door open and stepped in. He was sitting at the far end of the bar, hatless as always, deep in earnest conversation with another man. Looking up, he noticed her as she made her way toward him.

"Well, look. Here's my little girl!" He reached to put his arm around her shoulders. She stiffened. "Fellas, this is my Janie-girl!" The men all nodded to her.

"Come on, Dad," she said. "Dinner's ready."

"Dinner's ready, guys," he said. "I gotta go."

He finished his drink and followed her as she walked, self-consciously, out of the building to the car. They were silent on the short drive. It really did little good to bring him home. He walked through the living room and dining room without a word, and headed, first to the bathroom and then to bed. They heard the doors close.

"Well," said Marian. "At least we know where he is. Thank you, Jane. Now let's eat. We're late."

No one could think of anything to say. The usual pall had settled over them, the one that came like a silent fog to engulf them whenever Bill was drinking. Jane caught Marian's eye and smiled tentatively. Marian smiled back.

"Thank you again. I know you hate to do that, but it does help. Once he's home, I can relax. How was school today?" she asked, switching from the distasteful subject of Bill's drinking.

"Fine," Jane replied. "I like working on the newspaper. Mr. Moyer is a neat teacher. And for Spanish, did I tell you? Bill Gwinn is the teacher!"

"Not Bill Gwinn from the Ross Valley Players?"

"Same one! He's a real relaxed teacher, as you would imagine. At least to me. When I forget the Spanish and use a French word instead, he gives me half credit if my French's right!" Jane laughed and the mood lightened. The other children chimed in with their stories, vying for their mother's attention. For a moment they forgot the man sleeping it off in the bedroom down the hall.

And then, brief weeks later, the storm was over. Bill was back on track and, with typically forgiving memories, they ignored the bad times.

The Chevrolet they were driving dated back to 1927, the summer before the twins were born. It had seen better days and had endured many traumas. While they were at Estates Drive, Bill and a supposedly knowledgeable friend had overhauled the transmission. When it was all back together, there was a small hitch. Low gear and reverse had somehow switched positions. Bill explained it to Marian. "It won't be so bad. You'll just have to remember it's different."

"Don't be ridiculous," she snapped. "You and Bud will just have to redo it and get it right. There's no way I'm going to try to remember anything that stupid. Fix it." It took time but the job was finally done correctly.

Then they decided to paint the car. Bill suggested brown and Marian agreed. He purchased a gallon of house paint in a nice rich brown shade. Unfortunately, it only looked nice in the can. When it dried on the car's metal body, it had a definite lavender tinge, almost purple in some lights.

"What do you think?" Bill asked as they stood staring at it.

"Well, it's not quite as bad as a pink elephant," Marian answered. "I don't think it's worth doing over. Let's just call her 'Petunia.' Okay?" Bill was relieved not to have to repaint the car.

"Fine with me. Petunia it is."

A year later, this was the car that careened down the side of the hill in Woodacre without sustaining mortal injuries, but cosmetically she was battered. During the next few years, there was no money to put into luxuries such as a new automobile. Now the time had come. They could afford it and Petunia was definitely showing her age. Before she became terminal and dropped her transmission on the highway, Bill and Marian decided to turn her in on something younger.

Looking at used cars of a more recent vintage made them nervous. Neither knew enough about automobiles to make a wise decision. Most new cars were out of their league.

Then Bill fell in love.

Willys-Overland had reorganized the year before and renewed production of low priced motorcars. Sitting in the showroom corner was a new Willys. It stopped Bill in his tracks.

"Look at this, Marian!" He sounded excited.

"What is it? Looks like a beetle!" said Marian.

"It's a new Willys, brand new. New design, new everything."

Small, with a pointed nose and pointed tail, shiny black with no chrome, it did, indeed, resemble a bug.

Bill opened the door. "Come on. Get in the other side."

Marian walked around and opened that door. Ducking, she slid into the passenger seat.

"I feel like I'm sitting on the ground," she complained.

"Smell it. That new car smell. We haven't smelled anything like that for decades!" Marian looked at him. He was really excited about this strange unattractive little car! *Well, maybe,* she thought. *I'll keep an open mind.* Soon a salesman appeared, and sensing Bill's interest, produced facts and figures.

"What will you give us on trade-in for our old car?" Marian asked.

"What is it?"

"A 1927 Chevy. Good shape," she answered, crossing her fingers to cover her blatant exaggeration.

The salesman looked pained. "We'll do the best we can," he assured her. "Better than most."

Afterwards, Marian couldn't understand what had possessed her to go along with Bill on such an important purchase. Her initial antipathy toward the ugly little car grew, with knowledge, into downright hatred. And she was stuck with it! The Willys attracted attention wherever they drove. No vehicle like it had ever before been seen on the road. Marian felt conspicuous and foolish, not at all her normal mode, being associated with it. Bill and Jane didn't share her repugnance. They loved the Beetle and drove it proudly, enjoying the attention it brought.

As May 1937 drew toward Memorial Day, excitement over the completion of the Golden Gate Bridge reached fever pitch. The authorities planned to open the span to foot traffic the day before automobiles would be allowed to cross. Honoring California's Spanish heritage, all were encouraged to dress in appropriate Spanish attire. Nothing like this had been experienced before. Even the opening of the TransBay Bridge the previous year, linking the East Bay and San Francisco, had not been as wildly emotional. Spanning the Golden Gate, long thought impossible was actually coming to pass and the public went crazy..

Jane made plans with Helena MacKall, Aloha Jones, Helena's sister, Betty, and others from junior college, to walk across the span the morning the barriers fell. Billy was going with Rick Lloyd and Davey Pitman. When Marian broached the subject to Bill, he was, as usual, against going.

"It'll be a madhouse, no place to park. Too far to walk. The weather's lousy. No, I'll wait until all this craziness is over and then drive in comfort. When I have to. Next month, maybe. Next year!"

"Bill, you're impossible!" said Marian with a laugh. "I'm glad I don't have to depend on you to take me places. I'd never get out of the front yard. Thetwins and I'll go and see what happens."

Jane was up and out of the house at dawn May 27, dressed in a full turquoise skirt and bolero with a black satin shirt and a wide brimmed black caballero hat. She met Aloha, who was also dressed with a Spanish flavor, on the train to Corte Madera. There they got off and walked up the hill to Helena's. Her parents drove them to Sausalito where they pushed into a crowded jitney that chugged them up to the Bridge. Private cars were barred from the entire area that day. Bill was right: It was a madhouse. Everyone was excited, a festive circus air prevailed. This was a long-awaited day!

Jane and Betty MacKall, mid-span on Golden Gate Bridge, opening day, May 1937.

Helena, Aloha and Jane during festivities week before walk across Golden Gate Bridge, May 1937.

Fog was swirling overhead, almost obscuring the tops of the towers, making the curving cables mysterious in the mist. Jane found it impossible to simply walk down the middle of the bridge. She had to push her way to the sidewalk on the right to look down some 220 feet to the swirling blue-green water foaming below and out the Golden Gate to the open ocean. Then she raced to the other side again to stare straight down to the water far below, before raising her eyes to look toward the Oakland and Berkeley hills, the magical skyline of San Francisco. These were all views she'd seen from the deck of many ferry boats, but how different from this height!

At mid-span, Helena took pictures of them. They walked, sometimes arm-in-arm six abreast, all the way to the toll plaza before reversing direction. The sun was shining brilliantly by the time they arrived back on the Marin side, windblown but feeling truly a part of a memorable day, a historic event. Later they read that more than 200,000 individuals crossed the Bridge, between 6 AM and 6 PM that day, and they were, proudly, in that number.

School was out for summer vacation leaving the Rattray children with wonderful lazy time on their hands, long sunny days to fill. Marian

Jane with Tippy, Ross, 1937.

helped them with the latter. She always had projects they could undertake. The trick, they had learned, was to declare plans early and request permission to carry them out. In this spirit, Jane announced one evening, "I'd like to go visit Granny. I haven't seen her since Christmas. That's too long."

"Sounds good," said Marian. "How do you plan to do this?"

"Well," Jane answered, "I want to stay more than one day so I thought I'd call Ruth Rowland. She always has room and I'd like to visit her, too. Maybe stay two or three days if she's not busy. And see Granny part of every day. I'll go by train and ferry boat, like I used to from Woodacre to Piedmont. Won't be anywhere near as long a trip, just from Ross to Alameda! How's that sound?"

"Fine. Call Ruth. Set it up."

So Jane went to spend three days in Alameda. The first afternoon she climbed the stairs to her grandmother's room and knocked on the door.

"Come in," called a weak voice. Jane entered and found Susan sitting in a big chair, wrapped in a quilt, looking much smaller and more frail than she had at Christmas. Jane bent to embrace her. "Mrs. Beasley told you I was coming? I called her this morning. She said she'd come right upstairs and let you know." Jane sat in a straight backed chair opposite her grandmother and reached for her hand. "How are you?" she asked with a smile.

It had long been a family saying, "Don't ask Susan Murdock how she's feeling unless you really want to know. She'll give you a detailed medical report!" When she answered Jane's query with a soft, "All right, I guess," Jane looked at her in surprise.

"What's that mean?"

"I don't know. I don't know how I feel." She smiled at her granddaughter. "It's nice of you to come see me. I was hoping you would. I've been remembering the months you stayed with me in the apartment. Our nightly Ovaltine, the talks. We had fun, didn't we? How long ago was that? Ten years?"

"Not quite. Only seven."

"You've grown up. You're a young lady now. You were just a little girl then. And really *little* back when Billy was born. Remember the Creme of Wheat?" Susan looked at Jane. "Forgive me?"

"There's nothing to forgive. I was impossible, as I remember it. I'm sorry," Jane answered. "Do *you* forgive *me*?"

Susan smiled at her. "Oh, pshaw, of course! Now tell me what you've been doing. How's college going?"

Jane began to share the highlights of the past semester, answering Susan's questions, giving her the details she wanted. When she ran out of things to say she asked, "Do you want me to read something to you?"

"That would be nice. But I think I'd like to get into bed first, if you'll help me. And to the bathroom, too?" As Susan struggled to get out of the chair, Jane's heart sank. Her beloved Granny was old! When did this happen? In spite of her heart condition, she'd always been spry and quick. Now Jane had to almost lift her and support her to the little bathroom. Once Susan was in bed, leaning back on the pillows with the blankets pulled up to her chin, and the quilt spread over her, Jane dragged the chair close and chose a book from the table.

"Start anywhere," Susan said. "I'm rereading books I love. I don't have time to start new ones. It's much too hard to concentrate on anything I don't know! These are all old friends." She waved toward the books.

Jane was glad it wasn't one of Shakespeare's volumes lying at hand. They were impossible to read with the intonation Susan felt was proper. Jane hadn't read for more than five minutes when she realized that Susan was asleep, tiny snores punctuating her breathing. Jane closed the book, adjusted the pillows, kissed the wrinkled cheek and said, softly, "Sleep well. I'll be back in the morning."

On the way out she sought Mrs. Beasley. "My grandmother doesn't seem well. Do you take her meals to her room now?"

"Yes, I've been doing that for several weeks. It's too much for her to make the stairs. I'll take special care tonight to see that she's comfortable."

"Thank you. I'll be back in the morning." Jane walked the few blocks back to Ruth's house in the apricot twilight.

There was no answer to her knock in the morning. Jane opened the door and stepped in. Susan was lying still in the bed. Her hair had been brushed and swept into a wispy gray knot on the top of her head. Her leathery face looked strangely naked with neither glasses nor teeth to give it the familiar contours.

Jane moved closer and took one of the veined hands in her own. It was hot. She touched Susan's brow. It, too, was warmer than normal. She listened to the breathing and heard gurgles deep inside. Something was wrong!

"Granny?" she said, "Granny, can you hear me?" There was no response, not even the flicker of an eyelid. *She looks like an ancient Indian,* Jane thought. *I never realized her nose was like a beak. Oh, Granny, Granny, where are you?*

Jane went down the dark stairway to find Mrs. Beasley.

"My grandmother is really sick, I'm afraid," Jane said. "May I phone my Aunt Bess? She lives just across the street and she'll know what to do."

Bess arrived within minutes and found Jane sitting beside the bed holding Susan's hand.

"She's dying, Aunt Bess," whispered Jane with tears in her eyes. She had never seen death close at hand before, but she recognized it immediately, an unmistakable presence.

"I'm afraid you're right, Janie," said Bess as she touched Susan's brow, took her pulse and leaned to listen to the noisy, irregular breathing. "I'll go call the doctor and your mother. Can you stay with her?"

"Of course."

When Bess came back into the room, Jane stepped out to the little porch. She sank down on the wicker chair, gulping in deep draughts of the clean summer air. *She doesn't look like my grandmother anymore, and it's so hard for her to breathe. Does it hurt? How long will it take, I wonder? I'll miss her so much!* Jane felt tears on her face and reached to brush them away. She sat there for a long time, hearing Bess moving about in the room. Finally, there was a soft knock and the doctor's voice, greeting Bess. Jane moved to stand in the doorway to watch his examination. It was brief.

"You're right, Bess," he said. "Pneumonia. I'd say sometime tonight, or tomorrow, for sure. There's nothing we can do. Do you want me to send someone to be with her?"

"Oh, no," answered Bess. "Marian's on her way. Then we'll spell each other."

"Call me when she's gone and I'll come take care of everything." His voice was gentle and concerned. "She's not feeling any pain." He smiled and nodded toward Jane who was leaning in the doorway, listening. "Your grandmother was a fine woman."

Then he was gone. Bess dropped into the big chair. Jane sat near her. "Do you want to leave, Janie? You don't need to stay. There's nothing you can do."

"No, I'll wait till mother gets here." The only sound in the room was the labored breathing and the ticking of a clock. Jane couldn't stand it and went back to the porch where at least she could hear outdoor sounds.

Marian arrived an hour later. Bess brought her up to date, Jane told her about yesterday afternoon, about this morning. Then Marian watched as Jane walked over to the bed. She touched her grandmother's hands, her face. "Gooif I leave now?" Jane asked her mother.

"Of course, dear," Marian answered. "I'll phone you. I won't be home tonight. Take care of things."

"I will." With a tearful hug for her mother and her aunt, and another glance at the gaunt still figure in the bed, Jane left.

Susan clung to life for twenty six long hours, the heart she had worried about most of her life beating valiantly until her congested lungs deprived it of oxygen. The funeral was held at the Chapel of the Chimes that Saturday. Marian felt it was important for Jane to attend and insisted that she drive over with her.

Afterwards Jane said to her mother, "I'm glad you made me come. Granny looks so peaceful and pretty, with her hair all fluffed and her glasses on, and her cheeks rosy and smooth. How do they do that? She looks like she just fell asleep and is having a lovely dream!"

"I thought it would be good for you to see her this way. I was right, wasn't I?"

"Yes. I kept remembering the way she looked when I said good-bye. Like an Indian chief, not Granny. Now I have this."

They smiled at each other and went to join the rest of the family. Rill was weeping hysterically and being comforted by Oscar and Otis. Tone and Bess were in quiet conservation with the minister and motioned to Marian and Jane to join them. After a time of mingling and accepting condolences, Marian steered Jane out to the car and they drove back to Marin.

Life went on as it always does. Marian turned her thoughts to Jane's continuing education. She had one more year at junior college and would then transfer to the University of California. The next step, Marian knew, was to contact her cousin, Margaret Murdock, who was education credentials counselor at UC. Margaret had never married and took an active interest in the educations of her nephews, nieces, and her cousins' children, such as Jane. She had told Marian to get in touch with her before Jane's sophomore year at Marin.

Margaret lived with the Murdocks at Eighteen-Ought-Nine all the years she and Marian were in college, from 1913 until she graduated in 1918. Six months younger than Marian, Margaret was more like a sister than Rill had ever been. She was tiny, with long auburn hair, an infectious grin, and great musical ability. When Bill entered the scene, Margaret told Marian it was a crime to waste him on someone so totally devoid of talent and appreciation of music. Marian countered by saying with a laugh, "Well, you take him. You'll play lovely duets together!" Margaret paled at the thought. Although a popular friend to all the young men who made up their Sunday soirées, she refused any romantic overtures. In the beginning, Marian, twice, arranged double dates for Margaret, who tried to accommodate her cousin but instead became physically ill and had to beg off. Marian gave up and accepted Margaret's fear of men as a part of her personality that couldn't be changed. When Marian transferred to Mills College in her senior year, Margaret stayed at Cal and graduated in 1918 with a degree in economics. Upon graduation, she took a position at the university in the credentials department, where she stayed, moving up in authority through the years.

In the early 1920s, Margaret also became a carillonneur, ringing the chimes in the Campanile. Her frail looks were deceiving. She pounded the huge wooden levers of Sather Tower's bells, some weighing more than 4000 counterbalanced pounds, with flair and form. She played several concerts a week at 7:50 AM and at noon, for over sixty years! This was something that thrilled Jane every time she heard the peeling bells during her time at the University. She always wanted to stop a fellow student hurrying by and say, "That's my mother's cousin, playing the chimes. Isn't she wonderful? And she's putting me through college!"

A month after Susan's death, Marian and Jane went to the campus to meet Margaret for lunch at the Women's Faculty Club. Over dessert, Margaret cleared her throat and said. "Well, now, you're nearly ready, one more year there, and your grades are adequate." She smiled at Jane over the word "adequate" and continued. " I've put away enough to provide you with two years of study here. It will cover tuition, books, housing and a little bit of spending money. What do you think?"

Both Marian and Jane were speechless. Marian had expected help with the paperwork, maybe a cutting of red-tape, but such largesse was overwhelming.

"I think," she said, recovering her voice, "that you are generous to a fault!"

Margaret grinned. "It seems only fair. Jane is a favorite of mine. She's earned it. I have no children of my own so I've put my sisters' children through college. Now it's your turn."

"Thank you, Cousin Margaret," stammered Jane. "Thank you so much." Jane was overwhelmed by the generous offer.

When vacation ended, Jane went back for her last year at Marin Junior College with renewed enthusiasm an high hopes. She became editor of the school paper, *The Mariner*, took design and watercolor classes, and studied diligently on all her required courses hoping her grades this year would be more than "adequate" to justify Margaret's support. Her social life was centered in a group of girls, Helena and Aloha from high school, some newcomers. They dated casually, none had a steady boy friend, and the "gang" was still the social unit. Marian watched her daughter, hoping she'd find someone to erase the pain of Tommy's sudden departure over a year earlier but knowing how difficult that would be.

Family Gathering in Ross, Easter, from left: Steele McRitchie, Bill, Bella McRitchie, Suzanne, Marian, Marianne with Tippy, and Ernest McRitchie, 1937.

On Easter, Jane invited Aloha with a friend, Keith Askew, and Bruce Barker, a boy she had worked with on the paper. It was a big step for her, bringing male outsiders to a family gathering. She was glad that only the McRitchies, Bella and Ernest with Steele, joined them that year. Steele wasn't as much of a tease as Ronnie or Greig. He didn't rib or embarrass her as the other two would have taken delight in doing!

Jane's graduation took place on the expansive lawn of the college in the middle of May 1938, at a Saturday afternoon ceremony. It was a lovely warm day with Mount Tamalpais, crowned in fluffy white clouds, providing the backdrop. Bertha and Alec came over from San Francisco, Rill and

Jane and friends on side lawn, 1938. Garage in corner remodeled into the cottage years later.

Oscar drove from Piedmont, Ernest and Bella from Alameda. The graduation of their oldest niece was quite an occasion and all the family gathered at the Glenwood Avenue house for festivities afterwards.

"Well, Bill," Marian said when everyone had gone. "Jane is halfway there. Then it'll be one down and three to go."

"Good luck," replied Bill. This time he didn't snort as he had when she first broached the subject of four college educations. "You and your schemes!" he said with a laugh. "I bet you make it!" Marian felt this was high praise and wholehearted support considering the ice water he usually dumped on her plans. She was pleased.

Marianne and Suzanne viewed Jane as a creature from another world. To their young eyes, her university status raised her to unattainable heights. They were ten years old that summer, tall and skinny as Jane had been at their age, but prettier and more energetic. Marian was still buying matching clothes for them. It never dawned on her they might rather be seen as separate individuals.

Shopping excursions were totally traumatic. Both hated the clothes their mother picked for them to try on. Marianne, especially, managed to slouch and shoot out her arms so nothing fit. Marian, becoming frustrated, would pull the dress at the shoulders, smooth it across the back while Marianne's subtle shifts threw it out of kilter again. Lower lip sticking out farther and farther, a scowl between her brows, Marianne drooped and sulked until her mother was reduced almost to tears. Suzanne was more passive but just as uncooperative. Finally several of the less objectionable outfits would be purchased to no one's satisfaction. "But you have to have something to wear! And this looks really *nice* on you," Marian, the appeaser, would say. "Now let's go get a milk-shake. Okay?"

Grudgingly, the twins accompanied her to the drive-in and sulkily sipped their shakes, slurping the bottom of the glass with an eye on their mother to check her annoyance level. Marian gave up on small talk and prayed for patience. *This too shall pass!* she consoled herself. *And, hopefully, some day they'll take their daughters shopping and get the same frustrating treatment.* A bubble of glee burst forth at the thought and she smiled, much to the twins confusion.

The Youth Group at St. John's scheduled a summer conference at Asilomar near Monterey, in mid-July. Jane was given permission by Marian and Bill to sign up, and drove down with a carload from the church. The conference center was rustic with a large meeting hall, dining room, and kitchen under the windblown cypress and pine trees. Small wooden cabins were scattered in an informal semicircle among the sand dunes. The Pacific Ocean was within sight, sound, and walking distance. Jane loved it.

Days were spent in large meetings with speakers discussing the role of the church in the lives of teenagers. Then they broke into small groups, where they individually expressed their feelings about the general gatherings. Jane, of course, was silent. At every spare moment she slipped down to the edge of the ocean. Early evenings she walked along the beach with bright new ideas racing through her head. Back in her cabin, she wrote her thoughts into a poem. This was her gift to the conference. Home again, with shy pride, she gave a copy to Marian.

"Why, this is good," Marian said. "I'm going to copy it in my little book with the love poems you wrote a couple of years ago." Marian looked at the beginning words again. *Tonight I walked long hours on the firm hard beach of sand. The wind with a sharp salt sting touched my face, And God reached out to take my hand . . .* "I like it. I've had those same feelings walking by the ocean. But I've never been able to put my feelings into words. Thank you, Jane, I'll treasure this."

The next week Marian received a letter from Pauline DuBois asking permission to park their motor home in the front yard for awhile.

"Polly is so vague," Marian complained to Bill. "I didn't even know they had a motor home. She asks if she can come but there's no return address. I couldn't say 'No' if I wanted to. I thought they were still at Fort Baker. Maybe they are. But then, why not phone? And who is 'we'? The whole family – Pauline, Buddy and the three boys – or some combination, and if so, which ? How long is 'awhile' and when is 'soon' ? There's no date on the letter and I can't make out the postmark, not even where it's from so I don't know how long it will take to get here. If it's

Sausalito, they could be any minute. Damn!"

"Take it easy," said Bill with a laugh. "That's Polly! What difference does it make? They'll get here when they get here and there'll be whoever there is!"

"But I want to make plans!"

"Relax. She'd just upset any plans you made."

"I guess you're right. But I like to *know* what's coming and when so I can have things ready."

They didn't have long to wait. That afternoon a sleek motor home pulled into the yard. Pauline was driving with her son Bill beside her. After exchanging greetings, Marian said, "Why don't you back in, as far over by the lawn as you can. Then we can get our car past you."

Son Bill climbed out to direct her. Pauline backed up the hill. Then she drove down until the rear of the motor home was opposite the opening of the driveway. Following signals from Bill, she expertly swung the vehicle into place just inches from the edge of the lawn.

"Now, come in, come in," Marian said. "Tell us all about every-

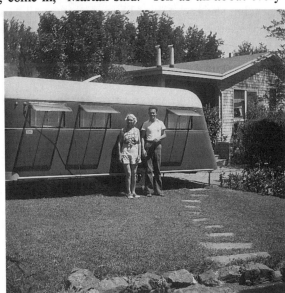

Pauline DuBois and son, Bill, visit Ross, Summer 1938

thing. Your note didn't say much and we just got it!"

Pauline took a deep breath. "Well, here we are! Bill and I are on our way to meet Buddy and the younger boys sometime next month. We just bought this contraption from a family who left for extended duty overseas. Got a great price! Isn't it handsome? Wait till you see the inside. It's amazing. Has everything and so compact you won't believe it. We'll be stationed back east for the next four years. Bill and Ted will finish college while we're there. Then, guess what? Buddy will have his thirty years in. He's going to retire. Can you believe that? I can't. Something will happen to spoil it. But we're making plans already. We'll buy a place in Laguna Beach and raise vegetables and dahlias in the back yard! Can you see Buddy puttering about in grubby clothes getting his hands dirty?" Polly laughed. "It's his idea. Pictures himself as a gentleman farmer, I think. You'll have to come down every summer and stay with us. Won't that be fun! Without the children. You won't have to bring the children, will you? Not in four years. I'm planning *not* to have room for children ever again." Pauline stopped for breath and smiled at Marian. "Hello, Marnie," she said. "We're here!"

Marian senses were reeling from this breathless monologue. She didn't know which question to answer first, which subject to seek clarification on. Go with her heart, *How s Buddy?* Be practical, *How long are you and Bill staying?* Be oblique, *What's the next duty station?* Start a history lesson, *Tell me about Laguna Beach.* Or ignore the entire confrabulation and start her own! One never knew with Pauline. And her mode of speech was deceiving. As Bill had remarked, "Polly may sound like an addle-pated nitwit, but she's got a mind like a steel trap. All those rushing words are just a smoke screen." *Covering what?* Marian asked herself now as she smiled at her friend.

"Well, Polly, it's good to see you. So how have these twenty-six years of military life been?"

"You don't want to know. Or do you?" Pauline was obviously deciding which tact to take on this large subject or whether to answer the question at all. "It's been wonderful. We lived all over the place. But one army base is the same as another, except for the weather, so it doesn't matter. I've played a million hands of bridge. I'm really a good player, champion caliber, actually. Do you play? Probably not, don't have time with all the children you have around underfoot. And no help! I've enjoyed having help. I hate housework. Don't you?" Marian nodded as Polly breezed on. "The boys are fine, I think. Buddy's very stern with them. He's always treated them like soldiers so I've been too soft. Poor kids! Bill's a strange one, I guess partly because he got his face smashed in that accident in DC when he was five. Horrible to confront life almost without a nose because the doctors couldn't do any reconstructive surgery until you stopped growing. And changing schools all the time. Having to explain himself all over again. He's made up some wild tales, believe me! He looks all right now, don't you think? Ted is so handsome. Even beats his father for looks. Actually he looks like me. I'd have been a great looking man. It's the planes of the face, androgynous. Looks good on both of us but basically masculine,

I've always thought." *Where is she going with this?* Marian wondered. *Should I break in or just let her go. She'll get to the end sometime!*

Pauline smiled. "It's been a been a good life and it's not over yet. Buddy's a difficult man to live with. Totally self-centered. But then, so am I!" She laughed. "We deserve each other. We'd have made anyone else miserable. He never talks. But then, I never stop!" She laughed again. "Enough. How are you?"

"Fine," answered Marian. "How long are you staying? We've rented a house on the Russian River at Summer Home Park and will be going up in ten days for a fortnight."

"That's perfect! I'd like to stay here a week. Okay?"

"Of course," Marian replied. "Now let's make plans!"

The time sped by in a flurry of activities. Young Bill DuBois, silent as a shadow, wandered in and out of the house, keeping himself occupied. He hiked the hills and toured the garden. Later, when cornered, he told Jane of his journeys. Marian kept Pauline busy. Bill enjoyed challenging her on anything dealing with intricate numbers – interest on loans, the stock market, and abstract problems. He was fascinated by her convoluted mind, her vague way of reaching concrete and correct conclusions. He was sorry to see them leave. Not so Marian! She was exhausted and ready to scream at the negative picture Polly painted of Buddy. Although she loved her friend, she waved good bye with a thankful heart.

Then dawned departure day for the River. The Pitmans were driving up, too, and would share the cabin. Marian was looking forward to peace, quiet and rest. She found it. Bill had Eric to talk to, Davey and Billy were in heaven, Jane and Betty were hitting it off, the twins had each other and Hazel was a joy, sharing work and play, making both enjoyable. It was a true vacation with morning and afternoon treks down the hill and across the bridge to their favorite spot on the sandy beach where the children swam and paddled a rented canoe while the grown-ups relaxed.

On the last afternoon, Jane and Betty had walked back from swimming and were swinging on the wide shady porch. They were much closer this summer. Betty had only a year to go in high school and then was planning to become a dental assistant or a beauty operator. She hadn't quite decided yet.

"So how do you feel about going off to Cal? I can hardly wait to graduate from Tam and get out on my own." Betty's blue eyes sparkled. "Ah, freedom!"

"I'm happy," Jane answered. "But living in a boarding house with a bunch of other girls and tons of rules is hardly 'freedom', at least, not like

Summer Home Park, Hazel, Eric and Davey Pitman, the twins and Billy, August 1938

Bill and Marian, 1940.

Marianne and Suzanne paddling at Summer Home Park, August 1938.

you mean."

"I know. But you'll be away from home and on your own, sort of. And your little brother won't be around to bug you. Davey's driving me nuts, teasing and spying and being a brat."

Jane laughed. "I know what you mean. Billy's better than he used to be. Or maybe it's just because I'm older. He doesn't get under my skin like he used to. Better times are coming. You'll see."

Betty doubted it. She changed the subject back to boys, her favorite topic of conversation that summer.

"So who are you seeing? Any of those cadets?" Jane brought Betty to a party for the young men from the California Maritime Academy last spring and they'd both had fun. Now Betty wanted an update.

"Not really," Jane answered. "A couple of them, Lou and Cy, are my good friends. And every time we had a dance at Marin last spring, I invited the whole class to come up from Tiburon. Usually about six or eight came." Jane laughed. "You'll love this, Betty. One of the guys is really tall, about six-six, and he was dancing with Elaine Erenfelt who's about four-eleven. She was sort of smothering down around his waist so he picked her up and was dancing, holding her about two feet off the floor and, of course, quite close to him. Some chaperone thought it was "indecent" and made them leave the floor. That upset the other guys and we almost had a brou-haha. What a commotion! I was even called in on Monday to explain what happened. I was sort of responsible because I'd invited them. The Dean of Women wanted to bar the cadets from the campus! We were lucky. That didn't happen."

"They are cute," Betty said. "Be sure you ask me next time there's an off-campus party." Jane said she would and they went on chatting about how the future would be "on their own."

It was soon time to return to Ross and prepare for the opening of school. Marian drove Jane and all her required belongs over to the boarding house they'd chosen on Piedmont Avenue. She was sharing a room with a friend from Marin JC, Dottie Winters. Theirs was a large room with an attached sun room built over the front porch. Jane chose the airy spot as a perfect place to sleep and they moved one of the single beds out there. This first week would be spent settling in, getting familiar with the campus, and facing "rushing."

Entering as a junior, Jane wasn't bombarded with as many invita-tions as the freshman but she had enough. Too many for her liking. Joining a sorority didn't matter one way or the other to her but the business of being on display, questioned and judged at a tea, was horrifying. She didn't per-form well, feeling clumsy, skinny, tongue-tied and out of place. Searching questions about her father's business, her mother's sorority, her own plans, brought forth the worst in her. She refused to put herself out to impress these elegant young ladies. They were reminiscent of her nemesis, the sun-tanned coeds during the summer at the River when she had been too young, too unknown, too unimportant to join the golden group holding court on the dance platform.

Marian, an Alpha Phi, was disappointed when her daughter wasn't invited back for a second round of inspection. Jane didn't care. If anything, she was relieved when no more elegant envelopes appeared in the mail. Now she could get on with important things!

The chore of mowing the lawns fell to Bill if he couldn't catch Billy to do it. One September Saturday, Billy disappeared for the day so Bill dragged the old mower out of the garage and up the drive to start the task. He began with the flourishing newer lawn since it was on a slope and took more push-power than the level one outside the front windows.

On the second downhill run, Bill pushed the mower over a hole where yellow jackets had decided to live. The mower passed the hole, Bill took a step. Unknowingly he positioned his left leg right over the hole. Indignant yellow jackets flew up his pant leg, stinging as they went. Bill's yell brought Marian to the porch. Bill was leaping about, trying to get his trousers off.

"What happened? What's the matter? Stand still!"

"Damn yellow jackets, they're up my pants," he shouted, hopping on one foot and kicking at his pants. "Ouch! "

"Stand still," Marian said again. "I'll help." Bill continued to hop and shout. Marian tried to get close enough to tug the trousers off. She finally caught hold of his waist band.

"Stop!" He did and she peeled the pants down. "Let me pull your shoes off. I can't get the pants over them." Yellow jackets were circling them, angrily. Marian was trying to hurry. The whole situation began to seem ludicrous to her. Finally, he stepped out, and she hurled the trousers, yellow jackets and all, away. The sight of Bill, standing in his underpants on the front lawn, shoeless, welts rising on his leg, still swearing and hopping, struck her as comical.

"I'm sorry," she said, laughing. "It must really hurt. Get in the house before someone sees you out here half naked. We'll count your stings and put something on them."

"What helps?" asked Bill, gingerly hopping across the gravel on his tender feet.

"Mud," Marian answered. "That's what I always use." She laughed again. "You go in. I'll make some mud and be right there."

Bill had seven stings that were already red and swelling by the time Marian reached him with her little pan of medicinal mud. "Soon as the sun goes down and all the yellow jackets are back in the hole, I'll go out and pour kerosene down it. That'll kill them so this won't happen again. I am sorry, really I am."

One more trip was planned before winter closed down the Sierra. The Pitmans had relatives with a cabin in the mountains. Hazel volunteered to spend a final weekend up there, battening down the house for winter. Eric would check the wiring and shut off the electricity. Bill and Marian were asked to come along to share the outdoors which they all loved, to help daytimes with the preparations for closing the house, and to play bridge or other card games in the quiet evenings.

It was Indian summer weather, warm midday and freezing at night. They had a great time, busy enough to feel necessary, relaxed enough for the trip to be therapeutic. There was even snow on the ground in shaded areas around the lake for them to make token snowballs. Too soon it was time to return to the routine of everyday living but they had bright memories to carry them into winter.

Hazel and Eric Pitman with Bill on trip to Sierra, 1939.

Marian was finding it less and less necessary to think about the deep and almost silent love she had shared with Philip. The memory of it was still there, a safety net, but her need for drawing strength from it was lessening. Besides, talking to Pauline and hearing tales of Buddy, had stirred long buried feelings about him. *I must be crazy,* she thought, *carrying these strange affairs in the secret darkness of my heart! Loving Buddy for so many years, based on so little contact, is weird! I can count on two fingers, no, one finger, the times we've talked together. Perhaps that's why Kim was so important. Part of me was actually talking and writing to Buddy through Kim. They're mixed up in my heart, They're mixed up in my mind. Part of me is all mixed up, too! I must be crazy. I hope it doesn't show.* Marian shook her head to clear it and pushed her foolish thoughts aside. The holidays were coming. Jane would be home for two weeks. There was much to be done to get ready for the holidays.

Marian, when she couldn't sleep, when she was soaking in the tub, when she was trapped in a moment of forced idleness, had a tendency to "take stock" and figure out where she was in relation to where she wanted to be. Such was the case on her 45th birthday, mid-January 1939. The day had been busy and satisfying but now she was lying in the dark, unable to fall asleep, reviewing her entire life, sizing up her achievements.

Twenty two years of marriage. Under the circumstances, that was an accomplishment. She'd never considered any other option. Bill was her husband and, except when he was drinking which was far from a constant thing, she was comfortable with him. She admired his sharp mind, enjoyed his humor, and was proud of his ability at the piano. She liked his looks and the way he treated her – and all women – with respect. Unless he perceived stupidity and then – male or female – he had no use for the individual. Since she shared his impatience with stupid people she couldn't fault him on that.

Another accomplishment: The four children. One approaching the last year of college, one, last year of high school, two with only three more years in elementary school. *I hope I can get them into Katherine Branson School as day students. It's great academically and so convenient, just a block up the hill from home.* Marian thought of the twins, so tall, so independent. *They have each other. They really don't need me, not the way Jane did at their age.* She compared the twins to her memory of Jane at eleven. *That's when I was in the hospital so long and basically deserted her for six months. I wonder if I've done right by her? Have I prepared her for life in college? Given her the right information? The right values? We've always talked frankly and I've answered any questions she had. Is that enough? Or have I made her too much of a confidant, dumped too many of my problems on her because there was no one else to talk to? I hope not.*

Then she thought of Billy. *Ah, Billy, my darling son. Bill says I've "mollycoddled" him and spoiled him rotten. That's not true. His needs are*

just different than his sisters' and when he gets sick with anything, he gets sicker than anyone else. He's been that way since he was a baby. That whooping cough! He nearly died. I have to take more care of him. But he's fine. He's still delivering the paper. I only drive him around when he's sick which isn't often. Otherwise, he's really responsible! No, I don't favor him over his sisters. Marian smiled, thinking of her son now almost as tall as his father.

And the house! *There is an accomplishment. I did that with the help of Franklin Delano Roosevelt, his New Deal and Home Owners Loan. And my own guts and perseverance. I wonder what would have happened if I hadn't gone after the house, if I'd just quit like Bill and not even tried? Where would we be? I hate to think!*

Marian relaxed and drifted toward sleep, on the whole pleased where she had gotten in forty five years. Just before she sank into oblivion, a sad minor note crept into her reverie, unbidden. *Oh, Doris, how I've missed you. There's so much we could have shared. I've needed you! We've needed each other. We had such a wonderful friendship. And Enid, my strong right hand. You were always there. Your absence crippled me in many ways. Nearly ten long years without a word from either of you. Why? Will I ever know? Will I ever find you again?* Sleep closed in on the question and covered the pain of their unexplained defection.

Off Yerba Buena Island, long a military stronghold, which, three years before, became the mid-Bay anchor and tunnel for the Oakland-San Francisco Bay Bridge, a man-made island took form. Over the years dredgings from the bottom of the Bay were deposited and slowly, slowly a new flat 400-acre island emerged . On it was constructed an art deco fairy land—the Golden Gate International Exposition onTreasure Island —which opened on February 18,1939 accompanied by tremendous hoopla and hyperbole. With the two new bridges in operation, it was possible to get from Marin to the Fair by automobile. From the East Bay, one could take the Key System Ferry directly to the site, or take the new bridge.

It seemed, during that year after the Fair opened, as though some family member was always heading to Treasure Island. Jane went with friends from the university several times a month, using the ferry. Bill and Marian drove over with the Pitmans in their car. The Willys was too small to hold four adults comfortably.

"Damn car!" Marian muttered every time she climbed in, ducking her head and folding her long legs. "This is an abomination." When all six Rattrays went together they felt like sardines.

To be able to use the two magnificent bridges was wonderful, however. That was part of the thrill of going to the Fair! Bella and Ernest McRitchie took their nieces, the twins and Betty Anne Panton, for a day-long outing that exhausted all of them. But they had to stay until after dark to see the light displays on the buildings, the statues, the fountains, truly a trip to fantasy land! All three young girls were awed. They enjoyed the magnificent outdoor production, *Cavalcade of the Golden West*, too. The stage was so huge that horses and wagons thundered across, followed by a live steam train, and as the story progressed, even San Francisco's famous cable cars.

At Treasure Island Worlds Fair, Betty Anne Panton, Suzanne, Bella McRitchie, and Marianne, 1939.

Marian in San Francisco, 1939

The theme of the Fair was exemplified in the tremendous statue *Pacifica* which dominated the main courtyard.. The spire of the Tower of the Sun was the central landmark. It was delightful to wander through the Court of Flowers, the Court of Moon, gazing in amazement at towers, statues, pools, fountains, bridges, waterfalls, beautifully landscaped with tall palm trees, lofty eucalyptus, dark pines, great beds of colorful flowers, and flying flags of all the countries that touched the Pacific ocean. There were lush tropical nooks, serene Oriental gardens, restaurants serving Mexican, Japanese, Chinese, or American food, in lavish style. A day at the Fair was a ticket to a half-dozen foreign countries. And thousands of people took the trip every day. The Rattrays tried to sample as many different ethnic foods as they could but it was difficult when Bill was along. He refused to stand in line for more than a few minutes. Since the better the restaurant, the longer the line, Marian had to either forego eating there and leave with him or take the children in without him.

Billy and his buddies found the Gayway the best part. There they took all the rides, enjoying it most after dark when everything was illuminated with colored lights.

"Your dad works for PG&E. Ask him what he thinks their electric bill is," Billy said to Davey one night as they looked down from the top of the ferris wheel on acres of brilliant changing lights, blazing in staggering glory. "I bet it's a pretty penny."

The boys also found much of interest in the side shows. They were forbidden to attend both the *Folies Bergere* and Sally Rand's exciting fan dance in which she was reputedly stark naked under those big white moving fans! They did enjoy Ripley's *Believe It or Not* and Billy Rose's *Aquacade*. And whenever possible, they attended the nightly performance at the outdoor theater. They could never decide which of the two shows they preferred: *Cavalcade of the Golden West* or the more broadly historical, *American Cavalcade*, with the redcoats in the Revolutionary War, the signing of the Declaration of Independence, colonial dancers, the move west, the Civil War. It was a colorful and exciting history lesson.

As Marian and Bill were strolling around one evening she said, "Remember our last fair years ago, the Pan-American Exposition? How do you think this compares?"

Bill thought for a moment. "Well, this is bigger. And *whiter.* That one, all the buildings were sort of terra cotta colored. And this is sharp, stark in spite of all the statues and towers, the trees and flowers. Art deco, whatever that means, modern. The other one was elaborate, rococo, *softer.*"

"That's true. The Palace of Fine Arts is still there, an example of what that fair was like. But I mean, how does it feel?"

"You can`t compare the feelings. That was, when? 1915? We were young, just engaged. . . "

"Whoa, back up," Marian interrupted. "We weren't engaged for years after that!"

"No? We were married two years later, so we must have been. As I remember . . ."

"You remember wrong." Marian cut in again. "You always have.

We were only engaged six weeks. I remember . . ."

"*You* remember wrong!" Bill countered, beginning to sound more than a bit heated.

Marian laughed. "This is silly. What possible difference can it make now? We've been married twenty-two years. Can you believe it?"

"It's a bloody miracle," said Bill with a smile. "Know what I like best about this fair? That bed of tuberous begonias. Now there's something to be amazed about! They're even bigger than the ones I grow." Bill was serious. Of all the wonders from all the countries in all the exhibits from the entire Pacific rim, nothing impressed him more than the flamboyant glory of the begonia bed. There was something he could relate to on a personal level. And he didn't have to stand in line to look at them.

Jane enjoyed being at the University of California. She found the short walk from the boarding house on Piedmont Avenue to the campus a pleasure. Most classes were huge. As a journalism major, she was required to take numerous courses in political science. The politics of Europe and Russia, both current and historic, she found difficult and disturbing. In her journalism classes, stories based on real events had to be written as though she were a foreign correspondent for *Time* or *Life* magazine. This was a challenge that often brought her close to tears for the sheer horror of what had happened or was happening. Sometimes she was so immersed in where the assignment had taken her that walking into the spring sunshine of Berkeley and seeing the happy carefree students hurrying to class was a jolt. *How lucky we are!* she thought. *How lucky I am!*

Jane tried a stint on the *Daily Californian* but was intimidated by the hustle and bustle of the busy office. She was too shy and unsure of herself to ask directions about assignments or procedure. She was ill-equipped to enter this hurly-burly world without a helping hand or a friendly voice. Her editorship of the weekly *Mariner* at Marin Junior College had been an entirely different thing, – small, orderly, comfortable – with Mr. Moyer standing by as a benign advisor. The *Daily Californian* was completely "student run" and everyone, it seemed to Jane as she stood around – lost and confused , knew exactly what they were doing. Finally, she just dropped out. No one seemed to care, or even notice, which didn't do her lagging self-esteem any good. Working on the paper was an extracurricular activity so it didn't affect her grades to give it up and it certainly improved her outlook.

Socially, she was having a good time. Mixer dances were held at the Student Union on Saturday nights. Everyone went "stag." She found it a bit intimidating to have the young men walk slowly by sizing up the coeds as though they were shopping for a bargain. Jane never knew whether to look nonchalant and bored, as though it meant nothing to her, or whether to smile in a friendly manner at the tall ones who looked relatively normal. Both attitudes seemed equally effective. She usually ended up having fun and dancing as much as she wanted.

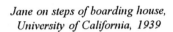
Jane on steps of boarding house,
University of California, 1939

The Masonic Club, in a big brick building a block off campus, held afternoon dances on Fridays. There were also ping pong and pool tables in a large airy downstairs room so it was a popular spot. Walking from the dance floor to the game room one day, halfway down the flight of stairs, Jane was stopped by a tall young man on his way up.

"Hiya," he drawled. "My name's Jerry. Let's dance." His blue eyes were laughing, his smile sweet and friendly. Jane reversed her direction and walked back to the dance floor, Jerry right behind her. They danced the afternoon away, exchanging statistics between numbers. Thus began Jane's first romance at Cal. Sweet and innocent, it lasted an entire semester. She brought him to Ross one weekend and the family were all well-behaved and friendly, for which Jane was thankful. Somehow she knew it was not a deep or permanent alliance. They had fun, enjoyed dancing together, laughed and talked long hours. Hugs and kisses were the extent of their physical loving. They were friends, buddies, devoted pals. And when the semester ended, so did they, without pain or remorse. Yet fifty years later, Jane could still hear the soft drawl of his voice, see the sparkle in his laughing blue eyes, and feel the solid warmth of this strong young body as they danced or embraced. As with Tommy Regan, four years earlier, Jerry carved a permanent spot in her heart, a gentle memory.

Billy was moving through high school, having his own first tentative loves. He attacked his senior year with less vigor than his sister. "Getting by" was his goal. He had postponed Oral Expression until the last possible moment and now his graduation depended upon passing that dreaded ten minute speech. Already he had given a talk that was too short to count and his teacher said he couldn't be rescheduled. Marian was exasperated that his procrastination had placed him in such an untenable position and took him to task in no uncertain terms.

"I'm going down to school and talk to Mrs. White. We have to work this out."

"No, Mom!" Billy pleaded. "Don't do that! What'll everyone think?"

"That you're a misguided lazy boy who isn't using his God-given brain, that's what they'll think. Do you know that your father, one of the most intelligent men I've ever known , doesn't have a high-school diploma because the week of graduation the authorities noticed that he hadn't taken all the required subjects! I'm not going to let that happen to you. You *will* pass Ruby White's torture test, you *will* graduate, and you *will* go on through college." Marian glared at him. He glared back. But he knew he was licked.

Marian made an appointment and the three of them met in the classroom after school a few days later. A plan was forged and a bargain struck. Ruby would give Billy another chance, Marian would coach and time him on his speech. And he would write, memorize and deliver the talk by the end of the following week. It worked and when June came, Billy wore a cap and gown and proudly accepted his diploma. Ruby White said it should have gone to Marian!

Billy also developed into a fine tennis player, the only sport that appealed to him. Neither football nor baseball suited his talents but he was a natural at tennis. In his senior year, he stopped delivering the paper so he's have afternoons free to practice. "You're like my brothers," Marian told him. "I polished their trophies every Saturday morning when I was growing up. Perce was a real champion, a runner-up in the State competition several years running. You'll be great, too."

Ross Grammar School, the two story wooden building that Jane attended for six years, Billy graduated from and the twins had been in since kindergarten, was being demolished and replaced with a modern U-shaped stucco structure. While demolition and construction was going on, classes were held in several private homes in the vicinity. Marianne and Suzanne felt themselves fortunate to be in a large three-story white Victorian right on the edge of the school grounds. They were in sixth grade the September work commenced. Marianne was pleased to find her desk in an overflow room through an archway and out of eye contact with the teacher although she could still hear her voice. She worked much better when she didn't feel under constant scrutiny but she had to get out of her seat to see the blackboard where assignments were written. When she realized how close she needed to walk for the words to be legible, she knew something was wrong with her sight. Eye examinations showed that she had a definite problem and glasses were prescribed. Marianne felt this was the final blow. Tall, skinny and now glasses: It was unfair!

Marianne and Suzanne, 1940.

Bill continued to look for employment in Marin, disliking the commute to San Francisco. He overheard talk after church one Sunday and hurried home to tell Marian.

"There's an election coming up in April for Town Clerk. It's a job I could fill. What do you think?"

Marian was surprised at his enthusiasm. "I think it'd be great. Right here in town. How much does it pay, do you know?"

"No, but I'll find out," Bill said. "I'll take a few hours off tomorrow morning and go see about it. I have to file right away. Then we have to get busy and campaign. We only have a few months." He was excited about the prospect which also startled Marian.

She wholeheartedly backed him and threw her fund-raising experience into action. She telephoned all her Ross friends, told them of his qualifications and asked for their vote. Bill designed notices which the twins and Billy delivered throughout the town. Connections they'd made through managing the Marin Musical Chest concerts, through doing publicity for the Ross Valley Players, through various Red Cross activities all paid off. They knew who to talk to, how to get work done. It was a busy three months. When the votes were counted, Bill had 333 to his opponent's 193 and was installed as Town Clerk at a salary of $90 a month.

He didn't give notice at his San Francisco job until after he'd won the election so for the first few weeks he worked both places. Since Town Clerk was not a full-time job this was no problem. The hours were flexible, so once he no longer had to go to San Francisco, he quickly filled his afternoons playing for Gladys Hodgson's dancing classes several afternoons a week. The twins often walked over to his office after school on the days he was there. Bill was always glad to see his daughters and pressed them into service folding notices and stuffing envelopes for which he paid them out of his own pocket. This had started during the campaign and the girls accepted both the work and the pay.

Jane, this spring of 1940, was preparing for graduation. She was well aware of the massive struggle underway in Europe. Her journalism assignments kept her involved. She read the newspapers and listened to Edward R. Murrow with the nightly news. Early in 1939 she wrote a paper on Prime Minister Neville Chamberlain's "Peace in Our Time" speech made after returning from a conference in Czechoslovakia. Then, as Germany invaded Poland in September, she chronicled the declaration of war by England and France against Germany. Jane was concerned about world turmoil but it was far away and separate from life on campus as the months wound down. Without putting it into words, the class of 1940 seemed determined to maintain the traditions of the University no matter what was happening elsewhere, postponing as long as possible the day when they'd have to become involved in the situation "out there."

Since 1912, every fourth year the Big C Sirkus was held. It was a carnival day for the University and the community, with a parade, a huge circus tent, and all the accompanying excitement and commotion. Jane was discussing it one weekend when she in Ross.

"I can hardly wait," she said. "It's going to be great! Our class has the egg-throwing booth. We get to hurl eggs at professors and campus big shots. Of course, it's all to raise money. But what fun. It'll be a colossal mess! Can't you just see it?"

Marian laughed. "I can remember our Big C Sirkus," she said, "in the spring of my last semester at Cal, 1916. That was the second one they held, not as big or crazy as yours is going to be. There was a war going on in Europe then, too. And a year later we were in it!" Marian shook her head. "Awful, all those young men going straight from campus right to war. So many of them died."

"Do you think we'll get into it this time, too?" Jane asked.

Bill had been listening. "Of course," he said. "War's good for the economy. Already we're making money on what's going on. It'll just take an incident, something to rouse the great American public from their normal apathy. Then the big boys in Washington will do what they've wanted to do all along. You'll see."

"Bill, you're positively revolting you're so negative," Marian said.

"I'm positively right this time," Bill replied. "I'm *positive* we'll be in the war as soon as one of the Axis makes a stupid mistake. How can you say I'm negative when I'm so positive?"

"Okay, you two," Jane cut in with a laugh. "This is developing in a semantics battle. Cut it out! What's to eat? I have to leave soon." They went into the kitchen to concoct a snack and then she left for Berkeley.

Sirkus Day was all she hoped for – big, brash, bold and blatant. Try as they might, they couldn't ignore the darkness falling on the world beyond the campus but on this day they rose above it. Everyone involved seemed trying to pierce that blackness with a bit of light, laughing hysterically so they wouldn't weep. A quote from the Sirkus program summed it up for all of them.

"Laughter and play are the privileges of the young, but today they are the privileges of only the favored youth of the world. We are thankful that we in United States are the fortunate ones.

"While young men of other nations march in military columns down roads that lead to misery and death, we happily join a carefree serpentine that winds its merry way to fun and laughter.

"We, the war babies of 1918, are thankful that the privileges of youth are not denied us. We hope that the four years preceding the next Sirkus will be unstained by the blood of the young men who participate in this one."

Senior Week found Jane already filled with nostalgia for what had been. Each time she heard the Campanile bells ringing out beloved songs, her heart saluted Margaret Murdock who was making the music and who had made Jane's education possible.

"Bill," said Marian, a week before the big day, "There's something we have to do before I lose my mind."

"What's about to drive you crazy?" Bill asked, amused to think of his sane and practical wife losing control.

"That damn little monstrosity of a poor excuse for an automobile," Marian answered. "I've put up with discomfort for three years. Now's the time to dump it. Okay?" Marian looked at him with her chin raised and her eyes steely. She was not joking.

"Well, I don't know. It's sure been a good little car," Bill replied with a smile, knowing he'd get a sharp reaction and unable to resist a chance to needle her.

"It's been a damn nuisance," she said falling for his teasing, "and an embarrassment. We can afford to buy a new car, a *real* car. Let's go. Right now."

"Okay," Bill said. "If you insist. But I'll certainly miss the Beetle."

"Then you can drive the idiot thing to San Rafael and we'll turn it in. I'll never drive it again!"

Marian had given this moment a great deal of thought. She'd already checked on cars and done a bit of pricing and research so she quickly found what she wanted. Bill didn't care one way or the other. He went along with her decision, feeling she deserved to make the choice this time having lived, although vocally unhappy about it, with his for the past three years.

She chose a new four-door 1940 Nash, gray-blue, fully equipped. Compared to the Willys, it was huge, spacious, and luxurious. Marian was delighted and watched Bill sign the papers with a happy heart. *At last, no more scrunching in and being jammed. This is a great day!*

At noon on May 25, Bill and Marian, with Billy and the twins, climbed into the new automobile and, with Marian proudly driving, took off for the Richmond ferry. It was a bright day, a California day, blue and clear. Once on the Berkeley campus, Marian parked the car and they hiked to Memorial Stadium where they joined the throngs of proud and excited people.

With more than 3,000 graduates, although they could see R designating the area where she was sitting, it was impossible for them to identify Jane but Marian was filled with happiness knowing she was there, in cap and gown, soon to hold a diploma in her hand.

They listened to the band, the predictable speeches, the echoing names as they called out the special honors. Then the graduates climbed the steps and walked across the platform to accept their diploma and shake President Sproul's hand. Names were called in alphabetical order. It was a long wait from "Aaron" to "Rattray" and 3,000 plus is an interminable number. But finally the ceremony was over and they headed down to the R section where they were to meet Jane. Even Bill was willing to push and shove his way through the masses to reach his college graduate daughter. Finally they were face to face.

"I'm so proud, so happy," Marian told Jane, giving her a big hug. "Congratulations, dear."

Bill, too, gave Jayne an embrace. "I'm proud of you," he said.

"We have a surprise in the parking lot. It's not for you – it's all of ours," Marianne blurted.

"What is it?" Jane asked.

"Can I tell?" Billy wanted to know.

"I think your mother should. She's the one who did it," said Bill.

"It's a new car, a brand new blue Nash," Marian said with pride. "You'll love it."

Holding on to each other to keep from getting separated in the crush, they pushed toward the exit. All together, as close as they could be, the Rattrays headed for the outside world where a new car waited, where the future waited. It was truly commencement day. Marian grinned at Bill and he smiled back, first at her, then at Jane.

"Congratulations," he said. "You did it." He was talking to them both. They each deserved the praise, he felt.

Later, after taking the Richmond ferry home, the family sat on the front porch in the twilight, reliving the day. The Nash looked well in the driveway, they all agreed. Jane would always remember that car as an exciting part of her graduation.

A gentle breeze blew and the wind chimes tinkled, softly.

"Listen," whispered Jane. "Listen."

Everyone became quiet. Another sigh of wind, another crystal jingle of the chimes. Marian smiled remembering the many times she'd heard that delicate sound.

It was the song of home.

Marian and her daughters

Marian, Jane, Marianne, Suzanne, 1942

Epilogue

There is no way to end the story of a family: It goes on and on as long as a single descendent still walks this earth.

The following pages, however, bring three lives to their conclusion and another three to the present. Also, shown are photographs of Marian and Bill's grandchildren and great-grandchildren, and an up-to-date family tree.

The rest of the story has yet to happen.

Bill

William Rattray

DURING 1941, BILL WORKED as Town Clerk of Ross, played piano for Gladys Kenny Hodgson's Ballet School, and continued on the Board of Directors for the Marin Musical Chest.

In early 1942, war having been declared, he became active in the Red Cross Disaster unit along with Marian and Billy. He also began practicing with the Marin Symphony to perform a Saint-Saen concerto at a concert May 25, 1942. This was a large event and a challenge to him. Much to everyone's relief, in spite of growing tension, he managed to stay sober throughout the months of practice.

On the day of the concert, with the entire family in the front row holding their collective breath, Bill walked briskly on stage, sat at the piano. He shot his cuffs out, a mannerism of his, and then flexed his fingers. The concerto starts with loud positive chord. Bill brought his hands down on the keys. One finger struck a wrong note. No one but the family noticed. And no one but Jane heard the "Damn," that escaped his lips. Afterwards, he said he hadn't sworn but Jane was sure she didn't just imagine hearing the word.

By late 1942, Marinship in Sausalito was producing Liberty ships. Bill worked the swing shift, and also, on occasion, played the piano for the ceremony when finished ships were christened and launched. All through the war, Bill continued at his several jobs. He hardly had time to drink and most of the time he was sober and happy. With the war's end in 1945, things began to go wrong for him. Marian increased her involvement with the Red Cross. As she became stronger and more powerful, he became weaker and less effective. By 1947, he was so down he attempted suicide, failing even at that.

Never the less, he was re-elected as the Town Clerk of Ross in April 1948. A month later the town Council accepted his resignation because of "health." Actually, the mayor, an old friend, arranged the resignation rather than exposing a discrepancy discovered in the monies handled by Bill. He again attempted suicide. Again, he failed. At the same time, checks he had forged were discovered at the Marin Music Chest.

Marian filed for legal separation and made arrangements to take him to St. Helena Hospital, run by Seventh Day Adventists in the Napa Valley of Northern California. He was there for two months. Upon his discharge, he went to Alameda to live, temporarily, with his sister Lottie and her family at the old home on Benton Street.

He became dedicated to Alcoholics Anonymous, finding a menial job at a bar in downtown Oakland with a room upstairs where he could live. He left Alameda and started to climb back to a new and sober life. He never took another drink, gaining strength though AA. Gradually, his situation improved. By 1949, he moved into a comfortable apartment in a converted two-story house in Oakland, close to the Berkeley line. Then he obtained a position selling pianos and Hammond organs in a San Rafael music store. He bought an old automobile and began commuting on the Richmond ferry.

In the fall of 1949, he approached Marian and asked if he could "board" at the Ross home while he looked for a room he could afford in Marin. She said he could. "But that doesn't change anything between us. You can stay as a boarder, not as a husband, understand?"

The arrangement worked well and Bill stopped looking for a place of his own. His piano had never left Ross. He was glad to be back with it and played more, for his own pleasure, than he had in a long time, as though losing access to the keyboard made him appreciate its importance to him.

In November 1951, he suffered a small stroke. As soon as he was able, he attended AA meetings again and conversed by the hour with other members on the telephone. June 1954, he had his second stroke, still not incapacitating. His third stroke happened nearly four years later, in January 1958. This time he stopped working. He gave his old car to Jane and her husband so they could turn it in to buy a new automobile

These strokes were followed, in August 1960 and May 1961, by increasingly serious coronary attacks. He was hospitalized at Ross General and went from there to his first nursing home. Marian visited him every Wednesday and Sunday afternoon without fail. Bill, who seldom complained, found fault with the care so Marian moved him to another facility. This, he said, was even worse.

The third convalescent home they tried, in Novato, was to Bill's liking. He settled in happily with his television and reclining chair. With no demands on him to do anything, he was more content than he'd ever been. The nurses loved him. He was intelligent, humorous and non-demanding. His room opened to a private patio where he could sit in the fresh air on warm days. Bill refused to go to the recreation room or have anything to do with the other residents. "Why should I go out where all those 'crazies' are?" he'd ask Marian when she suggested he be more sociable. "They babble," he'd say derisively. "Can't stand mumblers. I'd rather watch TV."

One afternoon, following a simple lunch, he said to the nurse who helped him into bed for his nap, "I feel so well today, I don't think I need a nap at all. I should take a walk instead."

They laughed together. She tucked him in, patted his hand and left the room. Bill didn't awaken from that nap.

He died in the early afternoon of July 23, 1964. He was 72 years old.

William Rattray, 1945.

Marian

Marian Murdock Rattray

IN THE MONTHS BEFORE the attack on Pearl Harbor, Marian was already deeply involved in many aspects of the American Red Cross, heading the canteen, in charge of the volunteers, part of the Disaster Unit and still running the annual fund raising campaign. Right after December 7, 1941, she put on a uniform, organized the canteen workers to serve at Hamilton Field twenty-four hours a day, and went to work in earnest.

She continued to run the house. With Bill, Billy and Jane working three different shifts at Marinship and the twins in high school on yet another schedule, Marian was serving meals around the clock and doing as much as she could on the outside, too.

As the war drew to a close, she resigned from the Board of Directors of the Red Cross, gave up all her volunteer positions and took a paid job on the switchboard in the office. She had heard there was trouble with the director and wanted to be on hand and available for appointment to the top position. Her strategy paid off and she became executive director of the Marin County Chapter, American Red Cross, early in 1946.

She heard from Polly DuBois that Christmas. Buddy's retirement had been postponed by the war but in 1946 he was finally out of the army and they purchased the planned home in Laguna Beach. Marian made a quick trip down to see them. This was so successful, she continued spending time with them each summer for twenty years.

In June 1947, on her first vacation from the Red Cross, Marian visited Jane in the Hawaiian Islands. Upon her return, she organized Marianne's wedding.

Right after that event, she realized how far apart she and Bill had grown. His attempted suicide shook her complacency. She began to pay more attention to him but things were unraveling. Uncovering the missing funds at the Town of Ross and his forced resignation, shook Marian to her soul and his second suicide attempt was the final blow. She acknowledged that the situation was beyond her control. The main thing was to get Bill whole and healthy, away from her. After 31 years of marriage, Marian was willing to release the reins. She filed for legal separation to protect her position at the Red Cross from whatever financial scandals Bill may have instigated. She took a loan on the house to reimburse the Town of Ross, cover the forged checks, and to pay for his care at the hospital. Then she packed his belongings, drove him to St. Helena and signed him in. She cried all the way home. *Why is it so hard to end things? Why do I feel so cruel?* she asked herself.

These were dark days for Marian. She had never been alone before and didn't enjoy it. Jane was in Honolulu, Billy on the high seas, Marianne had married and Suzanne was in her second year at UC Davis. With no one to care for, Marian had too much time to think about herself.

Then she located a beautiful neglected collie, Dawn, who needed a home. She and the dog became soul mates. Dawn slept on the rug beside the bed. Marian's hand sought her silky fur the last thing at night, the first thing in the morning.

Months later when Dawn died while undergoing simple surgery, Marian was devastated. All the unshed tears of her life came pouring forth. She was inconsolable. Only her responsibilities and commitment at the Red Cross forced her out of bed and into her clothes each morning. Habit took care of eating. Gradually, she found her footing again but Marian had never been so completely crushed.

By 1949, with Suzanne in nurses' training at St. Luke's Hospital, coming home weekends and Jane returning from Hawaii with her Marine husband, Marian was again on firm ground. She was even willing to accept Bill back into the house, although only as a boarder. It was great to have the rooms full again.

Throughout the 1950s, Jane returned home every other year to await the birth of a baby while her husband attended to Marine Corps business elsewhere. This delighted Marian. Eventually, the twins, too, provided her with grandchildren until she had ten. She continued her annual trek to Laguna Beach, planning it to coincide with the Living Art Show. Polly, growing progressively more deaf, was an unruffled hostess. Buddy and Marian had opportunity for long conversations. Although he remained a man of few words, and impeccable standards, those words he did say sustained her from visit to visit.

January 1960, Marian retired from the Red Cross. Six months later, Jane's husband received a medical discharge from the Marine Corps. Marian offered the Ross home to them on a permanent basis, moving herself to the little cottage down the driveway.

Then in 1961, Marian went on an AARP tour to Europe, a high point in her life. Funds for the trip came from the sale of Susan's engagement fifty-cent piece which brought $2,500. She wrote about the impact of the trip in the little red book, ending, ". . . all this made me a different person, nearer whole but still searching."

When Bill was hospitalized and convalescent care was looming in 1962, she found that the legal separation she had instigated 14 years before didn't mean a thing. She was still responsible for his welfare and expenses. This, the way things were, she couldn't afford. She solved the problem in a typical manner. She applied for a position as a house-mother at the University of Nevada women's dormitory and signed up for summer school classes in art appreciation to build on what she had discovered in Europe – the Impressionists, Van Gogh, Michaelangelo, Leonardo de Vinci. Then she drove to Reno where she settled in at college and filed for divorce. At the end of the summer she came home, tan and free. She moved Bill into his final convalescent hospital where his social security check now took care of everything.

With Jane's two youngest accompanying her, Marian visited Bill every Wednesday afternoon as long as he lived. Jane joined her for the Sunday visits with the little boys and news of the others.

Marian also worked at Katherine Branson School as alternate house-mother, spending three nights a week there in charge of one of the lovely homes that served as dormitories. Enid Hilderbrand was also working at KBS and although Marian didn't find out why things had gone wrong forty years before, she did re-establish a friendship with Enid. This gave her courage to seek out Doris Mayer. They had an emotional reunion. No explanation was forthcoming here, either, but Marian remained in close almost daily contact with Doris for the rest of her life.

She was the hostess for a Coterie luncheon in July 1964. Jane was sitting with the group in the lower garden when she saw their doctor, Frederick Coe, walking down the driveway. She went to greet him. "Jane," he said, "your father just died."

"Mother's in the garden with her oldest friends. Come and tell her."

Marian's first thought was *How appropriate that these dear people are with me!* Then she felt an unexpected stab in her heart. *He's gone, Bill's dead.* She was amazed at the wave of loss that washed over her. The meeting broke up amid hugs and condolences. Marian hurried off to take care of all the details connected with death. It took a surprisingly short time.

On Saturday, they had a memorial service at St. John's followed by a gathering in the lower garden. Jim Panton came with Ronnie, Jamie and Betty Anne. Bill's brother, Jim Rattray, Greig McRitchie, Bill DuBois, the Rattray children and grandchildren were all there.

In the summer of 1965, Marian sold the house to Jane's second husband and moved to a small apartment on Kent Avenue near the College of Marin. Her place opened to the oval swimming pool where her young grandchildren learned to swim and where the older ones cavorted and cooled off on hot summer days. Being alone here was comfortable. It was her own place, there were no ghosts of earlier days. She continued to work at Branson so was away three nights each week. Tuesday was still Gabby Girls, the Coterie still met monthly. She was busy and happy.

When she was told in the summer of 1969 that Billy's melanoma of a year before had not been successfully removed but instead had metasta-sized, something in Marian died. During the long painful six months, Marian was often the one who drove him to the hospital in San Francisco for chemotherapy. Later, when he was at home, she went to spend the agonizing days with him. During this time, he dredged up all the mistakes he felt she'd made in raising him, or in dealing with his father. Marian took the criticism without flinching, hoping it helped him. He was hospitalized after Thanksgiving and died on December 23, 1969. She had just been sent home by the nurse on duty.

"Children shouldn't die before their parents," Marian said. "It should have been me!" No service was held. Marian felt the joy of Christmas filling the church should not be disturbed by their personal sorrow and bid him good-bye privately, planning to have a memorial service after the first of the year. Somehow that never happened. She was always sorry her son had not been remembered and honored in that special way.

While working for the Red Cross, Marian became a member of Zonta International, an organization of executive women. She enjoyed their meetings and conferences, often being one of their speakers. It was enjoyable to be involved with so many intelligent challenging women.

Before the next planned trip to Laguna, Buddy wrote her a brief letter telling of Pauline's death. Marian sent a sympathy note. She knew that after a "decent interval" she would hear from him again. She looked deep in her heart. She studied her comfortable life. She made up her mind to leave the dream she lived with all her adult years undisturbed, to put it away forever. It was a decision she never regretted. Buddy, she thought, was relieved, too.

By the beginning of the 1970s, Marian's health began to fail. In 1971, she resigned from the board of the Marin Music Chest, having served for 40 years. She stopped working at Katherine Branson School in September 1972. "I'm falling apart," she said with a laugh. One little thing after another cropped up. Her platelet count was extremely high. They put her on cortisone which caused multiple problems. There was hemorrhaging in her left eye and the retina had to be "stitched" with a laser beam by a wonderful young doctor. A cancer in her palate was treated successfully by radiation. Living alone in her little apartment was difficult. She called Jane constantly and had her stop in both morning and night, to do the shopping, to walk the little Lhasa apso, Molly, to cheer and comfort her.

When school ended in June 1976, Jane and her family moved Marian back to Glenwood Avenue. They put stairs and an outside door into the big front bedroom for her friends to use. Marian chose the most treasured of her lifelong belongings to take with her. The rest she gave away to children, grandchildren, organizations. She moved in on the Fourth of July, feeling rather well. It was a happy homecoming

Sadly, by the middle of August she was hospitalized with stomach pains. An exploratory operation showed a massive invasion of cancer. There was nothing to be done. "She doesn't have long," said the doctors.

Jane brought her home to the front bedroom that had sheltered her for so much of her life. She became one of Hospice of Marin's first patients. Jane cut her hair. Without the coronet braid she'd worn so long, she looked like a waif.

"I don't know the rules," she said. "I don't know how to do this right." She wanted to follow protocol. Hospice people assured her that she couldn't do it "wrong" and she relaxed. (See *Until Death and After: How to Live with a Dying Intimate*)

Suzanne and Marianne came down weekends to relieve Jane. Marianne agreed to give the little dog, Molly, a new home which eased Marian's mind. The grandchildren were in and out of the room constantly. The radio played softly. Each day of the next to last week, she had Jane call specified friends to come and say good-bye. Most came although it was a difficult visit. She said to each of them, "I love you," words she'd previously found hard to use.

One day it was Vincent she wanted to see. He arrived with his second wife, Rita, carrying a potted chrysanthemum. "I forgive you," Marian said. "Everything turned out all right. The children are wonderful. And Rita got you to stop drinking." She smiled at him. "She was better for you than Jane!"

Before Vincent left, she asked a favor. "You're the only Catholic I know, even though you're not a very good one. Will you pray for me?"

Somehow, her Unitarian roots didn't seem adequate, even with her later Episcopalian conversion, and she wanted to cover all bases for the important journey she was embarking on.

A week later she stated, "Dying is the experience of a lifetime." There was awe in her voice.

Then as the Seminary chimes tolled three o'clock on Sunday afternoon, September 12, 1976, with Suzanne, Jane and granddaughter, Cathi, in the sunny room with her, Marian Murdock Rattray quietly and gently died. She was 82 years old.

Marian Murdock Rattray, 1960

Billy

William Murdock Rattray

BILLY GRADUATED FROM Tamalpais High School in June 1940, three weeks after Jane received her diploma from the University of California. He was halfway through his second year at Marin Junior College when World War II started. He stayed in school to complete his sophomore year in May 1942. Then he went to work on the graveyard shift at Marinship where he stayed for 18 months.

At this point, he applied for admittance to the California Maritime Academy. He was accepted and became a cadet there in mid-1943. In his first months at the school, he contracted mumps which everyone thought was amusing until he nearly died. Marian could have told the doctors he'd be the worst case they would ever see but no one asked her. Luckily, they pulled him through.

Upon graduation, he served in the engine room of merchant marine cargo ships for the rest of the war, plying the most dangerous waters of the world. The job, in the close hot dirty engine room, was hard and uncomfortable but he enjoyed it. When the war ended, he went to work for Matson Navigation Company, shipping from San Francisco to Seattle, Alaska to Hawaii.

In 1950, Billy married Nora Dole. Although they played great bridge together, the marriage lasted only a few years. By 1954, he was back home in Ross suffering from migraine headaches. He decided to remodel the garage into a bachelor pad. With the help of his friend, Shelby Martin, he made one large room, adding a cantilevered alcove using the three windows taken from the front room of the main house when new picture windows were added there.

On the opposite side of the structure, he built a bathroom and a work shop. These were both down a step to accommodate the required roof height. Billy slept and worked out there, bathed in his six-foot tub, showered under his high shower head, and slept in a large bed. Meals he still allowed his mother to provide. He probably would have lived out the rest of his life there, if he hadn't met Margaret Tate.

It happened in the waiting room of the orthopedic surgeon who was treating them both. Having seen each other there several times, they began to swap problems and experiences with their offending knees as they waited. They discovered more in common than their doctor and medical history, and soon were seeing each other outside the waiting room.

Margaret was tall, with hazel-blue eyes under heavy level brows, a handsome athletic woman and fine tennis player, always deeply tanned from her hours in the sun. She taught physical education at San Rafael High School when she and Billy met. They became close friends but Margaret, rightly, looked with alarm at his dedicated work on the bachelor quarters he was building, seeing it as a threat to any permanent relationship between them.

Christmas 1956, she invited him to her family home in Portland for the holidays. A year later, when she again asked him to go north with her, Marian stepped in. She took her son aside and said,

"It's not right to spend a second Christmas with Margaret's family unless your intentions are honorable and you declare them." Billy looked pained. Marriage hadn't worked for him. But the thought of giving up Margaret and all the good times they shared didn't please him, either.

Like his father, Billy had difficulty expressing emotions. He proposed at her apartment Thanksgiving evening. Margaret said later that his proposal was so oblique and round-about she thought they were breaking up! That straightened out, they went to tell Marian.

"Good!" she said. She left the room and returned in a moment with her diamond engagement ring. "Here, I want you to have this." Bill accepted the heirloom with a nod and slipped the ring on Margaret's finger. They were married December 28, 1957 in Portland, Oregon. Bill and Marian flew up for the ceremony, a church affair with Margaret's two sisters and brother in the wedding party.

Billy had a job with Bechtel Corporation. He applied to work on the Alaska Pipeline but the required physical showed a heart irregularity so he was turned down and confined to office work. He moved to Rucker Company in the East Bay as an engineer but the same thing happened. They wouldn't send him on jobs that required climbing ladders up many stories of buildings under construction. Marian convinced him to go into real estate. He passed the tests and was licensed as a broker. This was not an unqualified success. Billy wasn't a salesman by nature. Like his father, he enjoyed talking to people but didn't like to ask for anything. Selling houses was beyond him.

Margaret, however, was made the dean of girls at the new Terra Linda High School. She and Billy bought a home in the subdivision springing up in the hills and valleys just north of San Rafael, close to the school. From then on, any spare time not spent on the tennis courts was used in their garden. Both these outdoor activities, combined with his red-headed complexion, contributed to his death. Margaret, while massaging his neck to relieve one of the migraine headaches he was subject to, noticed a spot on the front of his right shoulder.

"Go to the doctor and have this checked," she told him. "It doesn't look right."

He did. The results came back: Melanoma. Their neighbor had recently died of what he referred to as "black cancer" so the word struck terror in their hearts. The spot was surgically removed, all of it, the doctors thought. He received a skin graft and a clean bill of health.

A year later, in the summer of 1969, Billy began to feel under par. Again Margaret convinced him to go to the doctor. X-rays showed strange shadowy masses. The doctor was cheerful but gave Margaret's arm an ominous squeeze. "We'll have to get some treatment going," he said.

Later he called to tell her it was hopeless. "Don't tell your husband, yet. We'll do all we can but its bad, really bad."

It was. Trips to University of California Medical Center in San Francisco for chemotherapy followed. Billy became friends with many of his fellow patients and was devastated whenever one died. "I'm not going to make any more friends over there," he told Margaret. "They'll just die and that hurts." They never discussed the fact that his turn was coming. Neither was good at words.

The long days at home when his mother came to tend him were a mixed blessing. He needed her help but he resented her presence. He vented his frustrations by telling her what he viewed as her shortcomings and mistakes as a mother, a wife, a person. Marian stoically accepted his diatribe.

She continued to visit him when he was moved to Marin General Hospital after Thanksgiving. He reached the point where he no longer recognized Margaret and she stopped coming to the hospital, finding it too painful. Jane accompanied her mother whenever she could.

On a cold wet December afternoon, she and Marian were in the room. Billy was babbling in the high excited voice of a child. Neither Marian nor Jane could understand him but he smiled into their eyes and moved his right hand across the sheets in a pushing motion, back and forth, laughing. Suddenly, Jane realized he was back under the towering redwood tree where they had built the Kingdom of OZ so many years before. Tears filled her eyes. "Oh, Billy-boy," she said. "We had such fun!"

He quieted down. Then began to moan and toss in agony. Marian rang for the nurse. "He's in terrible pain," she said.

"Well, it'll be time for his medication in another hour," said the nurse. "You better leave."

"Can't he have the medicine now?"

"Oh, no. He has to wait. And you two have to go. Regulations."

Marian and Jane leaned over him, stroked the tortured face.

"Good-by, Billy. We'll see you in the morning."

They reluctantly left the room with a backward glance at the frail figure moving restlessly on the bed

Billy died alone less than an hour later, before time for the medication that would have eased his pain. It was December 23, 1969. He was 47 years old.

William Murdock Rattray, 1942

Marianne

Marianne Laurilla Rattray
(Mare Rattray Shepard)

AT A PARTY FOLLOWING graduation from Ross Grammar School in June 1942, Marianne met her first horse. The girls in their class went riding from a stable in Fairfax, up the wooded trails and down again. For Marianne, it was a revelation, the door to a whole new world. Born instantly in her heart was the desire, the *need* to have a horse of her own.

Through her first years at Katherine Branson School, she spent every free moment working toward or dreaming of her goal. She badgered Marian. "I need a horse," she said firmly and often.

"You don't know the first thing about having a horse," Marian answered. "Find people around here who'll hire you to feed their horses and clean the stables. See what it's like. Save whatever you make. I'll match it and when there's enough, we'll buy you a horse." Marian thought nothing would come of it.

Dragging Suzanne, Marianne located two stables within walking distance and they were soon up to their rubber boots in horse care. They even brought sacks of manure home to benefit the garden. The first summer vacation from Branson, Marian located a dude ranch in the Valley of the Moon where they could work. They were to help the younger daughter of the family with maid duties and serving tables at meals. The rest of the time they had the run of the Ranch and the stables.

Irving and Mildred Shepard owned the Jack London Ranch in Glen Ellen. He was the nephew of the author/adventurer who had developed a model operation there in the early 1900s. The original ranch house still stood as did the ruins of the ill-fated Wolf House. Left over from Jack's time, too, were a long bunk house constructed over part of the tall stone walls of an old winery, and small guest houses, nestled under the eucalyptus trees on the side of the hill to accommodate his visiting friends. Jack's widow, Charmian still lived in the House of Happy Walls which she built in memory of her beloved husband in the early 1930s.

The Shepards had four children – oldest, Jack, then Jill, Milo, and Joy, who was the same age as the twins. Joy returned to the Rattray home at the end of the summer to board with them while attending Branson. The twins were on a fair way toward having their horses and in spite of the work involved, much to Marian's surprise, Marianne's interest didn't wane.

Penny and Lady were purchased during Marianne's third year at Branson., a monument to her determination. When she went to work at the Jack London Ranch that summer, the horses went too.

Following graduation in 1946, Marianne and Suzanne went to the University of California at Davis. Part of the time, they worked in the barns learning care of various animals. During one spring break, Marianne brought two active baby goats home. The kids won everyone's heart, bouncing, stiff-legged, on and off the furniture on their tiny black feet but no one was sad to see them go back to college. They had just begun to nibble everything in sight!

It was Marianne who looked at Tippy and said to Marian, "You're cruel, keeping that poor old dog alive. He's suffering. Put him out of his misery." This was a difficult a decision. Billy was especially reluctant. Tippy had been his constant companion for over sixteen years. Marian thought it would be easier on the children if they didn't know when it was to happen. Marianne came home from school one day and Tippy was gone. She never forgave her mother for depriving her of that final good-bye.

Shortly after that, Marianne brought Scott home. His mother, Jeannie, a Scottish border collie, felt – rightfully it turned out – that something was amiss with her pup and refused to work with him as she did with the rest of the litter. Scotty met his end years later trying unsuccessfully to "herd" a moving vehicle off the road! He was a well-loved, if somewhat fey, family member in the interim.

When it was time to get ready for the second year at Davis, Marianne announced to Marian that she didn't need any new school clothes: She wasn't going back. The reason, she said, was that she and Jack Shepard were getting married. This was a bombshell, totally unexpected. The entire family reeled under the shock. Marian took a deep breath and organized the wedding.

Marianne became Mrs. Jack London Shepard at a simple ceremony in Adele and Sydney Higgins' lovely home October 25, 1947. Back at the Ranch, they claimed the far-end rooms of the bunk house and set up their first home. Over the years, they cut doors in the walls between rooms as they needed more space. The Ranch no longer had paying summer guests. Instead prize Jersey cows were raised, the rich milk going to a cooperative for retail sale. Marianne took charge of the calf barn, frequently bringing a needy baby bull or heifer into the warmth of her kitchen for special nursing. She also helped with the milking, often assisting her brother-in-law, Milo, when he was home from agricultural college in San Luis Obispo, California.

In October 1951, her first daughter, Anne Paige Shepard, was born. Three years later, July 30, 1954, Ellen Greig Shepard, made her appearance. The girls found the Ranch a wonderful place to live, especially Ellen who was a fearless tomboy and kept up with, or ahead of, her many male cousins .

Marianne, having followed the interest in birds sparked by her first grade teacher, became an official bird-bander, Number 8788, in the early 1960s. For years, she has taken her nets to Yuba Pass in the Sierra for the summer census. She became an authority on western birds and was a volunteer helper and a "hanger-on" in the creation of the Point Reyes National Bird Observatory on the mesa above the pounding Pacific in Bolinas, California.

The night before school opened in September 1965, while Marianne and the girls were visiting friends, and Jack in the City, their house caught fire and was totally consumed, the blazing remnants falling to the ground between the walls of the old winery upon which it was built. Shaken and suffering a stunning material loss – everything except the clothes on their backs – she, Jack and the girls moved into the old ranch house across the road from the ruins of their destroyed home.

Two months later, on an November afternoon, with Jack driving the Jeep, Marianne, Ellen and Suzanne's son, Brian, went for a ride up the mountain. Jack lost control on the rough narrow dirt road and the Jeep rolled over. Brian was unhurt. Ellen's leg was shattered, Marianne suffered multiple painful bruises. Jack was seriously injured. He and Ellen were hospitalized, she with her leg raised and strapped in traction for long agonizing weeks.

In the afternoon, November 17, 1965, while seemingly on the road to recovery, Jack died of an embolism. As the little hospital went into a frenzy of activity, no one thought to shield or protect Ellen, lying immobile in her room, catching snatches of the horrible news as nurses bustled past her open door. One nurse called out in answer to Ellen's question, "Oh, Jack Shepard just died," and hurried on down the hall, leaving the eleven-year-old to wrestle with the enormity of her father's death alone.

During the next few years, Marianne, pulling their lives together, worked mornings in a pet shop and afternoons at the Greentree Nursery. In November 1969, she started as a rural mail carrier with the postal service, a position she still holds

In June 1972, Mildred Shepard, Jack's mother, finally was able to convince her younger son, Milo, to have the sheriff serve eviction papers on Marianne. There was no reason for such a cruel and unfeeling act except that Mildred had always resented Jack's marriage to Marianne and couldn't tolerate her presence in the historic old ranch house. She had dreamed of a socialite debutante wife for her son, not one who would wear jeans and milk cows.

Instead of fighting for her widow's rights, Marianne, devastated and angered almost beyond control, left the Ranch. The children were invited by their grandmother to stay on the property but they chose to leave with their mother.

After a gypsy year, Marianne found a little house she could manage to buy. Not long after that, Ellen ,having graduated from high school, presented Marianne with yet another challenge. After a lifetime of feeling out of step, Ellen decided to do something about it. She had always thought herself a boy and now wanted to undergo a sex change through Stanford University in Palo Alto to make it true. Much soul-searching and study had gone into this decision. Marianne supported her younger child throughout the long involved process. In 1975, Ellen legally changed both sex and name on the birth certificate becoming *Allen* Greig, called "Greig."

"After all, " said his cousins, "Greig always *was* a boy, right from the beginning."

When Greig married Constance Sharpe in June 1988, assembled family and friends burst into applause and tears, honoring the courage and wisdom that brought him to this moment.

Anne, in the meantime, deeply affected by her father's death, had taken her considerable talent as an artist to Hollywood. She came back to Glen Ellen occasionally for the solace she received being with her family and near the ranch of her childhood but usually managed to have an argument with her mother which negated much of the healing. Anne was a tall stunning blonde, talented, intelligent and tortured by demons. On August 24, 1985, she took her own life, tearing a gaping wound in the fabric of the family that can never be healed. She was nearly 34 years old.

Of all the blows that Marianne received, this was the worst. She found strength somewhere to go on, perhaps from the genes of her powerful mother. Under the façade of normalcy, however, there was, and still is, an indescribable pain. At present, Marianne travels as much as her job and finances allow, often with an Elderhostel group. She has gone bird watching in San Blas, Costa Rica and the southwestern states. Unfortunately, she usually knows more – especially about birds – than any leader so it's not always the learning experience she's seeking.

Back packing in the High Sierra, with its stark beauty and the simplicity of bare granite, appeals to her. "I don't like dark forests or jungles," she says. "They close me in." She also hates the cold gray weather of winter, preferring Baja's warm salt water and sandy beaches.

Or the uncluttered open well-defined cleanness of the Arizona desert.

She is still remodeling the little house she bought in 1973, her dreams always exceeding her time and energy. Greig and his wife, Constance, live on the property in a converted winery. They are slowly, by long-distance and infrequent visits, building a house in Cozumel, Mexico, where they all hope to take up residence someday.

In the meantime, Marianne lives in relaxed clutter with 27 beloved cats, an old dog, and an ever-changing evolving house and garden, planning her next trip, her next project, her next step.

Marianne Rattray Shepard, 1990

Suzanne

Suzanne Leticia Rattray
(Susan Rattray Shepard)

IT WASN'T UNTIL YEARS later that the pain of their twinship became apparent to both Suzanne and Marianne. When they graduated from Ross Grammar School in June 1942, they were still – and would be for five more years – yoked together in everyone's mind, marching through life in tandem. This was particularly difficult for Suzanne since she was more pliable than her volatile twin and was often swept along, not aware of the pressure being put on her. To become her own true self was a long journey for Suzanne.

During the early war years, Marian rented, then leased, a cabin on Silver Lake outside of Westwood in Lassen County. Adele Higgins was the first Gabby Girl to get a home up there, followed by the Rattrays. Ruth Hansen and Mabel Seimer often brought their children up to stay with Adele. Gasoline allotments were saved until there was enough to make the trip. Marian always started in the pre-dawn darkness to escape the valley heat. The last few miles were on a dusty dirt road so the first task upon arrival was to get as much dust off everything as possible. The lake water was icy but would do for hands, feet and faces.

Suzanne enjoyed the time at Silver Lake, sleeping on a cot under the towering pines, talking and giggling with Marianne until sleep finally overtook her. Usually the three Higgins daughters – Bobbie, Pat and Connie – as well as Patty Hansen, were in residence which added to the fun. Swimming in the glacier lake was impossible but on hot summer afternoons it was exciting to slip momentarily into the water and then jump out before the temperature registered!

With the summer job at the Jack London Ranch, their trips to Silver Lake became impossible. In the early summer of 1943, Suzanne was thrown from her horse and had a fractured skull. She was brought down to Ross Hospital where she remained for a week, under observation. The fracture turned out to be slight with no repercussions but it did scare the family. The first 24 hours were difficult: The doctors wouldn't let Susan fall asleep. They also insisted that she drink Coca Cola constantly. It's strange how soon you loose your taste for something you are forced to take.

Years before, when the twins were kindergartners and their father began playing for Gladys Hodgson's ballet classes, Suzanne and Marianne were enrolled. For the next 10 years, summers were the only break they had from their weekly ballet lesson. Suzanne enjoyed the discipline and the exercise. She even, married and a mother, took adult classes for several years, passing the love of ballet on to her daughter, Lisa, who, as a kindergartner was given lessons by Gladys Hodgson "because of your Grandfather Bill who played for us so many years."

The time at Katherine Branson School, just a block up the hill from home, was filled with learning for her. In the strict academic English class, she discovered rules of grammar that even her mother wasn't obeying and felt pride in correcting Marian and anyone else at the dinner table in whom she could detect imperfection of speech. Marianne aided in this familial education and everyone accepted it with good grace except Billy who resented being corrected by his younger sisters.

Although the twins took ballroom dancing, for which their father also played, in the community hall of St. John's, their boy-girl social life was limited. There was little opportunity to meet boys at the all-girl school they attended and the ones imported from Tamalpais Academy for school dances struck Suzanne as being impossible; too short, too fat, too brash or too tongue-tied. Only at the Ranch, where they were comfortable, did the girls find an opportunity to relate to males in a casual way. Jack's sarcasm and belittling manner irritated Suzanne but she liked Milo who was tall and quiet.

Arriving on the campus at Davis where there were more men than women students was a shock to Suzanne but she quickly adjusted. Here, too, the most relaxed friendships came from the people she met during her hours working with the animals at the barns.

When Marianne announced two weeks before the start of their second year at Davis that instead of going back to school, she was marrying Jack Shepard, Suzanne was as nonplused as anyone. It seemed a strange alliance and was totally unexpected.

Going off to school without Marianne was the first time in her life that she'd been a single separate identity. At first she felt lost. Then she took charge. She changed her name from "Suzanne" to "Susan" and started developing her own individuality and style. Deciding that animal husbandry was not really *her* choice, she made different plans.

In August 1948, after two weeks with Jane in Waikiki, she entered nurses' training at St. Luke's Hospital in San Francisco. There her roommate was Carol Fraser, a Scottish girl from Hawaii. Since Carol couldn't possibly get home on weekends or short breaks, Susan brought her to Ross. She endeared herself to the family by laboriously preparing meals of lamb curry with all the condiments – coconut, chutney, raisins, grated cheese, ginger, chives, bacon, hard-boiled eggs – each in its own small bowl on the Lazy Susan. Carol taught them the proper sequence of putting the condiments over the lamb, starting with the cheese so it would melt, ending with a sprinkling of the egg. The fact that it took her all day to prepare the feast made it even more special and appreciated. She did so with one eye on Billy if he happened to be around, seeking his approval, dreaming of his love. He enjoyed the curry but treated Carol like a fourth sister which was not what she had in mind.

While in Hawaii, Susan met a young ensign, Max Allen. With him she was able to converse, really talk and be heard, finding he took the same delight in life's inconsistencies and incongruities as she did. What might have come of it if they'd had more time, Susan could only wonder. Max did come to San Francisco. He looked her up and they went out to dinner. They stood on a street corner afterwards, entranced with each other, in deep conversation and laughter while streetcar after streetcar went by. Susan missed the last car and had to be taken back to the St. Luke's in a taxi. Then Max was gone again, this time permanently. She knew their paths would never cross again.

A week later she started dating Milo Shepard whenever he was in town. She completed her training and was "capped" in August 1951. Less than a month later, on September 15, she and Milo were married at St. John's Church. On the day of the wedding, held in the early evening to allow the groom and best man to finish the milking, Susan and Jane made a pilgrimage to Phoenix Lake for Susan to say good-bye to a treasured spot. Later, Jane drove her down to the church. Knowing she wouldn't register anything of her surroundings during the ceremony, Susan wanted to see it in all its glory with flowers and bows in place. They each said a silent prayer.

At the reception, held in Ruth and Harold Hansen's terraced garden on a full-moon night, Mildred Shepard announced, "Well, now that the wedding's over, I can tell you there's a baby expected." Into the stunned silence she added, "Joy and Bill are becoming parents next spring." Mildred was not pleased with Milo's choice of bride. Another Rattray killed her last dream of a more socially prominent *rich* daughter-in-law but she tried to be bravely civil at the wedding.

With her marriage, Susan was again close to her twin. Underneath the seemingly storybook tale of sisters marrying brothers, there was hidden pain on both sides. Marianne was upset that Susan would come live on the Ranch and spoil their *apartness*, and Susan felt Marianne's concealed antagonism.

Susan and Milo chose the little cabin on the hill under the eucalyptus trees that seemed to them to have the best location. Neil Murdock Shepard was born May 2, 1953. Two years later to the day, Brian James Shepard was born, and September 3, 1956, Lisa Jane Shepard made her appearance. As they grew, the cousins – Susan's three and Mare's two – had a wonderful time with the whole Ranch as a playground. Summers they were joined by Jane's children, sometimes for several weeks. Years later, tales of some of their childhood antics curled the hair of any listening adult, but they did have fun!

By the time Lisa was ten, Susan felt ready to pursue her career in nursing. She had worked, briefly, at Sonoma State Hospital while pregnant with Neil. Caring for the mentally disturbed and retarded when expecting a baby was difficult to handle. She could see first hand some of the many things that might go wrong and it distressed her. After Neil's birth, Susan happily stayed home, not going back until Lisa was in school all day. Then she worked at Warrack Hospital in Santa Rosa for ten years. A three-year break from nursing to work on medical records was followed by a seven-year stint at Brookwood Hospital in Santa Rosa. She has been at Friends' House, a care facility for the elderly, run by the Quakers, for nearly five years. The philosophy at Friends' appeals to Susan. She finds satisfaction in working with the dying and with Hospice patients. In spite of this, she is glad to reach a point where she can cut back on her work.

"I'm almost retired," Susan says with a grin, "just a few hours a week. It's wonderful."

Susan and Milo were divorced in 1972. She left the Ranch and moved into an A-frame summer home she was able to buy from friends. In 1989, she realized that she'd spent 18 years – more than half her life – building fires to keep warm in houses that weren't weatherproof and decided to change the situation. She sold the A-frame and bought a little place in Oakmont, a retirement community on the outskirts of Santa Rosa. It boasts "climate control" with a thermostat, miraculous to Susan after all the years of kindling and green logs and never being warm on both sides at once.

During her grammar school days, Susan began a list of places she wanted to visit during her lifetime. As history or geography classes introduced her to the wonders of the world, the list grew. The last place, added quite recently, was the Great Wall of China, which she read was the only man-made structure that could be recognized from outer space.

She took her first trip in October 1977, going to Mexico. It was actually a training trip in how to travel alone in a foreign country. Although apprehensive, she managed well. Two years later, Susan went to Peru. Here she viewed two of the places on her list: Machu Picchu and the Inca Ruins. She was enthralled by their age. These were *old* places, having been built between 455 and 1027 AD. Climbing the stone steps of the terraced city fulfilled a yearning in Susan.

A year later, in 1980, she went to Greece and Egypt and was able to cross two more names off her list, the Parthenon built in the 5th century BC on the Acropolis in Athens, and the Great Pyramid of Giza, the oldest thing she'd seen, constructed somewhere around 2900 BC in Egypt. Susan was staggered by the age, nearly 3000 years before Christ! *Now that's* really *old*, she thought

A trip to China in 1982 satisfied her need to view the Great Wall. It also introduced her to a culture more different from her own than any she had seen. That left one unvisited place on her list, Stonehenge. Going to Scotland and England in 1993 made this last experience possible. She stood in awe, wishing she could touch the stones, feel their texture, but realized the decision to keep tourists at bay is sound one. One million loving hands could do great damage. Erected between 1900 and 1600 BC, Stonehenge, Susan read, may be a monumental calculator to chart the movements of the sun, moon and planets. She was fascinated to be standing before the huge stones that she'd dreamed of seeing for so long.

So she fulfilled her list and was not disappointed in a single place. She still would like to go to Belize for more ruins, and France for the charm but basically she's satisfied.

"The underlying message I've gotten from so many places is how fortunate we are to be born in America, especially as a woman," Susan told her sister Jane. "Women are *nothing* in many parts of the world. We are lucky."

Her three children are married. Neil and his wife, Jenny Lord, have a home on the Ranch where they raise animals – Clydesdale horses and pot-bellied pigs – and enjoy working together. Brian and Kate Ortolano live in Sonoma with their three children, Eliza, Josef and Nicholas. Lisa married Jeffrey Stanbor and they are now living in Calistoga with their two daughters, Kaela and Lucy.

Susan sees them whenever possible but places definite limits to her grandmotherly duties. The entire clan attended a bottling at the Ranch in July 1993, which was a rare treat for Susan. Some holidays she sees them all but they have their own lives and aren't beholden to her. It's different than it was when Marian organized the family gatherings and no one dared *not* show up. *So many things have changed, most for the better,* thought Susan. *I would never want my children to do things for me because they felt "duty-bound." That's a terrible reason.*

Susan held out for 20 years, then bought a television so she can watch foreign films on the VCR. She also has an extensive collection of classical music which she plays by the hour when she's home. There is a small garden around her house and she looks forward to having more time to work in it. She enjoys the fact that a crew of laborers take care of mowing the expansive lawns and that the watering is handled automatically. Oakmont has a large pool so she often swims, and she hikes the many nearby trails.

Over the years, at home and on her trips, she has taken thousands of pictures, many of them exhibition quality. Lately, Susan has begun to study astrology, something that has long fascinated her.

She enjoys her beautifully appointed home, surrounded by antiques and artistic treasures, and looks forward to more trips, to watching her grandchildren grow, and to enjoying life which she does with style.

Susan Rattray Shepard , 1989

Jane

Jane Paige Rattray
(Jayne Rattray Murdock)

BEING IN THE REAL WORLD after graduation from the university, and looking for a job, was torture for Jane. Well-meaning people gave her letters of introduction to editors, business managers and advertising executives. When she finally came face to face with anyone whose name she'd been given, she kept hearing variations on the discouraging theme: One can't get a job without experience or get experience without a job!

In desperation, Jane created a niche at the *San Rafael Independent*, writing a column of trivia gleaned from the store managers on Fourth Street. For this she was paid $5 a week.

Then she entered a contest sponsored by *Mademoiselle Magazine*. Top prizes were positions in advertising at participating department stores throughout the country.

Months later, she won third prize and went to work at Raphael Weill's White House in San Francisco. She was placed on the Flying Squad, a group of special young ladies who were moved from department to department as needs arose. This, they said, was to prepare her for advertising. The closest she got to advertising, in her year there, was to be called in to stuff envelopes one day!

In the spring of 1941, Jane met Russell Callison, a lieutenant in the United States Army Air Corps. They spent the summer square dancing, folk dancing and falling in love. Russ had a sharp mathematical mind and a zany sense of humor. He and Jane were engaged when his squadron sailed for the Philippines the day after Thanksgiving, 1941. He was to be gone two years. They would marry upon his return.

December 7 changed all that. Instead, Russell landed in Australia, where, because of his special training, he was attached to the staff Five months later, he was killed in a sabotaged aircraft carrying a plane-load of top ranking officers. They were heading for a high echelon secret meeting.

Russell was the only second lieutenant aboard.

Marian and Bill received the telegram on a Thursday and chose to wait until Jane came home for the weekend after work on Friday to tell her. If they went over to the store, she would know something was wrong the minute she saw them and they wanted to tell her in private. It was an agonizing twenty-four hours.

When Jane walked in the house, Bill and Marian were standing side by side in front of the fireplace, tears bright in their eyes. There is no easy gentle way to break such awful news.

Their demeanor wiped the smile from Jane's face and filled her with apprehension.

"Russell's dead," Marian said, "He was killed in a plane crash on the twenty-fifth of May." She reached out her arms.

"No," said Jane, shaking her head. "No!" It was an anguished whisper of disbelief.

Bill moved close, put his arm across Jane's shoulder and with unaccustomed tears on his face said, "I'm so sorry." The three of them stood in a tight circle, weeping together.

Memorial Day weekend was long and difficult. Jane tried to continue with all normal routines, refusing to break down. Her bravery made it more difficult for the family: They worried about her. On Tuesday, Jane went back to San Francisco where she had an apartment with a friend, Tamara Comstock, and to work at the White House.

Two months later, she gave notice at the department store, moved home and went to work on the day shift at Marinship in the field engineers' office. "I have to do more for the war effort," she explained.

The shipyard still wasn't enough.

In July 1943, Jane enlisted in the United States Marine Corps. Across the country by train, five old coaches tacked on the end of a Santa Fe train to Chicago, then more miles, through Pennsylvania, down to North Carolina, a bus to Camp LeJeune for boot camp. Hot sticky heat! She'd never known such weather existed. Cherry Point, South Carolina, crisp autumn, more like home. Aerology school at Lakewood, out of Lakehurst, New Jersey, where clothes froze on the line and snow fell. Her first Christmas away from the family with her mind aching from the new things she had to learn. She spent that New Year's Eve standing in the midst of the milling mob at Times Square. Then she went to visit her Uncle Arnold, taking the train all the way to East Hampton Long Island. She met her cousins, Mary, Everett and young David, who was so excited – he was going to play the piano for her – that he threw up!

Back to El Toro in southern California, where the sound of planes brought Russell close. Down to the air base at El Centro where she was – Sergeant Rattray – when the war ended in August 1945. She was home by Christmas 1945. What a glorious holiday that one was! (See *I Painted On A Bright Red Mouth: The War Years*)

Jane, now a veteran as well as a college graduate, went to work as associate editor on the weekly *Marin Journal*, the county's oldest newspaper. She, the editor, Dick Hartford, and Jack Lawlor, in charge of advertising, were the entire staff. Jane loved the job. By the end of the summer, there was talk of the paper being consolidated with the daily, *San Rafael Independent,* and in the upheaval Jane took her leave.

She borrowed money from Billy and flew to Honolulu to attend the wedding of her college roommate, Dottie Winters, when she married Marine Lieutenant Barney Baxter in November 1946. They were transferred almost immediately to Midway. Jane stayed on, loving Oahu, for two and a half years. She found a job at the US Naval Station at Barber's Point.

In 1947, her mother sailed over on the *S.S.Lurline* to vacation with her. By then, Jane was in Waikiki, living in an apartment with Leah Weaver, a former WAVE from Kansas. The following summer, Susan flew over for two weeks before entering nurses' training. She was on hand when Jane met Vincent Cozzi, a handsome young Marine Corps Sergeant.

Jane and Vincent were married September 18, 1948 in a small chapel with Lee as Jane's only attendant. Eight months later, Vincent was transferred back to the States, stationed at Mare Island in Vallejo, California. They moved in with Marian which made everyone happy.

One Sunday, they borrowed Marian's car and drove to Oakland to see Bill. Vincent, who loved classical piano music, was instrumental in getting Bill back to Ross. He wanted to hear his father-in-law play Chopin's *Ballade in G Minor*, and talked Marian into inviting Bill for dinner the following week. Bill was quite rusty when he sat down at his beloved Steinway but since he was soon boarding there, he had time to practice. Eventually he played the piece, and many others, beautifully. His new son-in-law was impressed.

Jane went to work for Libby Smith at the *San Rafael Independent Journal* writing society items. Six months later, in December 1949, Vincent was transferred to Philadelphia Naval Shipyard. Jane followed by train as soon as he found an apartment for them on Broad Street in South Philadelphia. He was returning to his roots and Jane met all his relatives on his mother's side , uncles, aunts, cousins and his tiny Italian grandmother. They were invited weekly to Aunt Rose and Uncle Tony's for dinner. The entire family was amazed at Jane's ineptitude at the art of rolling spaghetti neatly against a spoon. She was embarrassed by their laughter and delighted the nights the pasta turned out to be little shells or butterflies.

They had a lovely Christmas and quiet New Year's. In the spring they attended a concert by Vladamir Horowitz at the Academy of Music. Vincent wore his dress blues and Jane a long gown. They had center seats in the front row. Horowitz played their favorite Chopin ballade. "Great," Vincent said, "but no better than your dad!"

Jane worked on the *Philadelphia Bulletin*, rode the subway and enjoyed Sunday bus trips with her husband to the end of various lines. She found Philadelphia "old" compared to her native California, and she liked the sense of history that permeated the place. One weekend they went to Washington DC and did the "sights." It was gratifying to be seeing things previously confined to the pages of books.

In early June, Jane was pregnant and Vince talked her into going home to Ross. He wanted to be free to ship out to Korea as soon as the opportunity came. Unfortunately, an altercation with his commanding officer landed him in the brig at Norfolk Retraining Command instead of on a troop plane to Korea.

A month before the baby's birth, Bill got two box seat tickets to hear Horowitz play in San Francisco. Marian had made beautiful Christmas dresses for her daughters, Jane's being a gold maternity gown, which she wore that night. She and Bill walked into their elegant box and were amused to see that her dress exactly matched the lavish curtains. It made her feel like Scarlett O'Hara.

Christopher Duncan Cozzi was born February 11, 1951, the same day that his father's confinement ended. Vincent shipped out to Korea and returned when Chris was 18 months old. They lived at Laguna Beach while Vincent was stationed at Camp Pendleton. Jane reveled in it. She wheeled her sturdy son down to the beach every morning, then loaded a bag of groceries in the stroller and Chris helped her push it up the hill to the apartment. Marianne bought her little daughter, Anne, down for a visit. Bill and Marian came by train for Thanksgiving.

Jane was pregnant again. Vincent, to her sorrow, accepted six months temporary duty in Hawaii just weeks before the baby was due. He dropped Jane and Chris at the airport, then drove all their belongings to Ross while they flew home. Bruce Hamilton Cozzi was born July 8, 1953, a week after his father left for Hawaii. Vince went on to Japan for additional duty and saw Bruce first when he was nine months old.

Two years of living near San Diego ended when Vincent decided he didn't want to be married any more. Jane, devastated, took the boys home to Ross. Her plans to carve a career for herself in the newspaper world died when she realized she was pregnant. Catherine Paige Cozzi was born March 14, 1956. Marian and Dr. Howard Hammond did a little dance of delight in the hall for the miracle of a dimpled daughter. Vincent sent pink roses and a tiny ruffled outfit.

Before Cathi had her first birthday, Vincent wrote that he was being sent to Guam. He asked Jane if she would bring the children and join him. She felt it would be better for them to be with a united family than to continue in Ross with Marian, Bill and Billy where there wasn't much gentle loving emotion expressed. Marian drove them to Fairfield for the plane to Hickam Field on Oahu. She watched Jane walk away with Chris, Bruce, and Cathi, *her* babies, and felt bereft. When would she see them again? They turned and waved one last time and Marian's eyes were brimming with tears as she turned to leave.

They loved Guam – the weather, the beaches, the relaxed life style. Jane became editor of the Naval Supply Center's weekly newspaper where she met Marilyn Crigger and her family. Their lives were to be linked forever.

In January 1959, the Cozzis sailed for home. It was a long trip, five weeks on a troop ship. Jane was, much to Vincent's disgust, pregnant again. He reported to the Marine base at Twenty Nine Palms, in the California desert. Jane stayed with the three children in Ross. Vincent drove up weekends when he could.

Before red-headed Steven William Cozzi was born on August 23, 1959, Vincent was discovered to have diabetes and received a military discharge from the Marine Corps.

Marian moved into the little house down the driveway to make room for the whole Cozzi family. Vincent went back to college and bartended nights. When Jane realized she was pregnant again, she didn't tell anyone except her doctor.

"I'm too old to be having a baby," she said to him.

"If you were too old to be having a baby," he answered, "you wouldn't be having a baby." She was five months pregnant before she mentioned the fact to anyone else, caring for her father without complaining through his most distasteful acts so no one would guess her secret. Both Vincent and Marian received the news with horror, but Jane was never sorry.

Jonathan Greig Cozzi was born June 8, 1961. He was a beautiful boy, with huge brown eyes, eyebrows with character from the beginning, a heart-tugging smile and charisma that was almost his downfall. He was connected to his mother in a special way.

But the marriage was in trouble. Vincent couldn't get away any more. He was trapped and concentrated fatherhood of five was too much for him. Jane, a quiet noncombatant Scot, found herself in verbal conflict with a volatile Italian alcoholic diabetic ex-Marine sergeant. She couldn't change him nor could she make peace. They were divorced just after Jon's second birthday, in August 1963, having been together less than seven years during their 15 years of marriage.

Jane enrolled at Dominican College in San Rafael to get her teaching credential with Marian taking charge of the children while Jane was in school. Still involved in student teaching at the end of her second year, Jane met John Edward May, a tall rugged Englishman who seemed to be the answer to her prayers. He was educated, cultured, ordered wine through long conversations in French with the wine steward, and owned a 36-foot boat which he let Steven, six years old, steer when they were out in the Bay. John had a zest for life, a sense of fun and an old Cadillac which he left with Jane when the dream ended nine months after they were married. (See *Brief Infinity – A Love Story in Haiku*)

Nothing in her entire life crushed Jane as much as John's departure. She came home from school one day to find every trace of him removed from the cottage. Shattered, she drove to Marian's apartment for their customary cup of afternoon tea. Before she decided what to share with her mother, the phone rang. Marian returned from answering it. "Jack just died," she said. "I'm going right up to be with Marianne."

Jane went home, carrying her own news like burning rocks in her stomach, searing near-fatal holes.

Vincent left her with five children: John left her with the house he'd bought from her mother. Luckily, the following spring Jane was hired by the Mill Valley School District where she taught first or second grade for 15 years, retiring in June 1980. During that time, she was part of the Ford Foundation/Esalen Institute project on confluent education for three wonderful years that changed her life.

A dozen Bay Area elementary school teachers were involved. The group was lead by Suki Miller and Marilyn Kreigel, with frequent meetings in San Francisco and monthly weekends at Esalen, Big Sur, where they experienced the various disciplines – gestalt, biofeedback, massage, encounter. Their task, as teachers, was to integrate the things they were learning into the teaching of reading. What it did for the curriculum was difficult to assess, but the change it made in Jane was obvious and positive.

In 1969, having taught the entire school to dance the Maypole, Jane invited a dozen friends to come weave their own magic Maypole on the side patio. This started an annual ever-expanding twenty-year tradition, ending with an all-out bash in May 1989. More than 300 near and dear friends attended the last festivities, weaving and unweaving the colorful pole six times.

At a family gathering July 1972, in the lower garden of the Ross home, Jane reconnected with her cousin, Dick Murdock. They fell in love and corresponded almost daily for the next two years, getting together whenever they could manage it. (See *Love Lines: A True Love Story*).

Jane's son, Christopher, a Marine stationed in San Diego, married Sue Taylor in the lower garden, March 20, 1976. His children, Jesse and Becky, and Sue's daughter, Lisa, were in the wedding party. This was the last family function that Marian was able to fully participated in, one of the few where four generations were on hand. Chris and Sue now live in Rohnert Park. He is a CPA with a firm in San Rafael.

Son Bruce had already married Paula Hunt on November 9, 1975, when he returned from Army duty in Italy. They drove up to Reno for the brief ceremony. "We don't need a *wedding*, we just want a marriage!" Bruce explained.

Dick was living in the cottage when Jane brought her mother home from Marin General Hospital to die in July 1976 and was a source of great strength and comfort to Jane during that painful month. (See *Until Death and After: How to Live With a Dying Intimate*)

From January 1946, right after the war ended, when Jane and Billy brought a station wagon full of rocks home to build a stone retaining wall for the side patio, Jane worked as a stone mason throughout the yard, building walls and steps to terrace what once was a sloping hillside.

To escape the stress of Marian's dying, Jane started her most ambitious project, a large fish pond with an island in the center, and in the far corner of the lower garden with three small pools forming a series of waterfalls with the water running back into the big pond. Getting help from her sons and their friends, Matt and Lars Hansen, who did the necessary wiring and piping, and a truckload of field stone brought by Neil Shepard from the Jack London Ranch, the pond was laboriously built.

This was during a drought so when the work was finished, Jane sent out invitations for a Pond Filling Party asking each guest to bring a container of water. Neil drove down from Glen Ellen with 200 gallons from the Jack London Ranch in a two-wheel tank-trailer. Marianne brought water from her 250-foot well. Anne Shepard and her French friend, Pierre, poured their store-bought imported bottled spring water into the pond. Dick and Jane added gallon containers from every northern California river they had visited during their recent vacation.

Throughout the afternoon, by ones and twos, friends made their way to Marian's room to say what they knew was their final good-bye. Pauline and Buddy's son, Bill, carried his father's love to Marian. For many of her grandchildren, this would be the last time they'd see her. She died a month later.

Dick and Jane were married in the same lower garden on February 19, 1977, five months after Marian's death, with 100 friends wishing them well. Susan and Marianne, all five of Jane's children and her two daughters-in-law were in the wedding party. Fifteen years later, wearing the same Victorian outfits, Dick and Jane renewed their vows at St. John's Episcopal Church with many of the old friends, and even more new ones, on hand.

In 1978, Jane put plans into effect to enlarge the cottage that Billy had started in 1955, doubling its size with the addition of a sky-lighted bedroom and a galley kitchen. In 1982, another 100 square feet were added, this time an entry area with a clerestory window, wood-burning stove and window seat.

Following a trip to England in May 1989 with their dear friend, Joyce Gibbs, Jane came home enamored with the English cottage concept and, in a tremendous upheaval, moved everything in the California-casual house, except the kitchen sink and the bathroom fixtures, to a new location! A huge beruffled Victorian bed, lacy curtains and memorabilia add character their bedroom/sitting room and the rest of the tiny house.

The old bedroom now holds two computers and a laser printer, an oak dining table (piled high with work in progress) bookcases and two wonderful blue tweed and oak executive chairs. Here, Dick and Jane are writing their sixteenth and seventeenth books.

In April 1980, Bruce and Paula, who were living in Mill Valley, asked if they could move into the house. Since Dick and Jane were in the cottage, Cathi away and Jon seldom home, there was room. Remembering how Marian had always welcomed her over the years, Jane said, "Of course."

Ryanne Lynn Cozzi was born November 17, 1980. On that day, Jane planted the five-foot redwood tree Dick had given her when she retired from teaching in June, five months before. Now forty feet tall, it, with two others, provides their own private redwood grove.

Two years later when a second baby was on the way, the house began to be crowded. Travis Vincent Cozzi was born March 14, 1983, filling the last bedroom. Bruce and Paula now work for the same company in Kentfield. Bruce is on the vestry at St. John's and active in the men's group there.

Before Travis was born, Steve left the house of his childhood to be on his own. Ten years later, manager of Marinwood Chevron Station, he is planning to purchase his own home soon.

Jon, a soldier of fortune, has worked in Alaska, the Virgin Islands, Australia and points between. He is a tree-trimmer and sailor. West Marin has been his natural between-trip habitat but in the summer of 1993 he decided to settle near Grass Valley in the foothills of the Sierra and put down roots.

Cathi moved to Washington state where, on August 23, 1983, she married Timothy Shriver. They live in Marysville, and have four sons born at 22-month intervals, starting January 15, 1985 with Zackary David, followed by Nathan Ross, Samuel Turner, and Alexander James. Jane flew up for the birth of each baby and always goes to spend Cathi's birthday with her in the middle of March. They talk on the phone for an hour each Friday night, if possible.

Important to Jane are the Science of Mind mediations that Dick reads to her to start each day, and Robert Schuller's Crystal Cathedral television broadcast which they watch each Sunday morning. Early in their marriage, they studied meditation, went to a marriage encounter weekend and, two years ago, attended Cursillo weekends in San Francisco. She and Dick, a retired locomotive engineer, belong to the Northwestern Pacific Railroad Historical Society and edited the organization's quarterly magazine, *The Northwesterner*, for its beginning years. Jane has maintained close ties with Hospice through its auxiliary, Friends of Hospice. She was instrumental in founding Marin Small Publishers Association and, through that group, has effected the lives of hundreds of authors and publishers .

Living in the same place for seventy years gives Jane a sense of continuity and roots that few are privileged to have. Remembering her childhood and her mother's struggles with her, she often wants to say, "Look, Mother, I'm standing up straight!" She is, in fact, determined to go into old age with head high, shoulders square, a smile on her face and love in her heart

Surrounded as she is with family and friends, that won't be difficult.

Jayne Rattray Murdock with her five, Christopher, Bruce, Cathi, Steve and Jon Cozzi 1990

Bill and Marian's Grandchildren

Lake at Jack London Ranch, 1978

Catherine Paige Cozzi

Anne Paige Shepard

Lisa Jane Shepard

Bruce Hamilton Cozzi

Christopher Duncan Cozzi

Jonathan Greig Cozzi

(Allen) Greig Shepard

Steven William Cozzi

Neil Hamilton Shepard

Brian James Shepard

Their Great-grandchildren

*Jesse & Becky Cozzi,
children of Chris Cozzi &
first wife, Mona Simmons*

*Travis & Ryanne Cozzi,
children of Bruce &
Paula Hunt Cozzi*

*Nicholas, Eliza & Josef
Shepard, children of
Brian & Kate Ortolano Shepard*

*Kaela & Lucy Stanbor,
children of Jeffrey &
Lisa Shepard Stanbor*

*Nathan, Alex, Zackary & Sam Shriver, children
of Tim & Cathi Cozzi Shriver*

CONTINUED FAMILY TREE
(Simplified)

William Rattray
b. June 1, 1892
d. July 23, 1964

Marian Paige Murdock
b. Jan. 16, 1894
d. Sept. 13,1976

married June 30, 1917

children

Jane Paige Rattray
b. Dec. 15, 1918
m. Vincent Anthony Cozzi
Sept 18, 1948
divorced Sept. 1963

William Murdock Rattray
b. Nov. 3, 1922
d. Dec. 23,1967
m. Margaret Tate
December 28, 1957

children

Christopher	**Bruce**	**Catherine**	**Steven**	**Jonathan**
Duncan	Hamilton	Paige	William	Greig
b. Feb. 11,	b. July 8,	b. Mar. 14,	b. Aug. 23,	b. June 8,
1951	1953	1956	1959	1961
m. Mona	m. **Paula**	m.**Timothy**		
Simmons	**Hunt**	**Shriver**		
Feb.14, 1969	Nov. 8, 1975	Aug. 22, 1983		
divorced 1972				

children

children

children

Jesse Lynn
May 26, 1969
Rebecca Marie Paige
July 12, 1971

Ryanne Lynn
Nov. 17, 1980
Travis Vincent
Mar. 14, 1983

Zackary David
Jan. 15, 1985
Nathan Ross
Nov. 22, 1986
Samuel Turner
Oct. 2, 1988
Alexander James
Jan. 1, 1991

Christopher m. **Susan Taylor** - Mar. 20, 1976
 step-children Billy & Lisa Taylor
Jane m. John Edward May - May 19, 1965
 divorced Oct. 1967
Jane m. **Ritchie McKee (Dick) Murdock**, first cousin (see Family Tree, Page vi)
 Feb. 19, 1977

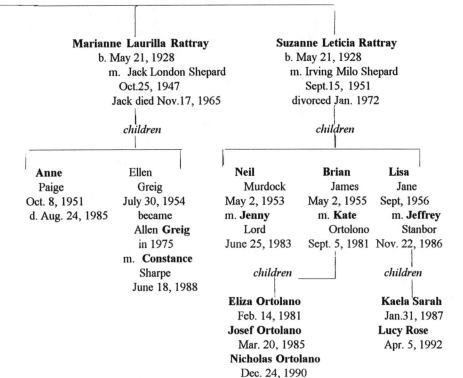

Marianne Laurilla Rattray
b. May 21, 1928
m. Jack London Shepard
Oct.25, 1947
Jack died Nov.17, 1965

children

Suzanne Leticia Rattray
b. May 21, 1928
m. Irving Milo Shepard
Sept.15, 1951
divorced Jan. 1972

children

Anne
Paige
Oct. 8, 1951
d. Aug. 24, 1985

Ellen
Greig
July 30, 1954
became
Allen **Greig**
in 1975
m. **Constance**
Sharpe
June 18, 1988

Neil
Murdock
May 2, 1953
m. **Jenny**
Lord
June 25, 1983

children

Eliza Ortolano
Feb. 14, 1981
Josef Ortolano
Mar. 20, 1985
Nicholas Ortolano
Dec. 24, 1990

Brian
James
May 2, 1955
m. **Kate**
Ortolono
Sept. 5, 1981

Lisa
Jane
Sept, 1956
m. **Jeffrey**
Stanbor
Nov. 22, 1986

children

Kaela Sarah
Jan.31, 1987
Lucy Rose
Apr. 5, 1992

Unto the Fourth Generation

Susan Letitia Fuller - 1879

Bruce Hamilton Cozzi - 1991
Great-grandson

Unbelievable resemblance that came to light during the course of preparing this book—Susan Letitia Fuller before her marriage to George Hamilton Murdock in 1879, and her great-grandson, Bruce Hamilton Cozzi, 113 years later, in 1993. Not only is every feature the same, even their hair styles look identical.

This seems almost positive proof that nothing is lost once it's in the gene bank. Generations may pass, but the chance is always there— that special face might appear again!

ACKNOWLEDGMENTS

To all who were tolerant of my single-minded tunnel vision as I worked toward completion of this year-long project.

To cousin Bob Murdock who answered questions about the Realty Syndicate Building in Oakland where our fathers and uncle held court before the crash of the empire in the early 1930s. Also thanks to Bob for his fine genealogy on the Valleaus (his mother's family) which contained information about Summer Home Park on the Russian River which I shamelessly used to augment my childhood memories.

To Paul Lawrence of San Anselmo who, several years ago, gave us a video he'd made from home movies of the 1939 Treasure Island International Fair. Playing it again was a true refresher course.

To Helena MacKall Skaer who carried an armload of photo albums to the house for viewing, as we looked for high school pictures to use. We found several, plus ones of our walk on the Golden Gate Bridge the day it opened to foot traffic.

To Wayne Lowrance, of AUTO*MAGIC* SYSTEMS, who took the text from my disk to his Pagemaker 5.0 and made it look just as I wanted. Special appreciation to him for creating the drop letters I had dreamed of and placing all the photographs exactly right. He deserves applause for all his creative work – and for being a computer genius.

To Joyce Gibbs, now of Willits, California, who spent hours finding typos and other glitches. I value her discerning eye and unflinching honesty.

COLOPHON

Typesetting: IBM Pagemaker 5.0.
Type: Times New Roman; Special headings, Lucida calligraphy.
Paper: 50# Glatfelter B-16
Printing & binding: Thomson-Shore, 7300 West Joy Road, Dexter MI

MAY-MURDOCK PUBLICATIONS
90 Glenwood Avenue
Ross CA 94957-1346

RAILROAD BOOKS BY DICK MURDOCK

SMOKE IN THE CANYON: My Steam Days in Dunsmuir
    144 pages, 63 historical photographs   hard cover $26.00
    original artwork by Charles Endom   perfect bound   16.00

PORT COSTA 1879-1941: A Saga of Sails, Sacks and Rails
    40 pages, historical photographs
    original artwork by Charles Endom   saddle stitched   6.00

HOGHEADS & HIGHBALLS: Railroad Lore and Humor
    64 pages, sketches by Charles Endom   perfect bound   5.00

LOVE AFFAIR WITH STEAM
    40 pages   saddle stitched   3.00

EARLY CALL FOR THE PERISHABLES, A Day at the Throttle
    24 pages   saddle stitched   2.00

WALNUT CREEK'S UNIQUE OLD STATION
    24 pages, 17 photographs   saddle stitched   2.00

BOOKS BY JAYNE MURDOCK

I PAINTED ON A BRIGHT RED MOUTH: The War Years
    December 1941—August 1945
    64 pages, vintage photo-collages   perfect bound   5.00

UNTIL DEATH AND AFTER: How To Live with a
    Dying Intimate
    64 pages   perfect bound   4.00

BRIEF INFINITY: A Love Story in Haiku
    64 pages   perfect bound   4.00

LOVE LINES: A True Love Story in Lyric Prose
    by Jayne May and Dick Murdock
    134 pages   perfect bound   5.00

OTHER OFFERINGS BY MAY-MURDOCK PUBLICATIONS

POINT BONITA TO POINT REYES: OUTDOORS IN MARIN

     61 Places to visit

     160 pages, 70 black & white photographs   perfect bound   10.00

LIME POINT TO LAWSON'S LANDING: OUTDOORS IN MARIN

     61 *More* Places to visit

     160 pages, 72 black & white photographs   perfect bound   11.00

REBIRTH OF THE VIRGINIA & TRUCKEE R.R.

     by Ted Wurm , 80 pages

     58 black & white photographs   perfect bound   5.95

SHANNON: WHAT'S IT ALL MEAN? 101 COMMENTARIES

     by Wayne Shannon, 128 pages   perfect bound   6.00

SEND FOR FREE BROCHURE
MONEY BACK GUARANTEE ON ALL MAY-MURDOCK PUBLICATIONS

Dick and Jayne Murdock, on hand to
sign books at the Marin County
Fourth of July Fair, 1993

What happened to the wind chimes?

When Billy was living at home after the war, he and
Marian decided to remodel the living room by knocking
out the front wall to the porch, making it part of the
room. At that point, the wind chimes were removed from
the spot where they had hung for a dozen years. Marian
carefully put them away in a safe place while construction was going on.

Years passed before anyone remembered to ask
about the chimes. By then, Marian had forgotten where
the "safe place" was. They have never been found.

Throughout the lower garden, however, hang several sets of large brass chimes, and smaller ceramic ones.
Although they looked, noonecould locate anywhere the
delicate painted glass wind chimes to replace the original ones. But, in honor of this book, a lovely modern
glass set has been hung on the redwood tree outside the
cottage door. Their sound is similar.

It is, as Marian said long ago, the song of home.

Glenwood Avenue home, 1993

"In the end, love is all that
matters. Only love."
Marian Murdock Rattray
Sept. 1976